THE COMANCHE KID

THE COMANCHE KID

JAMES ROBERT DANIELS

CUTTING EDGE

ISBN-13: 978-1-952138-94-2
Published by
Cutting Edge Books
PO Box 8212
Calabasas, CA 91372
www.cuttingedgebooks.com

To my wife, Patricia,
for her love, support and inspiration.
"One you can run the river with."

ONE

It was early spring when the ocotillo was in bloom that the raiders come down on us and killed everyone but me and Sally. I remember the ocotillo because the tiny red blossoms looked like splattered blood, even though the rains had washed most of the real blood into the earth by then.

I was down in the marsh with Jamie, maybe a quarter mile away, gathering leaf buds from the cattails when I heard noise up at the cabin. I figured it was Sally chasing after the chickens like the three-year-old she was, and I'd made a joke of it, saying either Sally or the chickens was getting the worst of it, but Jamie just held real still and listened, so I did too, and then I knew by the look in his eye it was something worse than that. The screaming was faint, from a distance, but it was high-pitched and a sort of wail, something panicky or painful.

Jamie threw down the leaf buds he'd gathered and started running—if you can call it running, trying to lift your feet out of the muck and push your way through the cattails. I threw down my leaf buds as well, figuring Ma would be mad at us for not bringing them in like she'd asked, but I threw them down and started after Jamie, running with all my strength, only it was like those nightmares where you can't run, no matter what, as hard as you try you can only go slow. The mud pulled at our feet and neither one of us looked out for cottonmouths, figuring they better just keep out of our way, unlike when we come down earlier that morning and slid off Buck, our eyes down and Jamie holding the Schofield, watching every step. It was cool so we had hoped they weren't around much yet.

Jamie got the lead on me. In spite of us being sixteen-year-old twins, he was stronger and faster and I kept yelling, "Wait for me! Wait for me!"

"Shut up," he whispered back. "Don't let them know we're here."

It was then I knew what he knew, that it was Comanches for sure, and my blood run cold because I knew the screaming for what it was—fear and suffering.

I thought at first Pa had got hurt or Sally got bit by a rattler or maybe Ma's frock had caught fire, but with his words I knew it was worse than that, and my heart was pounding and I couldn't breathe and the mud was pulling at me like it didn't want me to see what we were going to find. Then I heard a gun go off in the distance. It was Pa's Spencer for sure, the one he'd got off a dead Yankee, and he was trying to warn us maybe, or hold them off.

Then there were all sorts of voices screaming and I couldn't understand the words, and the reason I couldn't understand the words is because they were speaking Comanche. I started to weep and it seemed like forever before we were at the edge of the marsh, but just before we were out of the cattails Jamie turned and grabbed me by the arm and he said, "Don't you go up there, you hear?"

I tried to push past him but he jerked me around and he looked me in the eye and he said, "You listen to me. You stay here. There ain't no point in both of us going up there. Besides, I got the Schofield and you don't."

"I can help," I said.

"No, you can't. You're a girl—there's nothing you can do up there. I'll come and get you when it's over." And with that he pushed me back farther into the cattails and I fell back butt-first into the mud. Then he pointed at me like he was threatening me, but what he said was, "I'll be back, Jane," and he turned and pushed out of the cattails and ran up the hill toward the screaming.

I sat in the mud and I put my hands over my ears and I said to myself, *Stop the screaming! Stop that screaming!* Then the Schofield went off and there was another scream and then more yelling and I knew it was bad, and I couldn't figure out why the Schofield only went off once. I yelled at myself, *Go help them, get up there and help them!* Then I said, *No, you stay here, you're a girl, you can't help, he'll come back.*

There was no more screaming but there was shouting and hollering and it sounded angry. Then I smelled smoke and I knew they'd set the cabin and the shed on fire, and then the rains came.

It come on fast and hard, thundering and lightning and wind blowing and I couldn't hear if anyone was yelling or talking or calling. I pushed to the edge of the marsh on my hands and knees, trying to peek through the cattails, but it was pouring now, dark as night, and the lightning was so quick I couldn't get a clear glimpse of anything, so I sat back in the muck and I kept repeating Jamie's words, *Stay here, you stay here.*

So I stayed there but I said to myself, *You're a coward, go see what's going on. No, you could get hurt, there's nothing you can do, you're a girl.* And then I realized that even if I was a boy and if it was bad up there, without a gun what was I going to do, yell at them? Throw rocks at them?

The rain was coming down even harder now, pouring down, so I just knelt in the mud and I prayed, "Oh God, don't let them be hurt, oh dear God, don't let them be hurt," but I had a bad feeling that whatever I was praying for, it was all over and done with and the prayers wouldn't go for nothing unless they could work backward, and I wasn't even sure they worked forward. Ma always said they did, so I would pray and hope, and sometimes they worked out and sometimes they didn't, and when they didn't, Ma said, "*Gottes Wille.* That was just God's will."

"It would help if you could know what his will was ahead of time," I once told her, "so you don't waste time on something that's not to be and you don't get your hopes dashed."

"*Heidin!*" she'd said in German, slapping her hand down on the table. "Don't be a heathen!"

So I prayed and I tried not to cry but the bad feeling got worse and I wept and I froze because I was soaked through, and I didn't know how long I'd been in the mud.

Finally I couldn't take it anymore, so I got onto all fours and inched forward to the edge of the cattails, then I passed through them and up onto the limestone rocks. I couldn't see anything because of the rain, so I held real still and I waited for the lightning, and when it come, I saw, at the top of the hill, just for a second, something white on the ground, just outside the cabin. So I started crawling forward, and I worried that in the lightning flashes they might see me—but I realized I was so covered in mud I just might blend in with the earth, and even though I was crying and saying, "No, no, no," over and over, I ran my muddy hands through my hair so it wouldn't show up blond in the lightning.

I kept moving forward, looking for anyone moving in the flashes, but there was nothing and nobody, so I kept crawling to whatever was white.

Then there wasn't any lightning, but I kept on in the general direction, pushing rocks out of my way and crawling over wet stones and running into thorns and catclaw and feeling my way around the yucca. I was freezing from the rain and the fear and shaking so badly with a sick feeling in my belly, and crying, and trying not to cry, and holding my breath, and then panting like it was hot or I'd just run a mile and I thought I was going to throw up, so I just held my breath and kept on.

And then a bolt of lightning hit somewhere so close I liked to have jumped out of my skin, but it wasn't just the explosion and the flash that made me jump—it was Ma's eyes staring at me not three feet away, and in that flash I took it all in. She was flat on her back, stripped stark naked, scalped, her throat cut and her legs all akimbo. Jamie was on the ground next to her, his head bashed in like they'd pummeled him real good, and I knew in that flash what had happened.

When he saw what they were doing to Ma, he must have fired and hurt or I hope killed one of them, and then they swung around and jumped him before he got off another shot, and they thrashed him and pounded him and smashed his head in and scalped him. Then they slashed Ma's throat because they were angry, when they might have taken her with them like they'd done others, if he hadn't come along.

One flash of lightning and I saw it all and I was screaming and screaming, and then I began to throw up right there in the mud and rocks and I was weeping and screaming over and over, "Oh dear God, no, oh dear God, Ma, no!"

I ran out of breath screaming so I lay there panting, my eyes closed and my face in the mud, and then without looking at her I reached forward and found her face and closed her eyes. I lay there with my hand over her eyes saying over and over again, "Oh, Ma, I'm so sorry, oh dear God, no, oh, Ma, I'm so sorry."

And that was when the rains began to let up.

I don't know how long I lay there and I was just barely breathing. It reached a point where I couldn't sob anymore and the storm was moving on as fast as it had come, but I kept my eyes closed because I didn't want to look at them, and I rested my head in the mud and rocks. If the Comanches were around, I didn't care if I was seen anymore. I wanted them to kill me and have it over with.

As the sun come back out I opened my eyes and looked across from me, and that's when I saw the ocotillo, and I thought somehow the blood was still in the air, splattered, or maybe dripping from the branches, until I realized it was just their red blossoms, small, like tiny flags, waving with the wind.

I was going to have to look for Pa as well and find him dead too, and God only knew what kind of awfulness that was going to be. And I wondered where Sally was, and I knew that was going to be bad. She was either killed or stolen.

I crawled closer and I sat up and I grabbed Ma and I pulled her to me and I held her scalped, raw head in my lap. Her ma would have wanted her taken care of, I told myself, her own mother would have wanted her held and cradled and taken care of. Nobody would have wanted her child to end up like this. Nobody should end up like this. What was this world made of that anyone could end up like this, I thought, and what did it matter what prayers you said or what books you read or what you planted and harvested and ate or what friends you had or what games you played or songs you sang, if this was how it all ended up.

I don't know how long I held her. I don't know if the sun moved or just held where it was, as if time had stopped. The Bible says the sun stood still in the sky, so maybe this is what that was like. No time, nothing moved.

But I knew I had to move. I was like a stone, starting to move, if a stone could move. I laid Ma's head down and I was dry and hollow and I didn't know what to do. I looked down and the earth was all mud and blood mixed together, very little of it on their bodies because of the rain, and Ma's naked body almost clean, except for the scratch marks and cuts and bruises where she fought, at least for a time.

That's when I saw it, looking down at Ma's body.

A smashed eyeball in her hand.

So maybe that was what one of the screams was, and maybe it was that what got her throat cut. *Good for you*, I thought. *Somebody paid some kind of a price.*

I dragged Ma's legs together and I thought I'd never see my mother like that. I wondered if she knew when it was ending that I might survive and find her like that, and she must have felt nothing but rage and shame. Maybe in her pain and panic she didn't have time to think of any of that.

I couldn't look at Jamie. I was afraid to move him for fear his head was going to come apart in the mud, so I decided it was time to look for Pa and Sally.

Pa was in among the sandpaper oak. I can't say what they did to him but his clothes were gone and his eyes were staring at the sky and even though I didn't have anything to throw up, I gagged and heaved as I pulled it out of his mouth. I didn't know what to do with it, so I dropped it quick as I could on his belly, and I wept again even though there was nothing left to weep.

They must have caught him out in the open and he made a limping run for the oak hoping to hold them off from there, but they must have got in on him fast and that first shot was probably him trying to warn Ma and Sally and us. He couldn't have known it'd do no good, but he tried. They killed him, stripped him, scalped him, and then did that thing to him.

And Sally was nowhere in sight, not up at the cabin or with Pa, and I knew then she was gone.

I vowed I'd find her, and I vowed I'd kill any Comanche I ever met.

I looked down at Pa and I could see the scar on his leg from the war. I thought, how could this be? Second Manassas and Sharpsburg and Chickamauga and Little Round Top and all the others and then Appomattox, and now this. *You survived them all and ended up like this. Maybe it made you think you could survive anything. Moving out into this vulnerable territory, maybe you thought if the Yankees couldn't kill you for all their trying, then nothing could.*

Where is Buck? I suddenly thought. He was nowhere around, and that made me realize the cattle were gone as well, not a one of them in sight.

I shut Pa's eyes and I grabbed him by the ankles and began to drag him uphill and back to the cabin. *We're going home,* I thought, back to Ma and Jamie. He was heavy and I don't know where I found the strength but I got him there somehow.

I put Jamie between Ma and Pa because I figured that's where they'd want him, but I took Jamie's clothes off him first because I knew I'd need them. I buried all three of them in a shallow grave near the stand of chinaberry out back of the cabin, but just far enough away that I didn't run into the roots where I was digging. I covered them with a blanket from the cabin, scraped the dirt on top of them, then piled rocks on top of the grave to keep the coyotes and wolves away. God knows there were rocks enough.

It was getting on to noon and even though I had nothing left in me, I knew I had a journey ahead of me if I was going to find Sally and the cattle.

I stood by the grave and I figured, *You ought to say something. Tell them good-bye*, I thought, and I figured I should say something about God or heaven or the afterlife or forgive their killers for they knew not what they did, but I wasn't speaking to God anymore and the killers did know what they did, so I just promised them I'd find Sally, and then I sang "Wild Mountain Thyme." My voice was croaky but there weren't any tears anymore. I was feeling like a hollow shell, but I sang it and got through it and I wanted to tell them I'd get even, but I knew Ma wouldn't like that. And I knew there wasn't any even, so I kept it to myself.

I guess it wouldn't matter whether I said it or not because if there was a God he knew what I was thinking, and if there wasn't a God, then I couldn't help but think that Ma was still there and she'd hear it. "There's no virtue in vengeance," she'd say, "*nein Tugend.*"

I don't know if it was her actually talking to me or if I'd heard her speak good things so much that I was talking with her voice. Either way, I didn't want her to hear me say something heathen, but I kept remembering Jamie saying to me, "You're a girl, you can't help." And I thought back to him, *You ain't seen nothing yet.*

It was at that exact moment that Buck come ambling up.

We'd let him graze on the salt grass while we was picking the leaf buds from the cattails and he must have stayed down there through it all and only just now worked his way back up to the cabin, looking for some kind of a handout. And I thought, *Well, if there is a God, there's a sign, and what God wants me to do is kill every Comanche I meet until I get Sally back and I get the cattle back, and he just give me a horse to do it with.*

I went into what remained of the cabin to see what I could salvage.

They'd set the cabin on fire after they'd outraged Ma and killed Jamie, but the rains come on and they knew they had to get the cattle moving if they were going to steal that many of them. They'd thrown things around, but if they'd lost one of their own, then they were also dealing with taking the body home or finding some tree and scaffold to bury him on, so they didn't do a thorough search or finish the job of destroying the place, although they did find time to set the shed on fire and kill the mules and the hogs.

Everything in the cabin was knocked over or tossed outside, but I had the feeling it was more about being mad than actually looking for goods they could steal, so they missed the Sharps. They must have figured if they had Pa's Spencer and Jamie's Schofield they had everything, but I reached up high on the ledge where Pa kept it away from Sally's reach, and there it was, and there was the boxes of ammunition as well. I took all of it, and I knew that with Buck I was going to be able to get at least one of them before they got me, if they got me.

I threw off my mud-caked frock and I put Jamie's clothes on, wet and bloodstained as they were, and I put on his hat, and I knew I was a dead ringer for him.

Don't tell anyone you meet your real age, I thought. *Lie and tell them you're fourteen, if they ask. Maybe fifteen. No, fourteen. Make it fourteen, and they'll likely believe you're a young boy yet and not some sixteen-year-old girl.*

9

I still had some good hours of daylight left and I knew they'd be moving slow because of the cattle and carrying their dead, and Sally as well, and that was to my advantage. I dumped the boxes of shells into the saddlebags and I climbed aboard Buck, shoving the Sharps into Pa's scabbard. I pulled Buck around to the grave and we stood there, and I think Buck knew something was up because he stamped and shook his head and then he just stood real still.

"I'll be back," was all I said, and I turned Buck and we began to follow the track of the cattle. *Go real slow,* I told myself, *you got plenty of time, and don't give them a chance to skylight you.*

TWO

I knew they'd hurry at first, but hurry the cattle as they might, they couldn't afford to stampede them or they'd be hunting them all over the hills and through the brush while carrying a dead man across one horse and at the same time trying to keep Sally from slipping off and running away, if she had the sense to try that. And they had one man with his eye gouged out and more than likely in a lot of pain, unless the one-eyed man was the one Jamie shot.

He might have missed. I had to remind myself he might have shot wild, but I was hoping one was dead and one was hurt, and I swore I'd get at least one more and make them wish they'd never traveled south.

Because of the rain it was easy following the tracks and Buck was telling me to just hold on, but then I was always telling everyone what Buck was thinking. "Buck says he wants a handout," "Buck says he's thirsty," "Buck says he'd admire to have a roll in the dust and a day off."

"You don't know what that horse is thinking," Ma would say. "What you need is another little girl your age to talk to, *ein kleines Mädchen*, so you quit trying to read the mind of that buckskin horse."

My stomach tightened up when I thought of what Ma would say, so I stopped thinking in that direction, and Buck was telling me to pay attention and not get lost in my thoughts.

"You're right," I told Buck. "The last thing I want to do is ride right up on them."

We rode through mesquite and cedar and scrub oak and hackberry and around rocky ledges and through creeks, and I remarked how blue the sky was and how bright the sun, and it didn't seem like a day for death and dying. Spring flowers were opening up and there were bluebonnets and red paintbrush and white Mexican hat, but every time I saw ocotillo I had to turn away because it looked like blood that had splattered across the landscape. I thought I'd never get away from it.

The ground wasn't as churned up as when they were moving in the rain, so I knew this was about as far ahead of me as it took to gather up Ma and Pa and Jamie and bury them. What was that, two hours? Three hours? *That's how far ahead of you they are*, I thought. *You'll come up on them soon enough.*

I had Buck pick up the pace and he begun a fast run forward. I knew he was strong and I knew they'd ridden for days and days if not weeks before they come up on Pa and the cattle, so I was hoping their ponies were leg weary and hard used and I had the advantage on them. "Buck has bottom," Pa had said, meaning endurance, and I was counting on that.

I gave Buck his head and I watched the tracks to see what other signs there might be. If there was a band of ten or fifteen of them then I knew I didn't have a chance for sure, but I didn't see so many prints that I thought that was the case. *Good*, I thought, *maybe it's a smaller band that thinks it got lucky this day, killing a family and burning a cabin and kidnapping a young girl and making off with a small herd of cattle.* Only, one of them was dead, I hoped, and another one injured, so that was helping out with the odds—if they were a small band.

Buck kept it up as if he knew it was the mark of the cattle he was to follow, and I didn't weigh very much to make a hard burden for him. "You stay strong," I told him, "I'm going to need you."

I felt hollow inside when I thought back on Ma and Jamie and Pa, as if I'd left my insides on that rocky earth where I'd buried them, as if you could puke out your heart and your soul with your guts. I could feel muscle and bone, but I didn't feel grief anymore.

Maybe that would come back, but right now I could only feel the leather of the saddle and the reins and the warmth of Buck when I put my hand on his neck. And I could smell him and I could smell the clean washed air and the mesquite and the sweet fresh greasewood, and I could smell the crushed sage and the churned earth from the cattle tracks, and I could smell Jamie's sweat on his clothes I was wearing. At that I started breathing hard because I thought for a moment he was riding with me, and I had to remind myself, I rode alone.

I pulled Buck up and I got off and leaned my head against Buck and closed my eyes. I could feel his pulse against my head and I knew he had a strong heart and I only hoped mine was as strong as his.

I told myself, *Jamie is with you. You're riding with his blood on you, blood that just a few hours ago was inside his body and pushing through his heart and his brain and he was saving your life, telling you to stay behind. You're carrying him with you. He's riding with you.*

So take Jamie with you, I told myself, *and kill as many as you can, and if they kill you in the process, so be it. At least Sally will know someone tried, and when they get back to their camp maybe they'll think it was too high a price they paid for those cattle and one little girl.*

In that stillness I let my breathing slow down, and I touched Jamie's blood on his shirt.

And then I smelled the cattle.

Faint, like approaching the gulf from a distance and you smell salt long before you see water. And I heard a bellowing in the distance, and the bawl of a calf. Good, I thought. If they were going to drive the cattle without killing the calves, then that has slowed them down as well.

I took the Sharps and ran up a small swell and as I got near the top I lay down and crawled on my belly, struggling through the scrub, taking Jamie's hat off so there was as little to see as possible. When I got to the top, there in the distance was dust for sure.

"So there you are," I said, whispering it, as if whoever was riding drag at the tail end of the herd might have heard me if I'd said it any louder.

Some trees would be good, I thought. *If you've got some trees it might be easy to get one more after you've got the drag.* I knew I could get the first one for sure as long as there wasn't any rear guard watching. Maybe one of them might peel off just to check behind them, I told myself, so don't get too close, and keep a lookout left and right in case one of them comes in on your flank.

Pa would talk like that, in that Irish brogue of his. "Watch your flank," he'd say, if we were getting too close to some ledge or thick brush where a rattlesnake might be, or if a rider was coming in at an angle and we hadn't seen him to know if he was a neighbor or a drifter or a Kiowa begging or a Comanche on the scout. Watch your flank.

I looked around and the ground seemed a little rougher to my left than to my right. If a Comanche was going to double back he'd be coming in from the right to make it easier on himself, and he'd also figure if anyone was coming in on them, then that person would take the easier way as well, to the right.

So go left, I told myself, trusting that Buck was clear-footed enough that even if we slowed down because of the rougher terrain, we had a better chance of surprising them.

I crawled down the rise as fast as I could, grabbed Buck's reins, and told him, "We're going left." He jerked his head up and down and I thought, *He's agreeing with me,* and I heard Ma say, "That horse don't speak English," and I thought back, *Just you wait and see if he don't know English.*

I put Jamie's hat back on and pulled myself up onto the hurricane deck and Buck started out to the left without me pulling on the reins.

Buck and I circled around the rise, moving slowly over limestone outcroppings and around Spanish bayonet and then finding smooth and open paths every so often and breaking into a gallop whenever we could, so it was slow and go, slow and go. Buck moved like a shadow, slipping over ledges and skirting around scrub and cholla cactus and large stands of prickly pear like he'd been there before and knew the route.

I remarked to myself that even though the grief had left for now and everything felt empty inside, my heart beat faster whenever I thought of getting a Comanche in the sights of the Sharps. I tried not to think about how I found Ma and Pa and Jamie because I knew I needed to run cold now so fury wouldn't make my hands shake when the time come.

I kept my eyes on the outcroppings and the mesquite and I ducked under the low branches of the live oak as we rode. Buck was weaving in and out, then climbing slow, now stepping gingerly, then running for a fast stretch of good luck. I was circling wide and trying to imagine how far I'd gone since seeing the dust, and I knew by circling them I was making the distance greater, but it had to be that way if I was going to close in on them and not go plowing into them from behind.

Every so often I'd rein up Buck and slide off and throw Jamie's hat down and crawl up some bit of elevation and look for the dust. When I saw it, my breath would get faster and I'd tell myself, *Slow down, stay calm, keep your wits about you*, and I'd hear Pa saying, "Keep your head down, lass," which meant don't get spotted, but it also meant just do your job and don't get distracted.

I could hear the bellowing clearer now and I knew it wouldn't be long before I'd have to cut in on them and try to see how many there were and where best to take my first shot, and I knew I had to think it through if I wanted to get more than one shot off. If it was the drag that had Sally, I realized, I might be in trouble because I didn't know if I could be close enough and accurate enough to drop him and not hit Sally.

I hurried down to Buck. I calmed myself by just standing there and leaning into his shoulder again, and then he did that shiver horses do when they're shaking off a fly, telling me to get on with it. If we're going to do this, then let's get on with it.

I stroked his neck and threw on Jamie's hat again and mounted up and I checked the Sharps for about the hundredth time, and sure enough there was a shell in it. I put my hand on the saddlebag and felt the boxes of shells, more for assurance than to see if they was really still there. Then I clicked to Buck and he continued on, traveling north by northwest, swinging wide through the scrub mesquite and oak.

Good, I thought, *we're running into more cover. That's good for us and bad for them.*

I cut wide for quite a while, but slowly bore a little more to my right to edge in closer. The ground was rising and falling and I remember Jamie telling me the hills was actually giant fish and whales covered by dirt and rock, and we were living on top of a huge ocean that had gone dry, and if you dug deep enough you'd find old ships and the bones of great fishes. I thought that was nonsense, but every time I looked across the horizon and saw hills or bluffs or mesas, I'd think, *There lays a dead whale or some big ocean turtle.*

After what must have been an hour or so, I cut more easterly, keeping an eye out for a scout, seeing the dust get closer and hearing the bawl of the calves, hearing more clearly now and knowing I was closing in. If they were going slow enough I might be able to pick the exact spot I needed to be in order to kill the first one.

Buck and I kept moving in on them.

THREE

I found a small knoll that was well covered in rocks and cactus, soapweeds and scrub, and from the crest I could see the herd now. I lay flat, Jamie's hat beside me and Buck ground tied back below the crest, and I kept the Sharps down so the barrel wouldn't catch the light and warn them. I couldn't have timed it better. *Luck is with me*, I thought.

The cattle were lined out single file for what was maybe a quarter mile or so, and sure enough the calves and their mothers were at the tail end. There was one Comanche riding drag and trying to hurry them along, trying to keep them from straggling or spilling out, and all the while he was leading a horse with a body strapped over it.

Jamie did get one, I thought. *Good for him.*

The cattle were moving through a wide swale that curved off to the left, so I couldn't see the whole herd. Ahead of the drag, I could see one more Comanche riding flank on the left. There should have been one on the right, *so maybe they're short-handed*, I thought, *or maybe he's behind me somewhere.* I brought the Sharps up into position and adjusted the sights, the drag being a good seventy-five yards off at least, and I waited for the flank rider to take the curve of the swale and get out of sight. When the shot came, I didn't want him to know where it come from.

As they took the curve, I brought the Sharps down and rolled over onto my back and closed my eyes. I remembered Jamie pushing me back into the cattails and then finding Ma naked and then dragging Pa up to be with them, and I had to steady my breathing. When I opened my eyes, above me on the branch of a live oak was a scrub jay, looking innocent and simple and unworried, and I thought, *That must be nice, just sitting there and enjoying the shade, then flying off so free and easy.*

I rolled back over and brought the Sharps to bear on the drag and my breathing was easy and slow and I felt cool and bloodless, as if I was about to put in a normal day's work. The flanker was out of sight now and I gave him just a little more wait time, and I readjusted the sights.

Then I pulled the trigger. The Sharps went off with a boom and knocked into me hard like I expected it to.

I'd fired it lots of times before, the first time when Pa had shown Jamie how to use it, and I'd insisted anything Jamie could do I should learn to do too since we were twins, and there wasn't any reason not to show me just because I was a girl. Ma just shook her head, knowing we all had to be capable, but letting us know she didn't understand how things had come to this. How did she get here where her daughter was ramming a shell into what Pa called a Big Fifty, him saying that's what its caliber was, and then putting a hole in a cedar tree.

In spite of being knocked back, I saw the bullet hit and it was a lucky shot. I guess I figured the distance about right because it hit him square in the center of his back and his hands flew up and blood exploded and the round slammed into his horse's head as well, and I'm sure they were both dead before they hit the ground. *If I get out of this alive,* I thought, *I could have used that horse.*

The horse he was leading with the dead body shied back, then quieted down and looked for bunch grass to eat, having heard it all before, I guess.

That's one, I thought, and I didn't give any thought to the fact that I had just killed a man.

I threw the spent cartridge out of the breech and grabbed another shell from my pocket, jammed it into the Sharps, and closed the block. I knew the sound of the gun would carry far in the cool air, so I kept my eye on the curve where the cattle were rounding, figuring someone would be coming back fast to check on the noise, knowing full well what it was. If a half dozen or more came back I didn't know what I'd do. Maybe I'd get one or two of them before they got me pinned down and finished me off.

I steadied my breathing and I watched and I waited and I readjusted the sights for where I thought they might come, and sure enough the left flank rider come back from around the bend, looking for the source of the explosion, for powder smoke still in the air. At first he couldn't find the drag, then he saw both him and his horse down, and then he saw the horse with the dead body loose and wandering after grass.

The minute he saw all of that he reined up for just a moment. In that moment I pulled the trigger and the Sharps kicked hard and I wondered if I was ever going to be able to use that arm again, and at the same time I could see the bullet hit the Comanche's leg, blowing through it and then into his horse as well. I'd been aiming higher because I wanted the horse.

The Comanche grabbed his leg and the horse screamed and reared up and then fell sideways, taking the Comanche with him, then rolling right over his rider and then rolling back again. If the Comanche wasn't dead I hoped he'd have two broke legs and was bleeding to death, and if his legs wasn't broke then I hoped he was pinned down good, and sure enough he was. I could see the blood from both of them and he was struggling to pull free and he was looking to the copse of trees where I was, and he knew a second shot was coming his way soon.

I pulled the empty casing out and shoved another shell in, and I thought, *Serves you right, you son of a bitch.*

His horse was writhing and screaming and struggling to get up but making no headway, making it all the worse for the Comanche. I'm sure he was in a lot of pain but I didn't care and I was aiming to take another shot to put the horse out of his misery and leave the Comanche in his, when I heard a crack to my right, and at the same time bark and wood shattered off the oak behind me, both sounds together making a fearsome explosion.

I turned, and sure enough it was the second flank rider coming on toward me. So he had swung around to the right to look behind them, and I was glad I had swung to the left or he would have run straight into me as I was coming up from behind. I rolled over and rested the Sharps on a rock. He had Pa's Spencer in his hands and he was levering in another shell as he rode on hard toward the hill.

He fired and I knew he was just trying to get me to duck or run or hide, or hoping he'd get lucky and a wild shot would hit me, but I knew being on the move as fast as he was coming he wasn't going to be that accurate, and in that instant I realized he was the one who killed Pa, because the killer would have taken Pa's rifle as a trophy.

That made me angry, so I held my breath and aimed and because of his speed I knew I needed a big target to at least slow him down, so as much as I hated to do it, I hit his horse full in the chest and he stumbled and fell, and damned if the flanker didn't hit the ground running.

He saw the smoke from the Sharps and he screamed something high-pitched as he fired and the bullet hit the rock in front of me and scraps of rock and the splintered bullet went flying. I pulled the spent cartridge out of the Sharps and he was gaining ground on me and I was just barely able to jam another shell in, my hands shaking so. I waited just a moment for him to get close enough and as he was levering another shell into the Spencer I grabbed a rock and threw it as hard as I could.

He ducked, and he was only a few yards away, and he come back up and raised the Spencer and he fired and I fired and I felt his bullet fly by me and I saw mine hit him hard in the hip and it blew him back and the Spencer went flying. He lay there bleeding bad, and then, in spite of the pain, he was twisting and trying to crawl for the Spencer.

I rushed down and grabbed it before he could get to it, and there was a moment when he looked at me and he must have thought he was seeing a ghost, because in spite of his suffering he looked confused.

I said, "Look familiar?"

I figured he must have seen Jamie, and now here was Jamie back from the dead killing him, and maybe he had outraged Ma along with the others, so I dropped the Sharps and shot him with the Spencer and I thought, *That's justice*, and he shook and he trembled and he died with his eyes open.

Why is that? I thought. *Why do they all die with their eyes open? When you sleep at night your eyes are shut, so why don't they close when you die?* Ma's eyes and Pa's eyes and what was left of Jamie's face, they were all open. Maybe you see something when you're dead you don't see when you're sleeping. And now the Comanche was staring into that same sky like Ma and Pa and Jamie, maybe all of them seeing the same thing.

I ran back up into the trees and grabbed Jamie's hat and then ran down to Buck and shoved the Spencer into the scabbard, then climbed aboard.

I counted the shots from the Spencer. The tube held seven shells and it could hold an extra one in the chamber, but Pa never did that because it wasn't safe. So, the Comanche fired at me three times and I fired it once. That made four. Three left. No, two left, because Pa had got off a warning shot. Good to have remembered that, I thought. Two left in the Spencer. I had shells in the saddlebags but I'd reload it later when I had more time, if I had more time. I had killed three and that's better than I thought I might do. I slammed another shell into the Sharps as fast as I could and Buck got the message and took off at a dead run.

We headed north and I wanted to get ahead of the herd, or at least farther up alongside it. They'd think they were being hit from the rear now and that's what I wanted them to think, and who knows, if I should hit them from the side now or the front, maybe they'd think they were surrounded.

We swung wide, Buck moving fast and jumping rocky outcroppings and moving like wildfire, weaving around cholla and prickly pear and stands of yucca. When I thought we'd gone far enough, I cut back in toward the herd, looking for another rise to fire from and hoping I was near the head of the herd and looking to get a count on how many Comanches I had yet to deal with. No doubt some of them were falling back to the rear to see what was going on, and wouldn't they be surprised at the carnage.

Don't get cocky, I thought, *you could still end up dead and Sally lost.*

As I approached a rise, one of the Comanches beat me to it. He come up from the other side hoping to sweep around to the rear and see what was happening, and he ran straight into me coming up toward him.

I wheeled Buck around and yelled at him and Buck ran fast and now the Comanche was screaming an awful scream, "Hi-yi-yi-yi-yi!" and he was coming hard, both of us going downhill and tearing a hole in the wind, and I just had to hope that Buck was fresher and faster. We were in for a race for sure.

We hit an open stretch that fell away mostly flat. I leaned into Buck, keeping low, and he was weaving around the scrub, all at a dead run. I put a hand on his neck and told him he was doing good, when I heard the first explosion. It was the Schofield, and the Comanche had it and was firing at us.

So you killed Jamie, I thought. *All right, then, so now we know.*

I spoke to Buck and I don't know where he found it but he had more in him. The Schofield went off again and I thought, *Oh dear God, you can hit me but please don't hit Buck. I'm willing to die but I don't think I can take one more death.*

I glanced back and he was losing ground and I knew Buck's being fresh was to our advantage. *Just a few more yards,* I thought, *just a few more yards.*

We ran hard, and when I looked back again I thought the distance was in our favor, so I took a chance and waited for the Comanche to fire one more time, and when he did and missed, I called out to Buck, "Whoa!" I reined him back sharp onto his haunches and I twisted in the saddle as if maybe I'd been hit, and as Buck slammed to a stop I yelled, "Down!" and sure enough Buck lay down just like I'd taught him.

As he went down I rolled off and fell behind him out of sight, and as I did so I threw down the Sharps and slid the Spencer out of the scabbard. I hid behind the saddle, then I come up showing as little as possible and I brought the Spencer to bear on the Comanche. Buck looked at me as if to ask if I was sure this was what I wanted and I whispered, "Down," and he lay back, contented to do what I asked, figuring maybe I knew best.

I held steady and took careful aim and the Comanche wasn't sure what was going on, why we'd both fallen, and he started to rein up and he turned slightly sideways, looking hard, and I held my breath and fired and then I levered the last shell into the Spencer and breathed, and then aimed again and fired again, and then I threw down the Spencer and picked up the Sharps.

He was wavering on his horse and the horse was prancing back and forth, and I waited, aiming as best I could while he was trying to stay upright and control his horse, and when I felt I had a good shot, I hit him with the Sharps.

He went to the ground and he writhed and twisted in his death throes and I gave him space to die, and as I did so, I pulled the casing from the Sharps and slid in another shell, then I reached into the saddle bags and pulled out rounds for the Spencer, pulled the tube out of the stock and slid in all eight, levering one into the chamber so it would be ready to go just in case, all the while watching him go still.

When he had been still for a while, I rose and stepped over Buck and I approached him slowly.

His face was to the ground but his eyes were open, staring at who knows what, dirt and rocks or nothing, and there was a lot of blood all over. I reached down and picked up the Schofield and I fired one round into his head for pure vengeance and I said, "That's for Jamie, you son of a bitch," and I didn't give Ma a chance to say anything. I wouldn't have listened to her anyway.

No matter how still he was or how many times he'd been hit, I felt like I was standing next to something that might still be dangerous and deadly, like a diamondback on a cold day, so I backed up slowly to Buck, keeping an eye on the dead Comanche the whole time.

When I got to Buck, I broke open the breech of the Schofield to throw out the spent cartridges, then shuffled through the saddlebags, found the shells, and reloaded it, watching the Comanche all the while. Then I sat down and leaned my back into Buck's belly and felt him heaving and breathing hard, and I let myself be rocked for a minute before I realized I couldn't take time away from what was at hand.

This time I slid the Sharps into the scabbard, tucked the Schofield into my trousers, and held on to the Spencer. I stood up and I put my foot into the stirrup and I said, "Up," and Buck rose and I rose with him and I slid into the saddle as he got to his feet.

I rode up slowly to the Comanche's horse, a pretty black-and-white paint, talking to him real softly, and I grabbed him by his braided rawhide reins so he'd have to follow me and Buck. Then I turned Buck back toward where I thought the herd would be.

Lord knows what we're about to find, I thought, and then I remembered.

I wasn't talking to him.

⚜ ⚜ ⚜

There were only two of them, and Sally. I'd come into a copse of oak and there they were, right before me. And sure enough, there was John Bell Hood leading the herd.

"When we go north," Pa had said, "mark my words. John Bell Hood will lead the whole way, and when we sell them off we don't sell John Bell Hood. We bring him back with us, and when the time comes, he'll lead the next herd up as well. You don't sell off a good lead longhorn, and John Bell Hood is as good as they come."

And there he was, doing his job. "If a longhorn could be a ranahan," Pa had said, "then John Bell Hood is a ranny for sure. He don't quit."

When I saw Sally I thought my heart was going to explode out of my chest and I wanted to scream and tell her I was here, but I had to bite my tongue. The one who had Sally had a strip of cloth wrapped around his head, covering one eye. *So you're the one,* I thought, *the one who was outraging Ma when Jamie come up and fired. You all clustered around taking your turn and she took your eye out, and Jamie hit one of you and the rest piled into him and smashed him, and you cut Ma's throat, I bet.*

So you're the one.

I dismounted, and from the cover of the trees and the buck brush I released the paint and hit him on the backside hard with Jamie's hat and he run out of the trees and straight toward the two of them.

They'd been talking, I guess, and the one who rode alone had gone back and checked on what was happening and was now reporting on what he'd found. As the paint come out of the trees they both stopped talking and watched, and it was then that I dropped the one who rode alone, using the Sharps again. As long as I was good at judging the distance, I only needed that moment of stillness to pull the trigger and take the recoil into my shoulder.

It was after he fell that I ran into trouble. Instead of running, One-Eye grabbed his knife, reached around and cut the rawhide riata that bound Sally to the horse, and pulled her in front of him, his knife at her throat now.

She was screaming at the sound of the Sharps and she saw the one get hit and fall with blood splattering everywhere, and she saw his horse rearing and jumping and stumbling over the dead body beneath him, and she was scared to death. She cried and yelled and twisted but One-Eye held her tight and he turned and faced where I was, and there was no way I could get a shot off. I thought about killing his horse and getting him afoot, but he held his knife to Sally's throat and I didn't dare fire, even at his horse.

I shouted down to him, "I want the girl!" but I didn't know if he spoke English or not. He backed up his horse slowly and I yelled again, "I want the girl. I'll let you go if you give me the girl."

If he could understand me, he knew I was lying. He knew I'd kill him. He kept backing up, and when he was a little ways away he turned and headed into the cover of trees and scrub, and if I fired on him the shot might go through him and kill Sally, and if I followed after him I feared he'd cut her throat and take off.

I took a few steps closer and I screamed, "Sally, I'm here! Put her down and give her back!"

But he just disappeared into the scrub and I fell to all fours weeping and screaming and I didn't know what to do because I couldn't fire and I couldn't chase him, and I wanted to break something. I pounded the earth, and then I sobbed and lay down and I wanted to die, and I wished they'd just killed us all at the same time.

I wept for I don't know how long, then I rolled over and lay there exhausted and stared at the sky through the trees. There were clouds in the sky this time, thin straggly clouds looking like artillery shells had blown them all apart, shredding them. They looked like scars in the blue sky, I thought. They looked like my heart felt, and all I could hear in my head was how Sally had been screaming.

In the trees I saw a mockingbird perched high up with his gray body and his white-tipped wings and tail. What a name, I thought. Mockingbird. I stared at him and I thought, *All of this for nothing. Ma's gone and Pa's gone and Jamie's gone, and now Sally's gone,* and I couldn't think for the life of me how I was going to get her back. All loss, and nothing meant anything. Who knew what was in store for her, and as for me, I might as well be dead. Sing that song, mockingbird.

How could you lose all that and then go on living? If there was a God, then there was no justice, and there certainly wasn't any mercy. I felt like a hollow shell. And at the word "shell" I thought about taking the Schofield and just ending it.

I felt exhausted and sick to my stomach, so I curled up on the ground and I just lay there. If there was any Comanches left, then let them find me. Let them find me and finish me off.

I quit. I give up.

FOUR

I don't know how long I lay there, staring into the sky like one of the dead.

Then I felt something push my foot. I thought it was maybe one of the Comanches coming up on me and I thought, *Good, go ahead, have your way with me and do what you want, just get it over with fast.*

My boot was nudged again and I shut my eyes and waited for it to come, but at the third nudge I looked, and it was Buck checking in on me.

"I'm done," I told Buck, "I'm finished. There's nothing left in me."

He stood there and looked around and he just waited. So we both waited, and then he moved up alongside of me and his reins dragged across my body. I grabbed on to them and held them and I felt the smooth oiled leather, and I became aware there was something big and strong and breathing, with a heart pumping and blood running through him. I could feel it all coming down through the reins and into me.

Get Sally back, I thought. *Get help and get Sally back. Otherwise it's all nothing but loss.*

It took every bit of strength I had to get to my feet, but I did, and I put my arms around Buck's neck and leaned into him. He was warm and smelled like a horse and he was patient and he just stood there, and we were both silent for a while. Then I walked around him, touching him and checking him all over, making sure he hadn't been hit anywhere when the Comanche was firing at us, but he was in good shape.

I got aboard Buck and we rode down to the cattle, and since John Bell Hood didn't have a point man to follow he'd stopped and the rest of them had stopped and they were all looking for grass to eat. *Let them wander,* I thought.

I grabbed the reins of the paint I had sent off and then I went for the reins of the horse of the Comanche that had been talking to One-Eye, a bay that got all prancy when I approached him. I sweet-talked him and he danced all around and then he went along when I got his reins and pulled him up alongside Buck and the paint.

I moved back along the line of the cattle until I came to the Comanche who was pinned beneath his horse, and he had sure enough bled to death. I got off and went to his horse and checked through his parfleche and found some jerky and ate some of it up, realizing I was starving now, and I stripped his dead horse of his saddle robes and blankets, knowing it was going to get cold that night. I took a knife off of him and put it in my saddlebag, then I rode back to where I'd killed the drag and went through his parfleche, found more jerky, and took his robes and blankets. He was wearing leather leggings and I realized I didn't have anything to protect my legs when I'd be pushing cattle out of the scrub, so I pulled them off him, covered in blood as they were, and pulled them on over Jamie's trousers.

Grazing nearby was the horse carrying the dead man. I cut the rawhide strap that was tied under the horse's belly from his hands to his feet and pulled him off and he fell into the dirt, open-eyed, as if he was shocked at being dead, his arms and legs all akimbo.

Fuck you.

I knew Ma would have slapped me hard if she'd been there.

I took the reins of the dead man's horse and tied the parfleche and all the robes and blankets onto him, and now I had a string of four horses counting Buck. That would do me, I thought.

Then I did something I hoped I'd never have to do. I remembered Pa saying, "Calves do nothing but slow you down, and they'll be picked off by coyotes or wolves along the way. You can't have calves on a cattle drive." So I took the Schofield and there were I don't know how many calves wandering around the tail end of the herd. I shot all of them in the head, having to reload the Schofield more than once. It was awful. They went down and the mothers all started bawling but I had to do it if we were going to move faster now. I'd try and keep the mothers with the herd, pushing them even though they were grieving, but still, I hated doing it.

Holding the reins of my string I headed back up to John Bell Hood. I hurrahed him in a more northeasterly direction, then rode back along the herd, pushing at them and getting them in line. I rode back up on the other side, pushing them out of the scrub and driving them forward. *Keep them moving*, I thought, *and hope you find a larger herd going north to join before One-Eye comes back for you.*

And, God, help Sally. Keep her safe and don't let her be scared, and make them take care of her and not be cruel to her and help her to know I'll be coming for her.

There, I thought. *I talked to you.*

I rode point and John Bell Hood followed, and from time to time I'd ride back along either side of the line. It wasn't a large herd, maybe a hundred or so and too soon to be driving them north, but I didn't have a choice. Pa wanted the herd to grow and he had hoped to pick up more mavericks as well, but it was too late for that now. The last thing I could do was go back to a burned cabin and sit there with a hundred cattle and wait for the Comanches to show back up again.

I kept going over in my mind what I should have done about Sally but I couldn't see any way to have saved her. I thought about tracking her and One-Eye from a distance, and if he didn't spot me, maybe I could have picked him off, but what if I missed? Besides, he'd keep on the move as relentlessly as he could, day and night, not stopping at all. I kept telling myself there must have been something I could have done, but I couldn't figure out what it was, and I felt stupid and angry with myself.

Then I couldn't stop thinking about Ma and Pa and Jamie. Was it just this morning they died and how could that be? How could I be picking leaf buds one minute, then find myself with three Comanche ponies, a herd of cattle, and having killed five men the next minute? Yet here I was, dressed in Jamie's bloody clothes, a dead man's bloody leggings, and lost among some god-forsaken hills and draws and mesas, looking for salvation from a bunch of cowhands trailing a herd north who would probably want to do to me whatever the Comanches would do to me, if any of them found out I was a girl.

And at that thought I stopped and slid off Buck and I went over to the Comanche ponies. Other than pulling the blankets off I hadn't looked close at their saddles, but I found Pa's clothes tied in a bundle and I opened them up. They were bloody too, which made me sick to my stomach, and I have no idea what they wanted with them unless they were some kind of trophy. I had to stop and hold still for a moment, but then I took the knife I had recovered and I cut a long, wide strip out of Pa's shirt. I threw off Jamie's shirt and I stood there half naked in the setting sun and I wrapped the strip around my chest to flatten my breasts out so if I lied about my age and told someone I was a fourteen-year-old boy, then maybe there would be less of a chance of being noticed for a sixteen-year-old girl. I tied the strip off tight under my arm, and I threw Jamie's shirt back on.

I'm surrounded by blood, I thought, *wrapped up in blood.*

At that thought we moved out, and just before dark I saw a line of trees. Not just a copse of trees, but a line of ash and oak and cedar that stretched a distance and I thought, *That has to be water, the bank of a creek, surely.*

John Bell Hood smelled the water before I noticed the trees and he had been picking up the pace. I pulled back and watched the herd and like a line of soldiers they headed toward the water until they were trotting and bawling and sharing the word with each other that there was water ahead. They should have been guided in so John Bell Hood would hit the stream first and then all the rest shoved upstream so each one would be coming into fresh water, but I didn't have the strength to do it, and even if I did, more hands were needed to swing them in the right direction.

When they got to the tree line they plowed in and drank and the whole herd was milling about and bawling, but it was a shallow, clear stream running over a rocky bed so I figured they were all safe. I led Buck and the Comanche ponies farther upstream and they all drank their fill and I slid off Buck and I drank too.

Then I took all my clothes off, throwing them down on the bank, and I walked into the clear, cold water and I knelt down on the rocks and I scrubbed myself all over, as if it was the day's horror and not just the dirt and sweat and blood I was trying to wash off.

I still didn't feel clean. Maybe I felt dirty from all the killing, I don't know.

When I had washed off as best I could, I bound up my chest again and I threw Jamie's clothes and the leggings back on, and I tried to take comfort in the fact that Pa and Jamie were still with me in some way, maybe like some kind of shield, but it was cold comfort.

It was getting darker and the sunset was bloodred and I thought, *That seems just about right, the whole world is bloody, even the sky.*

I pulled jerky out of a parfleche and ate it, then I pulled Buck's saddle and blanket off and ran my hands all over him and thanked him and told him I'd brush him proper the first chance

I got. I pulled the saddles off the Comanche ponies and I took a rawhide strip from one of their saddles and made a hobble out of it for each one of them and Buck, then I let them go. The rising grass was good here and there was water, so I hoped they'd stay nearby. I was too tired to nightguard the cattle, so I figured if they wandered off or stampeded I'd just resign myself to the loss. I'd lost everything else so I might as well lose the cattle too.

It was getting cold as the sun went down, so I wrapped the robes and blankets around me as best I could and I sat up against a tree, feeling tired and sick at heart. I knew One-Eye wouldn't stop for the night and I knew Sally must be scared and cold and exhausted. I couldn't quit thinking about her and wracking my brain for what I should have done to save her, and I kept imagining One-Eye turning around and coming back on me in the middle of the night and he would discover I was a girl and do to me what he had done to Ma before he cut my throat, all for vengeance. Vengeance must make the world go round, I thought, and I tried to resign myself to it being OK to die out here.

Then I had to ask myself, why did I take after the Comanches by myself? I could have ridden for help, but it was miles to another farm and miles and miles to a settlement, and what could I do but gather up a few men who wouldn't have let me ride with them because I was a girl, and the men would all have farms and shops and families that had to be taken care of, so how long could they have tracked them in the first place, and if they had found them and attacked them, Sally could have been killed in the cross fire.

I kept going over it and over it, sick about Ma and Pa and Jamie and scared for Sally and afraid of One-Eye coming back, at the same time hoping the horses didn't stray and the herd wouldn't stampede, and wondering what should I have done other than what I did do. Then the words came to me.

"I have been assigned months of misery, and troubled nights have been allotted to me. My days come to an end without hope.

Remember that my life is like the wind. I shall not see happiness again."

I surprised myself because I sure couldn't remember ever memorizing those words, so was Ma speaking to me now, or was I dreaming her reading from the Bible by the fire at night?

Then I heard Ma say, *"Liebes Herz,* dear heart, Job was in the slough of despond when he said that, just like Christian in *Pilgrim's Progress,* remember, child? You're in the slough of despond."

She would have us read aloud from *Pilgrim's Progress,* to teach us better English than hers and to give us good instruction, but I was tired and bewildered and I couldn't figure out how Job got from the Bible into *Pilgrim's Progress.*

I awoke with the sun in my eyes.

I was panicked, as if I had been caught sleeping on guard duty and I just knew I was about to be shot or have my throat cut, but I looked around and all seemed calm. I could spot the ponies in the nearby distance and the cattle as well and they were all grazing and there'd been no stampede. I'd only need to swing around them and push them back in together and get John Bell Hood out front.

I went to get up but every muscle in my body ached and I couldn't even move my arm. I rolled over and pushed myself up on all fours, then stood up, using my good arm and hand to clutch the tree next to me. I felt as if I had been beat with a stick, so I slid right back down again, waited a minute, then reached over and pulled some jerky out of the parfleche and ate it. It tasted good because the Comanche women had pounded berries into the meat before it dried.

I got to my feet again and I tried to move my arm and the shoulder began to loosen up a bit. Then I did something I'd heard

Pa talk about, what he had done as he walked home from the war with a wounded leg. I took Jamie's shirt off and I walked down to the creek and lay down on my back by the edge of it and put my arm and my shoulder into the water, and the cold began to numb the pain and ease the swelling. While I was lying there my thoughts went back to Sally, wondering how she had survived the night and if they were still traveling hard and if One-Eye gave her something to eat and got her some water. There was nothing I could do about it, so I closed my eyes to it.

Finally I stood up and put my shirt back on and swung my arm some and I whistled for Buck and he heard me and came in from afar. I had intended to saddle up the paint and see how he rode and get him used to trailing cattle, but with my arm the way it was I couldn't take the chance of being thrown, so I had to count on Buck one more time before I could spell him. If I could get my arm moving and if I could get the other ponies used to pushing the cattle, then I could switch them out and keep them all fresh.

After I unhobbled Buck I had a hard time getting the saddle on him. I got the blanket on but I didn't have the strength to swing the saddle up on top of the blanket, so I got under the saddle and tried to push it up with my body but that just shoved the blanket off. I tried that two or three times before I asked myself what I thought I was doing, and I called out, "Down," and sure enough Buck lay down. I put the blanket on him, then with my good arm I dragged the saddle mostly on him and I called out, "Up," and as he rose I shoved the blanket and the saddle into position and there he was, standing, all saddled.

I tightened the girth and I bridled him as best I could, my arm starting to help somewhat, and that gave me some hope. "We may just get out of here yet," I said to Buck, and he nodded and shook his head, adjusting the bit and the bridle.

I checked the ammunition to all the weapons and tied my robes and blankets back onto Buck, then I managed to crawl aboard. We rode out to the Comanche ponies and I took off their hobbles, and instead of leading them I hoped they'd act like a remuda and stay with the herd as it moved out. Buck and I swung wide around the herd and slowly pushed them back together, singling out John Bell Hood and trailing him northeasterly. Then I doubled back and hurrahed the herd and slowly they lined out and followed John Bell Hood, and the Comanche ponies stuck together and followed along off to the side.

By God it's working, I thought, but I was begrudging in my attitude because I wasn't in a mood for giving him much praise.

We traveled that way for a few days, I don't remember how many, making maybe eight miles a day, before the blue norther hit.

FIVE

I knew my luck had been too good to hold. I felt the temperature drop, and then with every fresh blow the temperature was dropping faster. I pulled one of the blankets off the back of Buck and tied it around me as best as I could, and I rode out to the ponies and grabbed their reins to keep them with me. If it hit hard they would scatter, their tails to the wind, looking for shelter, and I knew I'd never find them.

I was freezing, thinking, what was I doing riding out without some kind of slicker or mackinaw? Where did I think I was going, on a picnic? I couldn't help but think I'd made every mistake in the book, and now things were about to get worse. The wind blew harder and it got colder and colder and the cattle were looking for some kind of shelter, all of them thinking it lay to the south.

I rode up and down the line, over and over again, trying to shove them back together. They responded to the shouting and hurrahing, but as soon as I got them back some other bunch would spill out from the line. It was like trying to catch chickens. I was scared and I knew this norther could go on for days if my luck was truly run out.

It began to snow heavily and it was getting harder to see and for a long time I couldn't even find John Bell Hood. When I did, he was headed for a shallow arroyo, so I doubled back and pushed as many cattle as I could in that same direction. The snow was getting heavier and I was freezing, my teeth chattering, the blanket hardly on me.

The snow was so thick I couldn't tell how many were in the arroyo and how many were still out on the plain. I got worried I'd get lost if I went looking for more of them, and I was remembering awful stories of travelers getting caught in the open and freezing to death, so I gave up and listened for the bawling and made it back into the arroyo myself.

It was still freezing but we were out of the blast. I slid off Buck and untied the other robes and blankets and gathered them all around me as best I could and hunkered down, holding the reins of all the ponies to keep them from straying and making them a buffer between me and the cattle so I didn't get trampled. I knew better than to unsaddle the horses. Pa had said when it got cold, the saddles and blankets would help keep the ponies warm.

I kept hoping it would all be over shortly and my luck would shift back, but it didn't let up for two days and they were the longest days and nights of my life. I thought, *They'll find me here frozen and the reins will be frozen in my hand and the four horses will be frozen and all the cattle will be frozen, and all of us will be found like some kind of ice statues in this arroyo.* Then I remembered more awful stories about buffalo and prairie chickens and pronghorns and such being found frozen stiff, or folks losing their way trying to get from a shed to their cabin and freezing to death only a few feet from a door, and even windjammers I'd heard about snow so deep horsemen and wagons rode over the tops of fences.

From time to time I got up and jumped up and down and moved around and leaned up against Buck, and I even crawled under him to keep the snow off me. I found myself wondering if I couldn't walk into the middle of the herd and pick up some warmth there, but they were shifting and butting up against one another, and with those long horns I figured I'd be lucky if I didn't get battered to death, so I just stayed under Buck and tried to make myself as small as possible.

When it got dark, I thought the nights would never end and the awfullest questions came to me all night long. How long did it take Pa to die and was he still alive when they scalped him, and did Ma see Jamie try to come to her rescue and did she see her boy get hit so hard it smashed his head and killed him, and did she wonder where was I, and when your throat gets cut how terrible is the pain and how long did it take her to bleed to death, and wouldn't that be like choking and drowning in your own blood, and did Sally see it all. The questions went on and on but I could only imagine so far before I had to close my eyes to it and just weep, it being so bad.

When I wasn't thinking about them, I remembered hearing that before you freeze to death you feel real warm and you just fall asleep. I thought maybe that wouldn't be such a bad way to go, and I kept waiting to feel warm but it didn't happen. I just shivered and chattered all night and all day.

At dawn on the third day the norther blew itself out. There must have been a good six or eight inches of snow on the ground and it was still freezing, but the sun come out and that gave me some hope, as if I could fool myself into thinking bright meant warm. I struggled to my feet and I led my string up and out of the arroyo and dropped their reins. Even they were too cold to go running off, and instead they started pawing through the snow looking for grass. I mounted up on Buck and took a look around.

Most of the cattle had already climbed out and were nosing through the snow for grass. A ways off, just as I feared, I could see several mounds covered in snow, cow brutes that hadn't made it into the arroyo and had frozen to death, probably the weaker ones, only one was still struggling to get up. I dismounted Buck and grabbed the steer by the tail and twisted it, and sure enough I tailed him up and he started nosing for grass too. A few had weathered the norther, gathering around trees or bunching together. It took all morning to circle around and find them and drive them in, and I was sure some had wandered far away, always moving south, being driven by the wind.

When I got the cattle back together, it looked to me like I had lost about a dozen or so and I decided I'd ride along the line and count them once I got them strung out and moving. After I ate some jerky, and before trailing John Bell Hood northeast, I slid off Buck and took his saddle and I approached the Comanche bay. After having watched all three, it seemed to me he was the mildest-tempered of the ponies. He was skittish sure enough as I approached, but not so much that I wasn't able to grab his reins. I talked to him for a while, and when he calmed down I threw a blanket on him and then I managed to throw Buck's saddle on him and tighten the girth.

He pranced around but he didn't get snuffy, so I mounted up slowly and again he pranced and danced, but before long he was responding to me and I knew I could give Buck a rest. I called him Dancer because of how he sidled and moved. I could deal with him dancing and I was just grateful he wasn't pitching.

We got John Bell Hood moving northeast and I rode up and down the line, calling out and hurrahing them. They slowly fell into place, and we were traveling again.

We rode that way for what I think was maybe four or five days, making slow time but finding water when we needed it. The weather warmed up and the snow melted, and the rising grass was coming on strong and they grazed aplenty when we stopped at noon to rest, then again when I threw them off the trail and we bedded down.

We moved steadily and I took the time to break in the other ponies to trailing the cattle. The sorrel I named Blood because of his color and he responded well to my touch and would make a decent cowpony, but the paint took more time, being ornery and objecting to the saddle and not liking me being on top of him. He even threw me twice and thank God I didn't land on my sore arm or among the prickly pear. I called him Paint because that's what he was, with real pretty black-and-white markings.

Over the next few days I'd switch them off and slowly Paint
got used to the idea he was someone else's horse now. He pitched
some, but I always knew when he was going to do it by the way
he bogged his head down right before trying to cut loose. I think
he got tired of me staying in the saddle, mostly. He'd usually do
it in the morning when he was feeling fresh and salty, so I learned
to line him out and get him into a run first thing, and that took
the rough off him.

Once Paint got used to pushing the strays back into line, he
got the idea and showed he had the makings of a good cutting
horse. He was nimble and he began to get in front of the cattle
before they could get hidden in the scrub, pushing them back
without me having to rein him into doing it.

The jerky lasted, so I figured the Comanches had come
from quite a distance because of how much of it they were carrying, and I found myself wondering what they thought they
were doing, showing up and attacking everybody. Sometimes a
Comanche or a Kiowa would come around begging or trying to
steal something, maybe making off with an axe or demanding a
beef or maybe just being bought off with biscuits or Ma giving
them a meal. We knew they could be dangerous and there was
always stories about someone being kidnapped, two kids being
stolen from a field or a wagon being stopped and the driver killed
and a woman outraged, so we knew to be wary, but it had seemed
to be safe enough, and we carried a weapon at all times.

What drove them to kill everybody and make off with horses
and cattle, I wondered, knowing they might be tracked and
caught? It baffled me. We were fools to think we were safe.

The nights were cold and I bundled up as best I could and I
would ride out two or three times a night on Buck and circle the
herd to make sure they weren't straying. When I bedded them
down I made sure they had plenty of room, hoping they wouldn't
get spooked and stampede, and maybe it was because they were a
small herd that they didn't spook. There was she-stuff with them

as well, and Pa always said she-stuff kept steers calm, and I was grateful.

During the day I was busy keeping them in line, so I didn't have much time to think. It was the nights that were the worst because it was cold, and that's when I couldn't stop thinking about what had happened to Ma and Pa and Jamie and going over and over it in my head, imagining it from every possible angle, getting angry and sometimes just feeling nothing, or having nightmares when I did sleep, and then weeping, and then just worrying myself sick about Sally.

I lost track of time and it was after I don't know how many days that I spotted the most magnificent sight I'd ever seen, and it took my breath away. It was a herd, and we were angling straight for it. I had topped a low rise, riding ahead of John Bell Hood, when the herd hove into view, the prairie sweeping away for a far distance, there being fewer arroyos and bluffs and mesas now.

And there they were, less than a mile or so away, some two thousand of them, I bet, a large herd some fifty yards wide, strung out for a mile or more. The trail boss was out of sight, probably far ahead, scouting the route, but I could see the camp wagon following alongside and there were the points and the swings and the flankers and the drags, all on either side of the line, and I could hear the bawling of the herd, and far on the other side I could make out a remuda of what looked like about a hundred and fifty horses and mules, with the horse wrangler nearby, snaking in what I guessed was wood or buffalo chips for the cook.

They were a beautiful sight, everything Pa had described when he told us what it was like to take a herd north. I remembered him taking a stick and drawing a long line in the dirt, saying, "Now, look here, that's the herd, see?" And he said, "The trail boss will be out front, scouting the terrain, deciding the route and looking for water and good bedding grounds." He went on, drawing an X on either side of the herd at the front, saying, "These are the point men. They're the two most experienced hands and they turn the herd, see? No one rides point ever but these two men."

Then farther back he drew two more Xs on either side of the line, saying, "These are the swings. They help guide the herd and push in strays." He drew two more Xs even farther back, saying, "And here are your flankers, keeping the herd in line and pushing in brutes that spill out, and back here..." And he drew two more Xs at the very tail end of the herd. "These are the drags," he said, "eating a lot of dust and pushing the stragglers and picking up beeves that got away from the swings and the flankers."

"Now, your remuda is here," he said, making a mark, "and the camp wagon is here"—making another mark in the dirt.

I thought it was a most beautiful picture, and until the winds blew it away I'd go out and look at it and marvel at the miraculousness of it all.

He'd been starting his own herd to take north someday, and he said Jamie would start out as the horse wrangler because that's where the newest and the youngest always started.

"What would I be?" I asked. "I could be a horse wrangler too."

"Girls don't ride with a herd, lass. The hands don't take to a girl hand no matter how bonnie she is."

He tried to cajole me into accepting it but I said, "That don't make sense. I can ride as good as Jamie, if not better, and I'm the one that rides Buck backward and stands up on him and teaches him tricks like how to count and how to lie down."

Then Jamie got all angry and told me that's what I get for being born a girl, and I tried to hit him and Pa stopped me and said I'd be needed to help Ma with Sally, that was a tough job too, and he winked at Ma and she just gave him a look and she asked, "What does a damn cowhand know about *die Frauen*, women?"

43

The only time I ever heard her use that word was when she would call him a damn cowhand, only she said it with the hint of a smile, never mean. She always said she was mad at herself, falling in love with a damn cowhand of all people, "and an Irish one at that." She said she couldn't imagine what she thought she was doing, and she'd give him that look, and he'd do that wink of his.

And now there the herd was before me, going north, the brutes black and brown and tan, yellow and red, some of them spotted and some of them striped, all of them like a box of colors, and their long horns swaying and looking all polished and glinting in the sun. There they were, the herd I'd been looking for, and it would provide me with some safety, for at least now, I hoped.

I ran my hand over my chest to make sure I wasn't showing, and then I realized I had forgotten all about my hair.

I got off Paint and pulled the knife out from my saddlebag. I hated to cut it because I liked my hair, how long it was, but I knew I couldn't hesitate. It was going to be a stretch, hoping they wouldn't recognize me for a girl anyway, so I cut away at it, as close as I could, leaving only a couple of inches or so, and when I finished, there it lay in the buffalo grass. I picked it up and held it and touched it and smelled it, then I tossed it as high as I could and the wind caught it and carried it south and I thought, *There you go, you're not a girl anymore. All gone.*

Then I remembered Jamie saying, "You're a girl, you can't do nothing, stay here."

So in my thoughts I said back to him, *It ain't your fault. You didn't know what I could or couldn't do. I'm a cowhand now and no one can say, "You're a girl, you can't ride with us."*

So here I go.

I mounted Paint and John Bell Hood was just coming over the rise, him following me and the herd following him. I told him, "There you go, John Bell Hood, there's our new family," and we pushed off the rise and headed toward them.

SIX

O ne of the swings peeled off and rode toward me, coming at
an easy lope, and I got scared, afraid he'd recognize me for a
girl, even imagining he'd send me back in the direction of One-
Eye. Then I got ahold of myself and said, *What are you thinking?*
The worst thing that can happen is you follow them at a distance.
They don't own the prairie any more than you do.

He was a Negro, a large man in a white shirt with a red scarf
around his neck and a black vest and a wide-brimmed hat and
worn chaps, and as he reined up he had a big smile on his face.
He said, "How you doing, son?"

At that my heart leapt because he didn't recognize me as a
girl right off, and I said, "I'm just fine, sir, how are you?"

"Doing fine. Where's the rest of your crew?"

"Ain't got no crew. I'm it."

He looked me up and down and said, "What the hell happened to you?"

"What do you mean?"

"You're covered in blood."

I had forgotten I was wearing Jamie's clothes and the
Comanche's leggings. I said, "You're sure right about that. That's
a long story."

He considered me and then asked, "What do you call yourself, son?"

That was exactly what Pa said they would say. You didn't ask
somebody what their real name was because they might have left
that behind them due to some kind of trouble, but I gave him

Jamie's full name and he leaned over and offered me his gloved hand. He said he was Bill, and it was the first time I ever shook a Negro man's hand.

"You look to be a long way from home," he said.

"I am, sir. Comanches made off with our herd but I got them back and now I'm trying to get them north and sell them."

"Why didn't you take them back home?"

"There ain't no home. Comanches killed my family and burned the cabin and took off with my sister as well as the herd. I got the herd back but not my sister."

"I'm sorry to hear that," he said. Then he asked, "What happened to the Comanches?"

"I killed them all, except for the one that got away with my sister."

I wasn't sure if he believed me or not, then looking at my string he asked, "Those Comanche ponies?"

"All of them but the buckskin. He's mine."

"You took them from the Comanche?"

"Yes, sir."

"That's where all the blood come from?"

I didn't want to explain to him it was Jamie's shirt and Jamie's blood, so I said again, "Yes, sir."

He just sat there a while longer, evaluating me maybe, and he whispered, "Well, I'll be damned." Then he asked, "How old are you?

I lied and said, "Fourteen,"

And he said again, "Well, I'll be damned."

"I'd like to join your herd. I can't trail these all the way north by myself. I need some help, and if you let me join up I can promise I'll be a good hand."

He kept looking me over and then looking the herd over, small as it was. If I had killed the Comanches and trailed the herd this far by myself, maybe I would make a good hand. At least that's what I hoped he was thinking.

"How many did you kill?" he asked, not even looking at me but maybe making a rough estimate of the size of my herd.

"Five. The sixth one got away with my sister."

"I'm sorry to hear that," he said again.

"I'll be going after her as soon as I can."

"Son, not by yourself you won't." He considered it all, then said, "Wait until we get past you and then fall in about a mile behind. I'll talk to the boss once he finds a bedding ground— then he'll be back to talk to you."

"Thank you, sir."

He smiled again and gave me a salute, then turned and galloped back to his herd.

Paint and I held John Bell Hood in position and the rest of my herd slowly closed in and milled around, content to stop and graze. I rode back to make sure the stragglers were with us, then I pulled Paint in front of John Bell Hood and we all waited for their herd to pass by.

When they were out of sight I felt lonely and scared again, as if they were going to forget about me, but I heard Pa say, "Hold steady," like he said when I come up on a rattlesnake one time without seeing it first, but he did see it, and he just said, "Hold steady." I turned to him and he said, "I want you to walk off to your left now real slow," and he was smiling like there was nothing wrong, and at that I knew there was something wrong, so I did exactly what he said, and then he pointed back at the rattler. It was cool out and the rattler hadn't struck or even coiled up to rattle and warn us away.

So I said to myself, *Just hold steady and do exactly what you are told to do.*

When I thought their herd was surely a mile or so away, I nudged John Bell Hood and he started out. I circled the herd, whistling at them and hollering and pushing them, and they fell in line.

The string followed along and we soon hit their trail. When we did, I turned north and John Bell Hood turned north and the herd turned north and my string of ponies followed alongside us. I thought, *Here we are, we're safe now*, and I tried to tell Sally such things as, *It won't be long now, honey, I'll be coming for you. You be a good girl and do what they say, and I'll be there as soon as I can to hold you and kiss you again. Hold steady.*

And I tried not to weep at the thought that I was leaving her farther behind.

We traveled that way for several hours, and late in the afternoon I rode ahead and caught up to where I could see them watering their cattle. Their bedding grounds would be on the far side of the creek, so I swung my herd farther to the west and we hit the creek about a mile upstream of them. While we were at the creek, in the distance, I could see a rider coming for us, so after I got a drink myself I rode out to meet him.

A ways out he raised a hand and I raised my hand and he come up alongside of me. He looked me over and he said, "So you're the kid, huh?"

"I guess so, sir."

"How many in your herd?"

"Eighty-seven, sir."

He appraised them and checked out my string and he said, "So you killed five Comanche?"

"Yes, sir."

"How'd you do that?"

"I sort of surrounded them."

There was a flicker of a smile. He was a broad-shouldered man with a battered hat and a face that had seen a lot of wind and rain, sun and hail and sleet and snow.

"Do you have a bill of sale for the beeves?"

"No, sir. They set our cabin on fire and any documents got lost in the flames."

Which may or may not have been true but who knew. The last thing I thought when I headed out was to look for Pa's bills of sale for the beeves he had purchased.

"Has your herd got a road brand?"

"No, sir, there wasn't time for that. This herd wasn't supposed to go north yet, and once I got them back from the Comanche I didn't have an iron, and even if I did I sure couldn't stop and brand them all by myself."

Again there was a hint of a smile. "So you think they're coming after you?"

I knew I was in trouble at that, because if they were coming after me that meant I was trouble for him too. I told him the truth and said, "Sir, I sure wish not."

I didn't doubt he was a hard man, but the slightest bit of a smile told me he wasn't cruel, or at least that's what I hoped.

"My name is Mike," he said, extending his gloved hand, and I shook it and his hand swallowed up mine. It was like shaking hard leather, his hand feeling big and tough inside the glove.

"I'm Jamie."

He asked how old I was and I told him the lie about being fourteen years old, and he nodded again and I was thinking, *This lie may just pan out after all.* I wanted to run my hand over my chest to make sure there was nothing to give myself away, but I resisted the gesture.

He said, "I'll tell you what." And there was a long pause while he ran his gloved hand over his face. "Move them across the creek and bed them down, then come in and get some bait, and you and I will discuss how we're going to handle this, all right? I bet you haven't eaten much, am I right?"

I told him I had some jerky I'd taken off the Comanches, but I'd been afraid to try and shoot a prairie chicken or a pronghorn for fear of stampeding my own herd. "Besides," I told him, "I didn't have anything to start a fire with."

He said, "Son, I think we can do you better." Then he caught me looking at the snakeskin tacked to the cantle of his saddle and he said, "Rattlesnake. Keeps away the rheumatism."

"Does it work?"

"It has so far." And there was that hint of a smile again.

At that he turned and rode back to his herd. As I watched him leave I started to weep because I was so relieved, and I thought, *Oh God, please don't let him turn around and see me crying,* so I quickly pulled Paint back to the herd. I dismounted and I pulled the saddle off Paint and as I crossed over to Buck I could hear Jamie say, "Just like a girl."

I got mad and I said, "You're goddamned right just like a girl." I saddled Buck and I said, "Yes, just like a goddamned girl," and I pounded the saddle with my fist until I made the tears stop.

I leaned against Buck and caught my breath, then tightened the girth and bridled him and I mounted up and pushed the herd across the creek, then circled them to make sure they were settled. I hobbled my string, then rode easterly to join their herd. I said to myself, *Don't go crying in front of them. Cowhands don't cry in front of each other and you're a cowhand now.*

I rode into their camp and it was a crew of about a dozen or so, two of them out circling the herd already as nightriders. The rest all sat on the ground or on their bedrolls with a tin plate in their laps and coffee nearby, their night mounts at the ready, and the bait sure smelled good. They had beans and biscuits and beef stew and stewed apples, and at the prospect of such a meal I realized I was starving.

One of them, a heavyset balding hand, looked up and said, "You the Comanche killer?"

I didn't know what to say to that and before I could think of an answer, this young hand who was tall and lean and didn't look much older than what I really was hollered out, "Small cheer and great welcome makes a merry feast, right?"

And then this small wiry hand spoke up, saying, "That there young man is Shakespeare, and Shakespeare likes to talk Shakespeare."

They all laughed at that and the Shakespeare hand come over and he said he was the horse wrangler, did I want him to take my pony for me.

He was a lot taller than me and he had eyes that were summer-sky blue and sandy hair that might have had a bit of copper in it if the light was right, and he seemed real friendly.

I said, "No, he'll stay ground tied right here and I'll be taking him back to my herd with me in a few minutes."

Then this Shakespeare character said, "'Tis an ill cook that cannot lick his own fingers, right?" He laughed at his own joke and then showed me over to the camp wagon, saying, "This here is Monty."

The cook, Monty, a burly Mexican with a limp, pretty much ignored me but handed me a plate and then doled out the stew and the beans from blackened and beat-up kettles and handed me three biscuits, then gave me a ladle of stewed apples.

I said, "Thank you, sir."

He nodded at me without looking at me and mumbled something, then pointed at the coffee and said, "*Cafecito,*" and handed me a tin cup.

I was trying not to shake I was so hungry and grateful. Shakespeare grabbed a rag to hold the coffeepot handle and poured it for me, and when he saw my hands shaking he said, "Whoa, kid." He dragged me over to the other men, giving me all the hands' names but I couldn't get any of them straight, other than the heavyset balding fellow was called Skinny and the small wiry one was Jack Straw.

Then this Shakespeare character winked at me, saying, "I almost die for food, let me have it, right?" and he laughed again.

I didn't know what to say to that, and then one of the men asked, "How'd you get the blood on you, son?"

Another chimed in, "That's Comanche blood, I bet. Is that Comanche blood, kid?"

And another said, "We hear you killed a bunch of Comanches. Is that true?"

My mouth was full and I couldn't answer, and the one called Jack Straw said, "Let the poor kid eat. I bet he's starving."

I was grateful none of them had identified me as a girl yet, so I just nodded yes to the questions about the Comanches.

One of them said, "What do they call you?"

I swallowed and I managed to say, "I'm Jamie," and then my mouth was full again. I looked over and Shakespeare had pulled Buck's saddle and blanket off anyway and had gotten a currycomb from the camp wagon and was brushing him down, and I wanted to weep to see someone taking care of Buck, but I knew I couldn't do that.

Shakespeare caught me looking at him and he smiled and did a wink and he said, "My kingdom for a horse, right?"

I didn't know what to say back but I figured he was telling me he knew how much Buck was worth to me, a kingdom, and I knew that was true, so I managed to mumble, "You sure got that right."

"Jamie nothing," Jack Straw said, going back to the subject of my name, telling all of them, "This here is the Comanche Kid!"

At that they all hoorahed and said, "That's good, Comanche Kid is good! How's that supper taste, Comanche Kid?"

I was aware I was eating too fast and looking like a starving beggar, so I tried to slow down and I said, "Jamie will do."

Skinny shouted out, "Hell no, Comanche Kid it is! Comanche Kid is good! I wish I could be called Comanche Kid instead of Skinny!" And at that he stood up and showed himself off, turning around, showing he was real beefy and not skinny at all.

Shakespeare looked over from the other side of Buck and he said to Skinny, "What's in a name? That which we call a rose by any other word would smell as sweet."

And at that all of them gave out a big guffaw and one of the hands said, "For sure Skinny looks more like a barrel cactus than a rose, and he sure don't smell sweet. I never knew a man so reluctant to take a bath."

Skinny defended himself, saying, "Baths is bad for the health, goddamnit. It don't allow the skin to breathe."

It was then that Mike, the trail boss, showed up with a plate. Sitting down on the ground next to me he said, "How's the bait, son?"

"This is just about the best I've ever had, sir."

"It always tastes better if you've been starving, don't it?"

"It sure does."

"So how about this," he says. "You got eighty-seven beeves with no road brand but you got your Pa's home brand on them, right?" I nodded yes, and he said, "When you get done eating, you and Shakespeare move your herd up into ours real slow and easy. I'll give you thirty dollars a month and you nightride the herd and you horse wrangle with Shakespeare and you help Monty, and when we get to Dodge you'll get full price for your beeves. How does that sound?"

I told him I was hoping to turn around as soon as I could to look for my sister. He said, "There's nothing you can do for your sister right now, son. You can't travel alone and there's no military outpost nearby that's going to start wandering over these plains looking for a lost little girl who is God knows where. Not only that, but I can't sell your cattle without a bill of sale, so I need you in Dodge to present your case to the stock inspector so we can get the proper paperwork. Once that's done you can figure out how to look for your sister."

I'd feared all along that was what was probably going to happen, but I looked at my plate and I couldn't finish eating knowing Sally was maybe eating nothing but jerky.

He said, "Indians like kids. They'll give her to a woman who's lost a kid and she'll take good care of her."

I figured he was probably lying to make me feel better. All the other hands were quiet now and just watching us out of the corner of their eye and pretending not to listen.

Finally, I just nodded yes.

"Good," he said.

I added in, "I can do more than nightride and day wrangle. I can pull my weight as a swing, flanker, or drag."

He asked, "You ever trailed cattle before?"

I lied again and said, "Yes, sir."

"What route did you take?"

I figured he was testing me, so I said, "Well, sir, starting at Bandera we crossed the Colorado, the Brazos, the Trinity, the Red, crossed at Doan's Crossing on the Red, then the Washita, the Canadian, the Cimarron, then the Arkansas, Smokey Hill, Solomon, the Republican. Never made it as far as the Platte, and I'd sure like to push into Montana someday and see that country." I had learned all the names from Pa, who used to recite them like they were some kind of a poem, so we learned them too and would say them with him.

He didn't say anything but I think he knew I was lying. He nodded, and when he stood up, one of the boys who'd been listening called out, "Hey, boss, go ahead and put him on the line and then maybe I can rack up some more shut-eye."

Another called out, "He can ride drag for me anytime, Big Mike!"

So that was what they called him, Big Mike. Big Mike just did that slight smile of his and said, "Shakespeare, get him Scotty's traps, then saddle up his buckskin and move his herd into ours, nice and easy."

He turned to me and said, "Scotty come all the way from Scotland to trail cattle and learn the business, then got hit by lightning a while back. You need to get out of what you're wearing, and I hope you don't mind wearing a dead man's clothes."

Nothing new with that, I thought, but I said, "Thank you, sir." I started figuring backward and I wondered if Scotty, whoever he was, was killed in the same storm when I was hiding in the cattails, and I remarked to myself how strange it all was, as if somehow everybody was all part of the same story.

I took my plate over to the wreck pan of hot water next to the wagon and when I saw the cook looking at me, I realized I hadn't finished my food and maybe he was insulted. Even though I'd lost my appetite talking about Sally, I shoveled it in real quick and nodded thanks to him. I scrubbed the plate down and he pointed to where I was to stack it.

Shakespeare come up leading Buck all saddled again, and this time he talked in English and he said, "Let me get Scotty's kit."

He climbed into the camp wagon and threw things around in there and then dragged out a bedroll and tossed it on the ground, hopped out and opened up the tarp, blanket and sougan. He pulled out a pair of trousers and a check shirt all rolled up and he tossed them to me and said, "There you go, change into these. Scotty was bigger than you but it's better than what you got on for sure. His slicker and his mackinaw are in here too. Storm come up before he had a chance to put his slicker on. Killed him and his horse. His possibles sack is in there, so you might want to go through it and see if there's anything you want, sewing kit, comb, flints, whatnot."

"Feels like I'm robbing a dead man," I said. "Don't seem right."

He shrugged and said, "Scotty's not going to need any of this stuff anymore, so you might as well make use of it." Then he said, "All that lives must die, passing through nature to eternity, right?"

I figured he must have gotten word I'd lost my family and he was trying to console me, but they were words to no effect. All I wanted was for more Comanches to pass through from nature to eternity.

"Getting hit by lightning is a rough way to pass through," I said.

"There's no good way to pass through, is there." It wasn't a question and he wasn't smiling anymore, and I had a feeling he was talking about something else. He stood there looking at me and I realized he expected me to change out of Jamie's clothes right then and there.

"Don't you need to get your pony?" I asked.

He said, "Oh yeah," and he turned and went to the remuda.

I looked around and found an angle where the boys and the cook couldn't see me and I pulled off my clothes real fast and threw on Scotty's clothes as quick as I could. I had to cuff my pant legs so they weren't so long and I rolled up the sleeves of the shirt as well. I looked like some kind of ragamuffin, but whoever Scotty was he must have washed his spare clothes out and put them away clean, and I was grateful for that.

I started to throw Jamie's clothes in the fire but I couldn't do it. It was like throwing Jamie away and I couldn't bear to part with him, as if he wouldn't be with me anymore, not that he was with me now, but somehow I felt if his blood was with me, he was still within reach. Crazy thinking, I said to myself, but I folded his clothes up real neat as if they were precious, thinking, *I'll wash these out later.*

Shakespeare come up with his horse and found me folding them and he said, "You're not keeping those, are you?"

"Never know when I might need a second set."

He laughed and said, "The soul of this man is in his clothes."

I looked at him as if he knew something he wasn't supposed to know, about it being really Jamie's blood, and he caught the look and asked, "What?"

"You always talk Shakespeare?"

"Ay, is it not a language I speak?"

"Why don't you just speak English?"

He laughed and said, "Words, words, words."

I didn't know if there was something about that I was supposed to get, but he pointed at Buck and said, "Mount up and let's get those cattle of yours up here. That good enough for you?"

"Well, at least that was in English."

"Listen up, Comanche Kid. Shakespeare is English."

"You don't need to call me that, my name is…" And I caught myself because I almost said "Jane," but I said, "My name is Jamie."

As he mounted up he said, "OK, Jaaaamie, now, why don't you quit whining and let's ride."

At that he spurred his horse and headed out toward my herd at a lope. I was all angry at him for making fun of me, because it was the kind of thing Jamie would do sometimes. I'd hit him, and he'd hit me back, and Ma would call out, "I don't want to see you two fighting anymore!" Pa would act like he hadn't noticed and call out some chore for one or both of us to do, and Ma would say something about ruffians, "*Rabauken!*"

I let it all go and I climbed onto the hurricane deck and followed after him.

SEVEN

We shoved the cattle toward the main herd. Two hands rode over and stood on either side of my herd as it moved forward, making a funnel as I led John Bell Hood through, Shakespeare trailing them from behind. As they passed through the funnel the two hands counted them, tying a knot in a rope for every ten.

They both wrote numbers in their tally books and agreed they had each counted eighty-seven, just like I'd said, and gave the count to Big Mike. Shakespeare and I moved them slow and easy into the main herd, then rode my string over to the remuda and turned them loose.

Shakespeare said, "Judging by the reins, those three are Comanche ponies."

"That's right," I said.

"What happened to the other ponies?"

I shrugged. "I killed them. One on purpose and the other two by accident."

He looked at me like he was trying to figure something out about me, maybe whether to believe me or not, but then he said, "O war, thou son of hell, whom angry heavens do make their minister, throw in the frozen bosoms of our heart hot coals of vengeance, right?"

"Vengeance is right," I said, but I got nervous when he said bosoms and I almost ran my hand over my chest to make sure I wasn't showing. "How do you know all that?"

"Some hands can't read and some hands, like Preacher, read the Bible and some read the *Police Gazette* or Beadle's Dime Novels, and some read Shakespeare. So there you are, simple as that."

"Who's Preacher?"

"He's the sin buster. You'll meet him."

Going back to the Shakespeare book, I said, "You sure remember a lot of it, but I guess no one goes around quoting from the *Police Gazette*, do they?"

"No, but they sure do look at the pictures over and over." And he just winked at me like Pa used to do.

He led me over to where the hands were bedded down near the wagon, pulling his own bedroll out, telling Skinny there were three new ponies in the remuda and to keep an eye on them because they were Comanche stallions and they might be snaky.

Skinny, the nighthawk, said, "Sure enough, boss," and left for the remuda. Pa said the nighthawk would be out there all night, watching the horses, sleeping in the camp wagon during the day. I thought it was odd he called Shakespeare boss, but I figured he was rawhiding him because he was the youngest and most inexperienced of the hands.

I spread Scotty's bedroll out, keeping Buck nearby, saddled and hobbled, just like all the hands did with their mounts, hobbled or tied to a ground pin in case there was some kind of an emergency. It felt scary to be sleeping next to so many men, and I just hoped my luck held out and they wouldn't figure me for a girl. I pulled the covers up around me and I thought how strange it was to be lying in a dead man's bedroll. I took a minute to think about Ma and Pa and Jamie and Sally, trying not to cry and wishing Ma could hold me, and I was starting to drift away when I heard one of the hands call out, "Hey, Shakespeare, I missed the first part when I was nightriding last night, so catch me up."

As he put his bedroll out Shakespeare said, "Well, she's in a strange land and her twin brother is dead, and she figures if she's going to be safe she needs to disguise herself as a boy…"

And then I was wide awake thinking, *What does he know about me?* My hands went to my chest, and I was thinking, *Could he tell after all?*

He went on, saying, "So she gets a job with this big shot and he doesn't know she's actually a girl disguised as a boy…"

Oh God, he knows!

Then he said, "This big shot is a duke named Orsino, and he's in love with this lady named Olivia, only she's not in love with him, so he asks this girl who's working for him now, who's disguised as a boy…"

And I thought, *Oh my God, it's not me, he's telling some Shakespeare story!*

"So the duke asks this so-called boy to go talk to Olivia and tell her what a great guy he is…"

And at that the hand said, "Oh yeah, that's where I come in, I remember that part when the kid was getting to Olivia's house."

My breathing had been all panicky, but when I realized he was catching them up on some Shakespeare story and it wasn't me he was talking about, it slowed down. Then I thought, *This is all real strange, Scotty getting hit by lightning the same day Ma and Pa and Jamie are killed and Sally stolen, and me dressing as a boy and sleeping in a dead man's bedroll, and Shakespeare telling some story about a girl dressing as a boy.* I just felt whipped with it all, wondering, *What has happened to my life?*

I fell asleep listening to Shakespeare's voice and I slept the sleep of the dead until I felt someone kicking my foot and saying, "Hey, Comanche Kid, it's your turn."

It was Bill, the Negro, coming off his shift, the man I'd met first off earlier this day. I rolled out and grabbed Scotty's mackinaw because the night was cold and I mounted Buck to go night-ride the herd.

I found the far edge of the herd and started riding slowly around it, singing as best I could, Pa saying that singing or talking kept the brutes distracted from odd noises during the night that might cause a stampede. I started out with "Wild Mountain Thyme" again, my voice all foggy, but slowly it got clearer. After a while I heard another voice farther away but coming toward me.

It was the other nightrider, and he was singing a hymn. I thought that was funny, as if the herd was a bunch of churchgoers being led to God by some odd preacher whose duty it was to save the souls of beeves, but he had a nice voice and pretty soon he hove into sight, heading for me. When I could hear the words of the song, I realized the tune was a hymn all right, but he was making up words about how dumb and ugly the brutes were and how he'd be glad to be rid of them once he got to Dodge.

When he come up alongside me, I could see he was the small, wiry hand and he reached over and said, "How do again, I'm Jack Straw, remember?"

We shook hands and I said, "How do you do, Jack Straw?" And I gave him Jamie's full name.

He said, "Now, that's an Irish name, isn't it?"

"It sure is. My Pa come over during the potato famine."

He looked a little confused and he asked, "A potato famine, now, what kind of a famine is that?"

"From what I understand they all ate potatoes in Ireland, but then one day the crop failed and they all started starving, so them that could, come over to America."

"Good for them," he said. "I don't want nobody starving to death."

And at that he rode on and I rode on in the opposite direction and I heard him switch over to some song about a little black bull coming down a mountain, and he seemed to enjoy entertaining himself and the herd.

The next time around he stopped and said, "So, Comanche Kid ... " but I interrupted him and said, "I'd rather be called Jamie."

"Son, it's too late now. You just don't change a man's nick-name, do you?" Then he changed the topic and said, "I hear you killed six or seven of them."

"No, sir, I killed five."

"Whoo-ee," he said. "You must be one real bravo!" And at that we rode on again, both of us singing, and new songs started coming to me so I wasn't boring the cattle with the same song.

Sometimes I'd just talk to them, singsongy, telling them wasn't it a beautiful night, like black velvet, and how bright the silvery stars were, and I realized I was talking to myself, trying to give myself hope, and it reminded me of how Ma would talk to us if we'd had a nightmare or couldn't sleep, and I started to choke up remembering how sweet and calm she was, so I went to another song to get away from the memory.

The next time Jack Straw come around, he said, "Now, how old did they tell me you was?"

"I'm fourteen, sir."

"Hell, I ran away from home when I was fourteen and I never regretted it. You're going to do just fine, son." And off he went, and that's how it continued, him asking questions every time we met up until he knew all about Ma and Pa and Sally. He was real kind about Sally, telling me all was not lost, or giving me bits of information about himself and how his father was a hard man and a drinker and his Ma died in childbirth and he wasn't in touch with his sister much, but someday he was going to go back to Iowa and find her, as soon as he got enough money saved up.

Just before dawn we heard Monty in the distance call, "Roll out, boys!" and Jack Straw and I rode into camp to get some bait. Skinny brought the remuda in and roped it off near the wagon so the hands could wrangle the mounts they would be riding that morning, and after getting some bait he climbed into the camp wagon to sleep for the day.

Jack Straw and I put our horses in the remuda and the cook nodded to us and pointed at the coffee, saying, "*Cafecito*," and he was handing out flapjacks and potatoes with gravy and fried salt pork, and there was airtight tomatoes stewed with sugar and bread, called pooch. Jack Straw and I sat with the other hands and the boys told me the biscuit buster here served up good bait, but with some outfits you were lucky if you didn't starve to death before you got to Dodge.

Shakespeare was throwing wood and prairie chips into the tarpaulin cradle under the camp wagon, so I threw down the rest of my bait and cleaned my plate off in the wreck pan. I jumped in and started helping Monty break down the camp, him just nodding and pointing and not saying much. Then I helped Shakespeare haul the mules out of the remuda to hook up to the camp wagon.

Big Mike stopped by and said I'd be riding drag. Then he told the two point men, Hard Luck Luke Bronson and Abraham, this Abraham being another Negro hand but with fearsome scars on his face, and he was Big Mike's *segundo*, to "string 'em out and point 'em north." Then he rode out to pilot the herd and scout the day's drive.

I decided I would ride Paint first, but I had a hard time getting my catch rope on him until Shakespeare come over, and with his riata he caught him in one easy throw. "Did you see that?" he said. "That loop was called a morning glory. Did you see how it didn't open until it got right to him? That's why it's called a morning glory, the loop doesn't open until it gets to where it's going."

He was oh so pleased with himself.

I was ashamed I was having so much trouble when all the other hands seemed to rope their mounts with such an easy grace. I was mad at him for helping me in front of everybody but I was also glad not to keep making a fool of myself, but that didn't make me any less mad at his showing off.

I saddled up, but Paint began to bog his head and pitch so I took my mad out on him and decided to ride the rough off of him by lining him out.

He took off at a dead run and I yelled at him and hit his rump with my hat and made him run even faster. We went out a good half mile or more, cutting through the cold early morning breeze as the sun come up, and when I thought he'd run enough that he would behave, I run him back hard to the camp wagon just to make sure.

Shakespeare was still there, turning the remuda loose, now saddling up his own mount, and without looking at me he said, "You can ride, can't you?"

I didn't say anything but I swear I felt my heart swell at the compliment and for a moment my chest didn't feel so much like a hollow shell, and I wasn't mad at him anymore.

Paint danced around, and as he mounted up Shakespeare added, "And he can run, can't he?" He did that soft smile of his that I thought seemed just a little bit sad, and he said, "Through his mane and tail the high wind sings, fanning the hairs who wave like feathered wings, right?" I noticed he always said, "right?" after every quote, like he wanted some kind of confirmation that he was speaking the truth, or maybe he just wanted you to admire him, but that sounded mean of me.

I said, "What did you do, memorize the whole book?"

"Just the parts I like," and at that he hurrahed the remuda away with a "Hi-yah, hi-yah!" and led it north alongside the herd as it began to string out.

I rode drag that first day, glad to be there in spite of the dust. Scotty had left a blue silk neck scarf in his mackinaw pocket and I found it and wore it like a mask to keep the dust out of my mouth and nose, and I was grateful for it. Paint was good at pushing the stragglers, then darting into the brush after ones that had spilled past the flankers, driving them back to the herd. I was grateful he was turning into the kind of horse Pa said all the hands would call a Joe Dandy.

Nearby was Preacher, the sin buster Shakespeare had mentioned. We didn't have a chance to talk, although I could hear him calling the stragglers slow devil brutes, telling them they'd damn well better catch up because they were being driven by an angel of the Lord.

Farther away also on drag was Shady, an Apache who seemed to be a particular friend of Monty, the cook, and I saw he wore a long red sash around his waist, but we didn't have a chance to talk much either. Preacher and Shady rotated up to flanker and other hands rotated back, taking their turn, me staying as drag, but I didn't mind, in spite of the dust. I hoped Pa would be proud of me now that I was a real hand.

At noon, when the herd stopped to rest and graze, I hurried over and helped Monty out as best I could, trying not to get in the way and waiting for him to nod or point and trying to read his mind as to how I could help best, then helping Shakespeare bring the remuda in so the hands could switch out their mounts.

While dinner was put out, I figured I'd start to ride the mounts in Scotty's string, and that would give all the mounts two or three days to rest before I put them back to work again. I soon discovered they were a salty string. When Scotty was killed, I learned, the hands divided up his best horses among themselves and traded in their saltiest, so now my string was saltier than even Hard Luck Luke Bronson's, who was the rough string rider, the rough string rider always riding the saltiest horses. He thought that was real funny and he told me, "You got here a day late and a dollar short, Kid."

That first day we moved out, John Bell Hood slowly worked his way through the herd until he was up front with their lead longhorn, Blackjack. The two of them argued about the leadership position and John Bell Hood won out and Blackjack fell into line behind him. Big Mike had come back in from piloting the herd to get some bait and told me about the challenge and he said, "That's one persistent brute you got there."

"Pa always said John Bell Hood is a ranny himself if ever there was one."

"That's what you call him? John Bell Hood?"

"Yes, sir, that's what Pa named him."

"Your pa fight with the Texas Brigade?"

"Yes, sir, he did."

"Not many of the Texas Brigade survived," he said. "Your pa was a lucky man."

"I guess so," I said, "and I guess not."

I think he knew what I meant. He changed the subject and said, "Let's hope that longhorn of yours is as good at river crossings as he is at leading the herd."

Big Mike trailed the herd slowly, maybe ten to twelve miles a day. They grazed in the mornings before being trailed out, then again at noon while everyone got some bait, then at night after being thrown off the trail and watered and bedded down. Big Mike said they'd be less likely to be ornery if they were fat and happy.

It was some days later when we were sitting around eating corn bread, beans, and salt pork with airtight tomatoes and corn and peas and onions all mixed together with lots of salt and pepper, and there were several apple pies sitting out as well, when someone called out to Shakespeare, "Hey, pick back up where she goes to that girl's house."

So he hauled a small book out of his shirt pocket and started speaking Shakespeare's words, reading from it and going on and on and explaining it as he went along. The gist of the story was that this girl who is dressed as a boy, acting as a servant to this duke, goes to this girl Olivia to tell her again that the duke is in love with her and that she should love this duke back, that he's a real good man. But this Olivia and her friends make fun of this girl dressed as a boy and won't let him talk, but she, or he, reprimands them back, and Olivia is so surprised and yet curious that she sends the other women away and gets this servant alone and lets him talk. He talks so pretty that this Olivia can tell something's up, and she starts asking questions about where this servant is really from, because she can tell by his accent that he's not from those parts and she can tell he doesn't act like he's from a servant family, and who is he really? And this girl, dressed as a boy, starts getting worried that she is being found out, because she is actually a noble person, so she tries to backtrack and throw Olivia off the scent, and pretty soon it becomes clear that Olivia thinks this so-called boy is an attractive boy, and she discovers she has a failing for him, not realizing that it's a girl in disguise.

It was very complicated. And I didn't like how close to home it was.

Shakespeare went on reading and knowing some of the words by heart, and pretty soon he's on his feet acting out all the parts. Showing off, I thought, but all the hands were laughing, and I couldn't help but wonder if he was trying to tell me something with that story, as if he knew something.

When Shakespeare was done, Jack Straw began singing that song "Get Along Home, You Spanish Girl," and right when I was listening to all that and about to fall asleep, one of the hands, named Cliff, him being a fellow that was always telling jokes and blanket stretchers, came fogging in fast and yelling, "There's hell in Georgia, boys!"

In an instant everyone was on their feet, throwing on their boots and unhobbling their horses and hitting the saddle as fast as they could, and so was I.

EIGHT

I don't know what set them off. Maybe it was a nightrider strik-ing a lucifer to light up his Bull Durham or the jingle of a spur or a jackrabbit jumping out, but the whole herd was off and run-ning, all some two thousand of them, as if they had a meeting planned and they all needed to get off at the same time and in the same direction. I heard one of the boys yell, "They're going north!" I got a grip on myself and I took off with the other hands.

As we caught up with the herd, they were a sight to behold, the moonlight shining on them and glinting off their horns as they ran. They held their tails high over their backs, their eyes wide and white and rolling and they bawled and the ground shook and I hoped Buck wouldn't hit a prairie-dog hole. I come up on the edge of the herd and I didn't have any idea about what I was supposed to do, as if there was some way to stop a runaway train all by yourself.

From out of nowhere Abraham, the *segundo*, rode up beside me, the one who had scars on his face, not pox scars, but scars that looked like he had been hit with something several times, or maybe knifed. He called out, "Don't ride too close or they'll think you're pushing them. Keep an eye out for those spilling off and push them back in. Anything you miss will be picked up by the hands behind you!" And he rode on.

And God help anyone who falls, I thought.

When they spilled out, I tried to push them back in but sometimes there were just too many of them. I kept a lookout for dangers but Buck saw everything before I did. I heard Pa say,

"Watch Buck's ears. They'll tell you what he's going to do." So I paid attention to Buck's ears, and Buck kept his head low as he ran and he watched the ground, and before I even saw any of it coming he was dodging around prickly pear and mesquite and yucca, their white blossoms shining in the moonlight, and sometimes he swerved so sharp it was all I could do just to stay in the saddle. He'd stop quick and I'd practically tumble over his head, then there was cut banks he'd somehow seen and I hadn't even known was coming up and he'd leap it without warning, or if it was too wide he'd clamber down one side and back up the other, then he'd slow down and step over some outcropping of rocks like he was a dainty old lady, and I thought I could have been killed a hundred times over.

The hands on the left whistled and hallooed and hurrahed and waved ropes and slickers, trying to push the herd to the right to get them circling around and back into themselves so they'd start to mill, but the herd wasn't having it and kept on the run, bellowing and wild-eyed, their horns clacking against each other so that the whole herd was making a rattling sound, like sabers hitting each other in some big battle.

I yelled at them too, and prayed I'd stay in the saddle and hoped Buck wouldn't fall. Even if we weren't trampled it would be a hard spill and God knew I could hit rocks or cactus, or even Buck could fall on me and there I'd be with broken bones or killed. Then I got scared Buck would stumble and I'd get knocked out of the saddle and my foot would get caught in a stirrup and I'd be dragged to death. I imagined Buck breaking his leg, and if I survived I'd be faced with shooting him, and I knew I couldn't take that loss.

And damned if the herd didn't keep it up all night long.

Right before dawn they finally just stopped. Bawling and clacking horns and breathing hard they came to a standstill, spent and just standing there, wild-eyed, their tongues hanging out, and maybe real proud of themselves for putting everyone on the run. Then they got quiet as if they all were coming home exhausted from some late-night fandango, then they bedded down and rested, as if nothing had happened.

The hands backed off and gave them space and you could hear the boys talking to them real low and sweet, some singing and some whistling, trying to keep them calm and reassure them everything was OK, talking to them as if they were kids who'd had a nightmare, like Ma did with us, stroking our hair and telling us everything was all right.

Dawn came on and the sky got lighter with streaks of gray and pink and gold, and the herd lay there like it was any other day.

Big Mike rode up and said, "You did good, kid. You may just turn into a ranny after all."

I felt good about that, knowing I hadn't really done anything but glad I hadn't made things worse or hurt myself, or Buck. I knew I had a long way to go before I was a real ranny, but then it occurred to me that by being a girl I couldn't ever be a real ranny, and at that I got mad and I was determined I'd do more than my share so I could be called a ranahan someday, even if I was a girl.

Big Mike spread the word that after we got some bait, we'd move the herd east a few miles to where they could get water and we'd spend the next week or so letting them graze while we rode back and rounded up the ones that spilled off and were God knows how many miles away and in every which direction.

Monty caught up with the camp wagon and I jumped in to help unhook the mules and get the fire going. The nighthawk, Skinny, showed up leading the remuda and Shakespeare rode with him, covered in sweat and dust. In spite of him looking worn and dirty I couldn't help but think, *Doesn't he look good, tall and slender and sitting light in the saddle like a horseman should, and pushing a herd of some hundred and fifty cow ponies.*

I told myself, *You can't think like that.*

Shakespeare and Skinny dismounted and hauled out yards of rope from the wagon, along with several iron stakes, then put the stakes into the ground to throw up a rope corral. I turned Buck into the remuda and helped them, and so did Abraham and the rough string rider, Hard Luck Luke Bronson. Between the five of us we got the corral up real quick, and it never ceased to amaze me that with only one string of rope circling around them withers high, the horses minded their place and wouldn't push through.

"That'll keep them," Shakespeare said.

I wanted to stay and talk with him but I knew that's what a girl would do, so I knew not to do that or I might give myself away. Then I thought, *Well, if I'm only a fourteen-year-old boy maybe it would be OK to stay and talk to him*, as if he was some kind of older brother and it wouldn't look funny at all. *You are on dangerous ground*, I then thought. *Don't even think about it.*

I started to walk off but he called after me, "So you stayed aboard the whole time, did you?"

I turned and said, "Yeah, but there were a few times I thought Buck and me was going to eat dirt."

"That your first stampede?"

"Sure was."

He tilted his head at me and said, "I thought you drove from the Colorado to the Trinity and so on."

I didn't know what to say.

"Not once any of those cow brutes stampede?"

And that is exactly why Ma used to say, "I don't ever want to hear you lie, do you understand me? *Keine Lügen!* No lies!"

I stood there silent, at a loss for words. Then he let me off the hook, giving me a head nod, and said, "You want Paint saddled up?"

I was real sheepish and I said, "Yes, sir."

As he shook out his riata, he said, "Whoa, listen to him, calling me sir. I just got a promotion. Heavy lies the head that wears the crown, right?" and he chuckled to himself at how clever he was.

I got real mad and wanted to hit him. I felt my face turning red and I was just as mad at myself for thinking he looked real handsome, pushing the remuda in. I wanted to turn and walk off before I said something to make things worse, all the while knowing he could tell Big Mike I'd lied anytime he wanted. I hated him having anything over me, and I hated that I had lied to Big Mike and that I was lying to everyone by dressing like a boy and lying about my name and my age.

Then I started understanding what that girl in his story felt like, having to dress like a man to protect herself, and I got mad at the world that you couldn't just be who you was without worrying about someone taking advantage of you or thinking less of you.

At that I grabbed my catch rope off my saddle. "I'll get him."

"You sure you don't want some help?"

"No, sir, keep your morning glory to yourself." Only I said "siiiiir" like he had said "Jaaaamie," but I threw and missed, and Shakespeare stood there and watched me, not saying anything.

I hauled the rope in and threw again, and after the third time missing he said, "You can sure enough ride but you need to practice your hoolihan." He threw out his riata, and even with the herd shifting back and forth he caught Paint so easily it made me even madder, and then he handed me his riata.

He watched while I hauled Paint out and saddled and bridled him. I tossed his riata back to him and I wanted to say, You think you're so smart, but I bit my tongue. I mounted up, and before Paint could pitch I yelled at him and swiped his rump with my hat and he took off at a dead run, as if he was as mad and angry as I was, Shakespeare just watching us go.

We rode east, straight into the dawn, the clouds now pink and red with streaks of blue sky coming up on the horizon. The wind in my face felt fresh and I leaned into Paint, hitting him on the flank again with the reins, and he went faster, rolling over the hills and through the scrub brush as if he had been waiting to cut loose from the remuda and the rope corral.

He ran like the Comanches must have run him, and I wondered what he had seen, where he'd traveled, what raids and killing he'd been part of. I wanted to outrun everything I'd seen and run so hard that maybe I could outrun time and go backward and save Ma and Pa and Jamie and Sally from everything awful that had happened, or run so fast I'd get far ahead of One-Eye and he'd never ever find me, even though I knew at some point I was going to have to turn around and go looking for him.

Deep in my heart I wished I could just leave Sally behind, but that was like thinking you could leave your right hand behind, and I hated myself for even thinking that, and I knew I'd be willing to die if it meant Sally found salvation. But what kind of salvation would that be, I wondered, with her ma and pa and brother dead and the cabin burned down. That would leave only me to take care of her with just a handful of cash from the sale of the herd, and how was I going to do that?

Finally I stopped thinking altogether and I put my hand on Paint's neck and felt his warmth, and I felt his muscles working beneath his hide, and I marveled at his power and his strength and his beauty. I eased up on him and he began to slow and I don't know how far we run or for how long, but sure enough we'd run straight to the creek that Big Mike was shoving the cattle to. It was a pretty creek with clear water running over smooth stones, with ash and cottonwoods lining its banks, and willows too.

I hauled back on the reins and I took Paint straight into the water. He splashed into it, dancing and circling as if the water felt good on his legs, and as he drank I leapt out of the saddle and threw my hat on the bank and kicked off my boots. The water felt clean and cold and I knelt down and splashed my face and washed my hair, then I threw off all my clothes, even the band I had wrapped around my chest. I splashed cold water all over myself, washing away the sweat and the dirt from the stampede, and the anger as well. I washed out my clothes and the band and I was freezing cold but it felt good.

The sun was coming up and I watched the light paint my body, and it felt strange and scary to be out on the plains naked. I wondered what that girl in Shakespeare's story felt when she went back to wherever her room was and she took her clothes off and found herself a girl again, knowing she would have to keep lying about herself if she was going to get by.

I wanted to ride back into camp and say to all the hands and Big Mike and Shakespeare, "Look, I'm a girl, but I can ride with the best of them and I've proved I can fire a weapon and defend myself and I can herd cattle and I'll learn to throw the hoolihan better, so let's just let it be OK that I'm a girl. OK?"

But I knew things didn't work that way, and after standing there naked in the water with the sun on me, I sat down and scooped up more water and ran my hands over my body one last time, as if to reassure myself of who I was. I even said my own name aloud just to hear it said. Then I picked up the band for my chest and wrung it out, and I started thinking about Shakespeare and how good he looked leading that remuda in and how straight and tall and lean he was, and how he sat a horse, and how was it he knew all those words from memory, what a marvel, and how was I going to explain getting mad at him and running off like that? It sounded just like something some dumb girl would do, but I hoped he'd write it off to me being an immature boy.

I sat naked in the dawn sun for the longest time, I don't know how long, going over and over all that in my mind, when I realized I was hungry and I wished I'd gotten something to eat before I'd run off, and then I felt real ashamed for not being there to do my job and help Monty.

I tied the band around my chest again, but when I looked up, there on a rise a little over half a mile away was what looked to be five riders in silhouette against the rising sun. My first thought was, *Oh my God, they aren't dead, they've come back for me.* But I knew that couldn't be true, because if they could come back, then Ma and Pa and Jamie could come back too, and I knew they weren't coming back.

I panicked, and I thought, *It's One-Eye, and he's come for me.*

Then the middle rider did something Pa had told me about. He pulled out in front of the other four, rode his horse to the left and then he turned and rode his horse to the right, then he stopped and watched me. I knew then they wasn't long riders like I'd hoped. They were Comanches.

He couldn't see me clearly enough to know what I was, and if I'd done the same thing back, he would have thought I was Shoshone or Kiowa or Comanche, and they would have taken their time riding to join me, but that's when I made a mistake.

Paint was a good thirty or forty yards away grazing, and if I had just walked over to Paint and mounted him and ridden out and turned Paint left and right like he'd done, then I could have lit out fast and I would have had a good head start on them. But I wasn't even dressed and they'd caught me naked, so I threw on my pants and shirt and leggings and I pulled on my boots, and if I had walked to Paint they would have waited, and I would have had that head start.

Instead, I ran, and the minute I ran they knew I wasn't Comanche and they come fogging off the hill at a dead run, coming straight for me. The yards to where Paint was grazing never seemed so far away and I was afraid Paint would smell them and race out to join them, and then they'd have me cold, and they'd kill me right in the middle of that creek.

He didn't run, but I slipped on the rocks trying to get to him and fell in the water and I was struggling to get out of the creek. I thought I was back in the marsh with Jamie again, both of us trying to run but moving so slow, like some kind of nightmare.

They were coming on hard and I finally got to the bank, my boots full of water. I ran for Paint as best I could, stumbling and falling and then rising and thinking I'd never get to him, and I could hear them screaming that "Hi-yi-yi-yi-yi!" I finally got to him and I swung into the saddle and yelled at him and hit his flank with the reins.

We splashed across the creek and climbed the opposite bank and started to run, when I realized I'd forgotten Jamie's hat, and I couldn't leave it behind. I whirled Paint around and raced back, leaned out of the saddle on the run and grabbed it off the bank, Paint splashing straight into the water again. I wheeled him around and we charged out of the creek and up the bank one more time and they were coming at me, all the closer now. I thought, *What a fool you are, riding straight out into Comanche territory, expecting everything to be all lah-dee-dah, and being so dumb as to not even be carrying a weapon with you, something Pa never would have let us do.* And me being so proud I had a Sharps and a Spencer and a Schofield in my possession, as if I was some kind of a real tough hand, a real hard case. And all of them, every single one of them, sitting back in camp wrapped up in my bedroll. *Some kind of a fool you are*, I told myself.

"Just ride," I heard Pa say, and his voice was real calm, a whisper. I thought, *I hear you.* What else was there to do but watch the ground and call on Paint's best. I was glad he was a Comanche pony because I knew he was used to hard riding, and he would have great endurance as well as speed. What the hands would call a lightning striker.

They were across the creek now. I could hear them yelling that bone-chilling shrill cry that made my blood run cold. I wanted to panic and scream and just give myself up and get it over with, but I heard Pa's voice again saying, "Just ride, angel," and it felt so good to be called that name again that I dropped the fear away and I said to myself, *Let's give these sons of bitches a run.*

I yelled at Paint and hit him with Jamie's hat and I remembered Shakespeare's words, "Through his mane and tail the high wind sings," and then something about "feathered wings," and I thought, *Yes, this, this is exactly what Shakespeare was talking about.*

Paint rushed over the ground as if he was a raging grass fire and he seemed to know the direction we were going. I only had to think right or left and he was ahead of me, slipping around scrub and rocks and even leaping a stand of prickly pear at one point, and all I had to do was hang on.

I ignored their yelling and their high-pitched screams and I talked to him and I told him he was a good horse, a fast horse, that they were only trying to scare us but we didn't scare, and didn't we love to run? And I called out loud, "Through your mane and tail the high wind sings!" I told him he was a Shakespeare horse, he was that powerful, and he could run as fast as angels with feathered wings could fly.

Then I heard the crack of a shot. One of them had a rifle, or maybe it was a revolver, I wasn't sure, probably picked up from a Mexican Comanchero, or off a dead man, someone they had killed, or maybe it was given to them by an Indian agent to hunt with or to protect themselves from Ute or Apache raiders when they were living on the reservation, and then they went on raids themselves and killed folks and stole horses and then pretended they'd never jumped the reservation, and just what was going on with all that?

Another crack rang out and I thought, *You were lucky once when they were firing at you. Can you count on being that lucky again?* And Paint called on even more from way down deep inside himself, running as fast as sunlight, and I never knew a horse could go that fast.

A lightning striker.

NINE

We topped a rise and I never saw a sight so beautiful. It was the herd slowly working its way east to the creek. Big Mike was in the lead with John Bell Hood and Blackjack, the rest of the herd spread out behind them. The sun made their colors so bright and shiny, reds and yellows and blacks, solids and spotted and striped, their long horns swaying and glinting. Even their bawling sounded like music.

The minute Big Mike saw me he knew something was up. He pulled out a big forty-four and fired it into the air, and at the sound of that and at the sight of me those hands carrying weapons left their positions and took out at a dead run to join Big Mike, and those that weren't heeled ran for the wagon to get their weapons.

I was going so fast downhill I couldn't stop in time and I flew right past Big Mike yelling, "Comanches!"

I reined Paint up by the wagon, dirt and rocks and dust flying he was moving so fast, then stopping so hard. I jumped in with the other hands and dug through the bedrolls until I found mine and I pulled the Spencer out. I jumped off the wagon and onto Paint and we ran to join Big Mike, just as the five Comanches come to the top of the rise.

I was up alongside Big Mike when I levered a shell into the chamber of the Spencer and aimed it. As I did, Big Mike reached across and grabbed the rifle and jerked it out of my grip, then he backhanded me right across the face and knocked me clear out of the saddle. I hit the ground hard and I started screaming, "Kill them! Kill every one of them."

I got to my feet and my nose was pouring blood and I tried to grab the Spencer away from Big Mike but he just kicked me hard, yelling, "You want to start a goddamn war?"

I fell onto my back and then I got to all fours, shouting at the hands, "They tried to kill me! Kill all of them, for God's sake!"

Big Mike yelled, "Someone shut him up!"

Abraham got off his horse and grabbed me by the scruff of the neck, pulling me upright and shoving me up against Paint and he said, "Shut up, Kid," only he didn't say it mean, he said it like it was for my own good, as if he was trying to tell me something I needed to know.

At that I started to weep and I went back to the ground, my face hurting really bad, and I hurt all over from hitting the ground so hard. Abraham knelt down beside me and he said, "No more yelling, son, no more yelling. You let Big Mike handle this."

"They killed my family," I said, "and they tried to kill me!"

He said, "I know, I know. Mine are lost too, and they tried to kill me as well. But they're gone now, yours and mine, and there's nothing we can do now, so let Big Mike handle this."

"I'll kill every one of them," I said.

"Not today you won't."

I was breathing hard and I felt ashamed to be there on the ground weeping, and I was embarrassed that I had run off like a spoiled kid. Everything kept going from bad to worse. I got back onto my feet, blood all over my face and hands, and I leaned against Paint and watched.

Big Mike was out front now with Shady, the Apache, and the two of them and the five Comanches were in a parley and they all were talking back and forth, and somehow they were hashing it all out, speaking English and Mexican and Apache and Comanche, I guessed. I couldn't believe they weren't trying to kill Big Mike, but instead they were all making some kind of a deal, I supposed. They talked for quite a while, and at one point

Shady pulled off the red sash from around his waist that he wore to look fancy and he handed it over to one of the Comanches, who held it up and admired it, then tied it around his own waist, then made some friendly signal to Shady, who made the same signal back, and they were all smiling and grinning.

I wondered how they could all be having a good time out there when I knew they were nothing but killers and were maybe even part of One-Eye's band. Maybe they even recognized Paint for one of their horses. Maybe they were on the scout, sent by One-Eye, looking for me. I thought it would be best if they were all killed right now so One-Eye wouldn't know where I was, but there was no way I could get the Spencer back, so I tried to steady my breathing and waited to see what happened.

As they talked, I looked around, and off a ways Shakespeare stood with the remuda, his Winchester upright and at the ready, the stock resting on his hip. The beeves and the horses and mules were all grazing, and most of the hands were now up in a line in a show of force, weapons at the ready in case anything broke out. I had a bad feeling there was danger all around us, and I couldn't help but think if I could just kill those five, all would be well, at least for a time.

Big Mike and Shady rode back to where we all were and reported in. Big Mike said they wanted fifty beeves to let us pass through, said if we didn't deliver them they'd stampede the herd at night. He said he talked them down to five and made them promise they wouldn't harm any of us when we were rounding up the strays. He told them if there was any strays we couldn't find, they could have them too.

Then he nodded at Bill and Cliff and he said, "Cut out five of the weakest ones, but make sure two of them are his," and he pointed at me.

"Why is that?" I said. "What are you taking my cattle for?"

"Because you got us into this damn mess."

"Even if I hadn't stumbled into them they could have come across us and demanded a toll to pass through," I said. "It's not fair."

"Point well taken," Big Mike said, and he turned to Bill and Cliff and he said, "Just take one of his."

I said, "That's still not fair!"

Big Mike reached down and grabbed me by the collar and said, "Consider it a penalty for riding off alone like some damn fool and being too dumb to carry a weapon with you, as well as not being here to help with Monty and the remuda and doing your goddamn job."

He tossed me back like some puppy and I felt ashamed and mad all at the same time and I could feel my face going all hot, and he added, "That's not all. Take your saddle off the paint."

I said, "What for?"

"They want the paint too."

"They can't have the paint," I said, "That horse is mine. You got no right to give him away!"

"You can have a horse out of Scotty's string but they want the paint and you're going to give it to them or you can take your goddamn eighty-six cows and drive to Dodge on your own."

I just stood there, my chest heaving and my jaw tight, all the hands watching me, and I couldn't think of anything to say, and I wished I'd never gotten mad at Shakespeare. None of this would have happened if he hadn't tricked me into admitting I'd never been on a drive before. I was mad at him, and then I was mad at myself because it wasn't his fault I'd lied about everything.

I knew I didn't have a choice, so I turned and loosened the girth on Paint and dragged the saddle off, letting it fall to the ground. I took his bridle off, and then the Comanche wearing the red sash rode down and slipped a braided rawhide riata around Paint's neck. As he started to lead him away, he turned and looked back at me, then he raised his hand and covered one eye with it. Then he took it away and just stared at me, and of a sudden I got a sick feeling in the pit of my stomach because I realized he was telling me he was with One-Eye, and they knew who I was, that I wouldn't have been riding that paint unless I was the one who had killed its rider.

That meant One-Eye was a part of several bands out raiding, and he must have run across this band and told them what happened. And to watch for me.

I turned and ran to the camp wagon and climbed in and dug the Schofield out of my bedroll. I jumped out of the wagon and started running for them, and then Shakespeare was in front of me on horseback, and he had Blood in tow.

I said, "Get out of my way!" but he began to crowd me with his horse, backing me up. I tried to get around him but his horse kept cutting me off like I was some kind of runaway calf, crowding me back toward the wagon. Then he leaned down from his saddle and grabbed the Schofield from me and I screamed, "Give it back to me, goddamnit!"

He threw the Schofield back into the wagon, and when I turned to go get it again he grabbed me from behind and he got off his horse and threw me up against the wagon and pinned me there. He said, "What's the matter with you? It's just a damn horse."

"I own my own string," I said. "My family's lives got traded for them. They got no right to take the paint back!"

He held me there until I stopped struggling, and then I told him, "They're with the band that killed my family. They're with One-Eye. He's taking my sister back to their camp somewhere, and then he's coming to kill me."

"Who's One-Eye?"

So I told him how Ma had taken an eye out of the one who had outraged her before they killed her, and he was the one who had survived when I killed the rest of them, and he had taken Sally.

Then he let me go.

I stood there, breathing hard, my face all blood and tears. Monty was watching both of us, not saying anything, then just nodding at me, so I stepped away from the wagon and he gave a click to his team and they headed out, moving to the creek to set up camp. I looked, and all the hands were back at work now and the Comanches were gone.

Shakespeare turned and led Blood over to where I'd dropped my saddle and bridle and I followed. He threw the blanket and the saddle up on Blood, saying, "All right if I help?" We were back to where we started from, and I just stood there while he saddled and bridled Blood.

He handed me the reins, saying, "You take the remuda to the camp and I'll join the boys looking for strays. It isn't a good idea for you to be out there on your own." Then he looked at me real funny as if he wanted to say something more, and I swear he almost touched my face, but stopped himself.

He mounted up and he said, "I'll talk to Big Mike." Then he stared at me until I nodded OK, and then he rode off.

The herd stayed by the creek for about a week while the hands brought in strays from miles and miles around us. They'd change out mounts and I got better with my catch rope, even figuring out how to throw a hoolihan, and I practiced the morning glory when no one was watching. When I wasn't helping Monty I tried to make up for being a fool by saddling and riding the rough off the mounts that needed it while the hands were up at the wagon getting something to eat. I got thrown a few times but I figured I deserved it.

I gathered wood and prairie chips for Monty and he began mumbling orders to me instead of just nodding at me, and even though he yelled at some of the other hands, cursing them out in Mexican for something stupid they'd done, he never lost his temper with me. I brought him berries and prickly pear fruit, quail eggs and wild onions and anything else he might use, and I washed out the towels and facecloths the hands used to clean up and I'd spread them out over bushes to dry. His nod always made me feel like I'd done something right.

Big Mike ignored me for the most part, although at one point when we were eating he looked at my face and he said, "That's quite a bruise you got there. Where'd you get that?"

I said, "I ran straight into some stiff-necked son of a bitch."

He laughed at that, saying, "That's just what I'd expect from someone called the Comanche Kid." Maybe that was his way of apologizing, although I doubt if he felt any need to. Then he asked, "You reckon they're around?"

"I know they are."

"Shakespeare told me about this One-Eye fellow. You think he'll come for you?"

"Yes, sir, I do believe that."

"Damn," he said. "I never should have taken you on. I should have left you to drive those cow brutes to Dodge by yourself."

"You can cut me loose anytime."

He did that slight smile and said, "Well, a deal's a deal, isn't it?"

When the herd was back together as best as possible, Big Mike told Abraham and Hard Luck Luke Bronson to "string 'em out and point 'em north." As the drive began, the swings made a funnel on either side of the herd and as it passed through they counted the beeves. I stood with the tallymen and counted Pa's brand as well. The main herd lost about a dozen or more, and my herd lost one, plus one that had been cut out and given to the Comanches. With the blue norther losses I was down to eight-five now. *If this keeps up*, I thought, *by the time we get to Dodge I'll be lucky if I have a dozen left.*

Shakespeare took back over as wrangler, and when I wasn't snaking in wood or chips I was helping Monty cook, clean, and pack up, then hooking up the mules. Then I rode drag, eating dust, even with my neck scarf up around my mouth and nose.

When I was nightriding the herd, the hands would stop and share bits and pieces of stories about themselves, Cliff always telling jokes or blanket stretchers. Tommy Deuce, a real hail-fellow-well-met type, told me he was raised by rattlesnakes and wildcats and he ate cactus for breakfast. They all told me they were sorry to hear about my family and several of them told me if I got the chance to kill more of them, they'd be glad to help me, some bragging that they'd killed someone once upon a time, or how tough they were and how many they'd kill if they got the chance, or who they wish they had killed back in the day.

One of the hands, Preacher, would pray aloud, saying, "Oh, Lord, be with me now and keep us safe and take good care of this herd and bless my ma and keep my sister Susannah in your gentle embrace. Thank you for her suffering being over and may the sun always shine on her, and please let there be no twisters or prairie fires." In between sermons he'd sing one hymn after another, "Old Hundred" or "Nearer, My God, to Thee" or some such.

Shakespeare would come riding along with a book of Shakespeare in his lap and he'd be reading it aloud by moonlight to the herd. Sometimes he knew the words by heart or he'd be teaching himself the words, repeating them over and over. When we crossed one night, he stopped and said, "Hey now, Kid, listen to this speech," and it would be all lovey-dovey, or the next time around it might be all about glory. One time as he came back around he said, "Here's a good one," and it was about a mangled, dying soldier saying something like, "Why, what is pomp, rule, reign, but earth and dust, and live we how we can, yet die we must." He was looking at me to see what my reaction was, when he realized it was about a body dying and he'd made some kind of a mistake reading it to me, who had a family that had been killed and scalped. He looked real sheepish and said, "Sorry, Kid."

I told him it sounded like real good writing and I admired how it rhymed.

Then there was a silence and he didn't know what to say, and he rode on.

One night, when I was passing Hard Luck Luke Bronson, who always wore his hat at an ace-deuce angle, I asked if he was called Hard Luck because he was the rough string rider and got thrown a lot.

"No," he said. "I never get throwed."

"Then why do they call you Hard Luck?"

"Is Skinny skinny?"

"No, he's a big fellow."

"I never get throwed," he said, "and I never get hurt. That's why they call me Hard Luck. Same reason they call a bald guy Curly." And he rode away without a smile or a nod or a how are you, whistling some tuneless song.

When I was nightriding, I'd sing songs I'd heard Ma sing, German songs, and I'd sing Irish songs Pa had taught us, or ones I'd heard at some fandango when we went to a neighbor's farm miles and miles away and spent the whole night there and danced or played party games like Snap or Pig in the Parlor. Sometimes I'd sing lullabies, thinking if I sang them, wherever Sally was maybe she'd hear them in her memory somehow and they'd bring her hope, or they'd be like a prayer and peace would enter her heart, or what Ma called *Anmut*, grace.

I didn't like thinking of them as prayers because that would mean I thought there was a God, and I didn't much believe in him anymore. If there was a God, then I thought he was pretty much useless if things happened like they did to God-fearing people like Ma, so what was the point? Or if there was a God, then I didn't much respect him anymore, much less like him or love him, and I figured we are all out here pretty much on our own, thank you very much.

I could hear Ma saying, "You'll grow out of that attitude, *Liebling*, darling."

I thought, *Bet me*, and I felt bad about back talking her, but I wondered what she would say now about God's love if she could see herself naked and outraged and scalped and her throat cut, and I realized that was an ugly, mean thing I was thinking.

She said, "God didn't do those things, don't go blaming him," and I thought, *Well, someone God is supposed to love surely did them*, and I couldn't imagine God loving the Comanches.

I tried to stay away from Shakespeare as much as I could because I could tell I wanted to talk to him about God and such, and just be around him, but it was the feeling of a girl. I was afraid if he caught on, he'd be thinking I was one of those boys who only like their own kind and if anyone thought that, then I'd be in as much trouble as if they found out I was a girl.

In camp I'd sit away from him and eat my bait, and he'd pick up with the story about that girl dressed as a boy. It turned out the girl dressed as a boy was actually in love with the duke, so it was real hard for her to tell Olivia the duke loved her when she loved him herself. And wouldn't you know it, Olivia was falling in love with the girl who she thought was a boy, and it was all one big mess and I didn't like hearing it because it all felt too much like what I was living.

When Shakespeare wasn't telling his story, some of the hands would sing or Preacher would preach. The hands all said when Scotty got killed by lightning Preacher led a real good service with readings from the Bible and then a sermon, and then kind words about what a hardworking, good man Scotty was, even if he was from Scotland, and how he was helping to civilize this country, and how he knew Scotty was where there was nothing but good ponies and tall grass and cool, clear water, and then he led them all in heartfelt hymns.

Once Jack Straw got up and showed how he could dance and they all laughed at that and Tommy Deuce would join him and they'd dance together, one of them making like a girl, or they'd do some clogging step together.

Some knew jokes and they would tease each other like a bunch of hands will do, and sometimes they'd get into a fight because one, usually Tommy Deuce, might brag about his reputation with the soiled doves, and then Hard Luck Luke Bronson would say, "The only reputation you got is among sheep who are scared to see you coming." Then there would be blows and the other hands would be pulling them off of each other. It reminded me of how Jamie and I would get into it with each other sometimes. I felt badly we'd ever hit each other or called each other names, and I wished I could take it all back.

If the hands were real tired they'd lie back on their bedrolls, their hands behind their heads, and they'd get into contests reciting from memory the labels from the airtight cans of tomatoes or the words on the tins of sardines or the sacks of beans, and whoever made a mistake had to pay a nickel. Sometimes they'd just speculate about what they were going to get with their coupons from their sacks of Bull Durham or from the tins of Arbuckles' Coffee.

I mostly stayed silent, and if someone asked me about those Comanches I killed, I'd say, "Naw, I want to hear Bill sing that song 'One More River to Cross,'" and he'd bail me out, sitting there with a cup of coffee, leaning forward, his elbows on his knees, his face to the ground and his eyes closed, and he'd sing away.

Truth be told, most times they didn't say much of anything they were so whipped. When they slept, there was a lot of snoring and breaking wind and some of them talked in their sleep, but I seemed to be the only one that had nightmares, and someone would throw a rock at me to wake me up or kick me and tell me I was going to stampede the cattle with all that caterwauling. I was always ashamed when that happened.

One night I was asleep and I was dreaming I was in the middle of a battle with artillery shells falling everywhere and I didn't know what direction to go and I was screaming for help ... and I woke up and there was explosions all around, only it was thunder and lightning and Preacher was yelling, "Everybody up or it's all going to Jericho!"

TEN

I threw on my boots and grabbed Scotty's slicker and boarded Buck as fast as I could. The sky was exploding and the wind was high and hard, and the next thing I knew it was a lashing rain that blew horizontal, the tarp on the camp wagon being thrown around so much I thought the wagon was going to set sail, or be blown over sideways at the very least.

The cattle were nervous and on their feet, bellowing and shifting around, a stampede just waiting to happen, and the storm turned into something awful. There was lightning so close and so fierce it seemed the ground was on fire with it, like blue snakes crawling all over, and there was St. Elmo's fire on the tips of the horses' ears and on our hats and running along the backs of the herd.

The whole crew spread out and we pushed them as if we were going up the trail, but as soon as they started to move the points and the swings shouted out, "Crowd 'em! Crowd 'em!" and "Hi-yah! Hi-yah!" and shoved them to the right so they'd turn in on themselves. Pretty soon the whole herd was milling in one big circle, the hands making sure not to press them in too tight or the ones in the center would be crushed to death. One bolt of lightning or the crash of one of Monty's kettles falling over might set them off in any direction, and with all the lightning exploding I'm sure everyone prayed they wouldn't get hit like Scotty did, but there was nowhere to hide and there was a job to do. We got soaking wet even with our slickers on, and water poured off my hat like a waterfall.

At one point, Shakespeare rode past me and he leaned over and he yelled, "Why now, blow wind, swell billow, and swim bark, the storm is up and all is on the hazard! Right?" Then he laughed real big and he said, "That's good, isn't it? The storm is up and all is on the hazard!"

I yelled back, "What, are you crazy? If we don't get hit by lightning we all might just drown! Do you think this is fun?"

"Try it out!" he yelled back. "Say it yourself! The storm is up and all is on the hazard!"

So I just said, "The storm is up and all is on the hazard."

"No! You've got to yell it! It don't work if you don't yell it!"

So I yelled real big because I was angry at him for acting so crazy in the middle of something that could get us all killed. Even Tommy Deuce had said one night, when everyone was talking about catastrophes—twisters and flash floods and such—that he'd seen thirty or forty steers killed with one lightning strike. So I yelled it out, "The storm is up and all is on the hazard!" But what I was thinking was, *What is the damn matter with you? This isn't some kind of a game!*

And he said, "Now, don't that feel good?"

Then he was off as quickly as he had come up, pushing some beeves back into the mill, then riding farther on, and I had to ask myself what was it about him I liked when all he did was act like some kind of a fool.

It wasn't until dawn that the storm let up and turned into a steady rain, and everyone was as exhausted and wet and bedraggled as they could be. Monty had the fly up on the camp wagon to keep his cooking dry and he doled out a hot plate of bait as the hands took turns coming in. I came in and helped him, and Big Mike told everyone as soon as they'd gotten some bait we would go ahead and string the herd out and keep them moving north.

"You can sleep when it's winter," he said.

So that's what we did, and day after day the rains came and went and came and went, and I imagined we were like soldiers slogging through mud, just like Pa said they used to do during the war, no resting up and seeking shelter or running away just because the weather was bad, just keep moving forward.

And Pa said, "Yes, ma'am."

I lost track of how many days it rained, but as long as there wasn't thunder and lightning not all of the hands had to be out all night watching the herd. It was possible to rest for a few hours, but nobody got dry, and it was miserable.

Jack Straw said, "Be glad it's wet. At least we ain't fighting a prairie fire. Now, that's hell on earth."

We had a bad river crossing a few days after the rains let up. We'd crossed rivers before and Blackjack and John Bell Hood acted as if they were no big deal, the herd following them easily. The hands loosened the girth on their saddles so the horses could breathe better in the water, then they took their clothes off and threw them into the wagon so they'd have dry clothes on the other side, then they plunged in naked on horseback off to the side of the herd to keep them moving straight, hallooing them and hurrahing them and yelling, "Hup! Hup! Hup! Move along, you big old beef!"

I got a real education.

When the boys asked me why I didn't take my clothes off, I said, "This is all I've got, so the only way I'm going to get them washed is if I keep them on."

Shakespeare would take the remuda across and wasn't he a sight, sitting so light in the saddle and leading some hundred and fifty horses and mules into the water, them splashing the water high and the sun glinting off the drops in the air and making a rainbow. Next to the bluebonnets in the spring, I didn't think I'd ever seen a sight so beautiful as him trailing a herd that size through the river, all of them wet and glistening and Shakespeare hurrahing them on and yelling words such as, "God for Harry, England, and St. George!" As if they could understand him. Maybe they did, because they always did what he wanted, and I thought to myself, *It must be he speaks horse like me*, but who knew horses spoke Shakespeare.

The bad crossing came when we got to one river that was swollen from heavy rains up north. Big Mike and Abraham and Hard Luck Luke Bronson stood by the bank, talking it over, and they called Shakespeare over and talked to him as well, and that made me curious because he was only the horse wrangler, so why would there be a parley with him involved? I figured maybe they wanted to know if he thought it would be a problem crossing the remuda.

They talked and then spread the word that the herd would wait a few days to see if the water would go down before we chanced a crossing. "We're not in any hurry," Big Mike said, "so let's go slow and easy." I admired him for not taking chances. We put the herd out to graze and it gave them time to eat and get fat, and the weak and the sore-footed could rest up.

It gave the hands a chance to relax some too. They played mumblety-peg or dominoes or washed out their clothes or went swimming naked. I always found a reason not to join in with the swimming, helping Monty or helping Shakespeare snake in wood and chips for the fire.

One time Shady and Tommy Deuce came over and said, "Hey, Kid, why don't you come swimming?"

They grabbed me and as they hauled me down to the bank I started yelling, "I can't swim! I can't swim!"

Tommy Deuce said, "Well, it's time you learned!" and they threw me into the river. I was lying about not being able to swim, so I flopped around pretending to get the hang of it and I was grateful they hadn't pulled my clothes off like they'd done to Skinny, claiming he smelled too bad to sit next to. Skinny said he didn't like taking a bath because it was contrary to the ability of the skin to breathe wholesome. He fought back, but they took him and stripped him, telling him, "Don't be so damn wrathy!" and they threw him into the water and then threw his clothes in after him and said, "Now, wash these out!" They stood on the bank and wouldn't let him out until he'd done what they said, so it could have been a lot worse if they'd done the same to me.

It took a few days for the river to go down some. When it was looking better, Big Mike parleyed with the boys again and they agreed to give it a try.

Shakespeare and I took the remuda over first and they swam across without any trouble, their necks held high and churning away as if they were born to it. We moved them over to good grazing land and Shakespeare left me near the bank and told me to keep an eye on the remuda, then he went back across and joined the hands who were putting the wagon onto a raft they'd built.

They tied ropes to the raft front and back and then strung the ropes across the river like the raft was a ferry, then they rolled the wagon onto it. The boys on my side had harnessed up the mules to pull, and those on the far bank had ropes to hold it steady, and slowly it made its way across. It landed where the bank was too high so they had to ease back on the ropes and let it float downstream some more, calling out to each other, "That's it!" "A little more rope!" "Whoa now!" and sure enough they found a low spot and the mules pulled it the rest of the way out. The raft was floated back across the river and left on the bank so another set of drovers might use it if they needed it.

The herd had been strung out a ways back from the river so when they got to moving forward they'd just plunge right in like they'd done elsewhere, and they wouldn't have time to calculate how deep the water was, how fast it was moving, or how far across it was.

Big Mike called out, "Start the swim!"

Several of the hands drove Blackjack and John Bell Hood to the edge, but they both sulled, figuring the odds didn't look good. The boys hurrahed them and waved ropes and hats and slickers and tried to nudge them forward, but it didn't help, so they pushed them back from the bank and circled them around, and the rest of the hands held their places, waiting for the big push, keeping the herd still. They drove Blackjack and John Bell Hood forward again, but the minute they got to the bank they turned right around and headed back for the herd.

Hard Luck Luke Bronson and Abraham cut them off, turning them with a big, "Heehaw!" and slapping them on the rump with their hats, and they drove the two of them straight for the bank and got them running so fast they plowed right into the water, not having time to ponder the safety of it all.

Damned if the two of them didn't start swimming across, and at that Big Mike and the swings drove the herd straight toward the river at a fast clip. Sure enough they all plunged in and started following Blackjack and John Bell Hood, figuring if the two of them thought it was OK, then it must be OK. Then every single drover pushed and hurrahed, and the herd funneled into the water, playing follow the leader, and it was all going smooth.

Swim as they might, they drifted downstream because of the current, but Big Mike had figured on that, calculating how far they'd drift and then arrive at a low bank on the far side of the river where they could climb out easy, the rest of the herd following behind. It was working out just as he had planned, and about a third of the herd was across when a tree come drifting downstream.

ELEVEN

Cliff saw it and I don't know what he was thinking but he must have figured he could stop it from hitting the herd, so he and his mount swum straight for it, maybe trying to get a hand on it and drag it to the bank, but he didn't realize how big it was under the water and some branches or roots must have plowed right into him and his horse.

The two of them went over and the horse rolled, taking Cliff with him, and when the horse come up Cliff wasn't in the saddle. Some of the hands could see his foot was caught in the stirrup and he must have been under his horse, who was all panicky now and thrashing, so Jack Straw, Tommy Deuce, and Preacher rode quick into the water to try to rescue him.

Jack Straw slid off his mount and got to Cliff first and tried to pull Cliff out from under his horse, but he had trouble because Cliff's horse kicked wildly and they were all tangled in the tree by now. Jack Straw got Cliff's head above water, but the tree begun to spin and it plowed right into the herd, taking Jack Straw and Cliff with it, and Tommy Deuce and Preacher had to pull back.

The herd began to panic when the tree struck and several of the beeves decided to turn around and head back for the bank they'd started from, only it was too crowded for any of them to turn, them running into the beeves still heading into the water, so they all began to mill right there in the middle of the river, a hundred beeves or so milling and drifting downstream at the same time, the tree and Jack Straw and Cliff now drifting into the middle of them. Hands yelled advice and tried to get to Cliff and Jack Straw, but there were too many longhorns in the way.

Cliff's foot was still caught in the stirrup and he come up choking, his face all bloody from being kicked by his horse, but he managed to grab hold of his saddle horn to try to stay above water, but as they struggled his horse rolled again and both went under, somehow going deeper now and then drifting under the milling herd.

Jack Straw kept trying again and again to reach him, but with all those longhorns knocking into one another he couldn't manage. Big Mike and Preacher and Bill and Tommy Deuce and the other hands were in the water as well, trying to fight through the brutes and get to Cliff, but they couldn't make any headway. I rode back and forth on the bank, holding my breath, as if it would help Cliff hold his, and I felt helpless and desperate all over again.

Abraham and Hard Luck Luke Bronson and Shady, still on the bank, halted the rest of the herd to keep them from going into the river and making matters worse. Everyone shouted and yelled and Jack Straw choked and struggled himself and he finally had to reach out and grab his horse's tail and hang on to it, and his horse headed for the bank, threading through the herd and pulling Jack Straw along, and when they got out of the river Jack Straw fell to the ground coughing and choking and throwing up water.

Meanwhile Cliff and his horse suddenly come up in the middle of the herd and me and the other hands all yelled, "There he is! There he is!" Then they went back down under again, being all tangled up in each other, and the herd closed over them. All the hands either tried to swim into the herd or were on horseback following the herd downstream and looking for a chance to ride in and pull Cliff out. All of them yelled and shouted and asked if anyone saw Cliff or knew where he was now, but there was no way anyone could get far enough into the herd and then go under and look for the drowning cowboy and his horse.

Then everyone just followed along and waited for him to come back up again so they could spot him and try to save him. Some of them called for him as if they thought he could hear them from underwater because it was all they could think to do, and as the herd milled the current continued to carry it downstream.

Some of the hands tried to hurrah the herd into changing directions to drive it toward the far bank, but it was dangerous work because they were on the downstream side of the herd. If they went into the river too far they'd get caught in the mill themselves, so they yelled and waved hats, but to no effect, and some of them went into the water farther downstream to look for the lost rider, hoping he had drifted away from the herd and would surface.

It was then I saw Shakespeare ride along the bank and get ahead of the herd. He dismounted and tossed off his boots and his vest and his shirt, then he dove straight into the water and swam straight toward the steer in the lead. When he got to him, he grabbed him by his horns and pulled himself up onto its back and then he turned the head of the steer toward the opposite bank and kicked him in the flank and hurrahed him like he was some kind of cow pony, and damned if the steer didn't change direction and head for the far bank, and that broke the mill.

The brutes behind him followed, as if Shakespeare was Blackjack or John Bell Hood, taking them all to the promised land. When they reached the bank, the steer shook Shakespeare off and suddenly Shakespeare was surrounded by all the other longhorns climbing up the bank and crowding in on him and he was slipping in the mud and trying to push the brutes away so he didn't get trampled.

I rode along the bank watching it all and feeling sick about Cliff, but when I saw the dilemma Shakespeare was in I rode straight down into the herd, yelling and hurrahing them and driving them away. When I got to him I held my hand out and took my foot out of the stirrup and he grabbed my hand and got his foot in the stirrup and hauled himself aboard, him sitting behind me all wet and covered in mud and holding on to me.

I liked how his hands felt on me, and I wanted to turn around and tell him I'd never seen anything so brave, and tell him I had these feelings inside of me for him that I'd never had for anyone else before, and was there a chance I was leaning against an open door, but I kept my mouth shut. I rode both of us out of the herd and up the bank and over to a lone black walnut tree. Shakespeare slid off and collapsed against the trunk, exhausted, and he said, "Thanks, Kid."

I said, "What, you can't talk in Shakespeare words anymore?"

And he came back quick, saying, "I rest much bounden in thee," and he gave me a little salute with two fingers of his right hand.

I was on Dancer and he pranced all around the same way my heart jumped at the sight of him all wet and muddy. I wanted to tell him I admired him, and even though he was covered in mud, I wanted to confess I found him handsome, but I stopped myself because they were the thoughts of a girl, and besides, I was feeling just awful about Cliff. I nodded at him and I said, "That's better," and then I left the remuda behind and rode farther downstream, joining the boys who were looking for Cliff.

He didn't come up, and we couldn't find him or his horse.

When the beeves were climbing the bank, the rest of the herd was sent in and they crossed over as if there wasn't anything to worry about and they had wanted to get over all along so they could go to graze again, and what had been the delay?

When the whole herd was finally across it was late afternoon, the sun getting low. I helped Monty get the fire going and the coffee on and the bait ready, and the boys went back and forth to the river, looking farther downstream on both banks and calling out Cliff's name, but they didn't find anything. When it got dark they finally came in and they were as bedraggled as wet hounds and looked so sorrowful.

None of the hands said anything, and I'm sure everyone was thinking the same thing. I know I was thinking what a horrible death drowning was, and how scared Cliff must have been and how he must have suffered. There was times when I had stayed underwater too long and I felt panicked about getting back to air, and how good it felt to break free and take in that first breath. What hell it must be to realize you aren't going to make it, and I found myself holding my breath, as if I was the one underwater.

I started breathing again when I heard Big Mike say, "Jack Straw, that was good work you did today."

Jack Straw muttered, "I couldn't get his foot out of the damn stirrup."

Big Mike said, "That's OK, Jack Straw, you were the only one who got to him and you did everything you could." Then he said, "You too, Shakespeare. Good work."

I felt proud for Shakespeare but there wasn't any way to glory in it because Cliff had tried to do the good work you'd expect from a ranny, but it had gotten him drowned instead. A few of the hands murmured, "Good work, Jack Straw, good work, Shakespeare," but Jack Straw didn't say anything and Shakespeare had the good sense not to start quoting from some play.

Then there was silence, and I'm sure everyone wanted to say something good about Cliff, but it was hard to say anything because there wasn't a body, so it was as if he wasn't dead yet, but everybody knew he was, but still you didn't want to act like you knew it was so.

Tommy Deuce asked, "Cliff got a family?"

"He's got a sister in St. Louis," Preacher said, and then there was silence again and everyone knew Big Mike was going to have to contact her at some point, maybe by going through Cliff's kit and finding a letter with her name on it.

Skinny nighthawked the remuda even though he'd been up all day, and the nightriders changed off throughout the night. When I was stretched out in my bedroll I kept wishing I was closer to Shakespeare's bedroll, wanting to tell him how much I admired him. I loosened the band around my chest so I could breathe easier, glad I was alive and reminding myself that I was a girl, my hand resting on my breast.

The stars were bright that night, and out there on the prairie they never seemed so close and yet so far away, and there were a million of them. I couldn't help but think what a strange world it was we lived in with all the death and dying and struggling, all the while taking a herd of cattle to Dodge so people in the east could eat more beef, and me not being able to tell the truth about myself, and the sun coming up every morning as if you could count on it. Yet you couldn't even count on waking up the next morning, none of us could, not my family and not those Comanches I killed, not Scotty or Cliff, and I wished I could move my bedroll over by Shakespeare and tell him everything I was thinking and ask him what he thought about death and dying or being alive, and did he think there was a God. And if he did think there was, then just what did he think God was doing with everybody, and did he think it mattered since everyone just seemed to live and die the same whether or not there was a God.

I don't think I slept that night, but I was surprised when my foot was kicked and it was my turn to ride nightguard, and when I got up I almost forgot to tighten the band around my chest.

The next morning we were up before daybreak and got some bait and all the folks were real quiet unless it was something like, "Let me have some more of that coffee" or "I think I'll have one more of those biscuits, Monty."

Big Mike and Hard Luck Luke Bronson were gone, Monty saying they'd left long before dawn and were going to ride down the river again for a few miles, which was about the most I'd heard him say in one sentence in the time I'd known him.

Abraham had been left in charge and he said who was going to be riding drag, flanker, and swing. We cleaned off our plates and broke down the camp, and Shakespeare and I got Monty's team of mules hooked up and he pulled out.

We drove all morning and we were on our noon break, grabbing some bait from Monty, when Big Mike and Hard Luck Luke Bronson caught up with us, and Cliff was slung over the rump of Big Mike's horse. They'd found him several miles below, his body hung up in some low-hanging branches or maybe it was some roots sticking out of the bank.

"Damnedest thing," Big Mike said. "You'd think we would've found the horse too, but he must have gotten hung up underwater somewhere. Damnedest thing."

Hard Luck Luke Bronson dismounted first and dragged Cliff off Big Mike's horse. The hands came over and they all eased him to the ground and Big Mike just sat there for a while watching, then he got off real slow and he helped Hard Luck Luke Bronson and the boys stretch Cliff out straight.

He said, "Somebody get me his bedroll," and he took Cliff's empty holster off and tossed it to me and he said, "Here, use this for that Schofield of yours."

I picked it up, and it seemed everything I had come from somebody dead.

Shady came over with Cliff's bedroll and Bill pulled the quilt and sougan out of it and Shady spread the tarp out, then Hard Luck Luke Bronson and Big Mike placed Cliff's body on it and folded the tarp over him. Slowly the hands gathered around Cliff and I don't think there was anyone watching the herd or the remuda, but they were content to graze. Everyone took their hats off and just looked at the rough shape of Cliff's body under the tarp. His feet stuck out and he had one boot on and one boot had been lost, maybe the one caught in the stirrup.

Big Mike looked around and he said, "I don't want to bury him close to the creek. If it floods he might get washed away.

No reason for him to go through that twice." He pointed to a spot about fifty yards away from the wagon and he said, "Get the shovels and we'll bury him there."

He looked at Preacher and he said, "Can you help us out here, son?"

Preacher said, "Yes, sir, boss," and he left to get his Bible.

Tommy Deuce and Shady went for the shovels and Abraham and Bill went to pick up Cliff, but Big Mike said, "No, Bronson and I got this."

Abraham said, "That's a heavy load, boss," so Big Mike relented and all four of them picked up a corner of the tarp and carried Cliff over to where they wanted him buried, the rest of the hands following along in a procession.

When they got to the spot, Tommy Deuce and Shady started digging, Jack Straw and Skinny spelling them. When they hit rocks, the other hands and I got down on all fours and helped pull them out. While we were doing that, Big Mike and Hard Luck Luke Bronson opened up the tarp and went through Cliff's pockets and found a pocket watch and a tally book with a pencil, but that was all, other than his Bull Durham. Then they folded the tarp over him real neatly. I was glad when that job was done because a man dead by drowning don't look good. I had to look away, and it was a relief to have him covered.

Then they put him in his grave.

I imagine the funeral was like the one they did for Scotty. Preacher knew just what verses to read, about life and ashes and dust, and he gave a brief sermon about life being short, and we know not when, like a thief in the night, and what a good man Cliff was and how he too was bringing civilization to the world, and he was riding now where horses were fast and the air was fresh and it was summer always.

All the boys were asked if they wanted to say something. Several of them spoke up about something Cliff had said or done, or a blanket stretcher he'd told about it being so hot and dry when he was a kid that the frogs never learned how to swim.

There was silence, and then Bill said, "Shakespeare, what's Shakespeare say?"

Shakespeare just thought for a moment or two and then he said, "Death doth close his tender dying eyes."

And that was it.

Everyone was silent again and maybe embarrassed about the tender part, everybody always bragging about what hard cases they were. Then Preacher sang "The Shining Shore" and several of the boys knew it and joined in, and I knew it too. Preacher ended it all with the Lord's Prayer.

Dirt was shoveled in on top of Cliff and several of the boys took a handful and threw it in as well. When the grave was filled, everyone gathered up as many rocks as they could find and covered the grave with them, making a rocky mound, protecting Cliff from wolves and coyotes. Skinny had made a sturdy cross out of branches, tying the pieces together with rawhide, and it was pounded into the grave.

Then Shakespeare said something else about "flights of angels sing thee to thy rest," which I thought was real pretty.

Big Mike said, "OK, boys, string 'em out and point 'em north."

As we moved out, I looked back to where Cliff was buried and it looked high lonesome all by itself, and I wondered if anybody would ever stumble across his grave and wonder who was there and how he died. I was glad he'd had a decent send-off, but I felt bad that Ma and Pa and Jamie hadn't had the Bible read and a sermon preached and hymns sung and good words said about them as well, and friends to pray for them and tell memories of them, and what a poor job I had done, being in such a hurry to get Sally back. I told myself, maybe I could go back and do it over someday, do it better, although I also felt like I never wanted to go back there again for the rest of my life.

TWELVE

We drove north and the heat was coming on hard now and the winds were constant and powerful, but there was a glory of flowers waving across the windblown prairie, verbena and sunflowers and pinwheels and primroses and such, and when the sun set at night you could have sworn both the sky and the prairie were all aflame.

Things went smoothly, although there was one bad hailstorm where everybody had to get under their horses to keep from getting knocked out of the saddle by hail the size of rocks. There was rain off and on and there were creeks and river crossings and sometimes there were even bridges to cross. The herd would come to a halt by a bridge and Big Mike would call out, "Cowboy!" and a hand would lead twenty steers over the bridge, and when they were across Big Mike would call out, "Cowboy!" and another twenty would be led across, until the whole herd was over. All in all, Big Mike took it slow and easy.

The evenings got back to normal and one night the boys started talking about rattlesnakes, and Bill said he knew a fellow who cut the head off a rattler and still got bit by it. Then they all had stories about rattlesnakes crawling into someone's bedroll and there was a debate about the best treatment for snakebite, most of them agreeing that Spanish dagger was best. Tommy Deuce said a rope around your bedroll would protect you from snakes, but Hard Luck Luke Bronson spoke up, saying, "Hell, that isn't any more true than saying you can stop a stampede by throwing salt in front of it." Then the two of them would start arguing again. Then someone told a windjammer about a road-runner shoving prickly pear cactus into a snake's mouth to kill it, and Skinny said a roadrunner would surround a rattlesnake with prickly pear and the snake would bite itself to death rather than crawl over the thorns of the prickly pear, and Tommy Deuce said, "Is that true? Is that true?"

Shakespeare went back to his story about the girl cast up on the shore and disguising herself as a boy, and sometimes he'd tease the boys and get them to say the words, him telling them what to say, and they got into it, one acting like a prissy butler and another acting like some lady talking in a high voice, and one acting like a big fat bragging drunk named Belch, and everybody laughed at that. Then he said, "Hey, you, Kid, read this speech here," and he tried to hand me his book.

I said, "No, I don't want to do that," but Shady grabbed me and dragged me out in front of the boys, them saying, "Yeah, read it out loud, Kid!"

Shakespeare said, "It's real easy, everybody's been doing it, so you go too, just read this part here."

So I took the book and I started reading where he pointed, and it was a speech to the duke where she, or he, says, "Say that some lady, as perhaps there is, hath for your love as great a pang of heart as you have for Olivia ... " and I thought, *Boy we are on dangerous ground here given how I feel about Shakespeare.*

Then Shakespeare, as this duke, has this bragging speech about how no one can love as great as he can, and I thought, *Don't that just sound like some man so full of himself, like Tommy Deuce bragging about his way with the soiled doves.*

I continued on where Shakespeare was pointing, saying, "My father had a daughter loved a man as it might be, perhaps, were I a woman, I should your lordship ... " And again I thought, *Is Shakespeare*—and by Shakespeare I meant the cowhand not the writer—*is Shakespeare trying to tell me he knows something about me? Is he trying to hint at something?* I went on to read, "She never told her love..." And then she goes on to talk about being melancholy and being someone named Patience who smiles at grief, and I thought that was pretty dumb because who smiles at grief?

And then Shakespeare, as the duke, asks if my sister died of grief, and I read back to him—and here all the hands are real quiet and leaning forward—I start reading, "I am all the daughters of my father's house and all the brothers too..." And then all I could think about was me being Pa's daughter and Jamie being my brother, and now I was saying I was Jamie when I really wasn't, and none of these boys even knew my real name, and I started getting all choked up and I thought, *Here you go, what fourteen-year-old boy is going to break down weeping in front of a bunch of Texas cowhands?*

Then Shakespeare took the book away and said, "Sorry, Kid. I keep thinking you're some tough old Texas ranny, and I keep forgetting what happened to you."

I said, "It's OK, Shakespeare."

Then he told the boys how the scene ended so I didn't have to read it, and I went off and sat down and tried to gather myself together, wanting to run away, but I knew that would make me look even worse.

Everybody was silent around the fire, and then Abraham started singing some spiritual song, singing, "When death has come and taken our loved ones leaving our homes so lonely and drear..."

And Bill joined in with him, singing, "Often I wonder why I must journey over a road so rugged and steep..." and then there was a part that went, "Farther along we'll know all about it, farther along we'll understand why, cheer up my brothers, live in the sunshine, we'll understand it all by and by." I realized it was something they might have sung by my family's graveside as a way of saying good-bye, and they were telling me everything was going to be OK. I appreciated the effort, but in my heart I thought, *That'll be the day. There'll be no understanding.*

Later on we were all in our bedrolls and Shakespeare was only a few feet from me, and I heard him say real quietly, "Sorry, Kid."

I whispered back, "It's OK," even though it wasn't.

He was silent, and then he asked, "How'd they die?"

"Badly."

I turned away from him and closed my eyes, wondering how it was that I could like him and still be mad at him so much of the time.

One night we were eating supper by the campfire when Big Mike sat down by me with his plate and said, "I got something for you to think about."

I said, "What's that?"

"Fort Griffin is a little over a day's ride from here and the weather looks like it's going to be fair. If you want, I can give you a few hands for protection and you can ride to the fort and talk to the commanding officer about the bands that come in for their annuities, and you can ask whether or not anyone has seen your sister and they could send out word to the other outposts and the civilian authorities to look for her. What would you think of that?"

I almost choked on my bait. In my heart I'd almost given up on finding her, even though I knew I'd never give up looking for her. I said, "I'd appreciate that, but how would you get by with so few hands?"

"Oh, we'll manage, you just make sure you turn around and head back as soon as you've talked to them."

I said, "We surely will."

"OK," he said, and then he turned to the hands and told them what we were talking about and he asked for volunteers to go with me.

Right away Jack Straw said, "I'll go."

Shakespeare said, "Count me in," but Big Mike said he would need him as horse wrangler, but Shakespeare pointed to Tommy Deuce and said he could do the wrangling just fine, and he said, "Besides, I owe the Kid a favor," and he tapped his shirt pocket where he kept one of his small Shakespeare books, and he winked at me.

Tommy Deuce just shrugged, so Big Mike said, "OK."

Then Abraham said, "I'll go," and Shady, he was the one who took his red sash off and spoke to the Comanches the time they took Paint back, said he would too, and that made four.

Big Mike told us to take our bedrolls and our weapons and he told Monty to make sure we had some bait. At that he got up and cleaned off his plate.

There was silence around the campfire and I said, "Thanks, boys."

Jack Straw said, "Always glad to help the Comanche Kid."

I finished everything on my plate knowing I'd need my strength, and I had to quiet my heart from hoping something good might come of this. Little red sparks drifted up into the sky from the campfire, and I asked myself if they were the flicker of hope I felt in my chest, or were they just burning embers that would spark out and turn into nothing in the black night.

And Pa's voice said, "She has to be somewhere, angel, and if she's somewhere, she can be found."

That was just like him, even with the war being lost and him being wounded, he always thought things were going to be OK, and whenever things were hard he used to say, "Now, look at me, made it back to all of you with a bullet in my leg, didn't I?"

At the time I was just a kid and I believed him, thinking, if you just believed everything would turn out all right and worked hard enough, everything would be OK. Now I knew that wasn't the case, that it didn't matter what you believed. Nothing got guaranteed. Ask Scotty. Ask Cliff.

We were up long before dawn and Monty had coffee and flapjacks and salt pork and airtight peaches ready. I chose Buck for the journey because he'd already proved himself when things got hard, so I trusted him the most. I also didn't want anyone recognizing Dancer or Blood, just in case we run across the band they come from.

We tied our bedrolls on the back of our saddles and stuffed our saddlebags with biscuits and dried apples and fried salt pork. I holstered the Schofield in Cliff's gun belt and I put the Spenser in Pa's scabbard and checked that I had shells on board. When we were all mounted and ready, Big Mike came up and said, "Damned if you all don't look like a bunch of hard cases."

Jack Straw piped up and said, "Hell, we look just like a bunch of horse marines or one of those Texas Ranger outfits, don't we all!"

"Damned if you don't," Big Mike said. "If you stop for the night, no fires. Keep a guard out and keep your mounts tied to you. You don't want to end up dead or afoot," and to Abraham he said, "Keep an eye out on the Kid."

"Hell, he's already killed five of them," Jack Straw said. "It's his job to keep an eye out on us!"

Big Mike did that half smile of his and he said, "Good luck, hurry back." Then he nodded at Abraham and said, "Ride on."

We pulled out of the camp and it wasn't long before the sun was rising, making a bloodred dawn. We rode at an easy lope, the wind in our face and Buck's black mane shining so beautifully. I ran my hand down his neck as we rode and he talked horse to me, saying it was good to be out and to run. I told him he smelled good, just like a horse smells, and I felt almost giddy, as if something good was coming.

The prairie was a world of flowers, all of them at their fullest. There were poppies and coneflowers and Indian blanket, and I swear blue and red and white and purple and yellow and orange had never seemed so bright. That's what hope will do, I thought, make everything seem alive and possible. *Don't trust it*, I kept telling myself.

We stopped and watered our horses at a small, clear-running spring creek and threw water on our faces and run water through our hair and put a wet neck scarf around our necks. We ate a biscuit and a few dried apple slices, then mounted up and headed on. All the boys kept an eye out on the ridges and hills, and once Shady pulled up and stared into the distance and Abraham said, "What?"

"Maybe nothing," Shady said, "but keep your eyes open."

Then a few hours later on Abraham did the same thing and said, "Two of them. I think we're being scouted."

"Not surprising," Shady said. "What we don't want is to run into fifteen or twenty of them."

Late afternoon we come across a burned-out wagon on its side, what wood was left looking like blackened bones, and nearby were the whitened bones of four oxen. Pretty wildflowers and green grasses were growing up through the remains of the wagon and the bones, so the attack must have taken place a year or two ago, maybe more. We all rode over to look at it and it looked awful, like the violence was still there, still happening.

Shady surveyed the ruins and he said, "They shot the oxen, killed the men, burned the wagon, and outraged the women." He made it all sound so simple.

We dismounted and walked around it and Jack Straw asked, "What was they doing all alone way out here?"

And Abraham answered, "What are any of us doing way out here?"

I thought to myself, *What were Ma and Pa doing way out where something so awful could happen to us,* and it made me mad at Ma and Pa, and terrible words kept coming to me. I felt ashamed for feeling that way, like I was betraying them to think those things.

We kicked at the burned wood and looked around us and up into the hills, as if whoever had done this might still be around, then Shady said, "Look at this." He stood by a charred wheel, the rear one, facing the sky, at the end of a burned axle.

Abraham said, "What is it?"

"Right here," Shady said, and he pointed at what was left of the rim, and there was the burned remains of rawhide cords. He said, "See, there's four of them," and he pointed them out, all four, spaced around the rim.

Jack Straw said, "Dear God."

Shady walked up to the front wheel, just as badly charred, and he said, "There's four here too."

I asked, "So what? What's that mean?"

"They tied them to the wheels and then they burned them alive," Shady said. "Someone's come along and taken the bodies away, or more likely buried what was left, probably somewhere near here."

At that I just felt sick and I had to turn away, thinking of their screams and wondering, did they burn them at the same time or did they burn one and make the other watch before they burned that person too? The hands stood there looking at it all, and I couldn't help but think, at least my family didn't have to go through that.

With my back to them I asked, "How do you know they were burned alive?"

"If it was you," Shady said, "how else would you do it?"

And at that they all turned away and we mounted up and rode on in silence, leaving the remains there in the middle of the bright green prairie grasses, the flowers colorful all around.

When the sun was going down, Abraham said, "We'll ride until it's dark. There's not much moon, so if they're watching it'll be harder for them to see where we are. We'll look for a grove of trees and pull in there so if we get hit we'll have some cover."

And that's what we did. We pulled our bedrolls off our mounts and had our weapons handy, and everyone cut off a piece of fried salt pork and ate that with a biscuit and more dried apples. Abraham gave me first shift as guard and he said, "You know what happens if you fall asleep on guard duty, don't you"?

I said, "They shoot you."

"That's right," he said, "if you're lucky."

"What happens if you're not lucky?"

"They burn you alive." And at that he rolled out his bedroll and lay down, but I doubt he slept at all, keeping an eye out on me, on all of us.

When I finally got a chance to lie down I pulled Buck over close and I don't remember going to sleep, listening for noises in the grass or in the trees or in the brush, or hearing something sliding across the rocks. Sometimes it felt like an army was swirling around us, or maybe I was just dreaming and imagining it all, I don't know.

THIRTEEN

It was early morning when we come across the buffalo runners. We found the carcasses first, huge and naked, mountains of red meat and white fat, looking as if God had said, "Let there be buffalo," but then quit halfway through, saying, "Oh well, that's close enough." They were scattered across the prairie, waiting for the sun to bloat them and make them stink. A little ways on we come across the runners themselves with their wagons and mules and the skins stacked up. When they saw us—there were three of them—they dropped the skinning and came walking over.

One of them, a tall, lean one with a long handlebar mustache, said, "Well, how do? What have we got here? You all long riders or maybe just lost? You all look like a bunch of Texas rawhiders but I don't see no cow brutes. Lost your herd? What're you all about?"

Abraham had reined up and he said, "On an errand to the fort, herd's behind us a ways."

The runner called out, "You the trail boss?"

Abraham nodded and said, "I am today."

The runner turned to the other two and laughed real big and he said, "Look at that, I seen nigger punchers but I never seen a nigger trail boss before!"

Then he turned back to Abraham and he said, "Whoo-ee! You coming up in the world, boy, congratulations, let me shake your hand!" He held out his hand for Abraham to shake but it was all wet from the skinning and all their clothes were stained with blood and fat.

I wondered what was going to happen if Abraham refused to shake the man's hand, but he reached down and shook it and said, "Thank you, partner."

The runner said, "By God it's good to see someone out on these plains!" Then taking us all in he said, "Now, what all do we got here? A nigger and a savage," and then pointing at Shakespeare and Jack Straw he said, "and two Americans." He looked at me and with a toothy smile he asked, "And what's that? Some kind of child? Maybe a little girl you got riding with you?"

I panicked at that and I thought, how is it that of all of them he's the one who sees through me?

He laughed real loud at his own joke and he looked at the two with him, and one was smiling big but the other just stared kind of flat and empty.

Jack Straw spoke up and bragged, "Why, this here's the Comanche Kid! Maybe you've heard of him? He's a kid all right but I wouldn't offend him like that, calling him a little girl. He's one real bravo. He's killed more Comanches than the rest of us put together. Why, he could make short work out of all of us if he wanted to!"

At that the runner said, "Whoa!" and he come over and clapped his wet hand on my knee and said, "Now, that deserves a cup of coffee! How 'bout you all join us at the wagon and we'll all have a cup of coffee together. And, little child, you can tell us how you killed those Comanches. Then maybe if you all have seen any buffalo in your travels you can tell us where they are, because they are in short supply. Damn buffalo runners so thick now we've had to search high and low just to find these, and damned if even the soldiers from the fort don't come out and kill them just for sport and take away our livelihood. A scarcity of buffalo. Why, just a while back there was plenty for everybody, and now look at this, so few and scattered so far apart. Who'd have thought it? No wonder the Indians give up and head for the reservations. Where else they going to get something to eat, huh? Lucky for them the United States government hands out sustenance, right? By God, they'd have to eat their own if not for the government. How about that coffee?"

Abraham said, "I'm sorry, partner, but we're on a deadline, due back to the herd no later than tomorrow and we've got a long way to go."

"Deadline," the flat one with the stare said. "That's what they called it at Andersonville. A deadline. Cross it and they killed you. I saw boys kill themselves on purpose by walking straight across the deadline."

He said it in a dull voice, but somehow it still sounded like a threat and I wondered if Abraham shouldn't take them up on their offer of coffee, because this one seemed a little addled in the brain, as if he'd snapped over at Andersonville, and who knew what he might do if we refused them.

Abraham changed the subject and said, "There's just three of you. You keeping an eye out for Comanches?"

The first one said, "We're too close to the fort. If they're going to raid, they leave the reservation after they got their rations and then go for weeks and weeks on a long ride and hit some farm or some family traveling, then hightail it back to the reservation with horses and scalps so no one knows who done it or where they come from."

I felt sick at heart because I knew firsthand what he was describing.

I heard Shakespeare's horse shift and paw the ground next to me, and I swear Buck understood it all because he took a few steps forward then backward and threw his head back and forth as if he was trying to shake the bit out of his mouth. I had to rein him in and I patted him on the neck and whispered to him that I wanted to get out of there too, get away from these men and all the dead, naked buffalo, away from that one buffalo that was half-skinned, looking like someone who'd been shot halfway through taking off his clothes.

Abraham said, "We appreciate the invitation but we can't stop, but maybe you all would enjoy this," and he reached back into his saddlebag and pulled out a sack of dried apples and handed it off to the first hunter, saying, "Take this and add it to the beans and salt pork you're eating."

The hunter said, "Well now, thank you! Whoa! Look at this boys, dried apples! Well now, we do appreciate that!"

Abraham said, "You're more than welcome," and then he nodded at us and as we began to pull out the runner called to him, "You keep it up, boy, I'll bet you're going to have a herd of your own right soon, then won't you be sitting high on the hog! We're all going to get rich and we'll all eat beef together in New York City!" And his laughter and the smell trailed after us as we moved out.

It was early in the afternoon when we come through a grove of trees and saw Fort Griffin before us on the open, flat plains. Several of the buildings gleamed white in the sun, built from limestone and looking clean and bright and well-ordered, the other buildings being made of wood picket logs, upright. They all surrounded a large parade ground but there was no protective stockade wall between the buildings. There were officers' quarters and several barracks and stables and such, and a limestone headquarters building that was two stories tall with a flag flying out in front of it. The flag looked good, giving some kind of significance to the place and making me think at least this part of the world has order to it, as if it was some landlocked north star.

Scattered outside the fort were wagons selling food and goods with teams of oxen and mules and horses grazing nearby. There were Murphy wagons and Studebaker wagons of emigrants, all with iron kettles and pots and skillets and Dutch ovens on campfires and smoke rising everywhere, as well as freighters loaded down with cargo, and more buffalo runners with wagons of hides. There were wagons of Comanchero traders and all about there was chickens and pigs in crates and small herds of cattle, and packs of dogs running about. It looked to me like a picture from a storybook about castles, all the peasants living outside the castle and the knights all inside.

A little ways off from the fort there was a large village of Indian tipis with horses tied outside each tipi, the women cooking and working hides and pelts and more dogs running around and kids chasing each other or play fighting with sticks.

Maybe Sally is there, I thought.

FOURTEEN

We rode onto the fort grounds, all five of us, me moving up by Abraham since this was my affair, and the two of us must have looked like quite a pair, him being so big and black and me being small and white. I felt scared, but I was glad he was with me because I thought maybe nothing could go wrong if he was there. The rest trailed behind us, all of us looking scruffy after so much time on the drive and no time to wash up and look presentable.

As we approached the headquarters building, Abraham said, "You tell them who you are and tell them you need to speak to the post commander."

I'd hoped he'd do that for me, figuring no one would pay attention to me, but now I knew I was on my own. I had to steady my breathing but I kept thinking, *Maybe Sally is here somewhere and they just don't know who to give her back to because she's too young to know who she is and where she's from.* Then I started kicking myself, thinking, *You're living in too much hope. Just make an inquiry and see what they say.*

There was a guard posted outside the headquarters building, and I'd never seen a Negro in uniform before. Abraham nodded at me, so I slid off Buck and all the others come to a standstill and waited as I walked up to the guard. I felt like I had some army behind me and Ma said, "You're just like Joan of Arc come to see the king." I thought, *Yeah, and we all know what happened to her.*

I stood before the guard, him towering over me, the four hands watching me, and I made sure to make my manners like

I'd been taught. I took off my hat and I said, "Good afternoon, sir." I told him I was on a trail drive headed to Dodge, but I'd come over to the fort because my sister had been kidnapped by Comanches and I was trying to find her and could I see the post commander to make an inquiry, please.

He was tall and all skin and bones with dark eyes and a narrow face and he had a stripe on his blouse, but I was never sure what rank went with which stripes. He looked me up and down and then he looked at the four behind me and he said, "Let me see what I can do," and he went through the door.

I stood there and felt the heat from the sun and I felt as if the eyes of everyone in the post were on me, so I kicked at the dirt and acted as if this wasn't anything important, this was just something I did every day. I glanced at the four and they were staring around at all the goings-on in and around the fort, and then I noticed there were troops and troops of Negro soldiers crossing to and fro and more troops of Negro soldiers being drilled on the parade grounds.

Abraham caught me staring at them and said, "They call them buffalo soldiers."

I was impressed and I said, "That's a powerful name."

Then I saw horses being led somewhere by several Indians. This time Abraham said, "Tonkawa scouts. They work for the army."

I marveled at that and I asked, "Indians hunting Indians?" He just shrugged.

The guard came out and said, "Go on in and tell your story to the sergeant."

Abraham dismounted but the guard pointed at me and said, "Just him."

So Abraham said, "Yes, sir," and I didn't like the way he said it, as if this skinny man with a stripe was his boss. He was Big Mike's *segundo*, and Big Mike didn't treat him that way and the two of them, along with Hard Luck Luke Bronson, always seemed to figure out things together.

Abraham took Buck's reins from my hand and he said, "Go on in." I walked through the door as the rest of the hands began to dismount and I heard the guard telling the boys where they could find something to eat and drink.

When I entered, I saw the sergeant at a battered wooden desk across from me. Still holding my hat in my hands, I said, "Good afternoon, sir."

He was a burly man with little hair and his eyes were red and squinty, and he said back to me, "Good afternoon, Sergeant."

That took me aback because I wasn't a sergeant, so I just stood there dumbfounded, and he said again, "Good afternoon, Sergeant."

Then I realized I was supposed to call him sergeant, so I repeated him, saying, "Good afternoon, Sergeant."

Again I stood there until I realized he was waiting for me to go on, so I rushed into my story, starting with Jamie's name and where I was from, and he interrupted me and he said, "You're looking for your sister, is that right?"

"Yes, sir. I mean, Sergeant. I mean, yes, Sergeant."

"Well, she ain't here. If they have a captive they don't bring them near the post for fear of having them taken away. They keep them wherever their main camp might be."

He sat there in silence, squinting at me as if I was some actor who didn't know his words very well, and at the same time I realized what a fool I was, thinking Sally would be walking around the fort in full sight.

I said, "Maybe I could speak to the post commander, Sergeant, sir."

He let the "sir" pass and said, "General Mackenzie is a busy man."

I had a feeling he was testing me, or just enjoying not giving me what I needed, as if he didn't have anything better to do. I don't know where it came from but out of the blue I asked, "Were you at Gettysburg, sir?" not remembering to say "sergeant," and he just looked at me like I knew some secret about him I wasn't supposed to know.

He crossed his arms over his chest and he said, "What if I was? What's that to you?"

"You boys kicked my father's butt good at Little Round Top," I said. "Pa told me no one whips John Bell Hood, but they got whipped good that day. Just plain outfought. Thought they had the advantage over Chamberlain what with the Yanks running out of ammunition and being left with nothing but bayonets, but he turned the tables on them with a right wheel march that shouldn't have worked."

He just sat there, silent, listening to me, and I added, "A few days ago, my Pa got killed and scalped by the Comanches and so did my mother and you can guess what they did to her, and they killed my brother and they took my little sister. Maybe you could throw a bone to my father and let me see General Mackenzie. After all, you're the one who come out on top."

He stared at me for the longest time, then without a word he got up, steadying himself, and walked to General Mackenzie's door, rapping on the doorframe, and a voice called, "Yes!"

He went in and there was muttering, and then he come out and he said, "Go on in, and you address him as General Mackenzie, and you call him 'sir' every time you speak, do you understand me?"

"Yes, Sergeant. Thank you, Sergeant."

As I headed for the door he stopped me with a hand on my arm and with a hard smile he said, "John Bell Hood got exactly what was coming to him," and at that he let me go and returned to his desk, and I went on in.

General Mackenzie was at his desk, papers and maps here and there, and bright sunlight from the window was spilling across both his face and the desk, and the first thing I noticed was one hand in the light that looked like it had been mangled and then healed up wrong. I caught myself staring at it, and then

I pulled away to look him in the eyes but he was putting some ledger to the side, and without looking at me he asked, "How are you, son?"

"I'm fine, General Mackenzie, thank you very much, sir."

Then he turned, his blue eyes bright and piercing, surprising me with how sharp they were.

"What can I do for you?" he said.

So I launched into the whole story about how I happened to be in the area on a drive and what had happened to my family and I was looking for my sister, throwing in the word "sir" as often as I could, and what a favor it would be if he could help me out.

He asked me my name, which I had forgotten to tell him, and he wanted to know how old I was, so I told him my usual lies and hoped the band beneath my shirt was tight enough because I had forgotten to check it. I tried to lower my voice a little bit to be more believable and I thought, *This must be what that girl in Shakespeare's story was feeling when she went to that duke to ask for a job and he hired her, thinking she was a boy.*

He seemed to take my story seriously, but he said, "Son, civilians are always trying to find captive children but the Indians lie about whether or not they have any, and they hide them if anyone comes near, even if it's just to parley. And often the children are traded away to other tribes, or sold, or, I'm sorry to tell you, son, they're killed. And sometimes they're used to buy wares or spirits or weapons and ammunition from Mexican Comanchero traders that come up from down south. Sometimes the Comancheros can get them back to their families, if they have the right information, and if there's a reward substantial enough. Do you have the money for a reward?"

"You mean a ransom," I said, and I think he knew I was angry that you'd have to pay someone to get a family member back, as if you were buying a mule or dry goods.

He said, "Either one."

I was daunted by everything he was throwing at me, but I said, "I figure I can get some money together after my cattle are sold in Dodge."

He asked, "Can you write?"

"Yes, sir."

He shoved paper and a pen and ink toward me and he said, "I want you to write out a description of her, how old she is, where she was stolen from, and say you are offering a reward. Then provide the information about how to contact you if she's found, and I'll make sure this is copied and sent to the other outposts."

He caught me staring at his hand and he held it up and said, "Shiloh." He added, "At least they didn't take it off."

I ducked my head real quick and mumbled, "Sorry, sir."

"The Indians call me Bad Hand. That's better than some other names I've been called," and his eyes glinted in the sun that spilled across his face and he gave a smile.

I tried to smile back. "Yes, sir."

He pointed to a chair and a camp table with books on it on the other side of the room and I took the pen and ink and paper and sat at it. I felt awkward trying to write in the same room with him, as if he was a schoolmarm looking over my shoulder.

He put his feet up on his desk and as I wrote he kept talking, saying, "The Indians around the fort here are Comanches and Apache and Kickapoo and Kiowa and Tonkawa, for the most part. Now, there are other bands out there who won't come onto the reservations, but they're going to be forced to come in, no matter what, and when that happens it will be easier to look for captive children. But you need to know," he added, "that often the captive children don't want to return to their families."

As I wrote I found that hard to believe, but that's what he said.

"Now, I need to warn you. If the captives end up in Mexico, then it will be impossible to ever find them or get them back, and even if captives are recovered, and if they're young enough, they might not know who they are anymore, or where they're from."

I felt sick at heart at what he said and I tried to keep my hand steady and not blot the paper with tears. It had been so long since I had written anything and I remembered Ma teaching sums and letters at night, her saying that none of her children were going to grow up *ungebildet*, ignorant, like some others she could name but wouldn't, no matter how far we lived from a schoolhouse. And her insisting we read aloud from *Pilgrim's Progress* and the Bible so we got good instruction and learned to speak better English than her. I was thinking these things when I realized the general was still talking. He had put a map down and he had asked me a question, and I said, "Excuse me, sir?"

"Why didn't you go to San Antone?"

I just looked at him.

"San Antone," he said. "Why didn't you go to San Antone instead of going after them yourself?"

"Too far and in the wrong direction," I said. "Besides, maybe I wasn't thinking. I was in a hurry to find Sally and get the cattle back and I thought I had a better chance of catching up with them myself than riding miles and miles trying to drum up enough neighbors or a troop of cavalry somewhere or other, and no matter who attacked them, the Comanche would have split up and maybe killed Sally in the process, or she could have gotten hurt or killed in the cross fire, so I thought I had a better chance going it alone."

There was another smile and I wondered if I had just insulted him about the cavalry.

"A kid as young as you going after a band of dangerous Comanches by yourself? They might have eaten you alive."

I got mad and I realized I hadn't given him all the details, so I said, "I did all right. I killed five of them. But one of them got away with Sally and I couldn't save her without risking her getting killed."

He studied me for a while and I don't know if he believed me or not.

"How did you manage to kill five?" he asked.

"I surrounded them."

I crossed the room and handed him the paper, and instead of saying anything back he just looked at me for a while. I was afraid I'd been too smart, or maybe I was showing through my band, but I resisted running my hand over my chest. He drummed the fingers of his good hand in the sunlight falling on his desk, then he turned to the paper and read what I had written.

"This will do," he said. "I'll send copies to McKavett, Clark, and Davis and the other outposts and to the civilian authorities and we'll get the word out, and if anyone knows anything they'll contact Fort Dodge. You can check in with them when you get to Dodge City."

"Thank you, sir." I put my hat back on and tipped it to him and started for the door.

He said, "You're lucky there weren't more of them."

I turned to him. "More of what?"

"Comanches. You're lucky there weren't more of them."

"Yes, sir. Had there been more of them, I'm sure I could have used a troop of cavalry."

He did that smile of his and wished me good day and good luck.

I said thank you to the sergeant as I went outside, then I said it again to the skinny guard at the door. When I looked around, the boys were nowhere to be found.

The guard said, "They'll be over at the wagons," and I think he knew what I'd find by the way he said it.

I crossed the grounds of the fort to where the travelers were. The knot from the band around my chest was chaffing me and I was wet with sweat, some of it from the sun and some of it from being in the presence of General Mackenzie and some of it from me worrying about Sally, and I wished I could just take it and all my clothes off and go down to some creek and lay back in the cool running water and forget about everything.

I walked among the freighters and the emigrant wagons and folks were bargaining or crossing back and forth carrying grain sacks or crates and kegs, or holding squawking chickens upside down by their feet, and some folks were bickering over goods and someone else was shoving a wagon wheel back into place.

Then there was a gray Appaloosa mare being led through the crowd, skittish and dancing and folks shied away from her and mothers shouted at kids not to get close. She caught my eye and I swear she stared straight at me, then she shook her head and bobbed it and snorted as if she knew me and was saying hello, and she kept looking back at me as she was led away.

Then I saw Abraham and Jack Straw and Shakespeare and Shady, all sitting cross-legged on the ground by one wagon with tin plates in their laps piled high with food, and what should have been coffee in tin cups at their feet, but I learned it wasn't.

Jack Straw saw me first and he called out, "There he is! There's the Comanche Kid, the toughest hombre east of the Pecos and west of the Mississippi!" He got to his feet, spilling his plate and weaving back and forth and shouting to the crowd, "Looky here, this here's the Comanche Kid! Damned if he ain't one real bravo!" and some folks turned to see what he was yelling about.

Abraham got to his feet and put his hand on Jack Straw to talk him down, only Jack Straw shook him off and yelled, "Hell no, these folks need to know who they got amongst them! This boy is a hero, a man among men!" Then his spilled tin plate got his attention and he said, "Damn! Would you look at that!" He got down on his hands and knees and tried to scrape the biscuits and beef and beans back on the plate with his fingers.

Shakespeare called out, "How'd it go, Kid?"

I could tell he'd been drinking by the way he was smiling real big. Too big.

Then Shady got to his feet, hanging on to the wagon, then turned his back to me and took a piss out in the open in spite of the crowd coming and going.

Abraham and Jack Straw got into an argument over whether or not the spilled food could be eaten. When I tried to get between them they shoved me back, but Abraham got a grip on himself and said, "If he wants to eat dirt, let him eat dirt," and he sat back down with his plate. Then I grabbed all their cups and dumped out the liquor and I threw the cups back at them, more out of anger over how hard it was going to be to find Sally than at them doing anything wrong.

I said, "A bunch of Texas ranahans can't go getting drunk on the job!"

Shakespeare smiled and said, "Dost thou think, because thou art virtuous, there shall be no more cakes and ale?" And at that he just laughed and laughed, and they were all laughing with him at what a good joke it was, and I wanted to kick him.

Eating a bite from his plate, Jack Straw said, "This tastes gritty. What happened?"

Abraham said, "I told you so," and by then Shady had sat back down and was eating. Then he looked around and wanted to know where his cup was.

I said to him, "I need you sober right now."

Shakespeare spoke up, making fun of me again, pointing at one of the empty cups on the ground, saying, "O thou invisible spirit of wine, if thou hast no name to be known by, let us call thee devil!" Then he laughed at himself again, thinking he was oh so clever, and they all laughed and pointed at the cups and said, "Devil! Devil!"

I got furious and I kicked all the cups every which way and I kicked one at Shakespeare, and of a sudden he threw down his plate and he got up and he grabbed me by the collar and shoved me up hard against the wagon. I could smell the liquor on his breath and it made me sick, and Abraham said, "Hey now, hey now!"

He said, "I had a brother too, you know, you're not the only one." And then he shoved me out of the way and leaned up against the wagon, his hands and arms outstretched and pressing hard against the wagon, as if he was trying to stop himself from doing something worse.

I didn't know what to say because I'd never seen him like that, but Shady said, "What do you need me for?"

I said to Shady, but watching Shakespeare, "You and me, we need to talk to these Mexican traders here."

"What about?"

"I need someone who can speak Mexican," and I backed away from Shakespeare. I said to Abraham, "Do what you can to get everyone sobered up, get coffee or something."

"What's gone and what's past help," Shakespeare said to nobody in particular, "should be past grief."

"I wish you would speak English," I said, "and besides, there ain't nothing past help yet. Now, sober up."

FIFTEEN

I grabbed Shady by the arm and he said, "Where are we going?"

"To talk to the Comancheros."

"I ain't finished eating yet!"

"That can wait."

I pulled Shady away and we began to weave through the crowd. I came to a wagon with a Mexican taking money from a line of men and soldiers and inside I heard groaning and grunting, and I realized it was some soiled dove plying her trade. I got all embarrassed and I could feel my face turning red, but I grabbed Shady and shoved him at the Mexican and I said, "Tell him we're looking for a three-year-old blond girl that was kidnapped by Comanches a month or two back, has he seen her."

So Shady spoke Mexican but the man just shrugged and said no, and I told Shady to tell him if he found her, to tell the commander at one of the outposts and there would be a big reward. He did so, then I pulled Shady away because he got too interested in the sounds coming from the wagon, and I was asking myself, *What kind of a world is this?*

We went from trader to trader, all of them selling pots and pans and kettles and some selling tobacco and bolts of calico and pins and needles and thread and all of them selling a little bit of everything and taking money, skins, or weapons in trade, then selling or trading their goods all back to someone else. One trader said he'd seen a couple of blond boys and another said he'd seen a ten-year-old girl with brown hair. Another said he'd seen a girl like that about six months back and another said he'd seen her up north and another said to the south and one said she was with the Apaches. I wasn't any better off than when I started, but I told them all about the reward, hoping something would turn up if they knew there was money in it.

When I got back to the hands, they were all drinking coffee and looking sheepish and they stood up when I approached, trying to steady one another. Shakespeare handed me a plate and said, "Here, eat this, Kid, you need something to eat," and I thought it was maybe a peace offering.

"Aren't you going to quote Shakespeare?" I asked.

"Unquiet meals make ill digestions, right?" and I felt he was reprimanding me for losing my temper. He added, "There, happy now?" But he still wasn't smiling.

I didn't answer because I felt embarrassed for having kicked the cups at him and the others, so I sat down and muttered, "Sorry," and the hands gathered around. Abraham asked what I'd learned from the post commander and I told them it didn't look good but he said he'd put the word out, and all Shady and I got from the traders and travelers and freighters was either nothing or information that didn't match up.

Abraham said, "At least that's a start. Good for you."

And Ma said, "He sounds like Hopeful, remember how he helped Christian to the Celestial City? *Hoffnungsvoll*, you have to be hopeful or you can't go on. It's that simple."

And I thought back to her, *Can't you stop that!* Between her quoting *Pilgrim's Progress* and Shakespeare quoting Shakespeare, I was getting pretty fed up with the two of them and wished I could just get to Dodge and then go home. But home where? The only home I had anymore was wherever Sally was, and that seemed to be nowhere.

Shakespeare said, "Stop what?" and I realized I'd said it aloud. Maybe even I'd snapped over. I was trying to figure out how to backtrack and make it look like I was just thinking aloud, but Abraham came to my rescue and said, "I'll tell you what. It's late afternoon now. Let's spend the night here outside the fort. You've done everything you can and early tomorrow we'll get a fresh start. The horses can rest and everybody gets something to eat, and no one drinks."

All the hands shrugged at that, begrudgingly. He said, "I'll send Shakespeare and Jack Straw to take care of the horses. Tomorrow we'll push hard and catch up with the herd."

I said, "That sounds good, Abraham."

"Why don't you crawl under the wagon and get some rest," he said. "This man here says we can camp by his wagon as long as we keep buying what he's selling."

"As long as it's bait and not spirits."

"Sure enough. "

I crawled under the wagon and stretched out and sneaked one hand under my shirt and loosened the band around my chest. I was asleep within minutes.

Sometime during the middle of the night I woke up and I lay there listening. There was an argument somewhere and I heard a woman crying and I could smell woodsmoke and beans and coffee and there was the occasional rattle of tin cups and plates. There was dogs barking and goats and pigs and mules crying out, and the sound of horses stomping or nickering. Someone was snoring and a wagon creaked from someone getting in or out. I felt the whole world was swirling around me and the only safe place was under the wagon.

It was strange to look up and not be able to see the stars after all the time on the trail, but I felt safe under the wagon and I was glad not to have the wide expanse of the night sky pressing down on me and reminding me how small I was, and I wondered what it would be like to sleep in a house again with a ceiling. I remembered Pa saying that as a soldier he had never wanted to sleep outside on the ground again, but he knew some who could no longer sleep in a house but would take their bedroll and throw it outside to sleep under the stars.

And then I remembered the gray Appaloosa being led through the crowd, dark gray and light gray and a black mane and tail and white spotted rump, and I swear she caught my eye, noticing me as well.

I was pondering all this when I realized somehow that Shakespeare was not too far away from me, so I whispered, "You awake?"

After a moment he said, "Yup."

"Sorry I kicked at you."

"It's all right, Kid. Sorry I had too much to drink."

"Too much? You were drunk."

He chuckled and said, "Yeah, that too."

I wanted to talk to him but I wasn't sure what to say, but something he'd said came back to me, so I asked, "What did you mean when you said you had a brother?"

We lay there quiet for a long time and I thought, *This is what it would be like to be married to him, the two of us next to each other in a bed in the dark.* I shocked myself so with such thoughts that I put my hand over my mouth as if I had confessed them aloud, and my face felt all hot.

"He was younger than me. Got sick and didn't make it."

I got a grip on myself and I said, "I'm sorry to hear that."

He didn't answer back.

I said, "For someone who quotes Shakespeare all the time, that isn't very many words." He didn't pick up on that, so I asked, "What was his name?"

"March."

"That's a real unusual name."

"It suited him. He was always on the march, always into something, headlong, determined, real curious."

"Sounds like you were close to him," I said, grateful he was talking now.

"Yeah."

"How old was he when he passed?"

"He was twelve, a little younger than you are now, right?"

I avoided the subject of my age. "How long ago was that?"

"A couple of years ago."

"I'm sorry," I said.

"Everybody's lost something, haven't they?"

"They sure have."

Then he said some long Shakespeare words about thy task being done, and how all golden lads and girls must come to dust, and about not fearing lightning or thunder and about how even young lovers must come to dust, and it ended with "renowned be thy grave." They were meaningful words, sad and beautiful and truthful, and I couldn't help but admire how he knew them all, and I wanted to take his hand and put it on my breast and tell him the truth about myself, but I knew I couldn't do that, so all I said was, "I wish you could say all that where I buried my family."

"Wish I could, Kid."

We lay there in silence listening to the sounds. Then he said, "You remind me of him."

"What's that?"

"My brother. You remind me of him."

At that I felt just awful. I knew he meant it in a nice way, but if ever there was a day I could tell him I was a girl and I had feelings for him, and ask if he could have feelings for me, then all he was going to think was I reminded him of his brother. That was just too confusing to go anywhere with, and I felt like one more road to hope was closed off to me. I was at a loss for words so I just asked him, "In what way?"

"He was a real ranahan too."

That was just about the nicest thing anybody had ever said about me. "He was good on a horse, huh?"

"Ranahan doesn't mean how good you can ride or trail cattle, it means you don't quit. Prairie fires, twisters, hail, rain, stampedes, the cattle come first. You don't quit. No matter how sick he was, he didn't quit. Just like you. You don't quit."

"Thank you. I'm sorry you lost your brother. I know what that's like."

We didn't say anything else but I figured, if a ranahan doesn't quit, then there's something else I surely should be doing to find Sally, and that's when one more idea come to me. I thought, *That's what we'll do tomorrow.*

I fell asleep and I dreamed about the gray Appaloosa, and in my dream we talked horse to each other.

I woke the boys before daybreak and told them we were moving out. They all grumbled and Jack Straw said, "Why does everything always have to happen in the dark?"

"I got a plan," I said. "Get mounted up."

They crawled to their feet and they all took a piss and I had too, earlier. They grabbed their saddles and gear and we all headed for the horses. Abraham said, "What you got in mind, boss?"

"Boss? That'll be the day."

Shady chimed in, "Boss is right. You're calling the shots, Kid. Why we leaving so early?"

"We ain't leaving. We're on a reconnaissance."

I always liked that word because Pa would use it when he was looking for something, maybe a lost tool or one more biscuit or mavericks he could add to the herd, and he would often throw out a military term like "provisions" or "advance," as if he carried his history with him. We were always reminded he was a soldier once, or that being a soldier had never left him, whether it was the words he used or the nightmares he had at night.

Up in the loft, Jamie and I would hear him mumbling, "Fall back, fall back, fall back," or sometimes he'd be yelling, "Rally to me, rally to me!" and then we'd hear Ma's voice, urgent at first, then going soft and talking him down, bringing him back home, back to us, away from some roadside ditch and him saying, "Oh no, oh no, oh no," or back from some shallow grave, weeping, saying, "The poor laddie, the poor laddie." Sometimes we would just hear him sobbing and her consoling him.

"What kind of reconnaissance?" Abraham asked.

I came back to earth and I said, "I doubt if we'll find anything, but I got a hunch."

Shady said, "Yeah?"

We bridled our horses now, then threw the blankets on and heaved up the saddles and tightened the girths. I said, "I'm looking for something. My sister ain't going to be anywhere near here, but I want to check their ponies. They've got to have a remuda nearby, and I want to find it."

"What you hoping to find?" Abraham said.

"I'm looking for Paint. Odds are he's not anywhere near here. He could be down in Mexico by now, but it's worth taking a look."

Shakespeare asked, "What are you going to do if you find him?"

"I'm going to take him back."

And at that Abraham said, "You can't do that. That pony don't belong to you anymore."

"He's my pony," I said. "Fortunes of war."

"He is not," Abraham said. "You gave him away so we could get past those Comanches."

"I didn't give him away. Big Mike took him from me and gave him away, and if he's here, I want him back."

"You are going to start some damn Indian war," Abraham said. "I ain't going to help you with this."

Everything came to a standstill and all the boys gathered around, reins in hand. Shady said, "I got a bad feeling about this, boss."

Jack Straw chimed in, saying, "Kid, they'll have guards watching those horses. You can't just shuffle in and take one."

Only Shakespeare didn't say anything.

"It's not the horse I want," I said. "It's One-Eye I want."

Then they all wanted to know who One-Eye was, so I told them about how Ma put out one eye of the Comanche who was attacking her before she was killed, and I told them about killing the five Comanches, but it was One-Eye who got away with Sally, and when Big Mike gave away Paint, the Comanche wearing Shady's red sash put his hand over his eye to let me know he was with One-Eye.

"If I take Paint," I said, "maybe somehow I can bargain and find out where they come from and where One-Eye and Sally are."

They were all silent after that and I went back to tightening the girth on Buck and checking the saddlebags.

"That plan don't make sense, boss," Abraham said. "And we could get killed doing this."

I didn't say anything but swung into the saddle and Abraham insisted, saying, "That paint horse is long gone by now, boss, and even if you find that red-sash fellow, he ain't going to tell you where One-Eye is."

"I'm just looking," I said.

I turned Buck away and Abraham shouted after me, "I ain't letting the boys ride with you! You're just going to get yourself and them into a whole lot of trouble! Besides, we got the herd to think about! We got to get to Dodge and not start some damn Indian war!"

"Get something to eat," I said. "I'll be back in a couple of hours."

The sun was just starting to come up behind me and it felt good to be on Buck. He tossed his head and danced, and he told me he thought we could find that ugly black-and-white horse. I told him he was jealous, that he was just as pretty, even prettier, and then the next thing I knew Shakespeare was alongside me, and then there was Shady on the other side, and then Abraham was following us and I could hear Jack Straw right behind me saying, "I think this is a bad idea, but if I get the chance, I'll kill old One-Eye for you!"

"Thank you, Jack Straw," I said, "but I'd just as soon do that myself."

And at that Jack Straw let out a whoop and said, "Look at us! Don't we look just like a bunch of them Texas Rangers! A bunch of horse marines is what we are!"

Shakespeare didn't look at me but he said, "You fucking ranahan, you don't quit, do you?"

We rode far away from the fort and the tipis, spreading out so we could still see one another but take in as much territory as possible. The dawn was coming on and there was pink and orange clouds and the trace of blue sky and I could tell already it was going to be hot. I wished I could take the band off from around my chest, but I knew I had to live with it, like some kind of curse keeping me from being myself.

Shakespeare was on the side toward the fort, then me, then farther out was Shady, then Jack Straw, then Abraham, all of us spread out and making as wide a circle around the fort as we could, as if the fort was the hub of a wheel and we were one of the spokes.

The plains were flat so it was easy to keep an eye on one another. We were in an easy lope, trying to cover as much ground as possible, as fast as possible, so that we could get back to the herd as soon as possible. I hoped to find the remuda when light was just breaking and there wouldn't be as many of the Indians up and able to protest what we were doing, although they'd soon find out.

Buck was his old self, cutting around outcroppings of rock or clusters of hackberry and scrub, like being on a hunt. I kept an eye on Shakespeare and Shady, on either side of me, and they'd catch my eye and shake their head no, and we'd press on.

The sky was lightening up fast, going from pink to gold and then to a bright blue rising. We had been out just a little while when Shady waved at me and pointed to his left, so I signaled Shakespeare, and we all headed in that direction, picking up Jack Straw along the way.

SIXTEEN

Abraham rode to meet us and he said, "Farther out's a creek, hoofprints all over, we're coming up on them. How do you want to play this?"

Your guess is as good as mine, I thought, but I said, "We'll move together."

Abraham took the lead, following the prints and the trampled buffalo grass, us following behind him. We followed the creek a short distance and soon we could hear them nickering. Buck threw his head up and his nostrils flared and he snorted as we rode into a copse of cottonwoods along the creek. We dismounted there, threading through the trees and trying not to get spotted, if anyone was watching.

We worked our way to the edge of the trees, leading our mounts, and there the herd was, spread out before us in an open field, a few hundred at least, grazing in what looked to be good grass and drinking from the same small, clear creek we'd been following. All the ponies were from the different tribes gathered around the fort and I figured they must trust nobody's going to steal from each other, something they'd do any other time.

Abraham said to me, "You see him?"

I'm sure he hoped I'd say nope right off so we could all turn around and head back for coffee and beans. "No," I said, "I don't see nothing," and at that I mounted up on Buck.

Abraham said, "What you doing?"

"Going to look."

Abraham said, "Damnation."

He started to mount up as well and I said, "No, you all stay here, let me look by myself first."

They all mounted up but stayed in the trees and they all checked their weapons as I rode out. I rode slow and easy as if it was no big deal, as if I was just out for a stroll and happened to stumble upon a herd of fine-looking ponies. Only they weren't fine-looking. Most of them were scrawny, ganted up and leg weary, their ribs showing, looking as if they had been hard wintered and then ridden too far for too long. Hard used they were, maybe coming from some place that didn't have good grass and water. They feasted now, but it would take a while before they were back to looking like prime horseflesh.

I got to the edge of the herd and checked back on the boys. I could see them in the shade of the trees, the sun above the horizon now, them all lined up and watching me. I turned and looked at the herd and there were several paints, most of them brown and white and there were a few black-and-white ones, but not with Paint's markings. I couldn't see to the far edge of the herd, so I started riding into the middle of them.

I came right across the gray Appaloosa. She looked up at me and tracked me as if she was curious about me, and I circled around her, taking her in for a moment, both of us looking at each other. I wondered how she got there looking prime and fit and better than any of the rest of them, when a young boy sitting by the bank of the creek saw me, and I saw him at the same time, as surprised as he was. He was eating something, and when he saw me he threw it down and raced over to a bridled bay grazing near him and vaulted up onto its back, and I could tell he didn't know what to do yet. His horse danced in anticipation, moving back and forth, then the two of them advanced toward me and then backed off.

I raised a hand in the air to signal I wasn't there to hurt anyone. I reined Buck up and held still with my hand in the air and slowly he advanced toward me, and I held up my other hand to show I wasn't holding a weapon. He raised one hand like I was doing and he edged toward me, and out of the corner of my eye I tried to check out the herd for Paint. I heard Pa say, "Don't take your eyes off of him," so I stopped looking and just watched the kid. I didn't know how old he was but he was young and skinny and looked like he could use a hot meal and a bath, but then so could I.

He got a few yards away and he started talking fast and gesturing. I couldn't understand a word he was saying, so I just listened to him and he pointed away from the herd, over and over again. He was telling me to leave the herd and he pointed at himself and at the herd and at the ground and at the sun. I was sure he was telling me this was his herd and these were their grazing grounds and I should leave and go in that direction. Then I noticed he carried a firearm tucked into his leggings and I heard Pa say, "You should have noticed that sooner, but whatever you do, don't reach for yours, at least not yet."

As much as I wanted to see all the Comanches dead, even I couldn't see my way clear to killing this scrawny kid, so I kept my hands in sight and I said, "I'm looking for a lost horse."

He just shook his head and pointed away from the herd, only more angry now. I kept my hands up and I said again, "I'm just looking for a lost horse," only he didn't understand me.

I tried to think how to make myself clear, so I turned back to the trees and I called for Shady, and I waved and gestured that he should come over to me.

At that the kid saw the boys in the trees and he got more excited. His horse pranced right and left and he shouted at me and pointed away from the herd, so I held both hands up higher. I stayed still until Shady got over to me, and the kid pulled back several yards, his hand on his weapon.

Shady started talking Mexican and Comanche, trying to calm the kid down, and I told him to tell the kid I was just looking for a lost horse.

Shady did that and the kid talked and gestured and Shady turned to me and said, "The kid says none of these horses are lost, they all belong to him. He means he's in charge of the remuda."

I told Shady to say again it was just one horse I was looking for, and maybe it got in their herd by mistake.

So Shady said it all again and the kid shook his head no and used a sweeping gesture to include the whole herd. I told Shady, "Tell him I'm just going to check the far side of the herd and then we'll leave."

Shady did that and the kid still shook his head no, but I rode off real slow, my hands still in the air, and the kid followed alongside me and then tried to get in front of me to block me. Shady followed along, talking real calm.

And then, just beyond the kid, I saw him.

Paint.

I turned to Shady and I said, "That's him."

"This kid isn't going to let you take him."

"I'm taking him."

"Do you want me to kill the kid?"

"No."

"Then pull that Schofield of yours now to scare him off," Shady said, "or he's going to pull his on you."

Shady pulled his .44 and trained it on the kid and I pulled the Schofield and did the same, and at that the kid wheeled around and took off, leaning low on his horse and riding fast, weaving right and left to make it hard for us to hit him.

Shady said, "Last chance."

"No. Let's get Paint."

We put our weapons away and I rode toward Paint, drawing out my catch rope and building a loop. Right when Paint looked up from grazing, as if he thought he maybe knew us, I tossed the loop and it was a good throw and I got him.

Shady said, "Let's get out of here fast."

We both wheeled around and I put the spurs to Buck and he got the idea and we headed for the copse of trees at a hard run, Shady on my left and Paint following fast on my right flank, the herd scattering as we barreled through them. All but the Appaloosa, who just watched us.

The boys in the trees saw us coming and they could tell we weren't going to stop, so they pulled back and cleared a path and I headed straight into the trees, Paint following me close and Shady right with us. As we shot past, the boys put the spurs to their horses and we were all weaving through the trees as fast as we could go. When we cleared the trees and got into the grassland, I pulled up for just a moment and I said to Abraham and the boys, "We need to get back to the fort before the kid warns the village and they send out riders to stop us!"

We all took off at a dead run, straight into the sun. As hot as it was getting to be we were moving so fast the wind kept us cool, and Buck was his old self, splashing through the creek or leaping over it when it narrowed and curved into our path again, then charging around rocks and scrub. The boys were on either side of me, Paint right in the middle. Across the flat plain we could see the fort before us, the sun smashing off the limestone walls and making the buildings look bright and clean, as if they were all newly washed.

I could see the Indian village near the fort and it was full of activity and the kid had come in from another angle and reached it just ahead of us. He raced through the village putting the word out, and the warriors leapt onto the horses they kept by their tipis in case something like this come up. They rode back and forth calling each other out so they could meet in force whatever threat we were. I realized we needed to make it through the village and onto the parade grounds before they got organized and were in front of us.

They saw us coming at a dead run and they called to one another and some started to ride out at an angle toward us, brandishing weapons, holding them high in the air to warn us or threaten us. We hit the village just in time so they couldn't afford to open fire at us or they'd hit their own.

We all broke apart and we wove through the tipis, each of us following our own path. Mothers shouted and pulled children out of the way, old men yelled at us, and warriors followed us with high-pitched cries. Dogs barked and nipped at the heels of the horses and I saw Abraham knock over a kettle and then jump the remnants of a wagon axle, broken beyond repair. Some Mexican trader was in the village waving his sombrero at us as if to stop us and maybe bargain awhile, then he ducked out of the way when Shakespeare drove past him.

Shady came from out of nowhere and was beside me again and Paint was still right next to me, both of them like shadows on either side of me, the three of us now weaving around broken kegs and old splintered crates that probably held rations at one time. We leapt over a bundle of pelts, then circled around more tipis, then barely around Indian kids too foolish to get out of the way, then drove through scattering crowds of families who came out of their tipis to see what all the noise was about.

I didn't have any idea where Jack Straw was, and then he appeared from around a tipi, leaning forward and yelling, "Whoo-ee!" or some such and I thought, *He's actually enjoying himself and not scared like me.*

All five of us and Paint spilled out of the village at about the same time, and we headed right between the sun-washed buildings and drove straight toward the center of the parade grounds. Guards called out to us to halt and blue-coated buffalo soldiers stood staring at us as we headed straight toward more buffalo soldiers drilling in the middle of the parade grounds. They all scattered out of their formation as they saw us coming and we drove straight through them, their white officers yelling at them and us. We pulled up and come to a stop right in front of the headquarters building, all of us swirling around in a tight group and looking in all directions to see if we needed to defend ourselves from the warriors on horseback that were charging in after us.

Travelers with their children and Comanchero traders and teamsters now hurried between the buildings and onto the parade grounds, curious to see what the commotion was all about, and officers with gold braid on their shoulders poured out of the headquarters building and joined the mob that was gathering. I didn't see General Mackenzie anywhere in all the chaos, but I heard Pa say, "Is this your plan?"

I said, "It is now."

I held Paint close and he danced about and Buck swirled around and we looked like we were at some crazy horse fandango. Indians, emigrants, teamsters, traders, officers, and buffalo soldiers all yelled at one another and pushed one another out of the way or shoved folks back to keep them from getting trampled or kicked.

Shady and Shakespeare and Abraham and Jack Straw milled about and tried to come to a standstill, at the same time keeping an eye on the warriors who were pushing their way to the front. The horses knocked into people afoot and folks yelled, "Watch what you're doing! Watch what you're doing!" and soldiers called out, "Get out of the way! Get out of the way!" The buffalo soldiers tried to push the crowd back and officers shouted, "What's this? What's going on here?"

I saw the hands all had their weapons out in case the Indians started something and the officers yelled, "Put those down! Put those away!"

One red-haired officer shouted real loud, "What are you people doing? Who's in charge here?" and it quieted down some.

Abraham spoke up. "These are all my boys here."

The officer said, "Who are you?"

Abraham told him what outfit we were with and said, "We're trailing a herd north, but one of our horses got stolen and we're here to get it back."

The officer's face was as red as his hair and he said, "What are you talking about? Whose horse? Whose horse got stolen?"

I remembered to say "sir" and I said, "Sir, my horse, sir, my horse got stolen."

While the crowd was milling and shoving he come over to me and he grabbed Buck by the bridle and Buck didn't like that and jerked his head back, but the officer insisted and held Buck steady. He said, "Who are you?"

So I gave him my name and I told him, "Comanches stole my horse a few weeks back and my sister was kidnapped before that and our trail boss let me come over to the fort to ask for help finding her."

He interrupted, saying, "Whoa, whoa, whoa! Slow down! Get off that horse and talk to me!"

Several Comanche warriors shoved in close and some had dismounted and were holding their horses' reins and several were still mounted but pressing in. The buffalo soldiers all raised their weapons just in case, and the officer turned and yelled at them, "Push the crowd and the Indians back! Push them away!" and the buffalo soldiers spread out around us and shouted at the crowd to stand back.

The Comanches yelled and protested and tried to edge though, but the soldiers, with their rifles across their chests, pushed folks back, and the Comanches resisted and pushed back against them.

Fistfights broke out somewhere between bluecoats and Comanches and other bluecoats tried to stop it, trying to pull them off each other. More buffalo soldiers arrived and joined in, pushing the crowd back, then pulled their own weapons on the Indians and told them to shut up and quiet down.

The Indians threatened the bluecoats with their own weapons and I thought, *We could have a battle royal on our hands right here*, when the red-haired officer yelled at the top of his voice, "THAT'S ENOUGH GODDAMNIT!"

Things got quiet, then my boys slowly dismounted. They gathered by me, holding their reins in one hand, a weapon hanging by their side in their other hand, backing me up.

The Indians remained still, then one of them held his hands in the air and stepped forward. He told all the warriors to lower their weapons, I guess, because that's what they did, and he did it in such a way that the bluecoats looked at one another and then let him pass because it seemed he was in charge, or at least had something to say about what was going on.

Then I saw he wore a red sash around his waist, the same one Shady handed off the first time the Comanches asked for a toll, and he was the one who took Paint and then put his hand over his eye.

The officer held a hand up to Red-Sash, telling him to wait, then turned to me and told me to start over. I changed the order of the story and told him about my family getting killed and my sister getting stolen, and I was here to get help from General Mackenzie, and after I'd talked to him I'd seen my horse in the Indian remuda, my horse that had been taken from me awhile back by this red-sashed Comanche, not telling him the part about Big Mike trading it away for safe passage, or that I had taken the horse when I killed several of the Comanches. I added that the red-sashed Comanche knew where my sister was and he needed to give her back.

Red-Sash must have understood some of what I said because he then launched into some big speech of his own, using some English and Comanche and Spanish.

Shady threw in some translation, but we all got the gist of it. He said the horse belonged to them, that I stole it from them and then they traded for it fair and square and got it back from me. Now I was stealing it and they wanted their horse back, and he didn't know where my sister was, and I was nothing but a horse thief. Somewhere in there he got in words about justice and the white men were all liars and their rations were no good and his people were starving. That was why they leave the reservation or don't come in at all, and no self-respecting Comanche wanted to be made into a farmer, and the cattle they got from the Indian agents didn't have any meat on them and they wouldn't eat them anyway because who would eat a cow after having tasted buffalo, and only Indians told the truth, or words to that effect.

I got furious and I said, "They killed my family and stole our cattle and they took my sister and they know where she is! Where's my sister, you sons of bitches?" And then I bragged, "I'm the one that killed your warriors when they raided our farm, and the one who rode the paint died like a dog."

Red-Sash rushed forward and grabbed me, and the boys grabbed me at the same time to pull me back. The bluecoats hit Red-Sash and knocked him down, then his friends tried to rush to his aid and the bluecoats pushed them back and knocked several of them down with their rifles. I screamed at Red-Sash, "Where's my sister, you fucking bastard? You killed my family, where's my sister? You know goddamn well where my sister is!"

Abraham had me by one arm and Shakespeare had the other and I couldn't stop screaming, "Where's my sister? You have my sister!" I was having trouble breathing but I shouted, "I'll kill every last one of them if it's the last thing I ever do!" and I yelled, "Where is One-Eye? Where is One-Eye, you son of a bitch?" I told Shady to ask them where One-Eye was and I tried to put my hand over one of my eyes to show them what I meant, but the boys held me too hard. The Comanches looked at one another, and they knew who I was talking about.

Red-Sash rose from the ground and with Shady translating he said I was crazy, they didn't know any Comanche with one eye, they hadn't killed anybody or stolen from anybody or taken any cattle, and I yelled back they were all liars, and he said back that I was loco and they only wanted their horse back.

I said, "You'll get your horse back over my dead body."

The officer tried to calm me down and the boys talked to me and Shady tried to talk to both sides as well as to the red-haired officer, but I couldn't get what they were all saying because I was shoving and pulling and telling the boys to let me go, and I tried to get away from being held. People in the crowd shouted and talked and asked questions and took sides, and the buffalo soldiers tried to keep the crowd and the Indians from all fighting one another or attacking us.

The Comanches acted all innocent, like I was crazed, like I'd snapped over, and they told the officer the horse was theirs, that they got it a while back, down in Mexico. Or maybe it was from a Mexican trader, a Comanchero, who knows? And then they started arguing among themselves, and one said it was a long time ago and another said no, they got it from a Tonkawa they'd killed who'd been down in Mexico, that's what they meant when they said they got it in Mexico. Someone else said no, they stole it from the Apaches down in Mexico, but it was theirs now, and Shady was translating as fast as he could.

The red-haired officer turned to me and he said, "Son, that horse could have traded hands any number of times."

I said, "Money stolen from a bank is still stolen money no matter how many times it's traded hands."

"I understand, son, but possession is nine-tenths of the law."

"Well, I possess this fucking horse right now!"

"Don't you dare talk to me like that, son."

I was out of breath and I tried to calm down. "So you think it's theirs?"

"Son, all these paints look alike. You could be mistaken. Besides, if you take this horse, you're not going to get far with him. They'll be after you, and you could get yourself and your men all killed. There's not much we can do to protect you. We can't march you clear back to your cattle drive."

Abraham and Shakespeare eased off me and I said to the officer, "So you think I should give him back?"

"I think it would be for the best. I'm sure you've got other good horses in your string, and it may just stop a war, because if you don't give him back, what do you think is going to happen here? Someone is going to get killed. We're lucky no one has opened fire so far."

So I turned to Shady and I said, "Tell them they can have their horse back."

Shady just looked at me, surprised, and I said, "Tell them."

So he turned and told them, and they calmed down.

I held the rope out and I said, "Here's your horse."

When Red-Sash took the rope, I pulled out my Schofield and put it to Paint's head and I pulled the trigger. The explosion was loud and blood and brains splattered over all of us.

SEVENTEEN

People screamed and Paint dropped like a rock. I watched the shock in Red-Sash's face as Paint went into his death throes, twitching and shaking and then lying still. At the noise women screamed in shock or wept in fear and men tried to shut them up or console them.

Abraham turned to me and said, "What the fuck did you just do!"

The red-haired officer said, "What do you think you're doing!"

I said, "Giving them their horse back."

I looked at Red-Sash, who held the rope to a dead horse, and I took one hand and put it over my eye and I said, "Tell One-Eye I'm coming for him."

Red-Sash backhanded me and then the fighting became general as the hands attacked him. All the warriors rushed in and the bluecoats swung their rifles and knocked the Comanches down and clubbed them. Men shoved the women and children away, pulled them back from all the fighting, afraid someone was going to get shot.

Suddenly there was a loud explosion, and in the midst of all the struggling and fighting Buck screamed and fell back onto his haunches. He buckled to his knees and blood blew from his chest and his nostrils and his mouth. He struggled to get back up but he couldn't make it, and he began to writhe and kick on the ground, and I yelled, "Buck! Buck!" and I screamed, "No, no, no!"

I rushed to him and held his head as he blew blood all over me and he heaved and struggled as blood came from everywhere, his chest pumping blood out in a spray.

Shakespeare put his Remington to Buck's head and I sobbed, "Oh God no, dear God no, no, no!"

Shakespeare said, "It needs to be now, Kid, he's drowning to death."

I wrapped my arms around Buck's neck as he thrashed, and I screamed I don't know what, all sounds and noises coming out of me I'd never heard before.

There was another loud explosion and more blood and brains and Buck tremored and shook, and then he was still, and he was gone.

I attacked Shakespeare, swinging at him and hitting him and I sobbed and said, "You killed him, you son of a bitch! You killed him!"

He tried to block my blows but he didn't hit back and all he said was, "He was suffering, Kid."

The crowd had backed off now and watched as I continued to scream and hit Shakespeare over and over again until he finally grabbed me by both arms and he said again, "He was in pain, Kid."

And in that moment I realized it was one of the Comanches who shot Buck. I jerked away and I turned my Schofield on the crowd and I screamed, "Who shot him? Who shot him? Which one of you bastards shot him?"

Everyone scattered back and I realized it didn't matter which Comanche did it—as far as I was concerned they all did it. I cocked the Schofield to fire when Shakespeare threw himself into me from behind and knocked me down and the Schofield fired into the dirt. He lay on top of me and he reached out and jerked the gun away and tossed it back to one of the hands as I struggled and kicked and screamed, "Get off me! Get off of me!"

He held me down with the weight of his body and I could feel his arm across my chest. I swore at him and I tried to get up and

I kicked and tried to elbow him until I didn't have the strength to fight anymore.

I wept and tried to breathe because of how heavy he was, then I went still and I gave up fighting, and after a long time he eased off me and pulled his arm away. I didn't try to get up, I just lay there with my face in the dirt until I stopped crying. He sat next to me with his hand on my shoulder and I shrugged it off.

The troopers pushed the crowd away and everyone was in shock and no one was yelling or fighting anymore. The battle was over now, so the women and children and the men all backed off and wandered away. The Comanches had revenged the loss of Paint so they all pulled away and trailed back to their camp, helping those who got battered by the soldiers.

I looked up and I saw Red-Sash turn and look back at me, and when he saw me looking at him, he held one hand over an eye, then he turned and kept on walking.

I heard the red-haired officer dismiss the soldiers, but he told someone to get two men and have them get mules to drag the dead horses away. Then he turned to me and he knelt down and he said, "I'm sorry how all this turned out. I hope you find your sister."

I didn't even nod to let him know I heard him.

He told Abraham we needed to clear out, and then he was gone.

It was silent, none of the hands saying anything.

Slowly I rolled over and I looked at the sky and it was a hard blue now. The sun was white-hot and the clouds were tall and billowy, like what I thought ships with sails might look like, if ships could fly across the sky. I felt like my insides were all gone and just ribs and skin covered me, and maybe some bones lashed together with dried hard leather straps. The dust and dirt on my face didn't bother me and I didn't even try to brush it away. Then something landed with a thud beside me.

I turned to look and it was my saddle and my saddle blanket and bridle, and Abraham was standing there. He'd pulled them off Buck and he said, "Get up Kid, you don't want to be here when they come for him."

What he said made sense, so I sat up real slowly and I looked around. Shady and Jack Straw stood together and Shakespeare wasn't anywhere to be found, and I wondered where he went.

Abraham said, as if nothing had happened, "Everybody needs something to eat, Kid. Let's go get something to eat."

"I don't think I'm hungry, Abraham."

Abraham knelt down. "Kid, these scars on my face, know how I got them?"

"No, sir, I do not."

"When they sold my family off and come to take them away," he said, "I tried to stop them. These are the scars of a bullwhip. I was tied to a whipping post, and these are the scars of that bullwhip. I got even more of them on my back. They hit me hard. Do you understand what I'm telling you? Are you listening to me? You tied to the whipping post, son. Do you understand me?"

That's all he said, and he looked at me as if that was enough, as if I ought to understand what he meant from that, but I hadn't any idea what he was talking about and I didn't feel like asking, so I just struggled up to my feet.

Jack Straw went to grab my saddle but I was damned if I'd let anybody carry it for me, so I said, "I got it." I hefted it up and slung it over my shoulder and it felt as if it weighed about a hundred pounds.

Shady handed me my Schofield and I holstered it, then I grabbed Buck's bridle and my saddle blanket and I took one last look at Buck. The ground was soaked in blood all around him and his face and chest and black mane was covered in blood and dirt, and I was beyond knowing what to say to him or how to say good-bye, or thanks, or I'm sorry, so I just turned and we all headed back across the parade grounds, the boys all leading their mounts and me walking in front of them without one.

I looked down and for the second time in my life I found myself covered in blood, and I wondered where Shakespeare was and if he could tell I was a girl when he had his arm around me and was holding me down.

When we got back to the wagon, there was the noise of the freighters and the traders and the emigrants and there was the smell of food cooking and coffee brewing. I threw down my saddle and my gear in the shade of the wagon. I sat down and I leaned up against the saddle and wrapped my arms around my knees and just leaned in, making as small of a ball with my body as I could. I was aware of people coming and going and some of them were staring at me, I was sure, and there was another line at the soiled dove's wagon. I wondered how much of that could she take, and I wondered how much it cost and how much of it she got to keep, and what her name was.

Emigrants threw supplies into their wagons or hauled oxen around and harnessed them, and I could hear the bray of mules and some kids chased one another. Some little girl about the size of Sally raced by, and for a second I thought maybe it was her, but it surely wasn't. Then I remembered Indians eat horse, and I wondered if they were going to eat Buck and Paint, knowing full well they were. That thought made me choke and I tried not to throw up, and I just wanted to curl up under the wagon and go to sleep forever.

None of the boys talked to me because they didn't know what to say, but they stayed nearby.

I realized how thirsty I was and I pulled my canteen off Buck's saddle and I took a long drink. Jack Straw watched me and he said, "Hey, Kid, let me fill that up for you."

He came over and I handed the canteen to him and he went to the water keg on the wagon and he filled it up and brought it back and said, "Here you go, Kid."

I poured water onto my neck scarf and poured it over my head and splashed my face with it and I tied the wet neck scarf back around my neck. Jack Straw said, "That must feel good, don't it? Here, let me fill that up again," and he took it and refilled it and then he knelt down and handed it to me.

I said, "Thanks, Jack Straw, you're a good man."

"Hey," he said, smiling, "nothing I wouldn't do for the Comanche Kid."

We sat there in silence and I didn't have anything to say and he didn't know what to say, so he got up and pulled out his Bull Durham and his papers and he rolled one and lit it, then just stood nearby, as if he was on guard.

Next thing I knew, Abraham sat down by me with plates of food and he handed me a plate and a cup of coffee. I said, "Who's paying for this?"

"It's coming out of your wages," he said.

I uncurled and put the plate in my lap and I just looked at it.

Jack Straw and Shady got plates as well and sat nearby, so I just picked at it and I said, "I don't think I'm hungry."

"I didn't think you would be," Abraham said, "but eat it anyway. We got a long ride and we'll be going straight through the night, no stopping, so eat up."

I said, "I don't have a horse."

"We're looking into that."

"Where's Shakespeare?"

"He's gone to see a man about a dog," Abraham said. "He'll be coming. Eat up."

I sipped the coffee and it was hot but I couldn't really taste it. I ate the hoecake and gravy and some of the beans but I couldn't eat the meat because I kept thinking of the Indians eating horse, so I put the plate down next to me and I stretched out on the ground with my head on my saddle. I put Jamie's hat over my face and I closed my eyes and I told Abraham to wake me when it was time to leave, figuring I'd be riding behind one of the boys.

I don't know how long I lay there but somewhere in my sleep I thought I heard Shakespeare's voice, but I couldn't tell what he was saying. It was just a sound I recognized and it felt good to hear it. He was talking with his mouth full, so he must have been eating, having come back from wherever he'd been, seeing a man about a dog. I almost smiled at that because it was the same thing Pa would say when he needed to disappear for a few hours or a day.

I pulled off my hat. It was high noon and hot and I was covered in sweat and my shirt had stuck to my body from all the blood drying. I squinted from the sun, and Shakespeare, sitting next to me, said, "Hello, Kid, welcome back."

I said, "Is that the best you can do?"

He was quick and gave me a smile and he said, "Trust me, sweet, out of this silence yet I picked a welcome."

I didn't know what to say to that and it scared me that he used the word "sweet," as if he knew I was a girl, so I just said, "Welcome back to you too," but he wasn't looking at me, he was concentrating on his bait and eating real fast. I wondered what he knew or didn't know, when Abraham said, "We're pulling out, Kid."

"Who am I riding with?"

"You're riding this ugly thing," Abraham said, "so saddle up now. "

I looked to where he pointed, and standing there was the gray Appaloosa, and I couldn't believe my eyes. "How'd you come by him?"

Shakespeare scraped his plate clean and he said, "Her. She's a mare. Bought her. You owe me sixty dollars, Kid. It'll come out of the sale of your herd in Dodge. Should have cost me forty because the Comanches don't ride mares, but they were pretty mad about the loss of the paint and they had a good point, so they raised the price and I wasn't in a position to argue."

"How'd you pick her?"

"I saw her go through the crowd yesterday, same as you, then saw her in the herd this morning and you circling her, and she looked to be in better shape than the rest. Didn't ask where she came from, didn't want to know. Figure they stole her off someone."

I got up and crossed over to where the Appaloosa was standing. Shakespeare's riata was on her and she was tied to the rear wheel of the wagon. All the hands were looking at me but it didn't feel right to touch her or even admire her with Buck's blood still on me, but I said, "She looks to be a fine horse."

"Who knows if she's a warhorse like Buck," Shakespeare said, "but she'll do for now."

I changed my mind and I reached out and ran my hand down her neck. Her skin did that shiver horses do when they're shaking off a horsefly, and I heard Pa say, "Shadow, that's what I'd call her, Shadow," and Ma said, "No, call her Spirit, because that's what she is." I was glad to hear their voices again but I thought, no, and I told them, "Ghost, her name is Ghost." I picked that name because she was gray, like how I felt inside with Buck gone. I felt like a ghost. A gray ghost.

Shakespeare said, "Good name, Ghost."

I didn't realize I'd said it aloud.

Abraham said, "Saddle up, Kid, we're moving out."

All the hands were already up on the hurricane deck, so I grabbed Buck's blanket and saddle and threw them on her as quick as I could. I got the bridle on her and adjusted it, got my gear on, and then climbed aboard.

As I rode past Shakespeare, I handed him his riata, but I couldn't look him in the eye because of what he might know, so I just whispered, "Thanks."

He said, "Sixty dollars, Kid."

Ghost wasn't salty at all, as if she knew me, and had been waiting for me.

EIGHTEEN

Abraham calculated where Big Mike and the herd might be by now and we headed a bit more north by northeast. The hands were silent and I was glad for it because I didn't feel like talking, and I stayed as far away from Shakespeare as I could. We stopped to water our horses and grabbed some dried apples or a biscuit from our saddlebags, but I was never really hungry and I didn't know if I'd ever be hungry again. When dusk came we kept riding, keeping on the move in case we were being tracked.

The night sky was deep and black and the stars all cold silver, and I wondered how could it all be so big and where did all those stars come from, and could we be any smaller than we were. I imagined lying out on a blanket beside Shakespeare, taking it all in and talking about the mystery of it all, but then I thought, *That'll be the day.* I felt lonely and buried, as if the sky and the stars were lying on top of me, pressing me down, just like the dirt and stones lying on top of Ma and Pa and Jamie.

Ghost rode easy and smooth but I couldn't take much pride in her because I kept thinking how I'd betrayed Buck and how he'd still be alive if I hadn't been so angry, and I wondered what Big Mike would say when Abraham told him what happened. I figured if he hit me again I'd just have to take it, because I deserved it.

We struck the herd early next morning, long before full dawn come on. We rode into camp right after Monty had gotten the bait ready and called, "Roll out!" God knows why hands always had to get up so long before dawn.

Preacher was on his feet and giving his morning sermon like he always done, saying, "Oh Lord, I'm sailing the River of Glory but I'm surrounded by all these heathen hands. Give me patience, Lord, and let these infidels see the light of your love so they can board our ship and beg forgiveness for their multitudinous sins, and I will welcome them like brothers to your truth and your justice and your mercy."

Tommy Deuce called out, "Oh Lord, give me patience so I won't whup Preacher's ass, and while you're at it Lord could you see that Preacher rides drag all day long and chokes on dust?" Pretty soon all the hands were calling out what they hoped the Lord would do to Preacher.

When Preacher saw us coming in, he called out, "Boys, the prodigals have returned!"

Then the hands called out, "About time you come back to work!" and "What did you see?" and "How did it go?"

Hard Luck Luke Bronson said, "Hey, Kid, where's Buck?"

"Buck's dead," I said. "Long story."

I dismounted and pulled my saddle and blanket off and tossed it near the wagon. Shakespeare rode up and he leaned down and grabbed Ghost's reins from me and said, "Get something to eat, Kid. I'll put her in the remuda. You want Blood or Dancer or one of Cliff's string?"

I said, "I don't care," but I didn't want to talk to the boys or to Big Mike and I didn't want Shakespeare treating me special so I just said, "Never mind, I'll take her myself."

I grabbed the reins back and it felt good to walk after being in the saddle so long. I was halfway to the remuda when I realized I was in such a hurry I didn't have my catch rope to lasso a remount. I felt like a fool, and when I looked up, there was Shakespeare riding along beside me while I'm walking, leading the other hands' ponies back to the remuda.

He didn't say a word but just rode beside me while I walked. It was the longest walk of my life because I wanted to ask him what he knew but I was too embarrassed to bring it up, and I was mad at him for not saying anything at all. On the other hand I didn't want him to say anything, so we walked along and he whistled some tune, and I wished I could crawl into Monty's camp wagon and hide or sleep or die or just disappear.

When we got to the remuda he released the mounts, including his own, and he still didn't say a word except for, "Which one?"

I just shrugged. "Blood."

As he built a loop he said, "Speaking of which, do you have another shirt?"

I looked down at my blood-dried stiff shirt and he said, "How about I loan you one of mine?"

And that quickly he had Blood lassoed and was reeling him in and I said, "Maybe I can get something out of Cliff's or Scotty's kit."

"Bad luck wearing a dead man's clothes."

"What do you think I'm wearing now?"

"Well then," he said, "see, it's true."

I slipped Buck's bridle onto Blood and started leading him back to the camp. He called out to me, "Make sure you get something to eat."

I'd just about had enough and I turned back and I said, "Would you quit talking to me like I'm a kid?"

He did that soft smile of his that I thought felt half-sad, and he said, "You are a kid, aren't you?"

I couldn't tell if he was taunting me or daring me to tell the truth about myself, and he made me mad, as if he knew something, or he felt sorry for me, or maybe it was something about his brother, or maybe it was all in my head because I didn't know what he knew or what he thought. Maybe I was just really mad at myself. I turned back and headed to camp because I didn't know what to say. I wasn't a kid but I'd acted like one by getting Buck killed and getting the hands and the herd in danger, and I was angry because he was right and I realized I was no ranny in spite of what he said earlier, and I was a fool to think I might be one. I got back to the wagon and the hands didn't say anything to me, and Abraham had for sure filled everyone in on what happened.

The horizon was getting lighter now, getting hot already, and I saw Big Mike hunkered down with a tin plate in his hand. As I come up the first thing he said was, "Get some bait, Kid," and I felt like every time I turned around someone was telling me to get something to eat.

I said, "Yes, sir," and Monty handed me a plate and scooped out beans and flapjacks and salt pork and stewed peaches and gave me a couple of biscuits as well and a cup of coffee, and it looked like more food than I could eat in a week. I still wasn't hungry but I knew I couldn't throw it away, and the boys were all real quiet, pretending not to watch me. Skinny was in from nighthawking and he tossed out, "Sorry about your horse, Kid," and I just nodded.

Big Mike tilted his head, telling me to sit next to him, so I did and I tried to eat. We sat there awhile and I wondered when he was going to start in on me, and I was glad he hadn't hit me again, yet.

He said, "You talked to them at Griffin?"

"Yes, sir, to General Mackenzie himself. The general says it's not likely she'll be found but he'll put the word out."

"Well, you never know. Good you talked to him."

We sat there in silence, but as he finished up, he said, "If they hit us, every cow brute we lose comes out of your herd, you understand that?"

I said, "Yes, sir," and at that he got up and took his plate to the wreck pan and scrubbed it off and stacked it, then he went over to Abraham and Hard Luck Luke Bronson, talking and conferring, then I heard him say, "String 'em out and point 'em north," as if there was any other direction for them to go. He mounted up and headed out to pilot the herd.

Abraham called out who was to start as swing, flanker, and drag. He looked at me and said, "You're going to be wrangling."

I said, "Yes, sir," and that meant I'd be spending the day with Shakespeare, switching out mounts as the hands come back and forth, or snaking in wood and dried chips for Monty. I was finishing my bait as best I could when a shirt landed in my lap and I looked up and there was Shakespeare. He was getting a plate now, ignoring me and getting coffee and going over to sit with those boys who hadn't got to their feet yet.

I stuffed the rest of the bait down as best I could, trying not to gag, then I cleaned off my plate and stacked it. I found a place on the other side of the wagon and I pulled off my bloody shirt and slipped on Shakespeare's shirt as fast as I could, and it smelled like him. It was a reminder of one more thing I couldn't have, so I pulled it back off and put my bloody shirt back on. I took Shakespeare's shirt and I threw it back into his lap and I didn't even look to see his reaction.

I helped Monty finish with the packing up and I got the mules and hooked them up to the camp wagon, then I helped the hands get their mounts from the remuda, Shakespeare and me not saying much to each other.

We drove for several days, me helping Monty and then wrangling the remuda with Shakespeare. I stayed away from him except to talk business, such as who would take the rough off of which horse or checking on some horse's limp. When I rode nightguard and passed one of the hands, they'd usually say they were sorry to hear about Buck and that was sure a fine-looking Appaloosa I was riding, and was it hot enough for me, and then we'd ride on.

One night I was singing songs and as I passed Tommy Deuce, he stopped and he said, "Hey, Kid, you been laid yet?"

I was shocked and I didn't know what to say to that. The hands were always rawhiding each other about women they'd been with or the lack thereof, their language even more profane than it usually was, and Tommy Deuce bragged he was called Deuce because the doves all told him he was twice the man of anyone they'd ever been with. Hard Luck Luke Bronson chimed in and said, "Aw hell, he's called Tommy Deuce because he ain't any bigger than that." Then they'd be at each other again, and it embarrassed me to hear them rawhiding each other about something so personal.

But I couldn't believe he was asking me that, about being with anyone, and I was embarrassed and I stammered around because I thought I ought to say yes so I'd be like one of them, but that wasn't the truth and I was sick at the thought of telling one more lie, but I felt awkward about saying no and admitting I was still innocent. I was also confused because I was a girl who wanted it to be special and not some boy out looking to have his way with just about anyone, whatever the opportunity. What I really wanted to say was it wasn't any of his business, but when I couldn't get an answer out he laughed real big and said, "Don't worry about it, Kid. You stick with me and we'll get that taken care of in the next town we hit for supplies. By God, the worst piece of ass I ever had was the best thing that ever happened to me. You'll see for yourself," and he rode on, laughing real big.

The next time he passed me, he asked, "What do you think? Would you like her fat or tiny or tall or what?"

I stammered out, "I'm just not sure about that yet," and off he went, laughing.

Then when we were in camp he announced real loud, "Boys, when we get resupplied, we're getting the Kid laid!"

And at that the boys began cheering and whistling and even Big Mike was trying not to laugh, and not looking me in the eye.

Preacher stood up and raised his arms and started in, "Oh Lord, protect this innocent child from these heathen and godless men. This child is a lamb, dear Lord, let not these ignorant wolves drag him down into the Den of Iniquity."

Tommy Deuce called out, "Dear Lord, let Preacher stumble upon some young innocent lamb of his own and then admit to himself what a fucking hypocrite he is!"

Everyone was catcalling and offering up their own prayers, some praying, "Oh Lord, bring me luck at the gaming tables," another praying for a hot bath and a shave and another praying for whiskey that wasn't watered down, and Jack Straw saying, "Cut it out, it ain't right to talk to the Lord like that!"

Big Mike got up and said, "If you all don't shut up you're going to stampede the whole damn herd!" At that they quieted down and began to turn in or go out on nightguard.

Shakespeare stayed quiet, his nose in a book, trying not to smile.

For the next several days I was scared stiff about going into town and being forced into a room with one of the soiled doves, and worrying how I could get out of it without looking like a coward when any other fourteen-year-old boy might have been scared but eager.

One night I was stacking my plate and getting ready to take my turn as nightguard when Big Mike told all the hands that tomorrow we should hit town. He said we'd bed the herd down outside of town and Monty and Shakespeare would be going in for supplies that first day with half of the hands and I'd be in charge of the remuda while they were in town. Then I'd go in the next day with the other half of the hands when that crew got back the next morning, no later than noon.

I felt sick because I couldn't imagine how I was going to get out of it.

When I circled the herd that night I felt all panicky inside and had a hard time even singing, so I just talked to them in some kind of low mumble. Then coming the other way was Tommy Deuce himself. As he came near me he said, "Hey, one day away, Kid! You are going to have the best time of your life, and if you need any instructions you just ask me and I'll be happy to help you out!"

He laughed real big and sure enough the next time around he started in again, saying, "Hey, do you like redheads, Kid? I can guarantee you, you'll never go wrong with a redhead. Now, that might be too much woman for you the first time out, but on the other hand, if you can handle a redhead your first time, then you can handle anything after that!"

I was surprised his laughter didn't stampede the cattle. Then I wished they would stampede so that looking for them would get me out of this fix, and I even caught myself considering stampeding them myself.

The next time Tommy Deuce passed, he stopped right next to me and he leaned in as if he had a great secret, talking real low and whispery as if there was someone else around, which there wasn't, or as if he didn't want the herd to overhear because of how personal this conversation was, as if they could understand. He said, "Now listen, Kid, it's OK to be a little scared your first time but don't you worry about that. These doves are experienced and they'll know just how to help you along. And another thing—" And he leaned in a little closer, and he said, even more whispery, "Now, don't you go fooling around with yourself while you're out here tonight or when you're in your bedroll because you want to save it for when it's needed."

I didn't have any idea what he was talking about but he clapped me on the shoulder real big as if we were best friends and we had a great secret in common. As he rode on he said, "You're going to remember this day, Kid, and you're going to remember Tommy Deuce and thank him for leading you to the promised land!"

Then he thought of something else and he rode back to me and he said, real businesslike, as if we were maybe partners in some big enterprise or maybe plotting to rob a bank together, "Now, we want to tell them you're the Comanche Kid and tell them what you done and how many you killed and by God, I wouldn't be surprised if they don't knock the price back."

He winked at me and he turned around and rode on, and I swear to God I was afraid I'd throw up right there in my saddle I was so scared and sick.

The next morning I had worried myself so that I figured I might as well get used to the fact that I was going to get found out and shamed in some awful way. That made me feel almost peaceful, like some people said they felt when they thought they were going to die and there was nothing to be done about it.

Big Mike told us there was a herd of about three thousand beeves several miles ahead of us and another herd of more than two thousand behind us, so there would be a lot of hands in town over the next couple of nights and we were to watch out for ourselves and not get into any fights.

Preacher then said, "Dear Lord, we pray there be no stampede or we will be separating them all out for days and days," and someone else called out, "Dear Lord, Preacher is right about that, let there be no stampede," and a couple of boys murmured amen to that. I'd noted before that when they weren't being foulmouthed they all could be real religious speaking.

We bedded the herd down at noon and Monty and the hands going into town gathered around Big Mike and he doled out a small portion of the pay they'd earned, telling them not to lose it all if they wanted to end the drive in Dodge and have enough to start their own herd someday. They all agreed to that, Jack Straw saying he was going to send money back to his sister, and they all had big dreams beyond just painting the town red and they sure weren't planning on spending it all, maybe just some new clothes and a shave and a bath and a game of chance or two and a few drinks. Big Mike reminded them we'd already lost two hands and he couldn't keep the herd hanging around while they went to court for fighting. They all swore up and down that getting the herd to Dodge came first, no matter what.

Monty drove the wagon to town to resupply and Shakespeare rode with him. I wondered if Shakespeare would come back drunk and if he'd be visiting any of the soiled doves, and that made me mad at him and he hadn't even hit the town yet. I had to admit to myself that I was jealous. I told myself I needed to get over it because there wasn't any hope for anything with him in the first place.

Big Mike went in with Monty and the others while Abraham stayed behind to oversee things, along with Preacher and me and Tommy Deuce, Jack Straw and Hard Luck Luke Bronson, and we all traded off riding nightguard on the herd and nighthawking the remuda.

When I had a chance to turn into my bedroll, I didn't sleep much, wondering what Shakespeare was doing and imagining the worst, then wondering if we were being trailed by Comanches, then fearing what the next day would bring me. I prayed for a stampede or hoped the herd behind us would stampede straight into ours, and then I wouldn't have to go into town. It was just my luck that didn't happen, and to make it worse, every time Tommy Deuce walked by my bedroll he'd kick me in the foot and say, "Tomorrow, Kid, I'm excited for you!"

The dawn came all red and hot like some inferno. I got up early and made coffee and biscuits and salt pork and it felt good to yell, "Roll out!" Then I went to the remuda and helped the hands get their mounts as they took turns on guard. It was all just waiting, waiting for the others to come back by noon, but I waited with dread in the pit of my stomach, like a prisoner going to be taken out and shot.

Monty came back first, late morning, driving the wagon with Shakespeare's horse tied to the rear. As I unhooked the mules, I asked, "Where's Shakespeare?"

At first Monty didn't answer me. He got down from the wagon real slow, then stood there for a while with his forehead leaning against the wagon.

"You OK?" I said, and he still didn't answer. He just stood there real quiet, taking his time. Then he went down onto all fours and crawled into the shade under the wagon and lay down on his back, his hands across his chest like he was being laid out for his funeral.

I leaned in to him. "You need some water or something to eat?"

He shook his head no and mumbled, "Take the mules to the remuda."

"Where's Shakespeare?"

He pointed at the floor of the wagon above him, then folded his hands across his chest again and shut his eyes.

I climbed up on the wagon and looked in. There Shakespeare was, sound asleep, spread out across sacks of onions and potatoes and flour and cornmeal and beans and Arbuckles' Coffee and crates of airtight cans of peaches and corn and peas and tomatoes and everything else Monty had purchased to continue the drive.

I climbed back down and I thought I saw a ray of hope.

The other boys came dragging in, all of them looking the worse for wear. Shady was in new clothes but looking disheveled, like he'd slept in them. Bill was muttering to himself, singing a song, but you couldn't understand a word he said. Skinny was walking his horse rather than riding it and walking none too steady, his face bloody, as if he'd maybe fallen out of the saddle a time or two and had resorted to walking to protect himself. Big Mike came in looking halfway decent and he said to Abraham, "Your turn."

Preacher, Hard Luck Luke Bronson, Jack Straw, and Tommy Deuce gathered around the boys and asked, "How was the town?" "How were the girls?" "How was the liquor?" but they were so eager they didn't even wait for an answer and they saddled up their own mounts, yelling, "This is it boys" and "Hoo-rah!" and even Preacher was hell-bent.

I took the mules back to the remuda and Tommy Deuce called out, "This is our time, Kid, mount up!"

I said, "I don't think I'm going to be able to make it, Tommy Deuce."

"Why not?"

"Shakespeare is in pretty bad shape. He's passed out in the back of the wagon and I think I'm going to need to stay here and watch the remuda."

"To hell with that!" he said. "Mount up, goddamnit!"

He headed back to the wagon and climbed into it and as I turned out the mules I heard him yell, "Get the fuck up, Shakespeare, you got a job to do!"

When I looked back, sure enough he had Shakespeare by the collar and had him on his feet and was hauling him out of the wagon.

Shakespeare stumbled and struggled to stay upright and Tommy Deuce yelled, "The Kid's got a date with a long-legged dove, Shakespeare, you need to do your job so he can become a man!"

I could see I wasn't going to get out of going into town, so I walked Ghost back to the wagon as slow as I could go. Shakespeare saw me and he come tripping over, weaving and trying to stay upright, and it made me mad to see him like that.

"Hey, Kid," he said, "did Big Mike give you your pay?"

"Yes, he did."

"Good. Give me two bucks."

"Why?"

"Good God, you owe me sixty, just be glad I'm only asking you for two."

So I reached into my pocket and pulled out two silver coins and gave them to him. He stumbled over to Skinny, who was now sitting by the fire with a cup of coffee. He said, "Here, Skinny, here's the ... " and then he looked at the coins as if he couldn't remember what amount it was, and then he continued, "Here's the two bucks I owe you."

Skinny took them and stuffed them into a shirt pocket without saying anything.

Shakespeare turned back to me and said, "Thanks, Kid."

"You lost everything you had?"

He ignored me and he said, "When we get to Dodge you owe me fifty-eight instead of sixty."

I said again, "You lost everything?"

I realized I sounded like an angry wife. He looked at me hard and he said, "So wise, so young, they say, do never live long." And at that he grabbed a cup and went to the fire and poured himself some coffee, then sat and leaned back against the wheel of the wagon.

Tommy Deuce clapped me on the back and shouted, "This is it, Kid!" and he almost knocked me into the fire. I climbed slowly into the saddle and he turned to Big Mike and said, "Boss, we are off!"

Big Mike told us to be back by noon tomorrow. Tommy Deuce mounted up and said, "Hell, boss, I'm coming back with so much money I'm going to buy the herd from you and you're going to work for me!" He did that big laugh of his and he wheeled around and slapped Ghost on the rump with his hat and the two of us took off so fast it almost jerked me out of the saddle.

The other boys followed, all of them filled with bluster and hoo-rah, yelling, "We're off!" and "Let's go!" and "Hi-yah, hi-yah!"

How long have I got, I thought, *before I have to face another hell?*

NINETEEN

We hit the town, the boys racing at a fast and reckless clip, calling out, "Here we are, the boys of the Rafter R! The toughest set of drovers to trail north from Texas! Lock up your daughters because we are here to raise some hell! Whoo-eee!"

We raced the length of the town, past dusty tents with signs out front, a plank across two barrels with someone selling kill-me-quick whiskey, a livery stable and corral, a hole-in-the-wall newspaper office, a dry goods store, several whiskey mills, broken-down wagons in an empty lot, and in one alley a go-as-you-please fistfight. There were horses tied to hitching posts, broken crates and staved-in barrels on the boardwalks, dogs barking and chasing after wagons and buckboards. A woman or two in sunbonnets ignored us, the boys calling out to them, "Is that your daughter, ma'am? My, my, don't let her come to the Full Glass tonight, but if you want to come we'd be happy to buy you a drink!" "Hey, girl, are you married?" "Hey, woman in the pink dress, can you sew?"

They all laughed and bragged about how dangerous they were and challenged each other to drinking contests or feats of strength or games of chance, and asked where was the richest pot, and Preacher was the noisiest of the lot. Hands from other outfits shouted back they'd be glad to take them on at arm wrestling or faro and be at this place or that place and they'd soon see they weren't the toughest or luckiest rawhiders from Texas like they thought they were, that they'd met their match in the boys from the Slash Diamond or the Circle C.

I didn't do any shouting but lay low and kept looking for an opportunity to get away. I leaned over to Tommy Deuce and told him I was going to take Ghost to the livery stable, hoping I could get lost in the melee and tell him later I had accomplished what he was hoping for me, but he immediately yelled out, "Boys, let's get these ponies off our hands!"

They all agreed and everyone headed back down the street, yelling and hoo-rahing folks, their horses rearing and kicking up dust. I had a feeling these folks had seen it all before and weren't paying it much mind, but the boys acted like they had the biggest audience in the world, parading along and making fools of themselves.

Everyone dismounted at the stable and the hostler asked for money up front to feed and water and stable the horses. All the boys grumbled at that but pulled out their wages and forked the money over, then pulled off their saddles and bridles and stacked them inside the stable.

With the horses gone, Tommy Deuce reminded everyone this was my big day. They all whooped at that and started guessing what kind of a dove I was going to pick, but Tommy Deuce announced, "There ain't going to be any visits to the doves until we get cleaned up! No dove is going to want to be with a hand that smells like a horse!"

Then he said to me, "We need to get you some new clothes and a bath and a haircut. You go into some dove's crib covered in blood like that and she'll think you're there to kill her." He laughed at his own joke, then took a look around and said, "Over here," and we headed for a dry goods store.

Hard Luck Luke Bronson said, "To hell with that, I'm getting a drink first," and he took off, Preacher and Jack Straw and Abraham agreeing with him and following after.

When we entered the dry goods store, it felt good to have some shade even if it wasn't much cooler. It was a new experience, being inside and looking out through storefront windows into the sunlit streets with horses and wagons and people passing by, and seeing merchandise on counters and shelves, and candy in jars, and kegs of nails and a black cast-iron stove over in a corner. The wide wood plank floors creaked as we looked around.

I couldn't believe I was in some place where goods were bought and sold and women made dresses out of bolts of calico and men bought tools and nobody got shot or stabbed or scalped or burned alive. What kind of a world was this, where people were safe and no one was looking for water or hoping lightning didn't strike you, or trying to hide from hail so big it could knock you out of the saddle. I wanted to sit down in that wooden chair in the corner and put my feet up on a keg and eat some crackers or pickles, and just watch the people come and go.

Then Tommy Deuce said, "Over here." I came out of my dream and he pointed at some ready-made shirts on a shelf and there were trousers next to them. He said, "Pick out something here, get you out of those god-awful bloody clothes." He pointed and said, "How about this blue one?

"No, I'll take the red," I said, but I didn't tell him it was because I was used to being covered in blood and decided I'd just keep it that way.

"Cow brutes don't like red," he said, "and only miners wear red."

I shrugged that off, figuring they'd just have to get used to it.

I picked a pair of trousers that looked like they would fit and I bought a vest so I'd look like all the other hands who used theirs to hold a pencil and a tally book or to store their makings. I wished I could get a new piece of material to bind my chest but I couldn't tell Tommy Deuce I needed a yard of calico or gingham, so I figured I'd just wash mine when I got a bath and hope it didn't disintegrate from all the sweat. That brought up a whole new fear, hoping I could take a bath alone and not be sitting naked in some tub next to Tommy Deuce.

Tommy Deuce bought the blue shirt he had recommended to me and we paid for our goods each and the clerk wrapped them in brown paper and tied them with a string. I hated to leave the store because they also had ribbons and lockets and rings and bangles. I wanted to look at them and touch them all and buy something pretty for myself, but Tommy Deuce announced real loud that a shave and a haircut and a bath were next.

As we walked out, I said, "I don't shave yet."

"I know that, Kid, but I do, and we both need a haircut and a bath if we are going to be presentable to the ladies, so we need to look for a tonsorial parlor." He added, "You can tell a tonsorial parlor because they'll have a red-and-white-striped pole out front."

Even I knew that but I acted like it was new information.

We strode down the boardwalk, which was washed away in some places and broken up in others. In front of some of the stores the lumber was all fresh and yellow but starting to buckle because the wood hadn't been dried properly. Tommy Deuce looked across the street and there was a small shop with an upright plank that had been painted with red and white stripes and he said, "Right there!"

We crossed over and went into the tonsorial parlor, and I'd never been in one before. Ma always cut our hair and I'd let mine grow until it was at my waist, and she'd tell me I looked like an angel in a picture book. I'd wear it up high when we were cooking or working so it didn't catch fire or get in the way, and we'd brush each other's hair at night, and it hurt me to remember that.

A plump, bald, but kindly gentleman put down his newspaper and got out of his chair when we came in and he said, "How can I help you fellow Texans?"

Tommy Deuce wanted to know where he was from in Texas and they got into a long confab about what town was where and did they know this person or that person. I was surprised he didn't ask Tommy Deuce home for dinner, they seemed to get along so well.

Then the gentleman said, "Now to business. What do you and this young rawhider need?"

Tommy told him and he said, "I'll tell you what. I'll take this young fellow first and cut his hair because he don't need no shave, do he? Then he can go on back for a bath and you and I can have a long talk about San Antone."

Tommy Deuce agreed to that and the bald gentleman stepped out back and said something to someone about hot water. I found I was holding my breath, and I let it out real easy because I realized if Tommy Deuce was staying behind for a few minutes then I was going to escape being in a tub at the same time as him.

I tossed Jamie's hat onto a nail in the wall and I climbed into the chair, the barber saying whoever I went to last must have been drunk or just about the worst barber ever, or I'd done it myself to keep some Indian from wanting to scalp me because no self-respecting Indian would want a scalp that ugly.

He and Tommy Deuce laughed and I pretended to find it funny, but I was thinking about seeing Ma and Pa and Jamie scalped, their heads all raw and bloody.

Tommy Deuce started in on how that barber didn't realize it, but he was cutting the hair of the famous Indian fighter, the Comanche Kid, and how I'd killed five Indians and lost my family and recovered my herd. Now I was driving to Dodge, and then I was going to recover my sister.

During it all the bald gentleman said, "My, my, my" and "Oh, I am so sorry" and "You do say" and "Well, I'll be." He said he'd put a sign out front that said, "Barber to the Comanche Kid," and "How about that?"

When he finished, he put a lot of something in my hair that made it smell good and he combed it like a boy would comb it, then held up a mirror for me to see myself. I tried not to gasp at seeing Jamie staring back at me, and I said that was fine, thank you very much.

Tommy Deuce called out, "Kid, you are almost good-look-ing! Those doves are going to eat you up! I wouldn't be surprised if you don't have to fight them off! Shoot, you might even end up getting two for one!"

Then he bragged to the barber, "This is going to be the Kid's first time with a dove!"

The barber raised his eyebrows at me and said, "Well, my oh my, there is a time for everything, isn't there? I wish you good luck, son. Now, go down the hall and into the first door on the left and there'll be hot water and a towel, but first you owe me four bits."

I paid him, and as I started for the hall he called out, "Now, don't forget your package!"

I was so nervous I'd forgotten both it and my hat, so I picked them up and told him thank you, and as Tommy Deuce climbed into the barber's chair he called out, "I'll be right behind you, Kid!"

I hurried into the hall and opened the door and there was a Mexican kid just finishing pouring water into the second of two tin tubs. He nodded to me and slipped out of the room so quickly it looked like he was being caught doing something wrong. It made me feel the same way, as if I was about to be caught stealing candy.

I kicked off my boots and threw off my clothes and took the band around my chest off as quickly as I could, and I stepped into the tub, taking the band with me to wash. As I slipped into the water, I looked down at myself naked. I was all skin and bones and I knew Ma would be upset and telling me if I was going to be working that hard on the trail then I needed to start eating more whether I liked it or not.

I soaped down the band and then let it soak while I scrubbed myself all over with a bristle brush, and as fast as I was working it felt good to have water all over me and to be free of the bloody clothes I was wearing. I wanted to just sit in the water for a long time, just like I wanted to sit in the dry goods store and look out the window, but I knew I couldn't take the time.

I splashed water all over myself to rinse the soap off, then I rinsed out the band and squeezed it real good and tied it back around my chest as tightly as I could. I stepped out of the tub and ran a towel over myself quickly, then I untied my package and threw on the trousers and the red shirt and the new vest and then my boots. Just as I got everything buttoned up, in came Tommy Deuce yelling, "Boy, am I looking forward to this!" and "Whoa! You're finished already! Well, sit down, Kid, and hang around and we'll both be out of here soon!" Tommy Deuce tended to shout most everything he said.

He pulled off his clothes and threw them on the floor, and then standing there in front of me stripped stark naked he stepped into the tub, me trying not to look. I sat down on a small wooden stool in the corner as he splashed water all over himself and he called out, "Oh my, would you look at that! I think it knows where we're going! Whoa there, Big John, don't get ahead of yourself!" He laughed real big and I acted like I wasn't interested, although I was curious, and I was shocked and ashamed at myself for being curious.

He scrubbed real hard and he talked away and I didn't think I even needed to be in the room for him to be having a conversation. He talked about other baths he'd had and how long between them and he said, "We'll get a drink first to loosen things up." Then he teased me and asked if I wanted him to be in the room for advice, and he laughed at his jokes about calico queens and ceiling experts and told me what his first time was like.

After a while I could hear him talking but I didn't listen to what he said, until I realized he was standing in front of me all dressed with his new blue shirt on. He'd asked me a question and I said, "Huh?"

"You ready to go tie one on?"

"Sure, Tommy Deuce."

We went back out through the barbershop and thanked the barber for the bath and said it sure was refreshing, and he thanked us both as he started working on a hand from another outfit. As we stepped out of the shop and into the bright heat, Tommy Deuce called back, "You're going to have to work awfully hard to make that puncher look good because he's plumb ugly."

The hand didn't take offense because they always rawhided each other that way. He called back, "Well, at least I'm rich!" which was a lie but we could hear his laughter as we started down the boardwalk.

Then Tommy Deuce pointed down the street, saying, "Now, that one right there looks to be the biggest and I bet they got music and games of chance and plenty of spirits and maybe a choice selection of doves with cribs out back, and maybe even dancing. So what do you say we try that one out first, OK?"

I said, "Sure, why not."

As we crossed the dusty and rutted street, he said, "Now, Kid, you ever played draw or stud or faro, blackjack, craps, or monte?"

"No," I said. "I have not."

"Well, faro is complicated as hell so we might start you out on draw or stud first."

"That sure sounds good to me." And it did because I thought if we did that, it would delay meeting any of the doves. I even had the idea I might get drunk and then get real sick on purpose and I could be excused from having any time alone with some poor unsuspecting dove.

We pushed through the doors of a whiskey mill called the Broken Bottle, and inside the air was filled with tobacco smoke and the smell of sweat. In a far corner there was a piano playing and some brightly clad women dancing with some men and a sign that said "Ten Cents a Dance." There were folks at tables playing different games of chance and there was a long bar and behind it a large painting of some maiden in a shameful state of undress. Jack Straw stood at the bar, having drinks and talking with some hands, and some folks were drinking alone. We spotted Abraham and Preacher and Hard Luck Luke Bronson at a table in the back playing cards with some other hands.

Tommy Deuce said, "This is on me." He went to the bar and bought a bottle and grabbed two glasses and he passed through the gaming tables and headed back to Abraham and Preacher and Hard Luck Luke Bronson, me following.

There were chairs up against a wall and we sat there and watched their game as Tommy Deuce poured out a drink for the two of us. Someone dealt out the cards and they all threw coins into the center of the table and then got more cards after they tossed some cards away, only some got one and some got two and some got three and some didn't get any, and it didn't make any sense to me.

Tommy Deuce leaned over and said, real quiet, "They're playing draw."

"What is draw?"

"Kid, you don't know anything, do you? Boy, you must have had real straight-laced parents." Then he whispered something about one pair, two pair, three of a kind, and it sounded like he was speaking some foreign language. He nudged me and said, "Drink your drink, Kid." I took a big drink and I thought somebody had set my mouth and throat on fire. I coughed and gagged and Tommy Deuce laughed real loud, saying, "Look at this, boys, he's never had rye before!"

Someone said, "There is a first time for everything," which was the second time I'd heard that today.

Hard Luck Luke Bronson was real serious and he said, "Hey, we're playing cards here."

Preacher spoke up. "There you go, the devil's brew is the first step down the road to degradation." Then he took a drink himself.

Abraham said to Preacher, "What about you, drinking the devil's brew and playing the devil's game right here?"

Preacher said, "Naw, I'm different because liquor don't affect me. Besides, I'm going to win real big and then I'm going to build a church and convert you and other lost souls like you and you can thank me later when you get through the Pearly Gates because you sure ain't going to get in now."

They all laughed and Hard Luck Luke Bronson was irritated and said, "Hey, we're playing cards here."

Tommy Deuce poured me another drink and he said, "Get used to it, Kid. I didn't realize it was your first time for everything." Then he told the whole table about what else was going to be my first time and the hands started whistling in amazement. One started singing a song that had filthy lyrics about being horizontal, and as profane as the hands were, I'd never heard men talk about women the way they were talking now. In the meantime someone had thrown their cards down and started pulling the coins on the table in toward himself.

The others were real disgusted or resigned and tossed their cards down, and another hand collected them and began to shuffle them and deal them out again. I drank the rye and tried to get used to the burn as they all tossed in coins and sorted their cards and passed their own bottle around. Some were real quiet and a couple talked about some stampede they went through a few days back and one hand said, "Hell, one time I got in front of a stampede and I had to shoot my own horse and hide under him to keep from getting trampled!"

Then they all got down to business, tossing coins in the center of the table and throwing down cards and saying how many they wanted. No one talked as they considered their hands, then made bets and said things like, "I'll raise you" or "I'll see you," and I had no idea how anyone knew what was going on.

In the meantime, I drank some more and it still burned going down and it took my breath away, but there was something about the burning that felt good, and when I threw down another drink, I caught Tommy Deuce winking at Abraham, who was trying not to smile.

We sat there watching and drinking, and even though I was baffled by the game, I leaned my chair back against the wall and closed my eyes. I swear something come over me, only it was strange, like I was in a dream, or another world, and the noise of the coins hitting the table and the music and the sound of the hands talking seemed far away. On the one hand I felt a wave of peace come over me, and at the same time I had this feeling like I wanted to hit somebody as hard as I could, and I couldn't explain how I could be feeling both things at the same time. Then I smelled this sweet scent, and it was all flowers, like roses and lilacs, but also prairie grasses and the wind through cedar and pine, but also sweat.

And then I heard a voice that said, "Who do we have here?"

I opened my eyes and there was this woman, more of a girl maybe, or maybe not. I couldn't tell how old she was. Her dress was bright colors and flouncy and it was low-cut and her breasts were large and they jiggled as she crossed toward me. I was shocked when she sat in my lap, making the chair snap back level, and I couldn't breathe or think and I didn't know what to say. She asked me my name, and she had large brown eyes and full red lips and red cheeks, and for the life of me I couldn't think of my name. Finally two come to me, Jamie and Jane, and I couldn't remember which was the one I should confess to. I was so confused I couldn't breathe and I couldn't give her an answer, so I went to get up but she grabbed the arm of the chair and said, "Whoa, puncher, there's no need to go anywhere, is there?"

I said, "No, ma'am."

She took off my hat and tossed it on the floor and ran her fingers through my hair and she said, "How old are you?"

I was real bewildered by that question as well because I couldn't remember if I was supposed to give her my real age or my made-up age. She turned to Tommy Deuce and she said, "You haven't brought a child in here, have you?"

Tommy Deuce said, "No, ma'am, I would not corrupt a youth. This here is the Comanche Kid, and he is more killer than the rest of us put together, I guarantee it."

Preacher called out, "Here it is now! This Cyprian here is the second step down the road to degradation!"

Only she answered back, "Shut the fuck up, Preacher, you damn hypocrite."

I didn't know how she knew him but all the hands laughed at that, saying, "Whoa! She sure told you!" and "Boy, did she get that right!"

I was shocked and couldn't believe what I'd just heard. I stared at her full breasts and it was so hot inside and the air was wet and heavy and there was sweat on her breasts and across her forehead and on her upper lip. I realized I was sweating too, pouring sweat, and her perfume smelled so sugary sweet I started to gag and I stood bolt upright and it threw her to the floor and she said, "What the hell!"

Tommy Deuce got to his feet and helped her up and steadied her, saying, "Take no offense, miss. Even though he is a genuine killer, he is a little inexperienced and he's never been with a woman before. This is the day we put an end to that."

Only now she was angry and she said, "Someone else can fuck him. I don't care how many Comanches the little bastard's killed. Bring him back when he's grown up." And at that she crossed away and headed for another table, and I couldn't believe such language coming out of her mouth.

Tommy Deuce said, "That didn't go too good."

Hard Luck Luke Bronson said, "Get him out of here. Take him down the street to the Red Feather if that's what you want. We're playing cards here."

So Tommy Deuce grabbed his bottle and he took me by the arm and led me away, saying, "We'll be back." He took a swig out of the bottle and handed it to me and I took one too. We went through the doors back out into the sun, and it was so bright I had to shade my eyes. I heard Tommy Deuce ask some drover, "Where's the Red Feather?"

Tommy Deuce then took off in whatever direction was pointed out, hauling me by my collar. I took a drink from the bottle again and I felt like I was being led into some fiery furnace of hell.

I realized I forgot my hat and I tried to turn around but Tommy Deuce said, "No way," and hauled me down the board-walk. It was so uneven I kept stumbling on it but he held me upright and my breathing got light and shallow and fast and I felt this panic, like I was a prisoner being hauled off to his execution.

I took another drink, hoping I'd pass out. I wondered if that's what sailors did aboard a sinking ship when they knew they were about to drown, drink so much that it wouldn't hurt when they were under the waves and sucking water instead of air.

TWENTY

We went banging through a door and it was all still and dark and the air had a thick mixture of heavy, sweet scents. Somewhere down a hall I could hear a piano playing and someone singing what I'm sure was a song about missing your mother or dying alone or the girl you lost. My eyes got used to the dim light and there was flowers in a vase on a table and the table had white lace on it and there were chairs on either side of it.

I heard the rustle of a skirt, and out of the shadows there came this older lady, heavyset with gray hair piled up high on her head and she said, "Well, hello, gentlemen, how are you?" She seemed real kindly and she smiled at me and I couldn't meet her eyes so I ducked away.

Tommy Deuce said, "Good afternoon, ma'am, we're doing just fine."

"I'm Miss Rose," she said.

Tommy Deuce put his bottle down on the table and he took his hat off. "Good afternoon to you, Miss Rose."

She eyed Tommy Deuce's bottle. "Well, I can see you are indeed doing fine. Maybe you two would like to get out of the sun and come sit down in the parlor?"

Tommy Deuce was as meek as a kitten and said, "Yes, ma'am."

She took me by my arm and leaned in closer. "And what is your name, young man?"

I could barely get the words out. "Jamie, ma'am," and I felt like I was doing some disservice to Jamie's memory, as if my taking his name into a place for soiled doves was staining his reputation, not mine.

Tommy Deuce gave his name and she wanted to know what outfit we were with and where we were up from. She had her arm around me as if we were best friends and Tommy Deuce followed behind giving her all the answers.

She said, "Oh my, we had some boys from that outfit in here yesterday, and just this morning too."

Then I wondered if Shakespeare had been in here and I felt angry about that. I wanted to ask her if one of them was tall and lean and had sandy hair with a little bit of copper in it, if the light was right, and if he quoted Shakespeare all the time. I couldn't get it out because Tommy Deuce was telling her I'm the Comanche Kid, a famous Comanche killer, and how I lost my family, and this is my first time.

She stopped and faced me and put both of her hands on my shoulders. "Oh, you poor thing." I couldn't look her in the eyes but she smiled sweetly and said, "Oh, honey, but life goes on, doesn't it? And isn't this a special time? But I'll bet you're as nervous as a long-tailed cat in a room full of rocking chairs, aren't you?"

I whispered, "Yes, ma'am."

"Oh, you are so precious I could eat you up myself." She ran her hand through my hair and gave me a kiss on the cheek. She shook her head and smiled real sad and touched my lips with her fingertips and she said, "Time, time, time."

Then she said, "Now, both of you come right in here."

We passed through a hallway door into another room and the air was heavy with perfume. There were stuffed chairs and a big stuffed sofa and flowery wallpaper and there were several girls, some of them full-grown women, maybe, or maybe not. Some of them even looked like girls my age but I couldn't tell for sure. All of them sat around waiting, I supposed, some of them with arms and legs all akimbo and some of them sitting up straight, real prim, and all of them wore bright, store-bought colors on their faces.

One of them rose and come over to Tommy Deuce and said, "Sweetheart, why don't you come over here by me?" She took him by the hand, leaving me behind, and led him to the sofa, sitting him down between herself and another girl.

Then this redhead with hair piled high pulled a pin and her hair fell down all across her bare shoulders. I thought it looked like blood spilling down. She was all skin and bones and her eyes were blurry and she said to me, "Young man, you come sit here," and she motioned to her lap.

I hesitated, so she got up and came to me and led me back to her chair and sat me down in it, then she knelt at my feet and said, "Now, I'm Charity." She pointed out two girls sitting near each other in a corner and said, "That's Faith, and that's Hope, and your friend is sitting between Irish Belle and Black-Eyed Susan."

Then Tommy Deuce announced to the whole room that this was my first time.

Some of them giggled and one of them did a half smile like maybe she was sorry, and then I realized there was a heavy, dark-skinned Mexican girl in the other corner. I nodded to her and I could barely get the words out, but I pointed and said, "Who's she?"

Charity laughed, but then she said real low, as if it was a secret, "That's Maria, she's a bean eater, and she's new here and just learning, so if this is your first time let me suggest one of us."

I was shocked to realize I was to just pick one out, and then Faith come over from the corner and she took me by the hand and pulled me up and away from Charity. She led me back to her chair, saying in a real slurry voice, "Come here, sugar." She sat down and pulled me onto her lap and she started to put her hand between my legs.

I didn't know what I was supposed to do but I jumped up and I mumbled, "Thank you, ma'am, but I'd just as soon stand."

They all giggled at that, and the one called Hope leaned over and whispered something to Faith, who covered her mouth and tried not to laugh, and then this Hope, and somehow I didn't believe I was getting their real names, she got up and said, "You're right, honey, and I'll just stand right here with you."

She faced me and she started pulling her garment down off either shoulder real slowly, standing right in front of me, and she said, "Sugar, would you like to touch this?" And she took my hand and put it on one of her bare shoulders and Tommy Deuce said, "Whoo-eee! This is getting good!"

I jerked my hand away and I didn't know where it came from but I blurted out, "I'll take the fat one," and there was silence in the room.

Charity said, "Oh, sweetie, are you sure you don't want to think about that? That's just going to be the blind leading the blind."

They all laughed at that, and Maria, the fat one, looked embarrassed and tried to smile, like she found it funny too. I said, "No, I like them fat."

Tommy Deuce said, "Hey, Kid, I like them fat too but not that fat! Besides," he said, "it's your first time! How do you know how you like them?"

There was more laughter and they all whispered back and forth. I just shrugged and said, "She'll do just fine."

Then Miss Rose, who had been watching all this, said, "If he likes Maria, then Maria it is. After all, that's why she's here, because we just knew she would appeal to certain people, didn't we know that?"

They all mumbled, "Yes, Miss Rose" and "Yes, ma'am."

Miss Rose took me by the hand and led me over to Maria, and she introduced us to each other, real proper, saying, "Maria, this is Jamie" and "Jamie, this is Maria."

Maria offered her hand and I took it and I mumbled, "How do you do, Maria?"

Neither of us could look at each other and Miss Rose turned and announced to the room, "Now, will you look at this. Aren't they just like young lovers?"

The girls all said things like, "Oh, they are so sweet" and "Don't they look lovely?" and one pretended to pout and said, "I only wish he had picked me!" They laughed and another said, "Well, don't we all wish he'd picked us?"

Miss Rose said, "Now, you two follow me," and as she led us away Tommy Deuce yelled out, "Ride 'em, cowboy!"

I didn't know what door we went through or down what hall because I was scared and everything was a blur and I swear the walls were changing shapes. There was banging and groaning coming from behind a door, and I was sweating as if the Comanches had staked me out in the sun. I tried to breathe and I couldn't imagine how I was going to get out of this, and the next thing I knew Miss Rose was closing the door behind her as she was leaving, saying, "Now, you two enjoy yourselves," and I found myself alone in the room with Maria.

We stood there in the middle of the room facing each other and I didn't have any idea about what I should do or say next.

Maria didn't say anything either, at first, but then in a heavy Mexican accent she said real quietly, "I need two dollar."

I said, "What?"

"I need two dollar," and then I understood what she meant. I thought if I didn't pay her I'd get tossed out and I'd be done with this, but I figured when Tommy Deuce found out he'd just haul me back and pay the two dollars himself, so I reached into my pocket and counted out two silver dollars and handed them to her.

"You can leave them by the washbasin."

I looked around and there was a small wooden table with a pitcher of water and a basin on it with a washcloth that looked like it was still wet. I put the two coins there.

When I turned around, Maria started to unbutton her dress down the front and I said real quick, "You don't need to do that."

"What?"

"You don't need to do that."

"You want to have me with my clothes on?"

She crossed to the narrow bed and began to pull her skirts up, and I said, "No, no, not that either."

She dropped her skirts. "How you want to have me?"

And I thought, *Here goes*, and I said, "I don't want to have you."

She sat on the bed. "Is something wrong you don't want me?"

"No, nothing's wrong."

"You want one of the other girls?"

"No," I said, "I don't want any of the other girls."

"You want your money back?"

"No, I don't want my money back, that's yours."

"Why you don't want me?"

And for the first time I confessed the truth. "Because I'm a girl."

She just stared at me. "What you mean you a girl?"

"I mean, I'm a girl."

"You mean you one of those boys who like boys?"

"No, I'm a girl who likes boys." She looked like I was playing some kind of a game with her, and she kept trying to figure out the right answer.

She said, "How can this be?"

I unbuttoned my shirt and opened it up and showed her the band around my chest.

She stared at me. "You have breasts?"

"Yes, ma'am, I do. I'm a girl."

She stood up and crossed over to me and she reached out and placed one hand real gently on my breast and then took it away. She said, "Why all this stain of blood on this cloth?"

"That's a long story."

She pointed and said, "You a girl down there too?"

"Yes, ma'am."

"For sure?"

"Yes, ma'am," and I took her hand and placed it there.

She pulled it away real quick, and she just stood there, looking me up and down, then crossed to the bed and sat on the edge and she asked, "You one of those girls who like girls?"

"No, ma'am."

"Then what we supposed to do?"

I went over and sat next to her on the bed. "I don't know."

We sat there for a time and I took in the wide plank wood floor and I wondered if Shakespeare had been in this room and on these bedclothes, and I felt jealous and angry and sick at the thought of it. I kept asking myself why did I care who he'd been with, when I heard her say, "So why you here?"

I began to tell her the whole story, starting with the raid, and I got a lot of the details mixed up and out of order. I started to weep when I told her about Buck being killed, and somewhere in there she held my hand. Then she put her arm around me, and I told her I was scared the hands would find out I was a girl and they'd leave me behind. She kept saying, "Is OK, is OK, I not tell anyone."

Finally I just put my face in my hands and sobbed and she patted me on the back and she said over and over, "Is OK, is OK." Somewhere during all of that I curled up with my head in her lap, and I fell asleep.

I woke up to a knocking on the door. I don't know how I got there but I was curled up on the bed with Maria behind me, alongside of me, and she had her arm around me and was holding me.

We both sat up and she said, "Quick, wash your face."

As I crossed to the washbasin she pulled the pins from her hair and shook it out so it fell down thick and black. Then she unbuttoned her dress so her breasts were showing. As Miss Rose opened the door and peeked into the room, she proceeded to slowly button her dress back up.

Tommy Deuce stood behind Miss Rose, looking over her shoulder, and Miss Rose said, "It's been an hour, Maria, how are we all?"

Tommy Deuce shouted out, "How'd the Kid do?"

Maria acted shy and embarrassed and she said, "Oh my, you would not know he is new, he have me several times. He wear me out."

Tommy Deuce said, "Whoo-eee, that's what I wanted to hear! Good for you, Kid!" He pushed past Miss Rose and clapped me on the shoulder and he said, "Not bad, huh? What'd I tell you! Just think, Kid, every town we hit to get resupplied, this is waiting for you! Proud of you, Kid!"

Miss Rose came over and gave me a hug and another kiss on the cheek and she said, "Now, don't be a stranger. Maybe tomorrow morning before you go back to camp you'd like to come by and see Maria again?" As she was talking she reached out and grabbed the two coins on the washbasin table and slipped them into a pocket in her dress.

"Yes, ma'am, I hope so, she sure was fine."

Maria was pinning her hair up again and I wished I could thank her proper, but Tommy Deuce pushed me out the door, saying, "Now we celebrate!"

He bragged he'd had the redhead and everything he'd said about redheads was true, and when he got alone in the room with her she didn't know what hit her. That was why he was called Tommy Deuce, but maybe it should be Tommy Tres or Tommy Cuatro or Cinco. Tomorrow morning he thought he'd go back one more time but maybe this time he'd try Maria to see what it was like with a girl that fat, and maybe I'd like to try the redhead to see if I liked them skinny. I felt sick at my stomach listening to him.

We were going down the hallway, and as we passed a door that was cracked open, for just a second I saw someone naked in the center of the room, his back to us, pulling his trousers up and talking, and I swear it was Preacher's voice. None of it made sense and I couldn't be sure of anything I saw or heard because I was so bewildered.

We passed the table that had the bottle of rye still on it and Tommy Deuce didn't see it but I grabbed it and we were out the door. The sun was low in the sky and the town looked even shabbier to me, even though there was new buildings being built from raw wood, even a brick building going up, maybe a bank, as if there was some kind of money somewhere.

Dust billowed up from farmers and ranchers going by in buckboards, some empty and some loaded down with crates and barrels and lumber and gunnysacks of something, and someone was pushing a handcart with dirt in it. I could smell beef cooking somewhere, and I wondered how a town could be built out here in the middle of nowhere while at the same time my sister was maybe a slave to the Comanches or being traded to the Apaches down in Mexico for horses or spirits or weapons. I asked myself, *What kind of a world are we living in?*

I stopped in the middle of the street and took a drink from the bottle of rye. Tommy Deuce grabbed me by the arm and said, "So tell me about it, Kid, how was she?"

I wished I was back at the camp where everything seemed simpler, helping Monty or getting ready to ride nightguard, and I said, "She was fine, Tommy Deuce, she was fine."

I took another drink and the liquid heat felt good burning down my throat. He took the bottle from me and took a drink himself and said, "Oh, come on, Kid, you've got to give me more than that! After all, I got you in there."

I took the bottle back and I just wanted to crack him in the head with it. Instead I said, "A gentleman never tells, Tommy Deuce, but just let me say it was so great that we're getting married," and at that he let out a big roar of laughter and he put his arm around my shoulders and together we headed back to the Broken Bottle.

The rest of the night was a blur. I remember when we entered Tommy Deuce announced to the room that I had done it and there were cheers and congratulations and someone returned my hat to me and someone else gave me a cigar that I struggled to smoke. Some hands bought me drinks and I threw them down and joined in with the festivities, bragging I was getting married and she'd bragged how I'd had her several times, and Tommy Deuce would vouch for that. I couldn't believe all the things that were coming out of my mouth.

Then Tommy Deuce was off drinking with some other hands, and somewhere in there Abraham taught me how to play draw and stud, saying that learning how to buck the tiger was too complicated for me just yet. He talked to me about one-eyed jacks and deuces wild and taught me straights and flushes and full house and all the combinations, but I had trouble remembering their order. I kept seeing coins coming and going across the tabletop as if they had a life of their own.

Afterward, several of us had supper at some place that served steak and potatoes, or maybe we had supper first and then I learned draw, I can't remember, but I ate like I hadn't eaten for days. Then I remembered being in an alley and throwing it all up, and somehow Preacher was there and he hauled me over to a trough and made me wash my face off. I wondered, how did I end up with Preacher in an alley? I asked which virtue he went with, was it Faith or Hope or Charity?

He said he wasn't with any of the doves. I called him a liar and at that he slapped me across the face and shoved me backward into the trough of water and told me to wash my mouth out.

I crawled out dripping wet and called him a lying hypocrite and I hauled off and started to hit him back, and then there were some boys on both of us pulling us apart.

At some point in all of that, half a dozen hands on horseback rode up and down the street yelling what outfit they were with, and someone fired a weapon into the air. Then the sheriff, or maybe he was the city marshal, was out in the middle of the street with a couple of deputies telling them all to go back to camp or to dismount and settle down or they'd be spending the night in jail and be facing a judge and a stiff fine in the morning for being disorderly and disturbing the peace.

Some other hands came to the defense of the riders and got loud about it, saying, "If it wasn't for these hands there wouldn't be no town here." Then one of the deputies cracked one of them in the head with the barrel of his pistol and he dropped like a swatted fly. The deputy called out, "Who's next?"

The hands backed off, but not before calling out some insults. After that, the crowd drifted away and the riders were gone, and I stood there soaking wet and wondered how I got there, and Preacher was nowhere in sight.

I thought maybe I should get a room somewhere, but when I put my hand in my pocket I discovered all my money was gone.

I wasn't sure what to do, so I headed for the livery stable, stumbling the whole way. When I got there, the stable doors were locked but there was a corral to one side, so I crawled under the rails and I sat down and leaned up against the wall of the stable, right among the ponies, and tried to shut my eyes. I didn't have any idea what time it was or how long it was until morning, but the smell of the horses and the smell of their piss and manure was good. I felt like I was home and safe.

As I sat there, I heard the clumping sound of hooves coming toward me slowly, and then stopping, and then there was that blowing sound horses make.

I opened my eyes and it was Ghost, just standing there, right before me, and I didn't think she'd know me because I certainly hadn't paid any attention to her, not trying to talk to her or listening to what she had to say like I would with Buck. I felt mean doing that to her, but after losing Buck I didn't feel like I wanted to know her. I just needed a horse to carry me, whether it was for nightguard or wrangling the remuda.

She moved a few steps closer, close enough that she was right by me, so close that I could reach out and put my hand on her hoof and her fetlock, and she felt strong and tough and smooth and warm, and she leaned down and she just nickered.

We stayed together like that for a while, then she wandered away when she thought she had been there long enough, and I told her thanks as she walked off.

I curled up against the wall of the stable, glad that the night was still warm given how wet I was, and I slept the sleep of the dead.

TWENTY-ONE

I heard angels singing, only they weren't very good angels, or maybe they were good angels but not very good singers, or maybe it didn't sound like good singing because I had a bad headache and it made the singing sound bad.

I could feel the heat of the sun on my face and I could smell the dirt on me from the corral as well as the vomit on my clothes from last night, and my head felt like a wagon had run over it. My face was sore from where Preacher had hit me, and I couldn't figure out why there'd be angels singing in this godforsaken town.

I opened my eyes to the glare of the sun and it was blinding already, and it was going to be another brutal day. I squinted across the dusty street and there was a tent, brown with dust, a wooden cross hanging from the top of the tent pole, and there were folks already up and sitting on benches. They were singing, and I realized that was the sound of the angels I'd heard.

I thought to myself, *Some angels. If that's the best that can be drummed up, no wonder God deserted Texas.*

I uncurled as slowly as I could, my head feeling like it was going to crack open, and I heard a voice say, "What the hell you doing?"

It was the hostler unlocking the doors to the stable, so I pulled myself onto all fours and I croaked out, "Catching forty winks."

"Good God," he said, "can't you do any better than sleeping in horseshit?"

"I been sleeping on the ground for weeks on end. This ain't no different. Besides," I said, "it's OK. I'm part horse."

"God forbid you should go and get a room like a decent person. Bet you lost all your money, didn't you?"

"Yes, sir."

"See? That's why I ask to get paid up front and then all you punchers complain, but I ain't no fool." He added, "Hell, you're just a kid, ain't you? You got no business getting drunk and losing your money. What the hell would your mother say?"

"She'd be mighty disappointed."

"There's a pump on the other side of the stable. Try to get yourself cleaned up, you damned fool child."

I couldn't argue with him about that, so I hauled myself to my feet and I had to steady myself with a hand on the stable walls as I walked around to the pump.

I pumped the handle until I got cool water and I threw it all over my face and hair and I soaked my neck scarf and tied it around my neck. I took a long drink and then splashed water all over me again. I wished I could take my new clothes off and wash the dirt and vomit off, and wash myself as well, but I couldn't do that.

Then the singing angels caught my attention again so I stumbled across the street, struggling to walk a straight line, my brain trying to pound its way out of my skull.

I stood outside the tent watching, and when the singing ended, lo and behold, whoever was leading the services introduced Preacher to the congregation of about a dozen souls. Preacher got up and said his text was from Matthew, and he read from his Bible the verses about the mustard seed.

He put the Bible down and sermonized about how hope and love and mercy and repentance and forgiveness live in all of us, but sometimes they're only the size of a mustard seed because they've been beaten down by life's sorrows, as well as by our own desire for vengeance, and the temptations of the flesh, and the temptations of pride and power and money. But the seeds of those virtues that live within us must be watered by the love of the Lord if they're to grow.

Then he got into how the devil's desires are the size of a mustard seed as well, and slowly he began to hop around and skip and talk in a louder voice and wave his arms around in big gestures, illustrating his words, saying, "Because we give into temptation, we pour water on those evil desires and vines grow from the seeds of those desires and they wrap around our heart and choke it, turning it into a dried-out, unloving, hard heart of stone."

Then he was on the ground and in the air and exhorting people to let the love of the Lord prune those vines away and fill that heart with the waters of redemption so the seeds of the virtues could grow, and people were saying "Hosanna" and "Hallelujah" and "Amen."

Then he pointed at me standing outside the tent and he said, "There, right there, is a young man who has given in to temptation because he is filled with the desire for vengeance as well as the desires of the flesh, but he is now filled with regret and remorse and shame, are you not, young man?"

I was looking around thinking someone else must have showed up and been watching and he was pointing at them, but I realized I was the only one there and it was me he was pointing out, and he was saying, "Look at this young man! This young man is no more than a child but his innocence has not protected him, has it, child?"

And that was the second time I'd been called a child that morning.

I wanted to blurt out, "I'm older than you think" and "You don't know who I really am" and "What about yourself, you hypocrite, gambling and drinking and having your way with whichever one it was last night, and how did I end up in an alley with you anyway?"

But I knew I had to trail a herd to Dodge with him and I figured I'd best keep my mouth shut, and the thought of keeping my mouth shut made me mad and I wanted to backhand him like he'd done me. But now I just wanted to back out of there.

He ran back and forth between the benches, inviting me into the tent and exhorting me to confess my sins, saying there wasn't a one of them sitting there that wasn't a sinner as well, and that included even him. I thought, *Well, at least that's the truth.* Then a gentleman with a beard and a large handlebar mustache, holding his hat in his hand, got to his feet, weeping, and said he wanted to confess his sins. Preacher turned to him and embraced him and led him up to the front, and I backed away as quickly as I could. I turned and I ran as best I could, stumbling all the way back to the livery stable.

I grabbed my saddle and my blanket and bridle and I hauled them out to the corral and whistled for Ghost and she nickered and ambled over to me. I was surprised she responded to me but she seemed to be throwing me a favor, so I bridled her and saddled her and then I let the two of us out through the corral gate. I hauled myself onto the hurricane deck and headed out of town before Preacher could see me and start in on me again.

It felt good to hit the camp even though the day was already blistering hot. I was bathed in sweat, more from the liquor, I guessed, than from the sun, but the cook fire was going by the wagon and Monty had coffee on. The hands were sitting around in the shade of the wagon since the herd wouldn't be moving until the rest of the hands got in.

Shakespeare was on the ground leaning up against his bedroll with his legs stretched out and a tin cup of coffee in his hands, his hat low on his head. He said something about the prodigal and asked why was I back so early, saying, "Did you get chased out of town for raising too much hell?"

The other hands called out, "Did you see the elephant?" or "Did you get all the circus you wanted?" and asked if I'd met Miss Rose and wanted to know who I picked, then laughing at that.

I pulled my saddle and bridle off Ghost and threw them down and Ghost turned and headed for the remuda by herself. Monty pointed to the flapjacks and fried salt pork and biscuits and gravy and coffee. I poured myself a cup and took a biscuit, not knowing if I'd be able to get it down. Even I was aware I needed to be eating something, so I thought I'd give it a try.

I sat down, leaning up against my saddle and stretching out my legs like Shakespeare, tipping my hat over my eyes like him, and I took a sip of the coffee and a bite of the biscuit, and Shakespeare said, "Well?"

With my mouth full I said, "I'm sure Tommy Deuce will tell you all about it."

Then the hands all said things like, "We want some details!" and "You a man now?"

Shakespeare said, "I'd like to hear about it from you, not from Tommy Deuce. Got to be a verrrry interesting story," and the way he said it I kept wondering if he knew something I didn't want him to know.

There wasn't any point dragging it out, so I said, "I spent some time with one of the doves and she bragged to Tommy Deuce about how well I done. Said I wore her out. I drank rye for the first time ever and I got drunk and I lost all my money playing games of chance."

At that the boys all said, "Whooo-eee!" and "Good for you, Kid!" and "Welcome to hard times!"

Shakespeare didn't say anything and I was glad he didn't do to me what I'd done to him, bullyragging him about losing all his money. At the time I'd wanted to reprimand him about drinking as well, and now I was glad I hadn't done that. He didn't ask me any questions about what I'd done with the dove I picked, and again I was sorry I hadn't had a chance to tell her thanks.

The hands left me alone and commenced to talking among themselves about their own adventures, and Shakespeare and I just sat there in silence. I was mad at him all over again because he was fighting back against a smile that made him look like a damned know-it-all. Once again I felt like some kind of a fool kid.

The rest of the hands made it in by early afternoon, most of them the worse for wear and some of them barely staying upright in the saddle. Not too long after they'd got something to eat and changed mounts, Big Mike moved the herd out, reminding us that there was a herd behind us and one in front of us, and if there was a stampede, there'd be hell in Georgia.

Things went smoothly, in spite of the relentless heat. For a day or two a couple of the hands were still in such bad shape they were called greeners because they used both hands to stay in the saddle, or took a spill when their horse got out from under them taking a tight turn to recover a stray.

At night the hands all regaled one another with their prowess with the doves using terrible language I'd never heard before, or bragged on the fortune they'd almost made, or bemoaned what they'd lost, or boasted how much they'd drunk, or vowed it was the straight and narrow from here on out. Preacher reminded them he had told them they were all sinners, and they all chimed in that he was the worst sinner of them all.

One night, when we were on nightguard, I passed Preacher as he was singing hymns and I asked him how I ended up in the alley with him. He said, "Hell, Kid, it was that or let you throw up all over the table."

I still felt like there was something I wasn't remembering and I was mad at myself for drinking so much that I couldn't remember. *You're a damn fool kid*, I told myself over and over.

Another night, when we were sitting around the fire, somebody reminded Shakespeare we hadn't heard the end of that story about the girl disguised as a boy, and for some reason I guess he didn't feel like putting on a show. I swear I caught him throwing a look at me, or maybe I just imagined it because I still didn't know what he knew. "Well, it all ends happy," he said. "The duke discovers she's a girl and he's fallen in love with her even though he thought she was a boy at first … "

At that Jack Straw said, "Now, that's not right!"

Shakespeare ignored him and went on. "So it turns out her twin brother is still alive and didn't drown to death after all, and when Olivia meets the twin brother she falls for him instead because he looks just like the boy who was actually a girl … "

And at that Tommy Deuce said, "This is getting real confusing."

Shakespeare ignored him too. "So the girl who's disguised as a servant boy is off the hook now, and she can reveal herself as a girl who is actually a noblewoman, and she can marry the duke, who realizes he was in love with her all along even though he thought she was a boy, and he isn't interested in Olivia anymore, and it ends with everybody happy, mostly." I swear he threw a look at me again, but in the shadows of the firelight I couldn't be sure.

Then Shady spoke up. "Now, there's a whole lot that ain't right about this story."

Shakespeare just left it all there. "Well, that's how it ends."

I thought that sounded like a bunch of nonsense and it made me mad. It was all so tricky and made up so that it turned out all right for everybody, not like how things happen in real life, so I spoke up. "You can't tell me that son-of-a-bitch twin brother survived the shipwreck. There's no way he could survive that."

Everyone was silent and Shakespeare just looked at me, then he spoke like he was trying to talk me down, as if I had a gun in my hand and was pointing it at someone. He said, "She survived the shipwreck, didn't she? And her twin brother did too. He just washed up on another part of the shore. That's not so hard to believe, is it?"

I said, "That's a bunch of nonsense. Good luck like that don't happen and it's not fair to make everyone believe the twin brother was dead and then suddenly he's alive again."

That was when the stampede hit.

TWENTY-TWO

We heard thunder first, or what sounded like thunder, but coming from behind us. Coffee cups were thrown down and Jack Straw said, "Looks like the lid is off, boys!"

Hats were grabbed and they all hit their saddles. It was too late to get the mules hooked to the wagon to get it out of the way. No one knew which way to take it anyway, and who knew if the mules would have survived if the herd smashed into them.

There was a peculiar high-pitched yell in the dark and Hard Luck Luke Bronson said, "Comanches!" They were hazing the herd behind us into ours, and that meant we would stampede and hit the herd in front of us. There were going to be some seven or eight thousand cow brutes on the run.

Shakespeare called out to me, "The remuda!"

My anger was gone in an instant and we got into the saddle and pulled away from the camp at a run, heading for the remuda to push it away from the stampede. Our cattle started running before the other herd even hit due to all the yelling and the commotion, and everything was moving one way or another.

Shakespeare and I hurrahed the remuda in an easterly direction, then swung them north, keeping the remuda alongside the herd so they would be available to the hands when they needed to change mounts during the run. Once mounted, the hands all pulled away from the herd, knowing there wasn't much they could do to stop what was coming at them, and they needed to get the lay of the land first.

When the herd from behind hit, riders from both outfits tried to turn the herds into a mill, but their efforts went for nothing. Turning the herd now was like trying to keep a flash flood from rolling down a dry wash. All they could do was let the herd run, keep apace, and look out for the herd coming up.

A few miles on they caught up with that herd, and now there were some forty hands from all three outfits on horseback, most of their efforts being spent trying to keep themselves from getting hurt. I told myself that Texas was bad enough, but if this is what hell in Georgia is like, I never wanted to go there.

It was a hot run. The day's heat hadn't let up when the sun went down and everyone was drenched in sweat and hands were coming in to change out mounts that were covered in lather. Dust was in the air and we were all choking on it even with neck scarves up around our faces, our sweat turning the dust on our scarves to mud. In spite of the dust, a full moon made it easier to see the terrain, and moonlight glinted off the clacking horns in some sort of hazy strange beauty.

Hands peeled off when strays spilled out and they tried to drive them back, leaving some behind and hoping the flankers and drags would catch them and drive them back in, but it was like Sally trying to grab the chickens.

The herds ran until dawn. The sun was getting close to breaking through a copper-colored horizon and the three herds must have decided they'd done enough damage and it was time to stop, so they all just stopped. They stood there with their tongues hanging out, looking like the stupid fools they were, thirsty and panting and hot, and all the hands reined up and canvassed each other, counting heads, making sure no one was lost or hurt, riding back along the line and checking on their outfit.

Early in the run when we knew we were clear of the herd behind us, Shakespeare stopped the remuda and cut the mules out and drove them back to Monty while I then trailed the remuda forward. He caught up and said the wagon had escaped being turned over because the longhorns, as dumb as they were, would rather go around something than run into it.

Later, when Monty joined us and was making bait and coffee and everyone was hot and exhausted, Hard Luck Luke Bronson claimed, "Once upon a time my pony gone down and I got caught on foot in front of a stampede. The whole damn herd went around me instead of over me, and it felt like God was protecting me, or angels was surrounding me."

Preacher said, "Now, see, boys? That is what you call the grace of God."

I was still mad about Shakespeare's story so I said, "That sounds about as believable as that twin brother being washed up onshore. If that was true, where was God and his angels when other hands got run down and trampled to death or got hit by lightning or drowned in a river crossing or burned alive by Comanches? For a man called Hard Luck, you were nothing but lucky." I added, "I'll tell you what. The next time we have a stampede why don't you go out front and get off your pony and show us how it works."

Then Hard Luck come at me. "Are you calling me a liar, you little bastard?"

I was so mad I didn't let him scare me. "Yes, I think you're a goddamned liar."

"So are you going to cry about it?"

"You son of a bitch!" But before I could hit him the hands separated both of us, Abraham saying, "Calm down, Bronson, there's no glory in beating up an ignorant child."

Preacher got between us, arms outstretched, but he said to me, "You got a problem, Kid. You don't believe in the grace of the Lord."

"To hell with your belief and your Lord and your grace, Preacher. You're a fucking hypocrite."

Then he came at me too and grabbed me by the collar. "I am a sinner but I believe."

"A lot of good it does what with you getting drunk and fucking a dove. Some kind of a believer you are, having it both ways."

And then he went to backhand me like he'd done before.

Now everyone grabbed at the two of us and pulled us away, saying to back off, and Jack Straw chimed in, "Now, that is no way to be talking about the Lord!" and Abraham told Preacher I was just a child who didn't know what he was saying, and for everyone to shut up.

Preacher still struggled to grab me and I tried to kick him, but the hands held the two of us back or got between us and yelled at both of us. Then Big Mike rode up and said, "What in hell is going on?"

Everyone fell quiet, and the next thing I knew, Preacher and me were standing alongside each other facing Big Mike.

No one knew what to say at first, so I said, "I started it," and I added, "I told Preacher his sermonizing was so bad it started the stampede."

Everyone was quiet and looking at the two of us, and then Preacher said, "He's lying, boss. The Kid said he admired my sermonizing and wished he could believe like me. I said there was hope for him yet but I just wished his singing was better, and I told him it was his singing that started the stampede. Then he got all riled up at the truth being spoken because he's a heathen who can't stand the truth. I pray for him every day, boss, just like I pray for all of these sinners here, and I pray for you too, boss."

No one said anything and Big Mike knew we were both lying. He just looked at the two of us but he knew better than to call us on it, so he dismounted and said, "Thanks for the prayers, Preacher," but the way he said it I didn't think he was sincere.

He changed the topic, saying he had talked to the other trail bosses and the trail boss behind us admitted the Comanches had stopped his herd and demanded cattle for safe passage, but he'd told them he was sure they already had plenty of cattle and they could all go to hell. So the Comanches waited until dark and then stampeded his herd, and they were now probably driving home quite a sizable bunch, more than they would have gotten if he had just gone ahead and paid the toll, like we had done, and the herd in front of us had done, earlier in the day.

Big Mike poured himself some coffee and said we were going to be there for a week or more sorting the three herds out, much less recovering all the strays that had spilled out over miles of prairie, then separating them out as well. He said after everyone got some bait and had changed mounts, Abraham was to divide the hands in half. One half would stay and work with the other crews sorting the cattle here, and the other half were to spread out and work backward, driving in strays. He reminded them they could all rest when winter came.

Then without even looking at me, he told Abraham, "Put Shakespeare with one of the two crews. The Kid is to stay here and wrangle the remuda by himself and help Monty."

I spoke up. "How come I can't cut the herd or look for strays as well?"

"Good God, someone has to watch the remuda, don't they? Aren't you the youngest and most inexperienced one here? Don't you realize we're surrounded by fucking Comanches who want your ass? I'm trying to save your goddamn butt when I really wish I'd given them you and your whole goddamned herd for all the trouble you've caused."

Then he looked at Preacher and said, "Sorry, Preacher."

Preacher said, "No offense, boss. The Lord understands and forgives, all that's asked is remorse."

I was glad Big Mike hadn't hit me, but with the way everyone was looking at me he might as well have. I told myself, *Things just keep getting worse and worse.*

I swallowed my coffee and without saying a word I got on Ghost and rode out to the remuda, pulled off my saddle and bridle, and turned her loose. I roped Blood and saddled him up and got aboard, then just sat there while the remuda grazed, waiting for the hands to come out and change their mounts. I tried to figure out how I could make things better but couldn't come up with anything.

The hands come out one at a time, but most of them ignored me or were just too exhausted to talk and just stuck to business, turning their tired mounts loose and saddling up a fresh mount.

Shakespeare come out after a while carrying a tin plate of bait and I said, "What's that?"

"Food," he said. "You didn't eat anything."

"Maybe I didn't want anything. I'm not a child, you know."

He just shook his head. "You're as stubborn as a blue-eyed burro."

"Is that another Shakespeare quote?"

"Shut up and eat something," he said. "It's going to be a long, hard day."

I was starving but I took the plate like I didn't care, and while he roped a fresh mount and saddled it and wasn't looking, I stuffed the bait down.

He rode over to me and he nodded to the remuda. "Don't let them get away from you." As he rode away he shouted back, "You can take that empty plate of bait you didn't want back to Monty!"

He rode off laughing and holding one hand high in the air as if he was victorious over something, and it made me mad all over again, him thinking he was so clever.

Shady was one of the last ones to come out and he was always real friendly, so I tried to make conversation while he reeled in his roan, hoping some one of the hands might not be holding a grudge against me for the way I'd talked. I knew earlier in the day some Comanche warriors had shown up and demanded a toll, so I asked him about the parley.

As he was saddling up, he told me they'd wanted too many cattle for safe passage and Big Mike had offered them only three or four, telling them they had a toll from the herd in front of us and they'd get a toll from the herd behind us, and that was all the cattle they could handle. Besides, Big Mike had told them, if they caused trouble there were some forty-five hands between all three herds, and we'd come after them. Shady went on to say they were all resentful at first, but Big Mike wouldn't give in. He said, "I didn't know if we'd get away with it because that red-sashed son of a bitch was tough as nails."

I said, "Red sash?"

"Sure enough. He was that same one I gave my sash to weeks ago to soften him up, remember? And he was in that crowd at the fort when you shot Paint, remember? Big Mike told him he couldn't go riding all over the country charging a toll again and again just to cross land that wasn't even theirs, and he shouldn't be charging us twice because we'd made a deal the first time. That made him mad. Most of them act real friendly like they want you to think they need a favor real bad, or that you should be grateful they only want so few steers, but this one acted like he was spoiling for a fight."

"And he was wearing that red sash you gave him some time back?"

"Yeah, same one." He put on his bridle and tightened the girth on his saddle.

"How many of them was there?"

"Three," he said, "but there could be larger raiding parties around somewhere. You never know."

When he was mounted up he gave me a salute, and then he was off.

I stood there like I'd been hit by a pole. When I come around to myself, I started thinking through plans as to what I should do. My first thought was to go to Big Mike and ask for some hands to track Red-Sash back to One-Eye, but I could only imagine him saying, Sure, we've got a mess on our hands here, but why don't you take half the crew and get them all killed by stumbling into a Comanche village that's refused to come live on a reservation.

Then I thought I could secretly ask some of the hands to join me, but I knew no Texas puncher would leave the herd like that, specially knowing we were on a fool's errand, riding into a hostile village with nothing to trade for a little girl, even if we could find the village.

Then I thought it was all too big of a mess for me to handle and I shouldn't do anything, just let One-Eye and Sally go. I tried to convince myself that Sally might have been sold or traded off quite a while back to Mexicans or the Apache, so even if I found the village, it'd all be for nothing if she wasn't there, so what was the point? But that just made me mad at myself for being such a quitter.

And then the thought came to me, *At least you can kill One-Eye.*

And that thought felt good.

It was a start. *You tracked them down before*, I told myself, *you can do it again. Red-Sash can lead you to One-Eye, and you can at least kill the son of a bitch who stole your sister. You'll get killed doing it, but maybe that wouldn't be so bad.*

When I was sure everybody had been out to the remuda to get a fresh mount, I checked my saddlebags for the shells to my Schofield and the Spencer, then I rode back to the wagon and thanked Monty for the bait and washed off my plate. I put some extra biscuits and dried apples in my saddle bags, telling him I expected to be out with the remuda for the rest of the day. I climbed into the wagon and stole some airtight tins of sardines, and from my kit I took the braided rawhide reins I had taken from the Comanche ponies.

When I mounted up, Monty looked at my weapons and I said, "Just in case," and he turned back to his kettles, stoking the fire and peeling potatoes.

When I got back to the remuda, I roped in Dancer and Ghost and put the reins on them, then checked that I was in the clear.

Leading the two horses, I left the remuda.

I knew they would stay bunched together and graze, and I felt bad about what Big Mike and all the hands would think of me, but I had reached the point that I didn't care. I figured since I'd lost everything, to include their good opinion, it didn't matter to me what else I lost, and if I got killed looking for One-Eye, then Big Mike could sell my herd and do whatever he wanted to with the money.

I felt bad about leaving Shakespeare behind. As mad as I got at him, I still wanted to tell him who I was and ask him if he had figured anything out about me. I wanted to know what his real name was and I wanted to tell him my real name, and I wanted to know if he had any feelings for me. That thought felt stupid because that would be like the so-called servant boy asking that duke if he cared for her, or him, and the duke would think that was a strange enough question, what with the servant being a boy, or so he thought. It was all too confusing, but in my heart I said good-bye to Shakespeare because I had misgivings about how this was all going to turn out. I was pretty sure I'd never see him again.

I couldn't see any other path, and if I wasn't going to get Sally back, then at least I wanted to stand over One-Eye's dead body, and to hell with whatever happened next.

I rode north first. If I had gone around to the rear there would have been too many hands out trailing in strays, so I figured north would be safer. If I could circle around in front of the main herd, I could then ride southwesterly and hope to cut Red-Sash's trail.

Blood and Dancer and Ghost rode hard and fast and I crossed spring creeks that come out of nowhere in the prairie and I'd stop and water them and switch mounts to keep them as fresh as possible. As hot as it was, there was a wind blowing and every chance

I could I threw water on my face and in my hair and I soaked my neck scarf, and that made things just a little bit cooler until the sun and the wind dried me off. No matter how shallow the creek was, I was always surprised by how cold the water was.

The prairie grasses were all sorts of shades of green, some fading and curing and turning the color of wheat. The grasses blew like waves I'd seen on the gulf, and there were blue cornflowers and yellow sunflowers and purple verbena and red and orange and white flowers whose names I didn't know, all of them in among the stirrup-high grasses.

We rode for hours like that and I began to feel how alone I was, out there on the rolling prairie by myself, and the feeling grew and grew. It was as if the emptiness of the prairie had weight to it and the great emptiness was pressing in from all sides. The blue skies and the towering white clouds and the colorful flowers seemed like signs of loss, not hope or happiness or joy, and I kept trying to remember during what part of his journey did Christian feel like this in *Pilgrim's Progress.*

"It's the Dark River you're in now," Ma said. "You must climb out."

"It's a pretty deep river, " I said, "and the banks are high."

"You could drown there," she said.

It all tumbled together and I could only remember that Christian seemed to make mistake after mistake, and then I felt like my whole life was some sort of mistake, that I was a mistake, and I knew for sure it was all going to end in death and disaster.

I reined up.

I sat there on Dancer and even he was still, as if he was waiting for me to make a decision about which way we would go. I wasn't hot anymore and even the wind had stopped blowing and the grasses were still and the flowers didn't have color and there weren't any butterflies flitting around, and no birds flew up from us being too close to their nests. I closed my eyes and I could feel the breath fall in and out of me, and I heard my own heart beat, and I imagined it stopping, my blood no longer flowing, my breath gone.

And then I heard Ma's voice again, still and small from somewhere deep inside me, and she asked, "What's my name?"

I was bewildered at the question. Why would she be asking me that when she knew very well what her own name was, and she knew that I knew what her name was, so why was she asking me?

Then I heard her ask again, "What's my name?"

So I said her name out loud.

"Grace."

And it didn't sound like my own voice coming out of me, it sounded like someone else's voice, but it was my voice, and I said it again, "Grace," and suddenly a killdeer burst out of the grass to lead me away from its nest and Dancer spooked and began to prance around and the flowers suddenly had color and there was a wind rippling the grasses, and the shadow of some giant ship of a cloud sailed past me. The sun was hot, blazing like an oven, like it said in Malachi, and I was covered in sweat, and the sweat felt wet and slick and good.

I steadied Dancer and I reached under my shirt and I untied the band from around my breasts and I said, "I am who I am."

I threw the band into the wind and it whipped away, carried like a bloody flag lost by some long-forgotten army. I said to myself, *If you can find One-Eye you can find his camp, and if you can find his camp, Sally will be there.*

I found their trail just a few yards on from where I'd stopped.

TWENTY-THREE

The grass was trampled down and the earth was churned up and it was clear they had a sizable number of cattle they were trailing. They knew it was unlikely they would be tracked because the hands would be too tied up sorting the herds out and driving in strays to go looking for them, especially not knowing how many Comanches there were and what direction they were headed. It had taken me quite a while to cut their trail, and the Comanche knew no trail boss could afford to send out a war party to cut for sign, track them down, and then enter into a battle to get the beeves back.

I hoped they were feeling cocky or arrogant at their success and wouldn't be paying much attention to anything coming up from behind them, but I reminded myself, they were warriors and they'd have an eye out in every direction, particularly toward their rear. I'd best not underestimate them.

They were headed in a northwesterly direction, but more west than north, so I swung wide to the northern side and moved off their trail and rode fast, keeping the other two mounts close to my right side. I edged in westerly until I cut their trail again, making sure they hadn't changed direction on me and gone south, then I swung back out to stay as far away from them as I could.

The prairie rolled and swelled but there wasn't any high hills or mesas like when I'd first tracked them, and there wasn't any copses of trees I could hide in like I'd done before, just a cottonwood or a sycamore now and again. I knew there was more of a chance they might see me before I saw them, so I kept my eyes on the horizon for dust from the cattle. If I found them I could then judge how to approach them, or how far back I needed to stay to track them to their camp.

I'd pull one of the ponies up alongside me while we were running and I'd slide out of the saddle and onto that pony, riding bareback, then later doing the same thing with the next one. When I could I'd stop under a cottonwood, then stand on the pony's back and reach up and grab a branch, hoisting myself up and climbing as high as I could, but I still couldn't see anything, so I'd climb down and ride on, keeping a sharp eye out. The last thing I wanted to do was ride right into them.

I thought about what I was going to do when I found them, and it dawned on me that because the Comanches had a long striking distance, they might be weeks away from their main camp, and I didn't have enough food to last me that long in order to track them for a far distance. Then like a fool I realized, if One-Eye wasn't in the camp for me to kill, I didn't have anything to bargain with for Sally, nothing to trade for her, and no money to purchase her in case I did find her.

At that thought, I pulled up. I realized I didn't know what I was doing, and I had boxed myself into a corner.

You've done it again, I thought. *You were too angry and too eager to think clearly and you were the arrogant one, thinking just because you whipped them before you could do it again, not realizing the first time you were more lucky than clever. Now your luck may be about to run out. Even if you come up on them and are lucky enough to kill them, you still don't know where their camp is, and you've gone and trapped yourself out in the middle of nowhere.*

I wished I had Shakespeare or Pa to ask, What should I do?

And I knew what they'd say.

Turn around.

I looked back to where I'd come from, and as bad as I wanted to go back, I couldn't do it. I didn't want to go crawling back to

Big Mike and apologize for leaving the remuda and have him yell at me for being a damned fool and what was I thinking? And I didn't want the hands looking at me like I was the fool kid I now knew I was.

And, oh, by the way, now that the band is gone from around my chest, I'm a girl.

So I told myself, *Just go a little farther and see what you can see. Maybe their camp is closer than you think, and you can then ride for help,* even though I didn't have any idea what direction help would be. *And if they discover you,* I told myself, *maybe you can get one shot off and at least kill Red-Sash, and if they come after you, maybe you can outrun them. Go a little farther and at least see how many of them there are.*

Just go a little farther, I told myself.

I moved more carefully now, feeling scared and knowing I was doing something more dangerous than what I should be doing. I remembered how Jamie dared me to walk out on the long branch of a live oak like he had done, higher up than either of us should be. The branch got thinner and thinner and swayed from both the breeze and my weight. I felt sick in the pit of my stomach because I knew I could get hurt, but I didn't want him thinking there was anything he could do that I couldn't do. I knew, in my heart, I could break my arm or my leg or my neck if I fell, but I had to do it even though I wanted to throw up and cry because I was so scared. I did it because I didn't want him thinking I was a coward. I figured it would be better to be hurt or dead than to be thought that. And Jamie yelled at me, "Go just a little farther, that's it, you're going to make it, you're doing fine, just a little farther."

And if Ma or Pa had seen us they would have raised holy hell and Ma would have said, "*Dummkopf!* If Jamie jumped into a fire would you do that?"

And now here I was, going out just a little bit farther and farther, and below me the fire was blazing.

It was Dancer that gave me away.

I was back to riding Blood now and leading Dancer and Ghost. There was a swell in front of us, just a gentle rise. I had crossed back in to check on their trail and I'd found it but I didn't hear any cattle lowing or bawling, or probably I was so lost in my thoughts I wasn't listening, so I figured they were still a ways ahead of me. All of a sudden Dancer gave a loud whinny. He began neighing and snorting and prancing all about like he was excited about something, and he whinnied some more, and then there was an answering whinny far ahead of me, and I knew I was in trouble.

Dancer jerked hard and pulled at the rawhide rein in my hand. I couldn't keep a grip on it, and in the excitement Blood pranced and called out as well, and then Dancer pulled loose and took out running, straight up the trail we'd cut across, as if he knew he was back with his old remuda and had missed them all along.

Only Ghost stayed calm, but she shifted and turned as if she knew we ought to get out of there. As I pulled Ghost in and got a better grip on her reins, I looked up, watching Dancer go, and there they were in front of me, three Comanches coming over the rise.

They only stopped for a moment to take us in. They saw Dancer but ignored him, saw me sitting out there in the wide open, then they whooped and hollered and screamed that chilling "Hi-yi-yi-yi-yi!" and took off at a dead run, fogging straight for me.

I spurred Blood and yelled at him and we took off, Ghost following by my side, all of us running hard. I had never put Blood to the test like I had Buck, but he moved now like he was born to run, and Ghost kept apace. I rode low in the saddle and leaned forward, putting my weight where Blood could use it best. I talked to him, and my heart beat so fast I thought it was going to explode. I don't know if I was breathing or not, I only knew I was falling, falling from that branch I'd gone too far out on, and any minute I was going to hit hard.

I wished I was on Buck and could rein him up and yell, "Down!" and take a steady shot over his saddle, but I hadn't taught that trick to Blood. I thought about reining up and taking the best shot I could with the Spencer, but I knew I'd be too unsteady to be accurate. If I missed I didn't want to give them a chance to gain any ground on me, and I knew my best chance was to just outrun them. I thought about pulling the Schofield and firing back as we ran, but I knew the shots would be wild. Even if I had wanted to do that, I would have to drop Ghost away in order to use a free hand, and I couldn't bring myself to let her go, as if her being near me provided some sort of safety.

You've got two horses, I told myself, *you can outrun them.*

So I told Blood to run, and I tried not to think about what they'd do to me if they caught up with me. Out of the corner of my eye I saw a cloud that looked like an overturned wagon and the last thing I wanted was to be burned alive. I remembered Jamie and I would talk at night and we'd ask each other, "How would you rather die? Drown or be burned to death?" I always told him I'd rather drown because maybe it would be quicker and less painful than being burned alive, even though choking to death underwater sounded awful. I thought, *If they catch me, maybe they'll just shoot me or cut my throat*, and then I thought, *No, they'll take me back as a trophy and they'll burn me alive with everyone watching and taunting me.*

I told myself to quit thinking that way, to just run and pray, and at that I almost had to laugh because I found myself saying, *Oh dear God, don't let them catch me. Dear God, let me survive this and I'll always be grateful and I'll do whatever you want.* I realized now I was so desperate I had to talk to God, because it didn't look like there was anything else that was going to save me.

It was then I heard a crack. I thought maybe somewhere near me a tree branch had broken, but there weren't any trees around.

Then I heard a crack again and I realized one of the Comanches was firing at me, that he had a Winchester or a Spencer or a Henry or some such, and then I heard another crack and I felt Blood stumble. He regained his stride, then he stumbled again, and I knew he was hit and he was struggling to keep going.

Then there Ghost was, pulling up alongside me, as close to me as she could get, as if I had talked horse to her and asked for help, as if I'd said, "My kingdom for a horse," and she had understood me, and there she was. At a dead run I climbed off Blood, dropping his reins. I climbed onto Ghost and I was riding bareback now and hanging on tight, my legs squeezing Ghost as hard as I could and one hand free to grab her mane as well.

Just as I got off Blood there was another crack and Blood screamed and went down, tumbling in the prairie grass. I wanted to stop and put a bullet in his brain but I couldn't do it and I was sick at heart at having to leave him like that, but Ghost and I had to run.

Ghost was fast, faster than Blood and moving like a gray shadow over the prairie. I realized I had never used her for much of anything except to nightguard, the hands saying that Appaloosas were clear-footed even over rocky ground, so I figured she'd be best for nightriding and she'd be reliable if there was a stampede. I began to talk to her, telling her I was sorry I hadn't talked to her before because I'd missed Buck too much to make friends with her. If she got me out of this, I told her, I'd talk to her forever.

And at that thought I felt like someone had slammed me in the back with a club, but I hadn't heard a crack, and the pain was sharp and terrible. I struggled to hang on but I couldn't and I dropped the reins and I lost my grip on her mane and I felt myself falling and falling, only it was as if I was falling real slow. As I fell, I could smell Ghost's sweat and hide and the leather of her reins and I could smell the prairie grasses and I saw towering white clouds and all their shapes, and the sky around them was just the brightest blue, and the colors of the wildflowers never seemed so bright.

Then I hit hard and I felt like my whole body must have broken. I couldn't stop myself from rolling and every time I rolled my arms and legs were everywhere, and I didn't even know if they were still attached to my body. As I rolled I felt this killing pain in my back, sure it was broken now, and I didn't think I'd ever be able to get up again. The wind was knocked out of me and I couldn't suck anything in, and I thought, *So this is what it is to drown and not be able to get a breath.*

I ended up facedown and it seemed like forever before the breath come back into me with a gasp, but in spite of the pain of the fall and the terror and agony of not breathing again, I found myself looking at ants and grasshoppers crawling in the grasses. I could see roots and leaves, and I swear there was a bluebonnet near me. I thought, *How can that be? It's too late in the summer and we're too far north.*

Then I heard "Hi-yi-yi-yi-yi!" and I knew they were almost on me. No one was firing at me, and that meant they had more in mind for me than just killing me.

I prayed again, saying, *Dear God, please let them kill me fast, let it be over with quickly. Tell Sally I'm sorry I lost her, tell Shakespeare I have feelings for him, tell Big Mike I'm sorry I left the herd, tell Ma and Pa I'm sorry I didn't come up to help, tell Jamie I love him.*

I found myself wondering where Ghost was, and then there she was. When I had fallen she must have pulled up and trotted back, and now she was standing over me and I could see her reins. I thought, *If I can just grab her reins I'll feel her strength come down into me. Even though it feels like my back is broken, I'll be able to get up and remount her and ride on.*

But I couldn't move. I couldn't grab them. I kept looking at her reins and thinking, *Dear God, let me hold her reins in my hand, let me hang on to something.*

Dear God, save me.

Dear God, I'm sorry.

And then they were on me.

The first one to me screamed that high-pitched scream and I couldn't tell if he was celebrating or angry or trying to scare me or just calling the others over, but he began kicking me and he kicked me in the face and he kicked me in the shoulder. I didn't want to scream but I couldn't help myself. I tried to curl up to protect myself, but then he kicked me in the back and the butt and in the legs, and then he knelt down and rolled me onto my back, lifting me up and slamming me into the ground hard for good measure. Where I had been hit or clubbed it hurt like nothing I'd ever felt before.

Then there were more of them and they dismounted and gathered around me and one of them was wearing a red sash. They called out what sounded like words but I couldn't understand them, and I was trying as best I could to protect my face from their blows.

Even though I was hurt too badly to stand, one of them yanked me up hard, pulled me up to my feet, and with one hand he backhanded me. When I fell back, his other hand was holding on to my shirt and it ripped open and tore away, and when I fell to the ground they saw I was a girl, and they yelled and whooped and hollered and laughed and celebrated their discovery. I was covered in blood from the injuries to both my back and my face and I hoped I would bleed to death before things got even worse.

One of them held my arms down, pinning me down on my back. Another one pulled off my boots and leggings and the other grabbed my trousers and started pulling them off of me. I wept and kicked, trying to stop them, and I screamed, "Get away! Get the fuck off of me!" That made them laugh and shout even more, and the pain in my back tore through me like wildfire, and I screamed a sound I didn't even know could come out of me, but it only seemed to make them more excited.

As I struggled against them I choked and gagged and I threw up as we fought and it got all over my face. I kept wishing they'd just put a bullet in my brain like I'd done to Paint, or like Shakespeare had done to Buck, and maybe if they did that to me there'd be light and sweet smells and everything would be clean and soft and there'd be no shame or rage, and there'd be glory, whatever glory was, or maybe there'd be joy, or nothing, but that nothing would be better than this, so I prayed one more time.

Dear God, please have mercy.

Dear God, let there be a bullet.

I heard the faint, sharp sound of a cracking tree branch again, and one grunted and dropped, falling on me, and I was pinned to the earth by the full weight of his body. I could smell the earth and the grass and I could smell his sweat and his breath and his hair and I could smell my own blood and vomit, and from the one lying on me I felt something warm and wet seeping all over my body.

There were more cracks and more cracks, and one of them fell right beside me, the back half of his brain blown away. He was still and open-eyed and stared straight at me, seeing God knows what in me, and then there were more cracks and I was hit with another weight. I couldn't breathe, two of them on me now, and I tried to crawl out from under the weight of the two but the weight was too heavy and there was too much pain and I couldn't use my hands or feet to crawl. I felt as if I was being buried alive, and I wondered why they had all fallen.

TWENTY-FOUR

Then there were horses' hooves around me and I heard horses chuffing and neighing and breathing hard. I thought the rest of the band must be showing up now, only the words I heard I could understand and they called me Kid, and the weight was pulled off me. When the last one was dragged off I could see he was wearing a red sash, and there I was in the grass, covered in blood and vomit with only a torn shirt barely on and a scarf around my neck and my trousers down around my ankles.

And there was Shakespeare, kneeling down close. I thought I was dreaming, or this was what death was like in some strange afterworld, only he said, "We're here, Kid, we're here. You're going to be OK. Can you hear me, Kid? Are you OK?"

I was in the here and now and I was half-naked and bloody and I didn't care because I was saved.

I whispered to him, "I'm a girl."

"Yeah," he said, "I've known about that a while now." Then he leaned in real close and he whispered to me, "Though she be but little, she is fierce, right?"

I wanted to kiss him and say, *I'm alive, I'm alive, I'm alive,* but I couldn't move.

Someone pulled my trousers up and straightened me out and then rolled me over so I was flat on my belly. I heard Big Mike's voice from the other side of me and he said, "That needs to come out now." He knelt down and my shirt was pulled the rest of the way off.

He said, "Hang on, Kid, this is going to hurt."

Shakespeare grabbed my hand and Big Mike had one hand on my back and then with the other he began to pull at something in my shoulder, and I was trying to scream but no sound would come out.

He pulled again and then he said, "It's hard to get a grip."

I heard Shady's voice, saying, "Use this," and he threw Big Mike something.

Shakespeare said, "You've got an arrow in you, Kid. It's been driven pretty deep into your shoulder blade and the shaft's broken off."

Big Mike must have gotten a better grip on what remained of the shaft and he pulled and I groaned some ungodly sound that embarrassed me, some kind of an animal noise. Then I managed to scream, "Oh dear God," only my throat was so raw from the screaming when I was attacked that I had a hard time getting the words out.

I grabbed at Shakespeare's hand and grabbed at the grass with the other, and there that same bluebonnet was, right next to me.

Big Mike pulled forever and it felt like he was pulling my whole shoulder out of my body and it was never going to come out. It was like being on fire and I thought, *So this is what it's like to be burned alive. Yes, I'm right,* I thought, *drowning would be better than this.* When I figured I was about to die from the pain, the arrow was out.

I heard Tommy Deuce's voice. "Put this on it," and he tossed Big Mike something.

Big Mike said, "You ain't supposed to have this."

"Well, use it anyway," Tommy Deuce said. "Medicinal purposes only."

Big Mike said, "I'll bet," and something cold splashed on my back. I could smell whiskey, and then the fire was back, burning deep into my shoulder. I remembered Ma reading from the Bible, saying it would be fire next time, and I thought, *This must be it, this is the fire they're talking about.* I felt like I was being hollowed out from the inside by flames.

I began to weep and Shakespeare said, "It's going to be OK, Kid."

"She's losing a lot of blood," Big Mike said, and whatever he had used to grip the arrow with he wadded up and held it to the wound, pressing down hard.

Tommy Deuce must not have seen what Big Mike and Shakespeare saw. He said, "She? She?"

I croaked out, "Get him away from me."

Shakespeare and Big Mike both said, "Get back, clear off," but Tommy Deuce kept yelling, "She? What the fuck are you talking about?"

I heard Shady tell him, "The Kid's a girl, Tommy Deuce."

Tommy Deuce said, "What? That's not possible!"

Shakespeare yelled at him to shut up.

They rolled me over, Big Mike pressing into my shoulder with one hand. I looked down and I was covered in my own blood as well as the blood of the Comanches.

Tommy Deuce asked, "Is that the truth? He's a her? Are you sure? How could that be?" Then he edged closer, saying, "You sure had me fooled, Kid. Should we still call you Kid? You got a name you want us to call you by?"

Shakespeare said, "For God's sake, shut the fuck up, Tommy Deuce!"

I felt ashamed at being found naked and dirty and bloody and messy, as if I had just been pulled straight up out of the earth, as if I had just been born, like Sally looked when she first come out, bloody and messy, and I just wanted to crawl back into the earth. I couldn't do anything to hide myself, so I turned my head away and shut my eyes.

I heard Shady say, "Put this on the wound."

Big Mike said, "What is that?"

"Prickly pear cactus. I scraped the needles off and split it open. It's good medicine, it'll help."

Big Mike said, "If you say so." He took the wadded up cloth away and pressed the prickly pear to the wound and it felt cool for a moment.

He told Shakespeare, "Tie it on with this." I looked, and while he held the prickly pear to the wound in my back he handed Shakespeare the bloody band I had thrown to the wind.

I managed to ask, "Where did you get that?"

Big Mike said, "That's how we found you."

Shakespeare put my left forearm tight up against my chest to keep it from moving, then he wrapped the band around my arm and my chest and my back, holding the prickly pear in place as well, keeping it all tight as he tied it off.

So I'm back to being bound, I thought, and it seemed funny to me, I don't know why, though I couldn't find it in me to laugh.

They put my good arm in my sleeve and wrapped my shirt around me and Shakespeare buttoned it up as best he could, saying, "How're you doing, Kid?"

I croaked out, "I'm alive, aren't I?"

"You sure are," he said. "Only the dead stay down. Right?"

Someone gave him a canteen and he gave me a drink and washed my face off as best he could.

Tommy Deuce asked the other hands, "Did you know about this? Did you know the Kid was a girl?"

I heard Abraham's voice for the first time. "Fooled me."

"Beats me," Shady said. "I thought he was some tough little kid."

"She's tough all right," Big Mike said, "but dumb as hell." He might as well have backhanded me again, but I knew he was right.

Big Mike held out the metal arrow with the broken shaft, and the arrow had a barb on it. He said, "You might want to keep this." Fingering the barb he said, "You're lucky it didn't get between your ribs. That barb is why it was so hard to pull out. It was driven in deep and it tore you up pretty bad."

I was too weak to take it but Shakespeare took it and put it in his vest pocket and said, "I'll keep it for you. Something to remember today by, right?"

As if I was in the mood for jokes.

Big Mike said to kill their horses and there were gunshots and screams and more gunshots and it seemed a waste. Abraham asked if they were going to look for the cattle and Big Mike said, "No, let them go. They'll only slow us down, and who knows, we might run into another raiding party."

Someone put my hat on me and someone else rode back and shot Blood and pulled my saddle off of him and was cinching it to Ghost. I whispered to Shakespeare, "Put her reins in my hand."

"You're in no condition to ride," he said.

"I don't want to ride, I want to hold her reins."

He put the braided rawhide in my good hand and I held it as they put my boots on me, and I spoke horse to her and told her I was sorry. Ghost just said, "I'm here," and I said, "Thank you," and she said, "You're welcome," and I could feel her strength through the reins.

Now the heat of the sun felt good no matter how hot it was. As I was helped to my feet I remembered to look for the bluebonnet I'd seen, but I couldn't find it anywhere, and that confused me. I knew I'd seen it, but it wasn't there, and how could that be? But I did see that the sky was like blue fire, the bluest blue I'd ever seen, and as I looked around I saw the prairie earth heave and roll and swell, and it all looked alive, as if the earth was rising and falling, as if it was breathing. *The earth is alive*, I thought, *it's breathing, and so am I. Alive and breathing.*

Shakespeare was aboard his mount and he reached down and held a hand out to me and I grabbed it. His hand was hard and strong and the boys hoisted me up behind him. He seemed taller than I remembered and his whole body was all muscle hard. He turned and smiled at me, his eyes the same color as the blue fire sky, and I wished I could pull his hat off and run my hands through his hair and look for copper.

Abraham took Shakespeare's riata and tied me to Shakespeare, knowing I didn't have the strength to hang on for the long ride by myself, looping it around my waist and Shakespeare's several times and then tying it off. I leaned into Shakespeare's back and it was all solid and wet with sweat and smelling like him, and I found myself wondering how he felt about me, knowing I was a girl. Even though my whole body was aching with pain, it felt good to be that close to him, and my heart pounded so hard in my chest that I was sure he could feel it through his back.

Big Mike said, "Let's get the hell out of here."

And at that we were moving across the prairie as fast as thunder rolling off a mountain.

It was a rough ride and the horses were pushed hard and I could feel blood draining down my back in spite of the band and the prickly pear. We'd stop at a spring creek and water the horses and Abraham would come over and make me drink as much as I could, saying, "Get this in you, Kid." I just wanted to stop and lie in the creek and let water wash over me and go to sleep in the coolness, but then we'd be off again, moving at a dead run.

The rough riding made my whole body ache and there wasn't any place that they hadn't hit or kicked. I hurt so bad I must have passed out, and then I came to and the sun was going down and we were still riding.

Big Mike pushed the horses hard but they were Texas mustangs, ranahans all of them, just like the hands themselves, and none of them faltered and none of them quit. I knew they'd run themselves to death if that was asked of them, so I prayed for the ponies to hold up and they did, and my prayers for the pain to stop were answered because now I mostly just felt numb.

We rode into the camp late at night. The hands got to their feet and Hard Luck Luke Bronson untied me from Shakespeare and I fell into his and Monty's arms. They carried me to the wagon and Bill pulled my bedroll out and helped to lay me down, and then Monty was over me with a wet rag and calling out for more water.

Big Mike told him about the arrow and told him I was a girl and Monty just said, "*Sí, sí.*" I couldn't tell if he meant he understood about the wound, or if he knew I was a girl all along.

All the hands gathered around and the word spread that I was a girl. Big Mike told them, "Leave her alone."

I could hear voices saying, "Her? Her?"

The other hands explained what they'd discovered and Monty began to take off my clothes but I clutched them to me. He said, "No, no, is OK, I have daughters." I figured there was no way I wasn't going to be embarrassed, so I might as well get it over with.

He undressed me and washed me all over and called out that he needed more prickly pear, then he covered me with my sougan and he went into the wagon and came back a few minutes later with some kind of cloth for my shoulder, a flour sack or a gunny sack, and an onion poultice for the wound. He placed the prickly pear on the wound over the onion mixture, then put the folded sack over that, then bound it all on with my bloody band again.

Bill tossed him some clothes and he and Monty dressed me, gave me more water to drink, then they rolled me onto my good side and Monty told me, "You rest now."

I whispered, "Thank you," and then he leaned down and he whispered, "Hey, I knew you girl all along, you no fool me. You tough girl. You call me you need something, OK?" Bill was standing there too but I was too embarrassed to speak to him or look him in the eyes.

I was left alone and the other hands stayed away. I found myself thinking about *Pilgrim's Progress* and thinking Christian had made so many bad decisions on his journey to the Celestial City, and I tried to figure out which valley or slough or river I was in now, like Christian. But I did know I was talking to God again. When I had asked for a bullet, one had come, but it hadn't come like I thought it would, and wasn't that just like God. You ask him to come sit by your fireplace but he shows up in the shed, and I wished he'd make it all a little easier. I felt bad for doubting him and deserting him, but I still didn't understand how it all worked. It was as much a mystery as it ever was. I was grateful the bullet had come, but I didn't understand why I got saved and others didn't. I'm sure Scotty prayed not to get hit by lightning, and when Cliff was underwater I'm sure he begged for salvation, and surely Ma and Pa and Jamie did too. None of it made sense and certainly none of it was fair, but I was grateful.

Shakespeare came and he threw down his bedroll next to mine. He kicked off his boots and he stretched out, lying on one side, and looked at me. He said, "How're you doing, Kid?"

"Does my face look as bad as it feels?"

He reached out to touch me but I pulled away, and he said, "It looks like you spent a little time in a back alley, but look at it this way, Kid, the other guys look even worse."

"I suppose so," I said.

He rolled onto his back and looked up at the stars. "You're going to be OK, Kid." And he said again, "Remember. Only the dead stay down."

He went to sleep looking at the stars, and I went to sleep looking at him.

The next morning when I woke up Shakespeare was gone, and I was in so much pain I could barely move. Monty came and got me to my feet and we hobbled away from the camp so I could relieve myself, then he brought me back. He gave me coffee and helped me to eat some beans and biscuits, and they all would have tasted good except I had a hard time opening my mouth and chewing.

While he was feeding me I mumbled between mouthfuls, "You said you have daughters?" He nodded, and I asked, "Where are they?"

He shrugged, "Apaches take them."

"I'm sorry."

"That's when I bought Shady. Comanches sell him to me so I could trade him to the Apaches down in Mexico for my daughters, if I find them."

"You own Shady?"

He laughed. "I tell him I own him but he say back, 'I'm in the United States of America, I'm free now.' I never find my daughters but he like a son to me."

Big Mike came over and asked, "How are you doing?"

"I'll be back in the saddle tomorrow."

He just snorted at that and walked away. I forgot to thank him for rescuing me.

Some of the hands came by when they were changing out mounts and they wished me well, or they were baffled and didn't know what to say and stood there with their hats in their hands and called me miss or ma'am. I told them they could still call me Kid, but I couldn't look at them. Some of them didn't come by at all and I wrote it off to them not believing any girl should be with a trail drive no matter what the circumstances.

Tommy Deuce came by and he hemmed and hawed and he started to ask something about Maria and the Red Feather, but I told him, "It's OK, Tommy Deuce, I figured out how to handle that."

"You sure must have been pretty damn clever."

"I try my best."

He apologized for swearing in front of a lady, and then he asked if he should call me Kid? Or miss? Or did I have a name I wanted to be called by, now that everything was out in the open?

I told him Kid would do, but I didn't tell him I didn't want to share my real name with anyone because I liked knowing there was something private I could keep to myself, even if it was only my name, and then he was gone.

TWENTY-FIVE

Shakespeare came by in the afternoon and brought me some water and he hunkered down next to me on his heels, it being obvious he wasn't there to stay long. He soaked a rag and washed my face and that was so sweet I started to weep and he said, "Rough day, huh?"

"Where are all your Shakespeare words now?"

"I'll think of some and get back to you."

I asked what was going on and he said they were going to be there for days and days sorting the herds out and I wasn't missing anything. He looked up at the sun and then he picked me up and I screamed and he said sorry, and he carried me to the other side of the wagon so I'd be in the shade. I wanted to stay in his arms, but I couldn't say that aloud so I said, "Please don't drop me," and I leaned into him, grabbing him hard because of the pain, holding on as tightly as I could.

"Don't worry," he said, "I got you."

He sat me down, then brought my bedroll around and moved me onto it, and even that hurt. He said sorry again and I told him it was all right, and before he left he did that gesture of brushing back my hair. Then he was gone.

That night Shakespeare and Monty moved me closer to the fire. I think they did it figuring it would be good for me to be around the hands and listen to the chatter. Some of them talked about times they'd been hurt, and I think they did it to let me know they'd been injured too. Jack Straw showed a long scar on his arm and said he got that when he was up on the Republican and Skinny said, "You did not. You got that when we was on the Canadian," and then they got to arguing about who would know best about where and when they were injured. Hard Luck Luke Bronson pulled up his trousers leg and showed a long scar, saying he got that when they were crossing the Cimarron and damned if some fool of a longhorn didn't hook him midstream and he liked to have drowned as well as bled to death, and that's where he got the name Hard Luck, because he survived.

Bill said I was lucky I was hit by a metal arrow and not a stone arrow because a stone arrow would kill you for sure. I didn't know why that would be but that's what he said, and others attested to the truth of it. Pretty soon it got into tales that had to be windjammers, about surviving being hanged or being run over by a buckboard or falling into a well or some such, each one trying to outdo the other, all of them loose herding the truth.

It got quiet as they fell asleep, but I was still awake. They made me smile once or twice, and then I discovered Preacher standing over me and I said, "What do you want?"

"I come to lay hands on you and pray over you."

"When I was being beaten I remembered what happened in that alley, Preacher. It was you grabbing at me and reaching into my pockets and taking what money I had left. You're a thief and a hypocrite. You lay one hand on me and I swear to God I'll take this Schofield here and I'll kill you." I pulled the Schofield out from my bedroll. He just stood there and considered things.

"You were too stupid drunk to remember things right, Kid. You got it all wrong. You lost all your money at the tables." He turned and walked away, calling back, "I'll pray for you anyway."

⚜ ⚜ ⚜

As they sorted the cattle and brought in strays, I got to where I was able to walk around. I stayed close to Monty and with one hand I helped him with the bait, grinding the coffee beans and cooking and cleaning as best I could, and as I got more strength I snaked in firewood or chips from nearby. The hands kept calling me miss or ma'am and were real cordial, but it was like we didn't know each other very well.

Sometimes I walked out to the remuda and stood with Ghost and talked horse to her. I told her I thought that, as badly as I wanted Shakespeare, there was no future in it. There was so much death around me he wasn't safe being anywhere close to me. It would be better for him if he left me alone, and it was best I stayed away from him for the sake of his own reputation, because he might be too dumb or careless to look after it himself, so I figured I had to do it for him. Ghost mostly listened and the more silent she was the more I talked.

My own reputation got brought home to me as well. One day I was walking back from the remuda and three hands from one of the other outfits was passing by and they stopped, and one of them said, "You the girl?"

I kept walking and said, "Most days."

They followed after me and one said, "So where's your frock?"

The others started laughing, so I just kept on walking and one of them yelled out, "You look too scrawny to be a girl, why don't you prove it to us?"

Another said, "Yeah, open your shirt, drop them pants! We want to check that story out!"

They were laughing real big and I kept walking, and then they rode up on either side of me and one of them started to dismount saying, "I just may check her or him out for myself and see what the truth is."

At that I turned and pulled the Schofield I carried with me all the time now and I pointed it at his face and cocked it and he backed up real fast and held his hands up. The other two reined up, all of them yelling, "Whoa now!" "Don't get so serious!" "You can take a joke can't you?"

I said, "Get the fuck away from me or I swear to God I'll blow you all to kingdom come because I don't give a good goddamn whether you live or die."

They backed up and the one remounted and they pulled away, and one of them said, "Listen to the mouth on her, I never heard no girl talk like that. I'll bet she's a boy after all."

One of them added, so I could hear it, "Sure as hell looks like one, and an ugly one at that."

I looked back behind me and I could see Shakespeare watching what was happening as he was changing mounts.

That night when Shakespeare came in, his face was bloody and he had a black eye, and the other hands were asking, "What the hell happened to you?"

He said, "I had to see a man about a dog."

I got a bucket of water and handed him a rag and when he turned away to wash his face, I said, "What happened? Did you get thrown?"

"Don't worry, the other guys look even worse. Well, at least one of them does." And he wouldn't say any more about it.

That night when we bedded down Shakespeare did his usual thing of trying to stay nearby to me, but I decided to put my bedroll under the canvas cradle we kept the firewood and chips in, slung under the bottom of the wagon, to sleep there in order to stay away from the other hands and to save Shakespeare's reputation. He just looked at me as I gathered my bedroll up, and when I thought no one could hear, I whispered to him, "I can take care of myself you know, I don't need your help."

And he whispered back, "Oh yeah? If you're so good at taking care of yourself then what were we doing out there on those plains looking for you?"

Well that made me mad again so I didn't say anything back and I threw my bedroll under the wagon and I gave him the cold shoulder. He was holding the rag to his eye and trying not to laugh, he thought he was so clever.

One morning I was cleaning up for Monty as Big Mike was mounting up, so I went over to him and said, "I think I could start out just riding nightguard—"

He interrupted me. "You ain't riding swing, flanker, or drag, you ain't riding nighthawk or nightguard, you're not taking the rough off any of the remuda, and you ain't roping them or hauling them in either. You're staying with Monty and the wagon and you'll do whatever he says until we get to Dodge, and if you mount that Appaloosa to go get firewood or wild plums or some such, you tell Monty where you're going and you stay in sight of the wagon. And if you don't do that, by God, I'll tie you to the wagon myself. Do you understand me?"

I said, "Yes, sir," and he was off, and I was left standing there, feeling like a fool.

They got the herds sorted out and the strays brought in after a week or more of hot, dusty work, then one after the other the herds were lined out and pointed north, a couple of days between each one to give them some space as they traveled.

At night, I had bad dreams. Several times I woke up screaming because I thought rattlesnakes were crawling over me. Shakespeare got to me first, but when I come to myself I told him to stay the fuck away from me, that I could handle myself. He'd back off, but the nightmares were so scary and so real all I really wanted was for him to hold me and calm me down and tell me everything was going to be OK. Often I couldn't go back to sleep and sometimes I'd try not to fall asleep, knowing the nightmares were going to come, and once I heard Hard Luck Luke Bronson say to Abraham, "She's going to stampede the herd if she keeps that goddamn caterwauling up. I liked her better when she was a boy."

Sometimes at night I'd go down to the remuda and stand with Ghost and lean into her and just breathe for a few minutes. I begged over and over again for the nightmares to stop, but after a while I was just repeating myself, so I leaned up against her neck and she put her head over my shoulder and I swear I felt the fear leave my body. For a while, there would be peace.

One time when I was visiting her during the day, I turned away from her to go back to the wagon and Shakespeare was standing there, holding the reins to his horse, just standing there and looking at me with that soft, sad smile of his, and I hadn't even heard him come up.

I was startled and I took a step back, and he said, "You see anyone around?"

I looked around and I said, "No."

"Does anyone see us?"

I didn't understand what he was driving at. "No, not that I can see."

He stepped in close and before I understood what he was doing, he pulled my hat off and tossed it down and then he put his hand in my hair and he drew me in and he kissed me, and then I was kissing him back, and then I stepped away real quick and I said, "You can't do that," but it was everything I had wanted ever since I had first seen him swim the river and turn the herd midstream.

He said, "No?"

He mounted up and I reached out and put my hand on him before he could ride off and I said, "I've never been kissed before."

He leaned way down, grabbed me by my good arm, hauled me up closer to him, and he kissed me again, and I kissed him back, and then he set me down. "Well, now you've been kissed twice."

He did that smile of his, turned his horse away, and rode off. He looked tall and lean and he rode with such an easy grace. I swore I could see the sun glinting off copper in his sandy hair, and I told myself I loved him and I put my fingers to my hair where he had touched it, and then to my lips, and my lips felt beautiful, and my shoulder hurt even though he'd hauled me up by my good arm, but I didn't mind because it meant I had been there, held by him, if only for a few seconds.

One night I was crawling into my bedroll under the wagon, when I saw Shakespeare coming up from the remuda leading Ghost. I thought, *What's he doing with my pony?* I crawled back out and I said, "What's this?"

He began to saddle her up. "What're you going to do if there's a stampede?" I hadn't even thought about that so I just stood there real dumb, and he said, "Hmmm?"

I said, "Get in the wagon, I guess."

"Yeah, that's real smart. Hope they don't knock the wagon over, right? Look around you. Every hand here has a horse saddled nearby so he can nightguard or mount up if there's trouble. What the hell kind of a ranny doesn't have his horse by him?" Then he corrected himself and said, "Or her." He handed me the reins. "So I saddled her for you, or are you going to get all salty and tell me you could have managed that all by yourself?"

He winked at me and he started to walk away but he turned back and he came in close and he said, real low, "I've seen you talk to that horse, haven't I?"

I got real embarrassed at that. "So what if I have?"

"Well, crawl into that bedroll and keep ahold of the reins and try talking to her. It might help with the nightmares."

Before he could leave, I whispered to him, "You can't stand real close like this and talk to me. It's not good for your reputation."

He laughed out loud and several of the hands looked over and he whispered back to me, "Reputation, reputation, I've lost my reputation," and he walked away shaking his head and laughing and I just knew he was quoting something from one of those Shakespeare plays.

But I kept Ghost hobbled close to me at night and I'd hold on to her reins and I'd lie there and imagine her heart beating and listen to her chuffing and breathing. I could smell her hide and I could smell the leather of her reins and sometimes there was a breeze that blew the smell of the cattle and the prairie grasses across me. I'd feel my heart slow down and I'd feel her strength flow into my hand and down my arm and into my body, and the hate I felt for the Comanches who had destroyed my family would ebb away. I'd stop imagining all the different ways I would like to have killed the three who beat me, and I'd start thinking about how beautiful Ghost was and what a mystery she was, so powerful and fast and graceful. Who was she that she was so patient and always willing to listen to me?

I remembered Ma telling me no horse could really understand what I was saying, but I knew she was wrong. I told her, "You said you talked to God and God talked to you, so what is the difference if I can talk to a horse? At least the horse is really there."

She got sharp with me, saying, "*Unverschämt!* Don't be impudent! God is not a horse!"

I tried to tell myself I was making things up, but night after night, as I held Ghost's reins, the nightmares eased off, and when I woke before dawn to help Monty, her reins wouldn't be in my hand anymore, but I could feel her with me still.

TWENTY-SIX

The days were hot and the drive was slow and relentless. There was rain sometimes and it was miserable getting the bait ready. When it wasn't wet there was wind, hard and constant, the dust blowing into the cooking and ashes from the fire blowing in as well. It wasn't any damn picnic.

I kept Ghost by the wagon at night but I rode one of the other horses in my string during the day, snaking in firewood and sometimes bringing Monty quail eggs or chokecherries or prairie turnips. I always stayed in sight of the wagon like Big Mike said. I'd wave to Monty and he'd wave back, and at some point during the day I'd drive the wagon myself, sitting next to Monty.

If we saw a herd of whitetail he'd send one of the hands out to see if we couldn't get some venison. Sometimes we'd stop the wagon by a creek and pick wild plums for jelly or pies, or some herb he could use in a stew or for medicine, such as greasewood leaves for colds or a sore throat. As my body healed I made a point of being up before him and already have the cook fire going and the coffee brewing. He'd smile and nod in approval, and I got to where I could hook up the mules by myself, with both hands.

As we rode he taught me words in Mexican, *la camisa* for shirt and *el guante* for glove and *el caballo*, and he'd ask me, "*¿Que es la vaca?*"

I'd point at the herd and say, "*La vaca es otro animal doméstico*," and he'd laugh and say, "*¡Sí! ¡Sí!*" as if I'd just given some big long speech in Mexican.

I pointed out flowers, him saying *girasol* or *primavera*, then he laughed at my pronunciation when I repeated him. One time I pointed out a plant and told him I was surprised to see it this far north, and Pa called it dead man's walking stick. I asked him what it was in Mexican.

He said, "*Ocotillo.*"

I said I liked that name better, but I got quiet remembering the bloody red blossoms on it when I found Ma and Pa and Jamie dead. We didn't talk anymore for a while.

One time I asked him what was his daughters' names and he said, "Angelina and Gabriela." I told him they were pretty names, but what I really wanted to ask was how he was able to go on after losing his daughters. It seemed to me if you lost everything, then you might as well put a gun to your head, because what was the point?

I'd thought of that off and on. There were times at night when I thought Sally might be dead or gone forever to Mexico, so why not kill myself, because there was nothing left. I'd put my hand on the Schofield and close my eyes and I wondered what the explosion would be like, whether or not I'd feel anything or even hear it, and I'd realize I couldn't breathe. Then Ghost would nicker or pull on the reins and I'd come to myself and breathe again, and I told myself I'd think about that another day.

One day I hinted to Monty that if I couldn't find Sally I didn't know what I'd do. He just shrugged and said, "Hey, you go on." That seemed awfully simple, if not impossible, but then Shakespeare's words came back to me.

Only the dead stay down.

At night, the hands played dominoes or read the *Police Gazette* over and over. Some of them encouraged Shakespeare to tell another story, so he started in on some comedy about two sets of twins who were separated at birth and then found each other, but there was confusion over which twin was married to what wife, the wives confused by it and getting it wrong. He acted out the roles and got the hands to say lines and everybody laughed and some of them called out insults to the characters. They told this one wife—who was mad at the husband, who wasn't really her husband, but she didn't realize it, her telling him what a bad husband he was—they told her, "Boy have you got the prod on!" or "What a highbinder you are!"

I found myself wondering why Shakespeare wrote about twins all the time. Didn't he have plays where kings were murdered or lovers ran away? Hearing about twins was a sore subject with me.

Shakespeare took the hint about staying away from me but he found ways to get a word in anyway, saying things when no one was around, such as, "Your hair is getting longer," but he said it like he liked how it looked.

I'd get beet red and say, "Well, whose isn't? We been out here long enough, yours is getting longer too."

Sometimes when I handed him coffee his hand touched mine, and I knew he'd done it on purpose, and sometimes when he was just passing by he'd wink at me and I'd turn red again and I'd get mad at myself for being so hungry for him to notice me. I told myself I needed to lock the door on those feelings.

We would stop outside of some town and Monty would go in for supplies. The hands would go in all rollicky and get drunk and visit the doves or play games of chance and come back looking like they'd been beaten with sticks. I didn't want any part of it, so I stayed back at the camp. Once the hurrahing was over, we'd push north again, crossing the plains, and the sky was high and blue and hot and the land level and the wind hard and constant. You could see for miles and miles, and day after day we got closer to Dodge.

Sometimes at night, when I was lying under the wagon, I'd close my eyes and run my hand through my hair where Shakespeare had touched it, or with my fingers I'd touch my lips and remember him kissing me. Sometimes I'd slip my hand under my shirt and put it on my breast and wonder what it would be like to have him touch me there.

One night I woke up with a jolt, hearing something moving under the wagon. I got panicky, wondering if it was a rattlesnake or a Comanche who knew where I was hiding, or some coyote or wolf edging closer to kill me like I'd dreamed before. I pulled the Schofield out and cocked it, and then I heard Shakespeare's voice saying, "Whoa, whoa, whoa, easy, Kid."

I whispered, "What are you doing here? You can't be here!"

He shushed me and said, "Put that thing away before you kill one of us." He moved up beside me and lay down on his back next to me. "Couldn't sleep. Thought I'd check in on you."

"You can check in on me during the day. You need to check out of here right now."

"Shush. You know very well if I try to check in on you during the day you won't talk to me. So just take it easy. How're you doing?"

I stayed silent, and then he reached up and touched the bottom of the tarpaulin cradle above us filled with wood and chips, "Whoa, sure can't see the stars from under here, can you?"

I stayed silent.

He said, "Now we're at the point when you would say, 'So how are you doing, Shakespeare?' And I'd tell you I had a close call when I was riding the rough off of that ugly sorrel this morning and damned if I didn't get thrown, but I fell where it wasn't so hard, so I'm pretty lucky, and you'd tell me you're glad I didn't get hurt, and then I'd tell you how the moon looked when I was out nightriding earlier this evening and wondering if you'd noticed it, and we'd both start talking about how full it looked coming up over the horizon. Any of this seem like a possibility to you? Just talking to each other?"

I didn't answer him.

Then he asked, "So how old are you really?"

"Fourteen, fifteen, sixteen, seventeen, eighteen, what does it matter?"

He thought about that for a minute. Then he touched my hair again, only just barely, so I let him do it. "What's your name?"

I turned and looked straight at him. "That's mine. It's all I got left."

"OK. Even if I knew your name I'd probably still call you Kid."

While he was touching my hair he eased the back of his hand up against my face, right against my cheek. I let him leave it there, then I reached up and grabbed it and held it to my face. "How'd you know I was a girl?"

"Easy," he said. "You're too pretty to be a boy."

He couldn't see me blush but I turned away because it hurt to hear something so sweet, and it was how I always hoped a man would talk to me. Then he turned my face to him and he ran his fingers over my lips and then he kissed me again. I kissed him back, and then I took his hand and slipped it under my shirt and placed it on my breast. His hand was rough and hard from hauling on ropes and wrangling horses and I liked how it felt against my bare skin. But of a sudden I started getting panicky and shaky and my breath was shallow and fast and I remembered the Comanches having their hands on me, and he pulled his hand away.

He said, "It's OK, Kid. Everything is going to be OK."

"It is not," I said. "I don't want you to touch me and I don't want you close to me. I don't want to be friends with you. You're going to get killed, and then where will I be? One more fucking loss."

"I'm Shakespeare," he whispered. "You can't kill me." Then he touched the cradle above us and said, "I always keep cases on the stars. Don't you miss the stars?"

"No, it's safe in here, and you need to stay away."

"I'll tell you what. Tomorrow night I'm going to come check in on you again. Now, you can stay silent when I try to talk to you, or you can talk with me, or you can tell me to leave. But it's too late. We're already friends, more than friends, aren't we?"

I didn't answer him and he added, "But I'll do whatever you say."

"I'm saying don't come under the wagon tomorrow night or I swear to God I'll shoot you and I'll say I thought it was a coyote."

He rolled over onto his stomach and propped himself up onto his elbows. "I'm going to put my hand on your face one last time, and I'm going to kiss you, and you're going to let me do it, OK? And then I'll stay away."

So he ran his fingers through my hair and then he put his hand on my cheek and he leaned over me, and I liked how much bigger he was than me and how strong he was and I wished I could have just held him against me that way, and he kissed me real gently.

Then he looked me in the eyes. "I don't blame you for being so hard. You've had a tough time." And he added, "You know you've got a failing for me, right?"

And with that he kissed me again, and then he pushed himself out from under the wagon, not waiting for an answer.

Every night after that I wanted him to crawl back under the wagon and kiss me and touch me, but I wouldn't tell him I wanted him like that, and he stayed away. But sometimes I crawled under the wagon and discovered he'd tossed prairie flowers in to surprise me. I kept them alongside me all night long and smelled them, then threw them away in the morning where he could see me do it.

At the wagon he'd casually start a conversation and tell me and Monty about some fox he'd seen, or about a nest of baby rabbits or a hawk in the air, or a black snake swallowing a frog whole, no different than the way he'd talk to any of the other hands. But he wouldn't take his eyes off me until I'd given him some answer, and then he'd act like what I said was just about the most interesting thing he'd ever heard.

One time I was coming back from some far-off cottonwoods where I'd gone to relieve myself and he come riding up from out of nowhere, reined up and took his foot out of the stirrup, and said, "Mount up, I'll give you a ride back."

"No, thank you, I like walking."

"No cowhand likes walking. Get the fuck aboard and quit being such a hard case," he said, and he wasn't smiling.

So I thought about it and it was unbearably hot, so I put my foot in the stirrup and mounted up behind him and I put my arms around him. At that he took off at a gallop, away from camp, and I said, "What're you doing?"

He didn't answer, so I held on to him and leaned into his back and he was wet and hot from the sun and I could smell him and he was just as lean and hard as when they had tied me to him, and I wanted to take his shirt off and run my hands all over the muscles in his back.

He took me a good mile away from the camp before he finally reined up, and I said, "What's going on?"

"It's too far for you to walk back," he said, "so I guess you're going to have to ride along with me and we're going to have a nice easy conversation."

"That's what you think." I slid off and started walking, but he just rode alongside me and chatted away about the weather and how dry it had been, day after day, but it sure had made the river crossings easier, the water being so low and not swift at all, didn't I think?

I stayed silent, walking as fast as I could, but the heat was getting to me and he seemed to figure that out, and without me even asking he handed his canteen down. I thought about not taking it but I was thirsty, so I stopped and drank out of it. Then I threw it as far as I could and walked away as fast as I could. He just circled out, leaned down out of the saddle and picked it up, then he rode his horse out in front of me and turned facing me. When I changed directions, his horse dodged right, and then left, then right, and then left, again and again, cutting me off, and I felt like some calf being edged out of a herd by a cutting horse.

I finally said, "What're you doing? Let me pass."

He slid off his horse and he stood in front of me. "Stop it. Stop it right now. What is wrong with you?"

"You want to know what's wrong?" I said. "I'll tell you what's wrong. Things can never be nice between us because you're going to be killed someday soon, or you're going to die somehow, sometime, and I'm tired of it all. What's the point of one more loss? You're only making it harder on me."

He put his arms around me and I tried to push him off but he wouldn't let go.

I struggled and I pushed, and finally I gave in and I just let him hold me, and then my knees went out from under me and he went down to the ground with me, both of us kneeling in the prairie grasses and flowers, and he held me.

I sobbed and sobbed, and he stroked my hair and kissed me on the top of my head as I leaned into his chest, and I said, "Who are you? What do you want from me? Why are you doing this to me?"

He held me and he didn't answer, he just held me, and I finally said, "I love you, is that what you want? I love you. There, I said it. Is that what you want to hear?"

"It's about time," he said. "Took you forever."

TWENTY-SEVEN

I t was late summer when we hit Dodge. The cattle were bedded down in good grass a couple of miles outside of town and Big Mike went in to make arrangements for them to be moved into the pens after they were tallied. The herd in front of us was being sold now, he said, and he would be negotiating a price with a stock buyer, depending on the final count and the buyer's inspection of the cattle.

I felt proud. I'd brought Pa's herd in, and I wished he could tell me good job and what a miracle it was we'd made it. It seemed like it had been years ago I had buried Ma and Pa and Jamie and started out to look for the herd, but now here we were, in Dodge.

Big Mike came back from town, and after the buyer inspected the herd and was given the tallies, Big Mike gathered us together and opened a strong box and paid everyone for their work, including me. In my whole life I'd never held that much cash in my hand at one time, over a hundred dollars. I felt as rich as any king.

He gave us all his speech about providing for the future and all the hands nodded in agreement, then they drew straws to see who would stay behind and watch the remuda and the herd while everyone else went into town. Jack Straw was one of the ones who lost, saying, "Now, don't that beat all?"

Everyone else headed off to spend their wages and hurrah the town, but not before swearing they were going to start their own spread or go in partners on some freight business or open a billiard parlor or some such. The boys shook hands all around and promised to have drinks together and said they'd see each other before they gathered up their kits and headed off in different directions. Then there was a lot of yelling as they mounted up and headed into the streets of Dodge.

Big Mike rode back in to receive payment from the buyer, taking me with him. Shakespeare was brought along as well, and I wondered why Big Mike took Shakespeare since he was just the horse wrangler.

We dropped our mounts off at the livery stable and Big Mike led us into the buyer's office, a Mr. O'Grady. He wore a fine-looking suit of clothes and he had fine black shoes that were now all dusty from being up and down the stockyards and then out inspecting our herd as well. He had hair that was plastered back from his forehead and parted in the middle and he had a large mustache that drooped at both ends, but he was very friendly.

With him was the stock inspector, a tall, lean, older gentleman with white hair and a white mustache and a weather-beaten face, and I could tell he'd been a hand once. Big Mike introduced me to both men as "this young lady," which took them aback, given how I was dressed. He explained that my herd wasn't carrying a road brand but I had quite a story to tell.

Big Mike backed up my story, saying they had come across me on the trail and testifying I even had a string of Comanche ponies with me that proved I'd had to fight to get the herd back. He said I was pretty fierce, "one you could run the river with," and those Comanches regretted the day I'd caught up with them, that I was a real ranny.

That shocked me because ever since I'd gotten into trouble I hadn't done anything but help Monty, and as badly as I had wanted to be called a ranny, it didn't seem justified. I didn't know if he was being serious or if he was just trying to impress the stock inspector, but in the back of my mind I didn't believe him and I wondered what I'd have to do to really earn being called a ranahan.

The stock inspector interrupted my thoughts and told tales of his run-ins with Indians. He pulled up his shirt and showed us a scar on his ribs, and then one on his back, and one on his temple, and then he pulled up a trouser leg and showed a scar on his leg. He then told about all the broke bones and injuries gained trailing cattle, saying he had a hell of a time getting up in the morning because not all the broke parts started moving at the same time. I think he liked having an audience.

Finally he shoved some documents toward me and I signed them, and then he signed them and handed them to Mr. O'Grady. He told a few more stories, one of them being about how he liked to tell greeners that to stop a stampede all you had to do was throw salt down in front of the herd, but the hard part was finding someone willing to get in front of the herd with all that salt to throw down. Everyone laughed at that even though we'd all heard it before. He wished us well and then he was out the door, walking like he'd ended up on the wrong side of an upside-down outlaw horse more than once.

Mr. Grady handed Big Mike a bank draft, and he handed one to Shakespeare, and that baffled me because why would he be giving the wrangler a bank draft? He told me he'd be giving me the same price as the others, that my herd looked good. I said that was because Big Mike moved them slow and easy so they could fatten up along the way. Big Mike gave a quick nod and I added, "Even if he is a mean son of a bitch." Mr. O'Grady laughed at that and Big Mike smiled as if he was proud of the complement.

Shakespeare was leaning up against a wall with that smile of his, watching me and folding his draft over and over until he tucked it away in a vest pocket.

Mr. O'Grady slid a piece of paper toward me, saying, "Now, I'm giving you the same price as these gentlemen so I'm assuming you'll agree to that." Pointing at the paper he said, "This is the price for your four-year-olds, and this is for your three-year-olds, and your two- and one-year-olds. And here's your total.

You sellers are having a good year this year, prices three or four times the fifteen dollars a brute goes for in Texas." He warned us, saying, "Don't think it will always be like that."

I looked down and I was stunned. It hadn't dawned on me to even ask what the herd might bring or what cattle prices were because I never thought I'd make it to Dodge in the first place. Even if I had considered it, the size of my herd was so small I never thought they'd bring much. No wonder everyone wanted to get into the cattle business.

Mr. O'Grady went on, saying Pa had been building a good herd for such a small shirttail outfit and I ought to be proud of him and it was a shame his progress had been cut short, but he was surely proud of me for bringing them in. He wanted me to know there were other women who had taken over after such a loss and ran good spreads, and he hoped I'd go back to Texas and start building another herd. I managed not to weep in front of him.

At that he sat down and began to write out a bank draft and he looked at me and said, "Now, miss, what is your name?"

The question caught me off guard because I was shaken by the amount. I didn't understand why Shakespeare was standing there with a draft in his vest pocket, and at the same time I was marveling at being called a woman, when all along I'd been thinking about myself as either a boy or a girl. I wanted to look at myself in a mirror and ask myself if I indeed was a woman, and here was a stranger calling me a woman, and he hadn't even asked how old I was. None of it made any sense.

Mr. O'Grady said, "Miss?"

I said, "Hmmm?"

He repeated himself and said, "I need your name."

I looked at Shakespeare. I had refused to give him my name and I was determined not to have him hear it now, so I said, "Yes, sir," and I pointed to the documents I had just signed for the stock inspector.

"Oh my, yes, of course, foolish me," he said. "There it is, right in front of me," and he wrote out the draft.

I looked at Shakespeare and he did that smile of his as if to say, Aren't you clever. I smiled back at him at him as if to say, What's mine is mine.

Mr. O'Grady came from around his desk and handed the draft to me, and he shook my hand just like he would with any other businessman. I didn't know what to say to him other than thank you. I kept looking at my name and the large numbers on the draft, and he told me to keep that money safe and not to go gambling or drinking or carousing and lose it all like some hand in off the range roistering around who only wanted to have a good time and didn't know the value of money or how to save for the future.

I told him, "No, sir, I understand."

Then Shakespeare chimed in, "By the way, don't forget you owe me fifty-eight dollars." Mr. O'Grady was curious and wanted to know what that was all about, and Shakespeare explained it was over some horse-trading that had gone on.

Mr. O'Grady said, "Aha," looking at Shakespeare, and then winking at me. At that there were more handshakes all around, and he wished us a good trip back to Texas.

Before we left the office I asked, "Is the herd going to Chicago?"

"No, ma'am," he said. "This herd is going to be wintered in Nebraska and then trailed to Montana in the spring."

"Your men will have two good lead longhorns, Blackjack and John Bell Hood. You see that they take good care of them and they'll get you to Montana. And if you don't mind me saying so, sir, if you bring them back to Nebraska, they'll take your next herd up as well."

He said he surely would hope to do that.

We left the office and the three of us stood in the sun outside. I counted out fifty-eight dollars from the wages Big Mike had paid me earlier and handed it to Shakespeare and said, "We're even."

At the same time, in my head I kept trying to multiply all the numbers and prices for my herd because I was sure the math was wrong and Mr. O'Grady was going to come find me and take the bank draft back, but I couldn't concentrate. Even though I was good at sums, I couldn't make the numbers work out.

Big Mike said, "Let's go get something to eat."

I was sure he was just talking to Shakespeare, but he nudged me on the arm and pointed up the street, and we all three started walking. I kept asking myself, *What's going on? What's going on?* and I was bewildered by wagons passing us loaded down with grain sacks or lumber and there were the sounds of saws and hammering. Mules were being led down the street braying and dogs were running past us in packs. There were children on the walks and ladies with parasols, all going somewhere, and hands from other outfits on the boardwalks or in the streets on horseback, talking loud or singing or rawhiding each other.

I passed a store window that had ribbons and scarves and shawls and bolts of cloth on display and I stood there and looked at it as Big Mike and Shakespeare walked on. I couldn't imagine what it would be like to dress like that, but the colors were beautiful and I wanted to touch the fabrics and feel how slick or soft or smooth they were. There was one bolt that was cream-colored with red stripes and little tiny red and pink rosebuds between the stripes, and wouldn't Ma have liked to have had a nice fancy frock like that. The next thing I knew Shakespeare was grabbing me by the arm and pulling me back up with Big Mike.

The street was noisy with sounds and ablaze with colors. There were buffalo runners with wagons of hides and blue-coated soldiers on horseback and folks coming in and out of stores, and men in long frock coats with expensive-looking shiny vests of bright colors, gamblers I guessed. Worn-out drunks leaned up against posts or slept on benches, all manner of horses and mules stood at water troughs, and alleys were filled with broken bottles and broken crates, or barrels with staves missing, and dogs fighting over the skull and antlers of a pronghorn. I was bewildered, as if I was in some foreign country and I didn't know the language or how to get along, and what would I do to get by if Big Mike and Shakespeare wasn't with me? I resolved to pay attention, but things were happening too fast, and I was still confused, trying to figure out if I was a girl or a woman, when all along I'd been saying I was a boy. I kept thinking, *Who am I?* and *Where am I?*

Then I heard a noise like nothing I'd even heard before, a roaring and a bell ringing over and over and over. There was a loud, screaming whistle sound that went on and on and I was terrified and looking around for a place to hide. Shakespeare yanked me back out of the way and a huge black train came rolling past, smoke pouring out of the top of it and steam pouring out from the sides of it. Kids waved and yelled at the men driving it, and they waved back and blew that piercing whistling sound over and over again and kept ringing a bell. Men were shoveling black coal into the engine, and then there was boxcar after boxcar of bawling longhorns, car after car of them, and then a bright red caboose, and then they were gone. It was so quiet I thought I'd gone deaf until Big Mike said, "They're going to Kansas City or Chicago." I'd never seen a train before and I was so scared by the size of it and the noise of it all, as if it was a black monster from one of Jamie's adventure stories. Then I looked across the tracks, and there were whiskey mills and houses with red lights, and I knew what that was all about.

"Big town, isn't it," Big Mike said.

We kept walking, I don't know in which direction, and slowly my breath came back to me and my heart slowed down, but I was bewildered by the noise and the strangeness of it all. I couldn't help but wonder how anyone managed to live in such a big city.

We walked some more, and then Big Mike and Shakespeare turned and we went through some doors, and as we passed through I saw a big sign with red letters that said "Delmonico's."

I could smell cooking and I realized I was starving, and a nicely dressed gentleman seated us at a table that had a white tablecloth and white napkins and shiny utensils, and there were menus, and when I looked at the menu I couldn't make out what I was supposed to do with it, and I felt sure people were staring at me.

Shakespeare was across from me and Big Mike was at one end of the table, both looking at their menus, and I just wanted to be back under the wagon where things were simpler and there wasn't even the stars above to complicate my thoughts. I could hold on to Ghost's reins and I only had to worry about whether or not I was going to have a nightmare.

A plump but nicely dressed woman came to the table and we ordered steaks all around and Big Mike ordered a drink called champagne, which I'd never even heard of before. A waiter brought us tall, slender-shaped glasses, and I couldn't wait to eat. Shakespeare and Big Mike talked about she-stuff and grama grass and winter die-ups and bulls and breeding with stock from Scotland, of all places. All around us there were tables of people dressed nicely, as well as hands like us out for a big meal. I felt out of place and wished I'd gotten cleaned up somehow.

The waiter brought a large bottle and he struggled getting it opened, and of a sudden there was a loud crack. I jerked because I thought we were being fired at, and then the bottle started to foam and Big Mike and Shakespeare laughed at my reaction. The waiter poured this golden liquid into our glasses and it was filled with bubbles like I'd never seen before. I stared at it and wondered how they'd gotten in there, and how bubbles could keep coming up out of nowhere from the bottom of the glass.

Big Mike raised his glass and he and Shakespeare touched glasses and I thought that was unusual, so I raised my glass and they touched mine with theirs. Big Mike said, "Here's to a long, hard drive."

They took a sip, so I did too, and it tasted like nothing I'd ever tasted before. It was cold but it burned in a good way as it went down, but not like Tommy Deuce's rye. Shakespeare raised his glass and he said, "Here's to Scotty and Cliff," and we all took another drink.

Big Mike raised his glass again. "Here's to our spreads."

I put my glass down. "What are you talking about?"

They took a drink again and Big Mike said, "Well, there's your spread and there's mine and there's Shakespeare's. Long may they prosper," and I'd never heard him talk like that before.

I looked at Shakespeare. "What spread? I thought you were the wrangler."

"I am," he said. "And I'm the owner."

I just stared at him. "How can that be?"

"It should be my father's spread, but he and my mother passed away in the influenza outbreak a year back, and I'd lost my brother before that, so the spread came to me as sole owner. I'm selling the three- and four-year-olds off, and since I've never gone up the trail before, I contracted with Big Mike to take my herd north with his, and I hired myself on as the wrangler."

I felt stunned for the second time this day, and already the sips of champagne I'd had were making me feel light-headed and confused, and I didn't know what to say, and I was bewildered by all the sounds around me and the smell of the food. How was it that I was sitting with someone who had backhanded me off a horse one day and rescued me the next? Now I was at supper with him, and I was sitting with someone else who had kissed me, and they'd both seen me naked, and I'd seen both of them naked in a river, and I thought this world was too strange. I wanted to hold on to the table and put my head down and close my eyes and go to sleep, when our plates came, and the steaks were big and made a sound like they were still on the fire.

There were potatoes piled high with some green vegetable I'd never ever seen before. Big Mike and Shakespeare went back to talking about the almanac, or how, because of Texas fever, the quarantine line kept pushing the drive to Dodge farther west, and about freight rates, and there was a need for railheads and shipping points closer to their home ranch, or maybe they should trail a herd to Wyoming or Montana themselves and start a spread there. I was eating like I'd never tasted food before when I realized no one was talking and they were both looking at me.

I'd been asked a question but hadn't heard it and I said, "What?"

Shakespeare said, "What are you going to do?"

"About what?"

He and Big Mike looked at each other and Shakespeare said, "You brought your herd through. What are you going to do now?"

I sat up straight and I put my fork and knife down. "I'm going to find my sister."

Shakespeare put his knife and fork down as well and Big Mike kept eating but he was looking at me. Shakespeare said, "How are you going to do that?"

"I'm going to buy her back. Or trade for her."

"Yes, but you need to find her first. How are you going to do that?"

I took another drink of champagne and it tasted even better with every sip and I was awfully thirsty. Big Mike reached over and refilled my glass. I said, "First I'll go out to Fort Dodge and talk to the commander and see if there's been any word about captives, and I'll ask him what he knows about where the Comanches might be who haven't come onto the reservations, and Monty tells me if I want to find her I need to travel as if I was a Comanchero trader. They're the only ones who know what's going on in the camps. If the cavalry comes anywhere near, even if it's just to parley, they'll hide the captives, but the Comancheros just want to sell or trade, so the Comanches aren't afraid of them."

Big Mike stopped eating. They were both looking at me and I kept wondering what the folks around us were thinking, seeing me at a table with two men who were so much bigger than me and me still dressed like I'd been dragged through the street. I must have looked like some kind of beggar they'd took pity on, but I kept wondering what they'd think if they knew I was sitting there with a bank draft for over four thousand dollars in my pocket.

Big Mike asked, "What are you going to trade with? Cash won't mean much to them."

"What are you going to do with the remuda, take it back to Texas?"

"No, we're selling it off here."

"Good," I said, "I'll buy it." I went back to eating my steak, and whatever the vegetables were, they were really good and covered in butter and I couldn't get enough of the potatoes, and I felt dizzy from the champagne.

Big Mike and Shakespeare went back to eating and I think they were turning things over in their mind, not saying a word. I was thinking about how to get a bath and about getting new clothes and maybe staying in a hotel room like I was some important cattleman, and also wondering what it would be like to wear a frock again. Even if I didn't buy one now I sure would like to look at them, and I wondered if my hair was long enough that maybe I could put a ribbon in it, and what would it be like to wear a sunbonnet again, even though I'd never liked sunbonnets, though Ma always insisted I wear one to keep the sun off my face. I'd grown partial to Jamie's hat and hated the idea of giving it up because it was the only way I had to keep him with me. What would everyone think if I continued to dress like a boy but still wore a ribbon in my hair?

Big Mike said, "You need to figure out how many horses you want, how many you think they'll take for her, and you need to buy a Murphy wagon as well, mules for the wagon, or oxen, and you need to pay for the trade goods and your own supplies. You need to hire several hands to go with you as guards to protect you, otherwise you're going to be taken advantage of once they find out you're a girl. You'll need to pay the hands for at least a couple of months because God knows how long it'll take you to find her, if you can find her at all. Remember, she could be in Mexico or she could . . . " He stopped at that and just shrugged. "Well, let's just hope she can be found."

He was being harsh and I wondered if he was trying to stop me from doing something foolhardy by overwhelming me with details. I said, "I guess I'm going to need a paper and pencil so I can do some figuring."

Shakespeare said, "I'm sitting here with a draft for over forty thousand dollars in my pocket. I'll throw in with you. And don't forget, half the remuda is mine. We can use them to trade for her."

"I don't know that I'll ever have the money to pay you back."

"Well then," he said, "I guess you'll just have to marry me instead."

TWENTY-EIGHT

Big Mike choked on his steak and threw down champagne to clear his throat. I looked at Shakespeare and I couldn't breathe, my heart beating about a thousand times a minute. Big Mike looked back and forth between the two of us and he was beet red. I was too.

Shakespeare said, "I'll give you a kiss right here if that'll seal the deal."

I found enough breath and my voice choked up and I said, "If you do that everyone will think you're kissing a boy and they'll take you out into the street and beat the tar out of you." I got up and threw two silver dollars down to pay for the meal. I left the table and walked outside.

The sun hurt my eyes and I felt wobbly, so I leaned up against the wall of Delmonico's until I could steady myself, then sat down on a bench next to me, and slowly my breath came back. I closed my eyes, and when someone sat down next to me a while later, I knew it was Shakespeare. We sat there in silence for the longest time until he finally said, "You said you loved me."

"Yes," I said, "I did say that."

"I do love nothing in the world so well as you—is not that strange?"

"That's another quote, isn't it?"

"Yes, it is."

"I don't want to hear it," I said.

And at that he was silent.

We listened to the noises of the street and watched the parade of people and animals going by, even a herd of longhorns being hurrahed through the street. Buggies pulled out of their way and their horses reared and neighed and folks shouted at the drovers.

"What am I to do with these feelings for you?"

"The same thing I'm doing," I said. "Shoving them aside."

"Seems like a waste."

"I told you, I'm not setting myself up again. I have something to do that's more important and I could get killed doing it, and anyone who is with me could get killed. So shove them away. Maybe someday we'll meet on the other side."

Big Mike came out at about that time and said, "You all missed a real good apple pie." Neither one of us replied. "I'm checking into the Dodge House for the night. I recommend you two do the same."

As he walked off he called back, "Good luck."

My chest hurt from my heart beating so fast and my shoulder ached from where the arrow had hit it and I wanted to ask Shakespeare to rub it for me, but I didn't dare.

After a while he said, "I'm still throwing in with you. What do you want me to do?"

"Talk to the boys and ask Monty to join us, if he's willing, and Shady too since he speaks the language, and a couple more, and warn everybody there could be trouble. We'll need the mules from your half of the remuda as well, and a Murphy wagon. We'll meet in the morning and go over the figures."

He got up and looked down the street with his back to me, and I said, "Thank you."

He reached back and held out a hand but I didn't touch it. He walked down the boardwalk holding that same hand high in the air, and he didn't look back.

I don't know how long I sat there but I didn't want to go to the whiskey mills and I didn't want to go back and sleep under the wagon, so I began to walk up and down the town, taking it all in.

I marveled at how big and sprawling it was and how many people there were and the number of dry good stores and banks and blacksmith shops and tobacco shops, land offices and lawyers' offices and saddle and boot shops and a newspaper office and more. Another train barreled down the tracks, the bells clanging and the whistle screaming and the cattle bawling, and when it cleared, there across the tracks were the saloons and the houses with red lights in their windows.

I walked to the Dodge House and got a room and I asked the clerk if I could get a hot bath. He gave me a key and had me sign the register and said he would send the water up, that there was a tub in the room. When I signed the register I tried to figure out what name might be Shakespeare's, but there were too many, and how would I know which one was his, and maybe he hadn't even registered yet because he was across the tracks. I ran my hand over the names as if I could touch him, thinking one of the names might somehow stand out.

The room was small but clean and the bed seemed almost too soft. I looked at it and thought, what a wonderful invention. There was a pitcher and basin on the dresser with a white lace doily under it and a clean washcloth and towel nearby, and an oval mirror on the wall above it.

A knock came, and when I opened the door a young Chinese boy carrying two large pails of hot water came in and bowed to me, then poured the water into a tin tub. He hung around the door instead of leaving and I didn't know what he wanted until he put his hand out. He smiled and nodded, and I realized he wanted to be paid for bringing the water. I felt rich so I gave him a silver dollar as if I was some important cattleman, and at that he smiled real big and bowed and bowed, saying, "Thank you, thank you," and then he left.

I had been surrounded by men for months and months during the drive, and now it felt both good and strange to be in a room by myself. It was getting toward dusk, so I lit an oil lamp on the dresser and I left the window open hoping for some evening breeze, but I closed the curtains. I took off my clothes, and I felt like a stranger to my own body.

I stepped into the water and it was hot, so I eased down slowly until I was used to it, and I sat there for the longest time. I remembered Mr. O'Grady calling me a woman, so I ran my hands over myself and asked myself if this is what a woman feels like, but all I felt were what seemed to be sticks covered by rawhide, nothing smooth or soft. After a while, I ran soap and water through my hair, then I soaped and sponged myself off and washed my face, then I sat back.

The lamp made flickering shadows in the room and a hot breeze blew through the curtains, and I wondered again if Shakespeare had gone to the whiskey mills and if he was going to see one of the soiled doves. If he was, then it was my own fault because I had turned him away.

As I got out of the tub, I turned and looked at my back in the mirror. The scar where the arrow had ripped into my shoulder blade and then been pulled out so roughly was long, red, and ugly. I had never seen it. I thought, *No man would ever want to touch that.* I turned back and looked at myself in the mirror one more time and I touched my face and my hair. *Some woman you are. Scrawny as hell, all angles, ribs showing, skin and bones, who'd want that?*

I dried myself off and I crawled into bed naked and covered myself up. I didn't have Ghost's reins to hold on to, so I talked to her as if she was there. "Please don't let the nightmares come, please don't let the nightmares come, please don't let the nightmares come."

I woke up, and in the darkness of the room I could smell the deerskin leggings and the leather breechcloths of the three dead Comanches, then I heard words I couldn't understand, Comanche words, and I could smell their hair and breath and their sweat. Then in the shadows I saw one of them coming into the room now, coming out of the darkness, covered in blood, and following him were the other two, bullet holes in all of them, one of them wearing a red sash, all of them smeared in blood, their blood dripping onto the floor. They walked toward the bed laughing and talking among themselves and pointing at me. I gasped and held my breath and tried not to scream, but they hit me in the face and kicked me again and again and they tore at my clothes, and in the middle of the beating, I woke up.

They were gone. There was no blood on the floor, and the sun was up.

I got out of bed, washed the sweat of the nightmare off me, and I dressed. When I left my room, Shakespeare was in the hall, across from my door, hunkered down on his heels, waiting.

"Let's get something to eat," he said.

"How'd you know I was here?"

"Thin walls. Figured it was you but I didn't want to come in for fear I'd be shot for a coyote."

"I don't remember making any noise." I didn't tell him about the nightmare.

We went to a small joint and ordered coffee, eggs, pancakes, biscuits, and potatoes. It seemed I just couldn't eat enough I was so hungry.

Shakespeare pulled a pencil and his tally book out of his vest pocket and we went over the figures on the men and the supplies and the wagon and the trade goods. When he stumbled over the figures, I straightened him out because I was always good with sums. It looked like we could split the cost down the middle, him matching what I put in, although the horses and mules would be all on him.

I said, "But this doesn't buy you anything with me, you know."

He got mad in a way I'd never seen before, even when he had shoved me up against the wagon, a quiet mad. Dead serious he said, "I don't need to buy your heart. I already own it. You just need to reconcile yourself with the delivery date."

He turned to his plate and I wanted to give myself to him so badly that I had to hold on to the sides of the table until the feeling passed.

While Shakespeare rounded up hands and made provisions for the journey, I picked up Ghost from the stable and rode the four or five miles east to Fort Dodge.

This time I didn't have any trouble getting in to see the commander. His name was Dodge as well, but not the same Dodge the town was named after, he told me, saying, "Who would have thought that was possible?" He was a burly fellow with a full beard, but he was more like some professor than a soldier.

I asked him first about Sally, if there had been any word, and he told me they'd had word on Mexican captives and Navaho captives, discovered when some of the bands come onto the reservations, but none of them could have been Sally, and he hadn't received any communication about her.

He dug through some maps and found one that was old and beat-up. He marked it up with lines and arrows and notes, going over where the reservations were and who hadn't come in yet and where it was suspected they were hiding, where they might be roaming, and where the various forts and outposts were located. He told me there were troops out in the field, and soon there would be even more, looking to parley with, or, if necessary, attack those that had refused to come in, in order to force them in. He told me what routes the Comancheros were likely to take and he seemed to enjoy talking about it.

He gave me the map to keep, and I thanked him, and then he said, "I need to warn you about something."

My heart sank. "Yes, sir?"

"You know some captives are tortured or made into slaves, or traded away, or killed. But you also need to know some of the captives don't want to be recovered. They like the way of life. They've learned to speak the language and they're often treated well."

"She's only three, sir."

"Then it's even more likely she may not want to come home. She may not remember home, or you, or her language."

That seemed pretty far-fetched to me, but I felt scared and heartsick. I thanked him for his time and he wished me good luck, escorting me to the door and holding it open for me.

When I got back to the stable, Shakespeare was already there, waiting. "What'd you learn?"

I showed him the map and he saw my hands shaking as I tried to repeat most of what I had been told, including the warning. He took the map from me and rolled it up, and he said, "We'll find her, don't worry."

"How can I not?"

"I don't know."

The boys joined us, and our outfit would be Shakespeare and me and Tommy Deuce and Monty. Shady agreed as well, and Abraham volunteered. Shakespeare said, "I talked to most of the other boys and Hard Luck Luke Bronson and Preacher are joining the hands taking our herd to Nebraska. Skinny and Bill are taking the train to Kansas City to see the elephant, and Big Mike is going home to Corpus. These are the ones that were willing to go with us."

He smiled and added, "We few, we happy few, we band of brothers."

Tommy Deuce took his hat off like he was speaking to some lady. "So are we to call you boss, or ma'am, or miss, or what?"

I said, "Let's stick with Kid like it always was."

"Yes, ma'am," he said, and he put his hat back on.

We spent the rest of the day planning our journey. Monty said he would purchase a Murphy wagon so we could pass for

Comancheros, and we'd have some sixty horses to bargain for Sally, if we found her. We spent the rest of the day helping Monty with the purchase of the trade goods. There would be rope twists of cured tobacco as well as packages of barbed metal arrowheads, the same kind that had dug into my shoulder blade, and pony beads, hatchets, knives, bolts of calico, gingham, and taffeta, pots and pans and blankets and tin lanterns, mirrors, geegaws, flints and steel for fires, molasses and coffee and other items we could use for trade or gifts. It would take a day or two more to finish buying all the goods, as well as our own food stores, then prepare the wagon and load up.

Bill and Jack Straw and Big Mike came by to wish us well and everyone shook hands all around. I thanked Big Mike for getting us through and putting up with me, and Jack Straw told me he had indeed saved his money and he was going back to his sister to help out, but he sure wished he could go on one more adventure.

I said it was a noble thing to help his sister and I admired him, and wasn't that going to be an adventure in itself, and I wished him well. We shook hands and he had to duck away because his eyes were all wet and he was still drunk.

Shakespeare had explained to the boys what their pay was to be, that we were looking for Sally and it could be dangerous. I told them we would be leaving in another day or two and they should get whatever supplies they needed for the journey and to not be so drunk that they couldn't ride.

Tommy Deuce said, "Hell, you sound just like Big Mike!" Then he apologized for swearing in front of a lady.

It felt strange to give orders. Even though Shakespeare had gone in halves with me, I realized it was my journey and they were hiring on with me and I was responsible for them, just like Big Mike was responsible for the herd and the dozen hands that rode with it.

When evening came, Shakespeare and I went back to Delmonico's for supper and I had him order a bottle of champagne. It tasted so good I had him order another, and he laughed at that and told me to slow down, but I told him for the first time in a long time I felt giddy and happy and I thought my luck was changing. He told me to slow down again, but he didn't try to stop me, and I couldn't see the harm in feeling that good.

We left Delmonico's and we walked back to the Dodge House. I said we should look at the map again and plan our route, so we went to my room, him holding me by the arm to keep me steady. I rolled the map out and we both sat down on the edge of the bed, holding it across our knees, and the idea of sitting on a bed with him seemed wild and dangerous. I didn't need to wonder what Ma would say if she could have seen us.

The room started to turn on me so I kicked off my boots and I threw the map on the floor and crawled onto the bed, leaning up against the headboard. Shakespeare kicked off his boots and did the same, the two of us sitting there like an old married couple, and we chatted away.

I asked him about his family and he told me his father had been a judge in Corpus Christi and that's why there had always been books around, but his father also had a large spread outside of town and that's where the cattle come from, and his mother was always reading and thought women ought to be able to vote and she was always helping neighbors or people in trouble and bringing home stray dogs. They were a family of raconteurs as well, he said, and I had to ask him what a raconteur was. He went on and talked about how the loss of his brother March had hit the family hard, then there was the influenza, and he was the only one left standing, for some unknown reason.

I told him I knew what that felt like.

I asked him what his name was and he did that sad smile. "You first."

"Maybe someday."

He said, "Same here."

I closed my eyes to try and stop the spinning. I told him about my family and about Pa coming from Ireland to Tennessee and then moving west from Tennessee and meeting my mother when he was working as a hand in Comfort. Her parents were Swiss German and they didn't want her marrying someone Irish, but that's how it happened after all. When he went to fight for the South they were done with him, especially after Ma's brother was murdered by Southern sympathizers when he was caught trying to sneak off and join the Union Army. I didn't remember my grandparents very well at all, and I was a twin. After the war they both moved farther west, and boy was that ever a mistake.

He said, "Well, I suppose so ... "

My stomach started to cramp and I said, "Oh dear God." Something hit hard and I scrambled off the bed and tried to get across the room.

He saw where I was going and got ahead of me and took the pitcher out of the washbasin. I was on the floor now, doubled over and heaving, and he got down on the floor with me and put the basin in front of me.

I gagged and choked and heaved and I felt like I was being knifed in the belly. Then it all came up, the supper and the pie and the coffee and the champagne. I heaved and heaved into the basin, and I swear I heaved up more than what could have been in me and I thought my ribs were going to break. I was bathed in sweat and even my shoulder hurt. I wanted to die and just be swallowed up into the floor I was so embarrassed. When it all stopped I lay there, and I couldn't speak.

Shakespeare sat on the floor with his hand on me, and he said, "I'm going to clean you up now."

I said, "Oh God no."

He stroked my hair and he said, "I'm sure you'd do the same for me."

I tried to cover my face as best as I could, just like I'd done when the Comanches beat me. He got the pitcher and the towel and washcloth and took my shirt off and pulled my soiled trousers off, and he began to wipe me clean. He said, "After all it's not like I haven't seen you unshucked before."

When he had washed me off, he picked me up and carried me to the bed and put me in it. I rolled away from him and turned my back to him, curling up into as small of a ball as I could make. He sat down beside me, and I felt his fingers trace the scar on my shoulder blade.

I flinched away from him. "Please don't."

"Looks like you had an angel wing removed right here."

"Yeah, some angel I am." He traced it again and I let him do it, and then he put his whole hand on it and just held it there.

"It's so ugly," I said.

"It's a battle scar." He went on, saying, "Coriolanus was supposed to go down to the town square and show his battle scars to the people in order to be appointed to some high office, but he was too arrogant to do it, saying everyone knew he was a war hero so what did he need to show his scars for, and it ended up costing him his life."

"Who's Coriolanus?

"A Shakespearian tragic hero."

"I don't think I qualify as a tragic hero."

"If your pride gets you killed, you just may." He leaned over and he kissed the scar, several times, over and over again. I grabbed the bed linen and clenched it with my fists in order to let him do it.

When I woke up, it was dark and he was sitting in a corner reading a small Shakespeare book by lamplight. He saw I was awake, and I couldn't think of what to say.

He stood up, putting his book away in his shirt pocket. Standing over me he said, "I wanted to make sure you're OK. You get some rest. Bang on the wall if you need me."

I could hear his boots hitting hard across the wooden floor and his spurs jingling and I heard his hand on the door, and I couldn't stand the thought of being alone.

I said, "Don't go."

He stopped.

"Stay with me."

TWENTY-NINE

I didn't turn to look but I heard him cross back. He sat on the edge of the bed and I heard his boots hit the floor. He lay down next to me and put his arm around me. He smelled like sweat and dust and horse and he smelled like prairie flowers and the hot wind off the plains, and he smelled like the night sky. I didn't even know what that meant but it was what I thought. I was glad he was bigger than me, and I felt as if now not even the nightmares could get to me.

I woke up long before dawn and the room was still dark, and I realized he was under the covers now, behind me, his arm around me and my breast cupped in his hand. At first I was shocked at how close he was and I feared what Ma might think, but I left his hand there. I began to breathe easy and I didn't want the sun to come up so we could stay like that forever. I loved his hand being on my breast, as if he was holding all of me, everything that I was, in just one hand.

I leaned into his hand and I whispered, "You can have me if you want."

I didn't know if he was even awake, but then I felt a kiss on the back of my neck and his hand moved to my other breast, and then it began to trail down my body and over my belly and I rolled onto my back so he could have me, and I reached back and grabbed the iron railings of the headboard as he moved up on top of me. He was still dressed and his clothes were rough and he was kissing me and I could feel his buttons and pockets pressing into me, and then I was scared. The fear was like a wave off the gulf, rolling over me, and I was afraid of what Ma would say and I imagined Preacher haranguing me and I feared the Comanches were in the room now and coming for me out of the darkness. My breathing froze up, and then Shakespeare was off me.

I curled up again and I said, "I'm sorry, I'm sorry, I'm sorry," and he said, "It's all right, it's all right, it's all right," and I felt ashamed for being so frightened. We were quiet then, and with his hand resting on my scar, somewhere in there, I fell asleep.

It was bright again when I woke up, and just like before, there he was in the chair, reading. I looked around, and there was a brown paper package sitting on the foot of the bed. I said, "What's that?"

"Look and see."

I felt as if every bone had been pulled out of my body, but I dragged myself out of the bed and I didn't even care if he saw me naked. I knew there was nothing attractive about me, so what the hell. I walked across the room naked and I got a drink of water from the pitcher, and then I opened the package.

He had been out already and he had bought me new clothes to replace the ones I had soiled. And there with the new clothes were ribbons, ribbons of different colors, pink and blue and red and yellow and green, and they took my breath away.

"Saw you looking at the ribbons," he said. "Thought you'd like them."

"Thank you," I said. "I'll pay you back."

"It's a gift. There's no need."

I put the new clothes on and I picked up the pink ribbon and fingered it. I said, "I'll wear this if I ever feel pretty."

He closed the book and put it in his shirt pocket and he said, "You're pretty now."

I just smiled at him, and I put the ribbons away.

⚜ ⚜ ⚜

We got something to eat and I had a hard time looking at him. When I did, he smiled at me and made small talk about how hot it was going to be that day, right? And the nights seemed as hot as the days, didn't they? And the wind across the plains never seems to stop, does it?

I didn't know what to say to anything he said.

We met Monty at the stables again and he said he would finish preparing the wagon and we could leave tomorrow, calling me "boss." I couldn't help but think again how the world was turned around and upside down, and that gave me an idea.

As we left the stable, I whispered to Shakespeare, "Follow me," and I led him back to the Dodge House.

We went upstairs and down the hall to my door and there were no words spoken as I let him into my room. When the door was closed behind us, I turned and pushed him up against the door and I kissed him and he held me and kissed me back, and then I told him to take off his clothes, and I began to unbutton his shirt.

He tried to stop me, saying, "Kid, I want to, but you don't need to do this. I understand."

"It's OK," I said. "I figured something out about being frightened."

Our hands were trembling as we started undressing each other.

We both stood there naked and we kissed again and he was tall and lean and his muscles from working the horses and riding all day were like cords. I ran my hands over him like I'd always wanted to, discovering him, and he touched me, slowly, all over. We were both covered in sweat, the day was so hot already.

I took him by the hand and I led him over to the bed and I said, "Lie down."

He did so, saying, "Kid ... "

"No, don't speak," I said, and I knelt on the bed beside him and I ran my hand through his hair, looking for the copper.

"Everything's been upside down and turned around ever since my family was killed. Every day I've been scared about something, whether it was Sally being lost or me freezing to death, or being hit by hail or lightning, or being run over by a stampede or drowning in a river crossing, or One-Eye finding me and cutting my throat, or Big Mike being mad at me, or whether or not you liked me, or what Ma would think about anything I was saying or doing, or if the horse I was to ride the rough off of was going to break my neck, or if the dead Comanches were coming back to haunt me."

I threw my leg across his body and I held on to his shoulders and I leaned down and I kissed him.

"I'm sick of being afraid," I said. "I'm done with being scared. If the world is turned around and upside down, then I'm turning things back around right now."

I began to ease down onto him and it felt like lightning was going through my whole body, and again he said, "Kid ... "

I was struggling to breathe but I said, "My name is Jane Fury. I'm sixteen years old. Fury is an Irish name. You can call me Jane."

He stared at me, his eyes wide and blue, then his hands went to my face and he ran his hands through my hair, smiling and saying, "Glad to meet you, Jane. I'm only a little older than you. My name is Roy Finnegan. Finnegan is an Irish name. It means fair one. Roy is French. It means king."

"You're king of my heart, Roy."

And he said, "Jane."

Light seemed to course through my whole body and I gasped. It felt good to hear my name on his lips and I touched them with my fingers like I'd always wanted to and I whispered, "Say my name again." He did, and I felt my name on his lips and I said, "I'm not doing anything I don't want to do, Roy," and I liked how it felt to say his name.

I looked into his eyes and he looked back into mine and he had the same look he had when he marveled at the stars. I remembered he pointed out a constellation of stars one time named Equuleus and he spelled it for me, saying it meant "little foal," and when I saw it I was struck by what a miracle and a mystery the world was, and that's how he was looking at me.

And as we touched each other, his heart beat so hard in his chest I swear I could feel it thundering against my legs, and the pounding of his heart and his blood rose into my hips and butt and spread up into my whole body until my heart was pounding with his heart, and he was bringing me out of the dark forest of fear and hate I was living in, and together we broke free of the dark forest and into the sun and the open air and we were flying high over a field of green grasses and prairie flowers. I was covered in sweat and my hands and arms were high in the air and Shakespeare's hands were in my hair and on my face and on my shoulders and then on my breasts and running down my ribs to my waist and hips and butt and legs. I was free and I could breathe because everything was air and sun and blue sky and flowers and open fields. Somewhere in there I was screaming, and then I was weeping because nothing could touch me or hurt me because I was free of all loss and fear and pain, and I was in his hands. He looked at me as if I was some kind of miracle, and that's what he said, "Thy life's a miracle," and I knew he was quoting from one of those plays.

I collapsed down on him and he was as wet as I was, as if we'd been underwater and just come up for air. I held him, and his hands caressed my back and his fingers traced my scar and he whispered in my ear, "Maybe you're not an angel, maybe you're Pegasus, but you've lost one of your wings. Pegasus and Equuleus. The winged horse and a little foal, both."

I whispered back to him, "If you die, I'll kill you."

"That doesn't make sense," he said.

"It does to me."

I don't know how long we lay there like that, covered in sweat, the hot sun pouring through the window and the hard wind blowing the curtains, but however long it was, it wasn't long enough.

When we got to the stables the next morning the hands were there, the wagon was ready, and Jack Straw was waiting for us, looking all sheepish. When I asked him what he was doing, he said he needed a job, that he was a fool and he'd gotten drunk again the night before and had lost all his money, and if I could afford another hand he'd like to hire on. He held his hat in his hands and looked at his boots a lot, and his kit and saddle were just behind him on the ground.

I looked at Shakespeare and he just shrugged. I thought, to hell with the money, why not? Who wouldn't want Jack Straw as a traveling companion.

"Sure, Jack Straw. Thirty dollars a month."

He said, "I'll save every penny of it."

We left Dodge, heading southwest, crossing the Arkansas River, Shakespeare trailing the remuda and Monty driving the wagon. I led the way with Abraham, Jack Straw, Shady, and Tommy Deuce, and we were following the direction General Dodge had drawn on his map.

We traveled day after day, the prairie stretching out before us, seeming so vast and empty, and the wind was relentless. The wagon and the horses and the hands could all have been swallowed up, and no one would ever have known we were gone. That's what I began to feel sometimes, a goneness.

At night, Shakespeare read from the plays. I didn't know if it was the words he spoke or the stories themselves or the sound of his voice, but when he read aloud I found myself thinking, we're not so lost and alone after all, here's where home is, here where I can hear his voice, as if his voice was the true center of the universe. When he wasn't reading or talking, I remembered how hard and lean his body felt against mine, but that made me lonely, like a pleasant memory of something I might never have again.

At night, when I got panicky about how alone I felt, I held on to Ghost's reins, desperate for her to calm me, but sometimes even she was quiet. Even the chatter of the hands or Shakespeare's voice didn't help, and often in the mornings I would be sick at my stomach and I'd throw up, and the feeling and the sickness would come and go.

Shakespeare threw his bedroll down near mine every night and we'd talk. The hands figured out we were partners, but we didn't do anything in front of them to act like we were in love. Sometime in the middle of one night it was raining hard and I felt his hands on me and he was unbuttoning my blouse. He had crawled into my bedroll naked and he was kissing me all over. I helped him slip my trousers off and he whispered, "Jane, Jane, Jane," between the kisses, and then he was on top of me and I held him to me saying, "Yes, yes, yes." He kept saying my name and he kissed my eyes and lips and cheeks and neck and ran his hands through my hair and over my body. Every time he said "Jane" I felt like I was being created anew, and every time he kissed me I felt like I was being touched by something holy. I felt the full length and weight of him, him holding me in his arms and my arms wrapped around him and I whispered, "Yes, yes, yes," and I bit against screaming, and then he was breathing hard and resting in me.

We stayed like that until just before the dawn, then he threw the bedroll off both of us and no one was awake yet. The rain was still coming down, washing me and pouring off of him, and he was naked and looking at me naked, and I've never felt so beautiful or seen anything so magnificent in my life.

We both got our clothes on, soaking wet. We had the coffee going and were drying off by the fire by the time the other hands were waking up, and I had pulled the pink ribbon out of my kit and put it in my hair.

The rain let up and we spotted several warriors out on the plains some days later, and all the hands kept their weapons at the ready. We had found a band in what was maybe northeastern New Mexico territory or northwestern Texas. I swear I could smell the wind off the mountains far to the west, carrying the scent of pine and cedar.

The warriors approached us slowly and Shady rode out to meet them, telling them we were friendly and wanted to trade. They came in cautiously and all the boys held their hands up and smiled real big and waved at them to show we meant no harm. The warriors talked with Shady and then circled our wagon, Monty throwing back the canvas to show them we were stocked with goods.

They rode out and looked at the remuda, then come back and said we were to follow them. Shady said they were Shoshone and they were friendly with the Comanches, so if we found that Sally wasn't in their camp, they might know where she was. We followed them for several miles until we came to their band, spread out for less than a mile along a creek lined with cottonwoods and willows and sycamores. The tipis were arranged in circles, Shady saying they were families camping together, each circle being a different family.

I asked Shady, "Why don't they just kill us and take everything we have?"

"Don't make them mad," he said, "or maybe they will."

Shakespeare kept the remuda outside the camp and the hands stayed with him so we wouldn't look threatening when we moved the wagon closer in. Monty and Shady drove the wagon to the edge of the camp, me riding alongside, and Shakespeare kept an eye on us from afar with field glasses. The warriors rode through the camp announcing us, and when we stopped we began to draw a crowd.

Little kids approached the wagon slowly and I kept an eye out for Sally while Monty pulled out some horehound sticks and gave them to the kids, then he spread out blankets by the wagon and placed goods on them for trade. Women began to show up, and when I dismounted Ghost they wanted to touch my hair, so I took Jamie's hat off and I pulled the pink ribbon off that Shakespeare had given me. I shook my hair out and they laughed and talked about it to each other.

Shady said, "Maybe they're talking about what a good scalp it would make."

I told him, "That ain't funny."

Several older Shoshone men with bear-claw necklaces and feathers and silver decorations in their long hair approached the wagon and looked like they were important because the women cleared back when they came near. Monty offered them rope twists of tobacco as gifts and Shady talked and translated. They were discussing trade, so I backed off and remounted Ghost and rode slowly into the camp, smiling and waving.

Everyone came out as if it was a big festival day because a Comanchero had arrived. I looked for Sally but I couldn't see a little blond girl anywhere, but I did see a tall redheaded girl that was with child, and when I spoke to her she couldn't understand me and just shook her head. I was baffled at that, her not understanding me, and she ducked away and disappeared into the crowd. I saw what looked like a young Mexican boy, then an older Mexican boy, but they both spoke Indian and not Mexican and were running and playing with the other Shoshone kids. I wondered where they had come from and who their parents were.

It seemed like I was riding through some foreign country, never having seen anything like this before with people living in tipis and speaking another language, and I realized they must have thought the same thing of us, that we were the foreigners, coming into their territory.

As I rode through the camp, those who were bold enough reached out to touch my hair and I leaned down and I touched theirs and told them I admired it, it being long and black and beautiful. Some understood a few of my words and spoke some English, and those who didn't still knew I was being friendly. They nodded and smiled at me, and I found myself wondering what farms their warriors had raided and who they had killed or outraged, yet they all were patting my knee or waving at me. I couldn't see killing these Shoshone even though I knew they probably weren't any more innocent than the Comanches, and everything seemed confusing.

One woman pointed to her tipi and insisted I come in, so I dismounted and ground tied Ghost and followed her in. Several women and young girls followed us and there was a small fire in the middle of the tipi with smoke drifting up high out of the open center. There were pallets with robes on them, and the women all circled around me and discussed something among themselves and gestured at me.

Then the one who had invited me said, "*am'bo*," and she reached out and pointed at my chest, and they all giggled, and I realized they were confused about whether or not I was a girl because of the way I was dressed. I told them yes, I was a girl just like them, a woman, *am'bo*. I pointed at her chest and then at mine and I gestured we were the same. They all gathered in closer and reached out to touch me, so I raised my shirt and showed them my breasts and said, "breasts," and they all gasped and giggled and said, "*pitsi*," and confirmed to each other that they had been right, or reprimanded those who had been wrong, or so I imagined. Then they all wanted to touch my breasts, so I let them, and then I touched theirs and everyone was laughing and giggling. All of a sudden I felt like I was home with women friends or neighbors or family.

A young girl about my age pushed her way to the front and put my hand on her swelling belly and she said, "*bibi*," and I said "baby," and I couldn't believe the words were so alike. We traded "*bibi*" and "baby" back and forth, all of the women murmuring and smiling. Then she took her hand and put it on my belly and she said, "*bibi*" again, and I laughed and shook my head no, but she insisted, nodding yes, and said, "*bibi*" again.

"Maybe someday," I said, and the two of us stood there with our hands on each other's belly. I thought, *This is what it would be like if I had a sister close to my own age, if we were both with child at the same time.* Then I was all bewildered, because I felt as if this Shoshone girl and I could be sisters, somehow.

When we all went outside, the warriors passing by stopped to look at me, and the women laughed and pointed out that I was a girl, an *am'bo*. They got off their ponies and wanted to touch me but I knocked their hands away hard. They thought that was funny and moved in to try it again.

The women yelled at them to stop that, sounding like a bunch of mothers or wives. The warriors smirked and pointed at Ghost and I didn't know what they meant until one of the women who spoke some English pointed out that Ghost was a mare, a "*piapeh*," and I realized the warriors were all on stallions and wouldn't be caught dead riding a mare. That made me mad, so I gestured and said my horse was faster than any of their horses, and that same woman seemed to understand what I was saying and she helped make my point clear, saying "*geta nuikwi.*"

They all laughed and pointed back and forth at me and Ghost, indicating we were both mares, "*piapeh.*" One of them mounted up and gestured at me to follow him, so I mounted up and the other warriors knew what he was going to do, so they yelled at everybody and rode through the camp making some announcement. I kept hearing the word "*na'natea.*"

People cleared out of the way and the one I was following led me to the far end of the camp. The whole way there I was looking for Sally because I was sure everyone was out of their tipis by now, but I didn't see her anywhere.

He bragged and yelled and gestured at everyone to get out of the way, and he pointed at me. I'm sure he was telling everyone I was a girl and I was riding a mare that I had bragged on. They all called out and lined up to watch, and when I realized he was challenging me to a race, I was just mad enough that I wasn't frightened. I thought, *Why not? I'll teach him a lesson for making fun of the fact that I'm a girl and Ghost is a mare.*

We reached the far end of the camp where there was a final circle of tipis close to the river and next to a long line of cotton-woods. He whirled his horse around and pointed to the ground next to him, meaning I was to come up alongside him, which I did. Then he pointed to the far end of the camp, less than a mile away, saying, "*Na'natea.*"

He looked at me and I nodded, and before I knew what was happening he hit me in the face with his quirt, and then he yelled and lashed his horse and he was off.

THIRTY

Ghost and I were left standing in the dust and I had blood coming down my face, but I yelled at Ghost and spurred her and hit her with the reins, and he had a good lead on us. Most of the Shoshone camp lined our path and shouted and cheered him on and jeered at me because I trailed behind. I wiped the blood out of my eyes as we ran and my face smarted, and I got angry as if I was tracking down one of the Comanches who had outraged Ma.

I spurred Ghost on and I whispered to her, "If ever you've run before, run now," and I swear she understood me. She picked up speed and we began to gain on him. He was looking back at us and some Shoshone just coming out of their tipis had to leap out of the way. Dogs followed after us and alongside us, barking and nipping, and mothers pulled children out of the way. Some other warriors had mounted up at the sight of us and raced right behind us so they could see the finish for themselves, all of us weaving through the circles of tipis and through the families who had come out to watch and had to dodge out of the way.

Halfway there, Ghost come up along the right side of him, and as we edged up closer he lashed at me again. I held up my left arm and blocked the blow, and when he tried it again I managed to grab the quirt and hold on to it. He tried to yank it back and it felt like he was going to pull my arm off and tear the scar on my shoulder open again, but I held on. I yelled at Ghost to "Go! Go! Go!" and the two of us raced along as if we were tied together.

I saw the wagon at the far end of the village and there was a large crowd at the wagon watching, and they pushed aside to clear a path for us. We were neck and neck and he was yanking at the quirt, and as Ghost began to push past him I let the quirt go and I said, "Now, now, now!"

She found more speed in her and we were out of his reach. He yelled at his horse, and I flew past the wagon first and he was right behind me at Ghost's rump, screaming something at me, or at his horse.

It took us almost a hundred yards to slow down and stop. Then he tried to lash at me with his quirt and he shouted at me and I ducked and reined Ghost away from him. The Shoshone warriors following us on horseback surrounded the two of us and everyone was yelling, and I realized they were rawhiding him because he had been beaten by both a girl and a mare. One of them pointed at the blood on my face and was berating him.

He yelled back at them, and both his horse and Ghost danced all around each other. I pulled up next to him and while he shouted at them I grabbed the quirt and threw it as far away as I could. All the warriors laughed at that and I could see he was going to hit me or kill me, but one of the warriors rode his horse in between us to stop him.

By then several of the older Shoshone men, the ones with the feathers and silver trinkets in their hair and bear-claw necklaces, had walked from the wagon to where we were and one of them spoke sharply to the warrior. Everyone quieted down and the one I had beaten ducked his head but I could see he was boiling mad.

The head Shoshone ordered someone to get the quirt and someone did, and the head Shoshone took it and handed it to me and gestured that I was to hit the warrior in the face with it. At that everyone fell silent and waited to see what I would do.

Shady had made it down to us by then and he caught what the headman had said and he looked at me too and waited. I looked at the one I had beaten and I knew as good as he did what it was to be shamed, so I held the quirt up high, and instead of hitting him I said, "I'm keeping this as my prize." I turned to

Shady and I said, "Tell him that, and then tell him that next to mine, his horse is the fastest horse I've ever seen."

Shady translated, and I said, "Tell him the only reason he couldn't beat me is because my horse came from the sky as a gift from the god of rain and thunder and lightning, that's why she's gray with a spotted rump, like storm clouds."

Shady translated and I added, "Tell him he is the noblest Shoshone warrior here because he was the only one brave enough to challenge a god horse to a race."

At that he brightened up and the others said admiring things to him, then they rode over and some said in English, "Good horse," and "Fast horse," and some of them dismounted and stroked her and felt her all over and looked at her teeth.

Shady said they wanted to know my horse's name, and I said her name was Ghost. When Shady translated it, some repeated "*gedukugan,*" but some shook their head no, saying, "*Tsoapittsi.*"

"*Tsoapittsi* means spirit, not ghost," Shady said. "They say Spirit is a better name." Shady then said, "They want to know why Ghost was given to you."

"She was a gift to make up for the Comanches killing my family," I said, adding, "The Comanches are dogs but the Shoshone are noble."

They were upset and arguing. Shady said, "The Shoshone are friends with the Comanches and don't think the Comanches are dogs."

"Ask if they think the soldiers who killed their families are dogs."

Shady translated, and at that they all nodded and agreed and some of them shrugged and stopped arguing, deciding not to push the discussion any further.

Then the headman made a speech, gesturing at me and Monty and Shady. The warriors nodded in approval and they all began to move back to the village. As we rode back to the wagon,

Shady told me we'd been invited to this headman's tipi, and it was a great honor to be invited.

Back at the wagon, I washed the blood from my face. I had been cut across my cheekbone and temple and I was afraid the wounds were going to leave scars. I never thought I was that pretty but I felt sick about the possibility of having scars on my face, but Monty dabbed honey on both cuts to stop the bleeding and said that would help. For a moment I felt like I was home again, because Ma had done the same thing with honey when we had hurt ourselves.

Shakespeare came in from the remuda and looked at the cuts and wanted to know what had happened and who he should kill. I told him it had all ended well and we were going to a fandango and he should wash up and be presentable. Abraham came in to keep watch over the wagon and Jack Straw and Tommy Deuce stayed to guard the remuda.

When the time came, Shady led us into the village. He said when we entered the tipi we'd be sitting in a circle that started on the left side of the entrance and ended at the right side of the entrance, and we weren't to talk until everyone had smoked the pipe that was being passed around. If anyone talked before everyone had smoked, then they'd have to start the ritual all over again. He told me I was to sit in the row behind the men, with all the women, and I wasn't to talk at all.

That made me mad, but Shakespeare said, "Do what Shady tells you because that's how they do things here, and when they come to your house you can make them do things your way."

I thought about that and I had to smile at the prospect of a band of Shoshone elders and warriors and women sitting around a long table eating and passing bread and talking about where they'd been and what they'd seen, and all of us asking questions of one another and laughing.

It all came off like Shady said. The tipi was dark and shadowy with the flickering light from the fire in the center throwing our shadows up against the hide walls of the tipi, and the air smelled of tobacco and woodsmoke as the pipe was passed around. There were other women in the second row with me, some with babies as well as older children, and dogs too, and once the pipe was passed there was a long silence. Then the men began to talk.

Shady didn't translate it because, he said later on, it was about weather or the proximity of their enemy, the Utes, or water and grazing and if it was time to move to a new location, and some asking why they couldn't travel or hunt as free and easy as the white men, and all of them wondering where the soldiers were, and there were fewer and fewer buffalo to be found anywhere and that was a bad sign, and even the antelope were scarce.

During all this talk, Shakespeare, Monty, and Shady sat quiet, then one warrior asked why we weren't trading horses. Shady translated as Shakespeare spoke, explaining about my family being killed and my sister being taken, and these were special horses that were only to be used in trade for her.

They considered that and talked among themselves and they wanted to know what she looked like. Shakespeare said she was three years old, and he turned and pointed at me and said, "She looks like that."

They asked if we would like to trade for a little Apache girl. He told them no, then they asked if we wanted to trade for a young Mexican girl, and he said no again.

I whispered to him, "Tell them about One-Eye."

Shakespeare hesitated, then told them we thought my sister was being taken care of by a Comanche with only one eye, would any of them have seen a Comanche with one eye? He told them we wanted to thank him for taking care of her, but now we wanted to trade for her with the horses.

The Shoshone talked among themselves and there seemed to be a disagreement, and they went back and forth. I felt we must have hit a nerve, otherwise they would have just said no, they didn't know him. My breath got real fast and my heart was beating faster and I whispered, "They know him, they know where he is."

Shakespeare elbowed me and said, "Shhh," but nodded yes.

Shady translated as the headman spoke, saying, "Yes, some know of this man. Some say he is far to the north and some say to the west. They say he is a brave warrior who was injured in a terrible fight, and even though he lost one eye, now he sees so well he can see into the future and he can see you coming to take his daughter away, and you will never find him because he will always see you first, so it's best not to look for him because he knows you come not to thank him and reward him with horses, but to kill him and take this young girl away from her Comanche family."

Some warriors spoke to the headman and he quickly added, "Some say she has been traded to the Cheyenne or the Kiowa, so you should look there."

Shakespeare thanked them for their good advice and said we did not intend to hurt the one-eyed warrior, we only wanted the little girl back.

I wanted to stand up and say One-Eye was no brave warrior, he was a dog who lost his eye to a woman who fought back when he was outraging her, and Sally was my sister and no daughter of his. Shakespeare must have known what I was thinking because he reached back and put his hand on my boot, and I had to hold my breath and bite my tongue.

The rest of the evening was a blur with more rituals. There was meat on a stick by a fire and we all pulled pieces off it and ate, and Monty pointed out later that we were eating horse. I almost gagged thinking about Buck, so he lied to me and said, "Maybe it was dog."

When we got back, I was so mad about the lies about One-Eye's bravery that I started pounding the side of the wagon with my fist and cursing, and Shakespeare said, "Calm down, we found out where she is."

I said, "What do you mean?"

"She's to the south, probably southeast."

"How do you know?"

"Because they want us to go to the north or to the west. They're sending us in the wrong direction. One-Eye's far to the east of Santa Fe for sure, probably still in Texas somewhere, and she's still with him, because they called her his daughter. We're going to find her."

At that I collapsed down, holding my face in my hands. Shakespeare sat by me and I said, "It's too close, it's too close, I can't come this close and then lose her again."

"You aren't going to lose her," he said. "We're going to find her."

After the meeting, festivities began in the village. There was drumming and dancing and singing and the warriors raced horses and the children played games, all in celebration of the Comancheros and the trading.

The next morning, the women came out to the wagon and took over the fire and made some hot brew and we all sat together and drank together, and the young girl with child sat near me. We all chattered away in Shoshone and English and Mexican about I don't know what, but it felt like I had friends. They told stories I struggled to understand and they teased one another and made one another laugh, and there were arguments and jealousies between them like any other group of women, and I found myself smiling the whole time. I admired how they dressed in soft deerskin frocks, not wearing corsets or undergarments or anything tight or confining, or sunbonnets, and I thought I might like one of those deerskin frocks as well, and I marveled at how free my body might feel in it.

But in my heart I couldn't help wondering what was going to happen to them and their children. I knew it didn't look good with the buffalo hard to find and the soldiers circling around somewhere. I wondered what life on a reservation would be like. I hoped the annuities and the rations would be plentiful and they'd have more food, and maybe they would learn to like farming, and maybe their children would learn English and become good farmers, but I wondered if that was at all possible. I knew if someone told me I was going to have to learn to like doing nothing but sums for the rest of my life, I probably wouldn't like it any more than they might like farming. I didn't have a good feeling about any of it, and I couldn't figure out how things could go well for anybody.

After several days of trading the women came out to tell me goodbye as we prepared to pull away from the village. I walked up to the young girl who was carrying and I pulled the pink ribbon Shakespeare had given me out of my hair and I tied it into hers. Again she put her hand on my belly, me shaking my head no, her nodding yes, and me laughing and saying no.

We said goodbye, knowing we'd never see each other again, and I mounted up on Ghost and waved to her, wishing her and her baby well. In my heart, I had my doubts.

THIRTY-ONE

We traveled for days, for weeks, for I don't know how long, and the season changed and the grasses dried and cured yellow and the sun rode lower in the sky. We come across a few bands and traded for several days at a time, and sometimes we traveled and found no one. One day we come across a small band, and like so many of them the trade wasn't good because they were poor and living on rough row. I made friends with the women again, but no one had seen a little girl like Sally. There was one Comanche widow with a baby and the mother looked thin and pale, so I slipped her some sardines and airtight tinned meat and some airtight peaches, but I knew it wasn't enough.

Like the other bands, the women told me they were worried about the soldiers looking for them. With the hunting so bad and winter coming on, they thought it would be best to move onto a reservation, thinking they could then jump the reservation when spring came like everyone else did, and maybe the hunting would be better. But they didn't have any say in the decision. They complained that when their warriors stole cattle, rather than eat the beef they traded them away for more horses, or for weapons and ammunition and spirits from other Comancheros.

One day scouts came in saying a raiding party would be coming in that afternoon, and everyone in the village was excited and made ready. Shady said if the raid hadn't been successful the warriors would have sneaked back in, but the fact that they announced their arrival meant they would be bringing back prizes and tales of bravery.

Sure enough, eight warriors rode in and there was a big to-do with drums and songs and dancing, and we were right in the middle of it. They brought back a dozen cattle and the cattle were branded and not just mavericks off the range. They were leading three horses, and there were two fresh scalps hanging from one of the warrior's shields. Another warrior was holding an open parasol and another had a red-checked tablecloth wrapped around him like a shawl, spoils from their raid.

The one riding up front announced his own deeds, Shady said, describing who he had killed, and the others in the party praised his bravery and bragged on how they had touched the enemy. "Counting coup," Shady said. I realized I was one of the enemy whose family had been touched and I was furious. I put my hand on my Schofield but Shakespeare grabbed me and led me back to the wagon. When Monty gave gifts to the raiders I was so angry that Shakespeare told me to go stay by the remuda, saying we needed all the goodwill we could get.

Shady and Monty were invited to the same ritual we'd been to before. They said after the pipe was passed around and the men had talked, Shady announced we would be leaving the next morning. Then he asked about One-Eye but didn't say why we were interested, only that we had heard about him and understood he might have a large camp we could trade with. He didn't ask about Sally, figuring it was best not to raise any suspicion.

The men discussed the question and they all agreed. One-Eye was to the southeast, camped along a creek lined with cottonwoods and willows. Pointing out several landmarks, they assured Monty and Shady they couldn't miss it.

We drove the wagon and trailed the remuda day after day to the southeast, running across a few more small bands and staying several days. We crossed creeks and rivers and it was getting colder, and from time to time we started to get snow, but never enough to slow us down.

At night, the stars seemed even more brilliant because of the cold. Around the fire the hands talked about good meals they'd had in the past, or they played dominoes and repaired their equipment, or oiled their weapons. Now that they knew I was a girl, they didn't talk about women the way they had before, and they tried not to swear as often. Monty pointed out that I wasn't eating much and I told him the smell of the cooking made me sick and I just wasn't hungry. He shook his head but kept encouraging me and brought me hot drinks made from peppermint or ginger or wild oats and other herbs when I was sick at my stomach.

Slowly the land changed and it started to roll and curve and there were more trees and outcroppings of rock and rock ledges. It was a land of divides and gullies and dry washes, ravines and arroyos, and I lost track of dates and time. It seemed as if this was our life, just moving on and trailing the horses and taking care of the mules and repairing the wagon. I began to think we were the only people on earth, and I regretted it was so difficult to give myself to Shakespeare because of how close together we were living, although there was one day when the wagon and the hands moved one way around some hill and Shakespeare led the horses another way and I was riding with him. When we were out of sight he reined up and dismounted and he hauled me out of the saddle and he pushed me up against a live oak and started kissing me.

I said, "Not here, we'll be seen," but I kissed him back and we didn't stop, and when it was over we were both on the ground, and then we pulled on what clothes had had to come off, and without speaking we rejoined the wagon as if nothing had happened. All that night by the fire he kept looking at me with that soft smile of his. I blushed and looked away, and when I looked back he would wink at me, then I'd blush all over again. I'd never known such happiness and hope and joy.

The hills got higher and the rocky ledges got bigger and steeper and the groves of pitch pine and scrub oak and mesquite got thicker, and it was a few days later when we found their camp.

There was snow on the ground and we'd been traveling alongside a wide creek, but it was so rocky that the wagon had to divert over a low hill, and when we crested it, there the village was down below us, spread out for quite a distance, curving with the creek until both the village and the creek and the cottonwoods and live oak curved out of sight. It all looked so white and beautiful and peaceful. The creek, clear and cold, spilled over rocks with small falls and pools. The tipis were painted with symbols and decorations and they all had smoke coming out of them, and in the air there was the scent of woodsmoke and bait being cooked. There were shields propped up outside the openings of the tipis and folks were moving to and fro, the women scraping hides or drying meat. Dogs were barking and kids were running and playing and horses were tied by the tipis. There was a vast herd of horses in the far, far distance to the south, all of them pawing through the snow and grazing.

We were surprised we hadn't been met by scouts and we didn't know if we were just lucky and accidently wove our way through them, or if they were being careless, or if we were being tracked the whole time. To be safe, we stayed at the crest of the hill and waited for the village to discover us rather than ride right down into it.

Sure enough, warriors saw us and mounted up and shortly a dozen or so came up the hill toward us. Then Abraham called out from the remuda watering at the creek at the foot of the hill, and we saw another half dozen or so coming up from behind us. They must have been following us after all, and we'd never seen them.

We all held up our hands to show both parties we weren't intending any harm. Those behind us circled our remuda as it grazed. Abraham and Shakespeare, down by the remuda, held up their hands and smiled real big and said "Hello!" and "Fine day, isn't it?" and acted like friendly fools.

The band approaching us from the village moved in cautiously, counting how many of us there were. Shady rode out with his hands up and began to parley with them, explaining we had been trading with other Shoshone and Comanche bands and they had told us how to find them, and we wanted to trade with them as well. Monty jumped out of the wagon, threw back the canvas, and showed them our goods, and they all rode up and swirled around us. The warriors talked among themselves, then half of them rode back into the village to discuss our arrival with their headmen while the others stayed, watching us.

Shady bantered with them, asking about buffalo and pronghorn and how was the hunting and had they had any trouble with the Utes or the Cheyenne or the Kiowa. He told them the Shoshone had bragged on what great warriors this band was, even though they claimed they were braver.

They laughed at that and said the Shoshone were women when it came to fighting. Then they confessed that the buffalo were few and far between and so were the antelope, and it had been a dry summer where they'd come from, and some time ago the horse soldiers had sent word they had to come onto the reservation, or else. The old men wanted to go in but they themselves weren't afraid of the horse soldiers. They wanted to know if we had spirits or weapons, and Shady said no, that the horse soldiers wouldn't let us travel with those, but we knew the Comancheros up from Mexico had spirits and weapons, but they had to be careful not to be caught by the horse soldiers.

My heart was beating so fast because I wanted Shady to ask about Sally, but I knew he didn't want to give us away yet. He knew they might be wary if he suggested it, or they might even turn on us if whoever had Sally felt threatened.

Riders came back up the hill and said the wagon could come on down. Shakespeare and Abraham stayed with the remuda and

Jack Straw and Tommy Deuce stayed at the top of the hill to keep an eye on us as Monty drove the wagon down the hill, pulling back hard against the brake. Shady and I rode alongside and I thought my heart was going to burst I was so scared. I reminded myself I had to be careful with how I reacted if I saw her. I didn't know what I was going to do if I saw One-Eye.

At the foot of the hill, and at the edge of the village, Monty set the brake and men and women gathered around and everyone talked all at once. The old men came over and Monty gave them tobacco and small gifts and you'd think we were the town square with all the news that was being traded, and them wanting to know if we had seen any bluecoats, and several conversations going on at once.

Monty had picked up some Comanche lingo from the previous camps, so he laid out the trade blankets in the snow and talked hides and tin lanterns, knives and mirrors and beads and such. Folks sat on blankets across from him and he and Shady bartered and made offers and negotiated, and you would have thought we were some big-city dry goods store. Kids were looking in at the goods and at the mules and the wagon, and they circled around me and pointed out my hair. They laughed and tried to grab the new blue ribbon I'd put in my hair from the ribbons Shakespeare had given me.

I rode straight into the heart of the village, passing dogs and children and old men and warriors and women, young and old, all of them gesturing and inviting me to join them, some acting suspicious and frightened. I smiled and waved and handed out trinkets and horehound candy and pointed back to the wagon as if I was promoting the goods, when I was actually looking for Sally. I rode through the circles of tipis and far into the village, and one woman came up and grabbed me by the leg and wouldn't let go, insisting I climb down and join her and her friends.

I did so, and several of them knew some English and we traded words back and forth. They wanted to know if we'd seen any bluecoats, and I told them no. I made it clear I wanted to see the village, so we began to walk and I kept Ghost with me, holding on to her reins, thinking her force would keep me calm. The women pointed out different tipis, and with a few English words they indicated who was a brave warrior or who had a nagging wife or what woman had a bad reputation and had had her nose cut off, or where some widow lived. I don't know how we did it but somehow we were talking to each other.

The whole time we were talking and walking I was watching kids run and play. Most were beyond the tipis in open fields, playing shinny in the snow with curved sticks and some kind of a stuffed leather ball. Some boys had small bows and arrows they were practicing with, and there were footraces and pony races and they yelled and wrestled and shouted and teased just like any kids would, some kicking through the snow and throwing snowballs at each other.

Warriors rode to and fro through the circles of tipis, calling out to the women and the women would call back. The warriors looked at me, only not with a friendly glance but as if I was some invader. It scared me because I knew what they would do to me if they had me alone, and I found myself getting panicky and frightened as they swirled around. I clutched Ghost's reins hard, fearing being beaten or outraged, and I wished I could pull my Schofield and kill as many of them as I could. I almost expected to see the three bloody Comanches come walking toward me to start in on me again, when I saw Sally.

THIRTY-TWO

It was just a flash of blond hair and it was farther down the way. She ducked inside a tipi and at first I thought I'd imagined it, but she came back outside as if she'd heard something. She stood in the sun for a moment looking around, then turned and went back into the tipi. I couldn't breathe and I couldn't believe my eyes, but I told myself I saw what I saw, and I didn't know what to do. I wanted to call to her and run to her, but I thought that might scare her, and I didn't know how the women would react.

I decided I would walk toward the tipi Sally had gone into, and I kept my eye on it as we continued down the path through the circles of tipis. The women in our little group tried to teach me their names, but I struggled to listen to them because I was watching for Sally. They wanted to know my name and it took me a while to understand what they wanted, but finally it got through and I said, "Jane."

They repeated it among themselves, but all the talk faded away and it was as if there was no sound at all, not any splashing of the river, no birds overhead, no horses neighing or warriors calling out or children shouting, just me walking silently toward the tipi. The women pointed things out to me and asked me questions, and I didn't hear any of them. They pulled on my sleeve and tried to get my attention and I tried to smile at them, but I kept on toward the tipi.

When I got there, there was a shield outside of it with several scalps on it. One was long blond hair and I wanted to gag, but I held back. I turned to the women and pointed inside, and I gestured to my own hair and they laughed and nodded yes.

One of them stuck her head into the tipi and called, and when Sally walked out the sound came roaring back to me. I was overwhelmed by the noise of horses whinnying and children clamoring and birds singing and crows cawing and the creek water spilling and splashing and swirling. People talked and shouted somewhere, and dogs barked.

Sally looked at me, and she didn't recognize me.

I knelt down and the women were interfering, pointing out our blond hair and blue eyes and chatting on and on. I touched Sally's face and caressed her hair and I said, "Sally." I wanted to be alone with her, but Sally was shy, as if I was some kind of stranger.

I said, "Sally, it's Jane."

She didn't seem to understand. A woman came quickly out of the tipi and scooped Sally up into her arms and held her tightly, and Sally clutched her as if that was her real mother. I felt angry with Sally, as if Ma was being betrayed. The woman looked at me, then complained to the other women about something and shooed us away. I wanted to grab Sally out of her arms and run with her.

I stood up and said, "Sally, do you remember me?"

Sally didn't look at me and instead she buried her face in this woman's hair. The woman reprimanded the crowd of women and then ducked back inside her tipi, clutching Sally to her. I felt as if my heart was being ripped out of my body.

I called after her, "Sally!"

The woman came back out of the tipi without Sally and confronted me and pointed that I was to go away, speaking angrily to me and to the other women and gesturing that we should all leave. I tried to push past her to get into the tipi but she shoved me back. The other women grabbed me and pulled me away and forced me back down the path we had been following, one of them now leading Ghost.

I didn't know what to do but I turned and I marked the tipi in my mind, what paintings were on it and where it stood among all of the other tipis, how far it was into the village and where it was by the creek. I let myself be pulled along but I looked back, waiting for Sally to come out again, and I continued to set the tipi's location in my mind as we twisted and turned through the circles of tipis. I kept imagining getting into a tug-of-war with the woman, yanking Sally away from her and getting her back into my arms and running with her.

The women talked on and on and one of them managed to communicate to me that that woman had lost a daughter, and now she had a new daughter, and how happy she was with her new daughter, and it all made sense. I remembered what the officer told me about captives losing their language, and maybe that was true after all and maybe Sally could no longer understand me, but I couldn't believe she didn't recognize me. I thought maybe it was the length of my hair or how sunburned I was or I wasn't in a frock, or all of the surroundings were too different for her to remember back that far.

I counted up the months in my mind since she had been taken, and maybe it was three months, but all the traveling since Dodge was a blur, and I thought, no, was it five months? So many things had happened that I was confused about the time, and she was only three, and how much could I remember from when I was three? It was practically nothing, but it seemed impossible that Ma and Pa and Jamie and me and Buck and the chickens and the farm were all gone from her memory. If I just had enough time with her, maybe I could bring it all back, and she would hold me and laugh and say my name and be glad she was rescued.

I tried not to weep as we walked along and the women looked concerned and confused as to why I would act that way. They were trying to console me and reassure me that she had a good mother and I needn't worry about her. I wanted to say, "She's my sister! She's my sister!" Most of them wouldn't have understood me, and those that did would tell the men, and then the village would turn on us and get us all killed.

I tried to think what to do, how to get her back, and at the same time I couldn't help but wonder if buying her or trading for her or stealing her wouldn't frighten her just as much as the first time she had been kidnapped. And now, to be yanked away from a woman she was holding on to so tightly, how could such a little girl withstand that much loss and fear and confusion? Yet I knew that was all I wanted, to get her back and bring her home, and I was still bewildered over where home was, other than I knew wherever home was, it was with me.

We were back at the wagon and the women nodded and smiled and tried to reassure me all was well. I tried to smile back, and there were still big goings-on at the wagon. Even with the snow, a festival had started and more blankets were on the ground with trade goods, and Monty and Shady were still bargaining.

I wanted to make myself scarce, so I mounted up on Ghost and waved to the women and thanked them, then pulled out of the crowd and raced uphill, scared about what would happen next. I rode down to where the remuda was watering by the creek and I dismounted and fell to my knees, struggling to get my breath. I crawled over and sat up against a tree. Shakespeare rode over and dismounted and sat down beside me, taking my hand.

"You found her?"

I couldn't speak and I nodded yes.

"Is she OK?"

I nodded yes, and he said, "Did she recognize you?"

I shook my head no and I began to weep, and he said, "Well, that was to be expected."

I jerked my hand away. "Why? Why is it to be expected?"

"She's so young, Jane, and it's been a long time."

He touched my hair but I shook him off. It wasn't his fault but I was mad at the world and at life and at God that things had to be so difficult. I wanted to hit somebody, so I turned and I hit him on the shoulder as hard as I could and I hit him again and again, and he let me do it until I was exhausted.

I fell back against the tree and I said, "I want to kill somebody, I want to kill them all."

"I'll bet you do."

I was even angry at him for being so understanding but I didn't have the strength to hit him again. I wanted to pull out the Schofield and just fire it into the village over and over, but I knew with my luck I'd probably hit Sally. He held my hand and touched my hair and ran his fingers over the scar on my cheekbone from when I had been hit by the quirt. I thought, *I've got scars on my back and on my face and on my heart.*

I said, "What are we going to do?"

He didn't answer until my breathing sorted itself out and he knew I could listen.

"We talk to Shady and Monty and we have them say the army is looking to recover a young blond girl, that we're authorized to trade for her."

"What if they say no?" And I told him what the women said about Sally being a replacement for a child that had died.

"Then we just take her. There are seven of us. We abandon the wagon and the remuda and we take her at night and we ride like hell."

"They'll come after us. Someone will get killed and I don't have the right to ask them to give their lives for her. It's not like we're a troop of Texas Rangers. It's not their fight."

"Then let's hope we can trade for her," he said. "We'll start there."

Monty and Shady were invited to the ritual in the headman's tipi and they brought Shakespeare with them. I rode down as well and the women took me into the tipi and I sat in the second row again, behind Shakespeare.

Sitting across from Shakespeare, on the opposite side of the tipi, was One-Eye.

My breath froze, and then my heart started beating so fast I thought my chest would crack open.

I ducked my head down and pulled my hat low and tried to make myself small behind Shakespeare so One-Eye wouldn't see me. Shakespeare reached back and put a hand on me but I knocked it away. What I wanted to do was pull the Schofield out and stand up and just fire every shot into him and see him destroyed like he destroyed my family, see him killed in the same way the three Comanches who beat me were killed, and if Shakespeare and Monty and Shady and me and all the rest of the hands were killed and I lost any chance of saving Sally, so be it. That one moment of seeing him die would be worth all the other deaths.

I put my hand on the Schofield and it felt big and hard and powerful and the metal was pure cold steel. In my mind I could see the brass cartridges and the lead rounds and even the grains of powder that would send the hate straight into him as they exploded, the bullets shattering his heart and his lungs and his brain. I would only wish for a moment when I could stand over him and speak Comanche and tell him who I was and why he was dying, and say to him, "How dare you, how dare you."

Shakespeare reached back again and he put his hand on top of mine, on top of the Schofield. His hand was strong and the same fingers that had caressed me and wiped away my tears and touched my scars were hard and tough from wrangling horses and gripping a riata. That same hand that had touched every inch of my body was saying no, and through his hand, clutching mine hard, I could feel his whole body on me and in me.

I whispered to him, "It's OK," and I released the Schofield.

His hand stayed on mine a moment longer, then let go.

I sat there, my breathing now fast and hard, and I knew I didn't dare look at One-Eye. I reached out and put my hand on Shakespeare's back and he leaned into it to let me know he was there.

They all smoked the pipe and then turned to talk, and after I don't know how long I heard Monty speak up, saying what we had planned, and Shady translated to make sure those who didn't understand English got it. I leaned in and listened without looking up, and I heard him say he was offering fifteen horses for the return of the little blond girl.

There was silence in the tipi, everyone looking to One-Eye, who realized why we were really there. He began to speak, and I watched him over Shakespeare's shoulder.

One-Eye was saying, Shady said, that little Sun-in-Her-Hair was his daughter and she belonged to him and his wife, Woman-Who-Waits. They had lost their own daughter, and Sun-in-Her-Hair was a gift from the spirits and she couldn't be bought for any number of horses.

Monty expressed great regret at the loss of their daughter and what a terrible tragedy that was, and no family should ever lose a child, and he himself had lost two of his daughters to Apache raiders and he hoped they had a father as good as One-Eye. He went on to say another family had lost their daughter too, and they wanted her back as badly as One-Eye wished he could have his own daughter back.

One-Eye replied that Sun-in-Her-Hair's family was gone, that he had killed them all, and there was no one to return her to even if he had wanted to return her.

When Shady translated that, Shakespeare leaned back harder into my hand and my hand was a fist now, pressed against his back. I could feel his muscle and bone through my fist, and I could feel Shakespeare staying calm and breathing into my fist, as if he could spread his own calmness into me.

Monty expressed great admiration for what a powerful war-rior One-Eye was. Now I wanted to kill Monty too, but he went on, saying there were still family members alive who wanted her back, and the Comancheros were authorized by the bluecoats to bargain for her. Out of admiration for what a dangerous warrior One-Eye was, and in sympathy for the terrible loss One-Eye had endured, Monty then offered twenty-five horses.

One-Eye tossed the offer away with a wave of his hand, say-ing he had horses.

There was silence in the tipi, then Shakespeare stood up and I didn't have anything to hold on to. He spoke, saying Sun-in-Her-Hair came from a very important family, so the bluecoats were looking for her as well.

One-Eye interrupted him and said he had seen their farm. They were not important, Shady translated, and the bluecoats wouldn't waste their time.

Shakespeare stood silent at that and I had my arms around my knees now, holding tight so I wouldn't touch the Schofield, I was so angry.

Shakespeare finally spoke up, saying he was authorized to give not only thirty-five horses but also all of the trade goods in the wagon to One-Eye. One-Eye could then distribute them as gifts to whoever he wanted, showing to all how rich and generous he was.

Shakespeare was hoping the others would start putting pres-sure on One-Eye.

He sat down and Shady translated and there was murmuring in the tent, warriors and old men whispering to One-Eye. One-Eye shook his head and made a speech about how this little girl brings comfort to his wife. To give the little girl away would be to stab his wife in her heart, and he would not be a man who would put a knife into his own wife's heart. She had one knife there already from the loss of their own little girl.

I hated One-Eye and wanted to kill him. For all of his talk about a knife in his wife's heart, he had put a knife to my mother's throat and into my heart as well. I didn't want to care about his wife, even though I had seen her anger and panic when I had talked to Sally. I knew only too well what it was like to lose family. I wondered how their daughter had died, through illness or accident or by bluecoats, and if she had suffered. And of course she had suffered, and so had Woman-Who-Waits suffered, because a loss was a loss.

I told myself it was all too bad but Sally was mine and I wanted her back, no matter how much pain it caused anybody, either Woman-Who-Waits or Sally.

Shakespeare stood up again and asked how many horses One-Eye would want, and he was authorized to offer five hundred dollars in addition to the other gifts.

I jerked up and looked at him. I had no idea what he was talking about because the only place that money could come from was the sale of his cattle, and we had never discussed that.

One-Eye just smiled at him and spoke. Shady turned to Shakespeare and said, "He wants to know where the store is that he should spend these dollars."

And I swear One-Eye caught my eye, but I looked away as if there was nothing being talked about that concerned me.

Shakespeare stood there for a few moments, then he nodded and sat down and the talk turned to other matters.

That night we sat by the fire and talked about what to do next. All the hands gathered around and Monty said we should give it a day, maybe One-Eye would think about it or discuss it with his wife, or maybe others in the village would persuade him.

Shakespeare thought there was little chance of that happening, that One-Eye seemed firm. He told the hands he thought we should abandon the wagon and the remuda and take Sally in the middle of the night and run for it.

Before the hands could speak up I said, "No, not yet. I don't want to risk the lives of everybody, and I doubt we can outrun the Comanches."

Jack Straw said, "Hell, we'd be just like a company of Texas Rangers, wouldn't we? They attack the Comanches all the time and outfight them even when they're outnumbered. We could fight a rearguard action and delay them while you get away with her."

"There's too many of them," I said. "They'll outflank you and you'll all get killed. We'll stay another day and see if anything happens, and if not, then we'll leave and find a fort and ask for soldiers to locate her and get her back."

Shady said, "They'll be gone by then and split up, long before any soldiers get here. Take her now or you'll never find her."

"They're trapped with the army out looking for them," Tommy Deuce said. "At some point they'll have to come onto a reservation and you can get her then. The reservation agents won't let them keep her. But if you want to run with her, I'm in."

I asked Abraham what he thought and he said, "I'd fight to get my own children back if I could, but after the war I couldn't find them. So I'm willing to fight to get your sister back. I got nothing to lose."

Shady spoke up again. "Take her tonight and run. We attack one end of the village and they'll come after us, and you run for it in the other direction. They'll never catch you on Ghost."

Monty nodded in agreement.

Here were men willing to risk their lives for Sally, I thought. Then I realized it wasn't for Sally, it was for me. They were rana-hans all, but what kind of a ranahan would I be if I got them all killed? I couldn't ask it, even for Sally.

I said, "No, they know now we want her, so they'll suspect we may try something. We'll wait one more day, and if One-Eye doesn't give in, then we'll talk about this again."

We divided up times to watch the remuda and the wagon, then we turned in. Shakespeare's bedroll was near mine and he whispered, "Tomorrow night I'll raise the offer to a thousand dollars and fifty horses and we'll see what One-Eye says."

"He won't go for it," I said. "The money and the horses don't mean anything to him, but thank you."

The light of the fire flickered across his face and he said, "You're welcome," and even though I wanted to crawl into his bedroll, all I could think about was Sally sleeping in her tipi, so close, but so far away.

I should have listened to Shakespeare's advice to take her and run. The next morning the bluecoats attacked.

THIRTY-THREE

It was before dawn and there was snow falling with a shadowy full moon behind low gray clouds. They must have moved into position during the night. I don't know why the village didn't have scouts out, or maybe they got the drop on the scouts and killed them, or maybe the scouts did discover them, only too late, and broke for the village, firing weapons to warn everyone. We woke to gunfire coming from the far eastern end of the village, near Sally's tipi.

"We're being hit!" I said, and the gunfire became a roar.

We pulled on our boots and I was in the saddle first. I called out, "I'm going for Sally and I'll be back with her. You all stay here and watch the wagon and the remuda."

Shakespeare mounted up and said, "I'll slow the attack down so you can get to her."

I wheeled Ghost around. "How are you going to do that?"

"Trust me," he said, and he was gone.

I took off at a dead run, down the hill toward our end of the village. Ghost was clear-footed as she barreled through the snow, and the next thing I knew Abraham was on my left and Tommy Deuce come up on my right, Jack Straw just behind him.

I shouted, "Go back! Go back!"

Tommy Deuce said, "Like hell!"

I said, "Then follow me!" and the four of us tore into the village.

I led the way, weaving through the first circle of tipis as women and older folks poured out, children in tow, all of them hurrying toward the fields that lay far, far to the south where their remuda grazed. Warriors were mounting up and riding to the sound of the guns to engage the cavalry and hold it back so the families could escape, and I was hoping we didn't get hit in any cross fire.

We passed by the creek and I looked to my left. Shakespeare was across the creek now, leading the remuda in a hard run, sixty horses exploding through the snow and weaving through the cottonwoods and oak along the far bank. I couldn't figure out what he thought he was doing but he yelled at them and hurrahed them and pushed them hard and fast.

I pulled away from the creek and ran through another circle of tipis and then another circle, one after another, the hands all with me, and the village was in an uproar. Tommy Deuce and Abraham and Jack Straw were now in single file right behind me, and we weaved and dodged and threaded our way through the growing crowd of escaping families. Dogs barked and howled and ran all about and families scattered to get out of our way, and I hoped the warriors would understand we weren't the ones attacking.

I knew exactly where Sally's tipi was and I was sure the soldiers hadn't gotten there yet, but they were coming on. I rode toward it as fast as Ghost would go, Tommy Deuce and Abraham and Jack Straw still following me, all of us racing through the chaos of warriors and panicked families.

I looked ahead and across the creek, and Shakespeare had gained ground on us. I saw him flank the remuda and he turned them and swung them into the creek. They exploded into the water and then came out and over the near bank, and they were going to slam right into the far eastern end of the village, right where the cavalry was attacking. I realized Shakespeare was driving the remuda straight into the cavalry to break up their charge so I would have time to find Sally, and he would be putting himself right in the line of fire of both the attacking cavalry and the Comanches who were trying to stave off the attack.

I prayed with all my heart, *Oh dear God in heaven, don't let him get killed.*

And as we ran I saw the remuda smash straight into the cavalry, and they hit so hard the sound made a crack. It was all hell, cavalrymen being knocked off their horses and horses running through the village riderless and other soldiers barely hanging on with both hands as their mounts went wild and ran dead ahead, straight into the warriors coming on. Some horses panicked and went mad, pitching and sunfishing and crowhopping, trying to get rid of their riders, and one man fell from his mount, his foot caught in the stirrup, and was being dragged through the circles of tipis. Soldiers on foot found themselves in hand-to-hand combat with the warriors.

The remuda scattered the charge, driving it apart, but from farther east, behind the attacking cavalry, artillery began to fire and shells exploded into the far western end of the village, most likely to keep the band from escaping in that direction.

Families screamed and clutched at one another and ran, and soldiers and warriors were engaged in a bloody struggle, and I rode past a woman facedown dead in the snow with a baby beside her crying and screaming.

The cavalrymen were trying to regroup as they straggled into the village, some on foot and some still mounted, trying to get back together, firing at the warriors and forcing them back, then pausing to reload. I saw one shoot an old man in the back and some of the soldiers began setting the tipis on fire, and I heard bullets scream past me and the boys as we ran. There were more explosions from shells hitting to the west, and I hoped Monty and Shady weren't being hit, if they had stayed behind to protect the wagon like I told them. In all the chaos I didn't have any idea where Shakespeare was now.

We got to Sally's tipi and I reined Ghost back hard onto her haunches and I jumped off and threw open the tipi covering and ran in. There was no one inside.

I should have known it.

Sally and Woman-Who-Waits were gone already and I might even have passed them while they were in flight, and One-Eye would have gone to help push back the attack.

I came out of the tipi as more shells hit the far western end of the village. I mounted fast, wheeled Ghost around, and shouted over the gunfire to Tommy Deuce, Jack Straw, and Abraham, "They're gone!"

Abraham said, "Then where is she?"

"In the crowd somewhere, heading for the horses. Now, get back to the wagon!"

He yelled back, "No, Miss Jane," and Tommy Deuce said, "If we go back now we'll just get hit by those shells."

Jack Straw said, "Whoo-eee! If this ain't like being a Texas Ranger I don't what is!"

I yelled over the gunfire, "You're a goddamned fool, Jack Straw!" Then I pointed to the escaping families, saying, "They've got to be in there somewhere."

The four of us spread out and weaved through the crowd of women and old men and children, searching for Sally, looking for her blond hair. There were so many fleeing I couldn't figure out how I was ever going to find her, but I knew I had to get her out of the line of fire and back to the wagon, if it was still safe there.

The sun began to come up and its rays looked like blood being smeared through the clouds on the eastern horizon. When I looked back, what with the snow falling through the smoke of the burning village and the sounds of the gunfire and the artillery and the screams of the panicked, the wounded and the dying, it all seemed like some kind of cold hell.

I rode through the crowd, looking for women who were carrying a child. Some of the women were wounded and bleeding and some were barefoot and some were naked, and some of the children being dragged along were naked as well. *How can they survive this?* I thought. Then I asked myself why should I care whether or not these Comanches survived, and it was bewildering, wondering who I should care for.

I leaned out of the saddle and grabbed one after another and turned them around, but I couldn't find Sally or Woman-Who-Waits. Tommy Deuce and Jack Straw and Abraham did the same thing, but we couldn't find her.

Then Abraham pointed and he said, "Look! There!"

Far away, by the Comanche remuda, I could see One-Eye. He was getting Woman-Who-Waits mounted up and she was carrying a bundle that I knew to be Sally.

Rather than ride to the sound of the guns, One-Eye had mounted them up on his horse by the tipi and rescued them first, taking them to the remuda. I realized he wasn't doing anything different than what Pa had hoped to do, but I shook that thought off.

One-Eye saw all four of us coming and he slapped Woman-Who-Wait's horse on the rump and she took off at a dead run. Then One-Eye mounted up on his own horse and he turned toward us, knowing it was Sally we were after.

Somewhere in the past several months he'd picked up a Winchester from a raid or traded for one from a Comanchero, and now he raised it, aimed, and fired as he rode hard straight for us, trying to stop us from following after Woman-Who-Waits. He levered in shell after shell, firing again and again, and Jack Straw was hit and tumbled backward off his horse.

I don't know where he had been but Shakespeare come out of the trees to the east and he had his own Winchester out. He dropped his reins onto his sorrel's neck so he could use both hands and he fired at One-Eye, all at a dead run.

One-Eye turned and began firing at him and then both of them fired at each other as Shakespeare closed in. Shakespeare gained ground, running hard and fast, firing over and over, and then he rode his horse straight into One-Eye's horse, slamming into him as hard as he could, just as One-Eye fired. They all went down in an explosion of snow, the horses screaming.

Shakespeare didn't get up.

Both horses tried to rise but their legs were broken and their cries were terrible and they couldn't stay up, try as they might. I rode toward One-Eye, screaming, "No! No! No!" and I fired the Schofield at him, over and over.

One-Eye was on all fours searching for his rifle in the snow. He found it and he struggled to his feet and he fired at me and missed and he fired again, levering the shells in fast. As we rode toward him Tommy Deuce and I both were firing at One-Eye and missing, the snow exploding all around him.

Then Abraham reined up sharp, dismounted fast, and took a firm stance, raising his Winchester. He aimed and fired, and One-Eye's head snapped back, blood exploding into the snow behind him. He fell, and then he was still, staring at the sky like all the others, I'm sure.

I leapt off Ghost and ran to Shakespeare and there was blood coming from his chest. I put both hands on his wound and pressed down hard, then Tommy Deuce was by my side and he said, "Here, let me, you go find your sister."

Abraham shot both horses quickly and Tommy Deuce said, "Go check Jack Straw!"

Abraham was off as I mounted up on Ghost, Shakespeare's blood on my hands, and I wanted to scream but I couldn't get a sound out.

I wheeled Ghost around and the women and the young and the old and the helpless were streaming past us, trying to get to the horses and get away from the soldiers. I rode hard in the direction Woman-Who-Waits took, riding straight through their remuda, their horses scattering, and about a quarter mile away I saw Woman-Who Waits.

She held Sally in front of her and she could ride as well as any warrior. She was headed for cover in some trees in the distance, when a lone cavalryman come out of the tree line, a picket or a scout maybe. I found my voice and I shouted as loud as I could, "Stop! Stop! Stop!" but he fired at them. They both were slammed off their horse, falling hard into the snow, then tumbling and tumbling in a spray of snow. I wailed, the sound roaring out of me, and maybe because I wasn't dressed like a Comanche, the soldier didn't fire at me.

I got to Woman-Who-Waits and Sally and I dismounted. I grabbed Sally up as Woman-Who-Waits struggled to get up, then collapsed, then went into her death throes, trembling violently in the snow. The bullet had gone through both of them and I didn't know how, but Sally was still alive. She stared at me, something scared or shocked or surprised in her eyes, and as I pulled her robe open to find the wound I begged God for her to be OK, and I said, "Sally, it's me, it's me, Sally, it's Janey, honey, I've come for you."

There was so much blood I couldn't find where she was hit and I didn't know if she could even hear me or understand what I was saying, she looked so confused and bewildered and stunned. She was covered in blood, blood coming out of her mouth and her nose and she was choking, and I tore at her robe and her deerskin dress. Something seemed to shift in her eyes and she tried to speak and I didn't know how much pain she was in and I thought, how can one so little have so much blood in her. I couldn't find her wound to stop the bleeding and I wanted to scream, Where the fuck is it! At the same time I tried to talk to her calmly, saying over and over again, "It's me, Sally, it's Janey, I'm here now, you're going to be OK."

She looked deep into my eyes and she struggled to say something. I thought it was "Janey, Janey," and then I realized, because my hair wasn't long anymore, it was "Jamie, Jamie," she was trying to say. I didn't want to confuse her or try to convince her I was Jane, so I just said, "Yes, honey, it's Jamie, it's Jamie, honey, I'm here. It's Jamie, and I'm here to take you home," and then just as I found the wound she gasped, and her eyes rolled back into her head, and she was gone, and I was too late.

I thought, if I hadn't ridden to Shakespeare first, *I might have saved her.*

I still pressed down hard and tried to staunch the bleeding and I begged her to come back and I insisted she was going to be OK, that we were going home. I kissed her and with my free hand I touched her face and stroked her hair and I tried to wipe the blood away, and I wanted so badly to see her chasing chickens again.

Her eyes came back and she stared at the sky, and I hoped it was Ma and Pa and Jamie she was seeing.

I held her to me and my heart beat wildly and I kept talking to her, saying, "No, no, no, I'm here, honey, don't go away, come on back, it's OK, come on back."

I felt as if a dagger was being slowly pressed straight into my heart and twisted. I couldn't breathe, and I wanted to scream but I didn't want to scream because if she could still hear me I didn't want her to die hearing me scream. I shoved my fist into my mouth and bit it until it was bloody, then I grabbed her robe and shoved it into my mouth to keep from screaming.

The cavalryman who shot them rode up to look at us and he said, "They were trying to get away."

I pulled the robe away and an awful scream came out and I said to him, "It was a woman and a little girl, you fucking bastard!"

I pulled out my Schofield and I shot him, and I found myself wondering whose side I was on. He sat there looking stupid and shocked, and then he toppled out of the saddle and fell face-forward into the snow. His horse shied away, and then there were I don't know how many bluecoats on horseback coming out of the trees, placed there to stop a retreat, I guess, riding toward us to contain the fleeing villagers.

A few of the women had managed to find a horse and mount up and make a run for it, but most of the families were still on foot and struggling to catch a horse. When they saw the blue-coats coming they abandoned the horses and turned to run to the west, but the cavalry was on them too quickly, spreading out and surrounding them. Some bluecoats fired into the air to stop them, but some fired into them and women and old men and children fell and screamed and the officers shouted, "Hold your fire! Hold your fire! You'll hit each other, you fools!"

Some of the soldiers were so eager to kill they continued to fire and they yelled, "Don't let them get away! Don't let them get away!" and others shouted, "Hold your fire! Hold your fire!" The children wept and screamed, and then everyone was on their knees, holding up their hands to surrender.

In the middle of all this horror, some officer rode up to me. I was holding Sally and I felt like I'd been hit in the head with a rock. He pointed at the bluecoat facedown in the snow and he asked, like a fool, "What happened to him?"

I said, "He got hit by a stray bullet."

He pulled away without saying anything else. I could hear the shooting still going on in the village, more slowly now, and here in the field the shooting had stopped and the families were being rounded up and herded back toward the village.

Another troop was rounding up the horses, and I didn't know what to do, so I held Sally tightly to me, feeling her body so limp in the robe. I rocked Sally back and forth and told her not to be frightened, that she was going to be OK, and I wept and I hummed a lullaby to her. And I was afraid Shakespeare was dying or dead, and I didn't want to see it or know it.

Two bluecoats came up and they slung the dead cavalryman over his horse and led him away, ignoring me and Sally. I heard a loud volley of gunshots and I looked up. The horses had been herded up against a long rock ledge that banked the creek at the far end of the tree line so they couldn't escape, and they were killing all the horses, shooting into the remuda, hundreds and hundreds of them screaming and falling and thrashing in the creek water and in the snowy field. A few tore through the ranks of the bluecoats and managed to escape.

I realized Shakespeare's horses were probably in there by now with all the others, and I couldn't help but do the sums in my head. Sixty horses at a hundred and fifty dollars a head. That's nine thousand dollars. Small loss, I thought, compared to all the other losses.

The sun was up but struggled to break through the clouds. The snow was trailing off, and it was a bloody, awful morning.

The women and children and old men being herded away clutched their wounded to them, but a few were suffering in great pain, writhing in the snow, family members by their side begging for help. Those in fierce agony were dispatched with a bullet to the brain by the soldiers, the family members screaming in horror. I wanted to throw up, it was all so ugly and violent, and I wished they'd put a bullet into my brain as well so I'd forget what I'd seen.

I felt like I'd been swallowed into hell, and the next thing I knew Abraham was kneeling in front of me and he said, "Is she … ?"

He stopped at that, not wanting to say the word, and I couldn't say the word either, so I said, "She's gone."

Then I asked him, "Jack Straw?"

And this time he said the word. "He's dead."

I couldn't ask the next question because I couldn't get the words out of my mouth, and I could feel the dagger being hammered even deeper into my heart.

Abraham knew what I was thinking and he said, "He's still alive."

I said, "He won't make it."

It was then that I felt the first fluttering in my belly, and I realized what it was, and why I had been sick so often in the mornings, and the young Indian girl with child had been right all along. Before Abraham could stop me, I was so full of anger and hate that I took the Schofield and pointed it at my belly and I pulled the trigger, but it was empty.

Even though I was holding Sally I began to reload the Schofield, only my fingers were cold and I was fumbling and the rounds fell into the snow. When I got two or three in, Abraham reached out and took it away from me and he said, "What are you doing?"

I tried to take it back and we struggled with the gun and he got it away from me. I was furious and I said, "It's not fair."

"No, it isn't, isn't none of it fair, no guarantee on fairness, but you go to kill yourself and what if he lives?"

I didn't know what to say to that. He tucked the Schofield into his belt and he took his neck scarf off and put it in the snow to wet it. He reached out and held me real still, and he began to wash Shakespeare's and Sally's blood from my face.

While he was doing it he said to me, "You listen to me, Miss Jane. You're tied to the whipping post. You remember me talking to you about that? You're tied to the whipping post and you're on your knees now. I know, I've been on my knees too, but you got to decide right now, this minute, this second, while you're here in the snow, holding Miss Sally, you got to decide right now whether or not you're going to get up. Do you hear me? Believe me, I know what that's like. But you got to decide. You going to stay down, or you going to get up?"

He put his neck scarf down and he took the Schofield from his belt and he finished loading it for me. Then he handed it to me.

I took it, but I didn't have the strength to lift it, much less fire it, and I couldn't look him in the eyes. I told him, "I'm done with hoping."

He ran his hands through my hair like Pa used to do to me, and gently he lifted my face back up to him. He washed my face some more, getting the places he missed, and he looked me straight in the eyes. His face was scarred from the whipping he took years ago and his eyes were the deepest dark brown I'd ever

seen. I thought, the two of us are just about the farthest apart
two people can get, him a black man and once a slave and me a
blond, blue-eyed, half-Irish, half–Swiss German girl, yet here we
are, and how did we end up together like this?

He smiled at me, and as he washed my face and brushed my
hair back he asked, "You a ranahan or not?"

I didn't answer, but I clutched Sally to me and I rocked her
and rocked her and he let me do that for a while. The horses were
still being shot and screaming and the snow was falling again. I
could hear gunfire off and on in the village, the warriors having
pulled back, and I could smell the smoke of the burning tipis.
Farther away I could see the women and children and old men
being driven like cattle.

Abraham put his hand gently on Sally, saying, "Let me … "

I said, "No, she's mine," and I hugged her close, but I holstered the Schofield and held out a hand, and he stood and pulled
me to my feet. He helped me mount Ghost, just like One-Eye was
helping Woman-Who-Waits, and then he mounted up, holding
Ghost's reins, and he led me back to where Tommy Deuce still
knelt by Shakespeare while I held Sally in my arms.

I could see the entire village was burning now. The warriors
had melted away and soldiers were throwing food and blankets
and robes and equipment and weapons and saddles into the
flames. I thought, no food, no clothes, no horses, no buffalo,
they've got no place to go now but the reservation.

Maybe they'll be happy on the reservation, I thought, but I
doubted they would, and behind me the soldiers continued to
shoot the horses.

THIRTY-FOUR

Shakespeare was breathing but he was unconscious and his leg was broken from slamming his horse into One-Eye. Tommy Deuce had taken off his own shirt and wadded it up to stop the bleeding and was still putting pressure on Shakespeare's chest.

I knelt down by Shakespeare, holding Sally, and I could no longer speak. Abraham told Tommy Deuce he'd take over and to go get Monty and Shady and bring the wagon.

Tommy Deuce mounted up and left. All I could do was watch Shakespeare breathe. One breath in, one breath out, one breath in, one breath out, and I waited for the last breath to fall out for good so it would all be over and I'd be left with nothing.

I thought, *That's right, God, take it all away. Don't leave anybody anything. Let them all die on their crosses and then say, "It's OK, it'll all be better after they're dead. There'll be angels and harps and golden streets and everybody will be happy. Like Christian in the Celestial City."*

Except for those who don't die. We'll be like some fish on a plank, our heads cut off and our bodies gutted, but we'll all be pretending we're still swimming around all la-ha-jolly, when actually we're all dead. Gutted, that's how I felt, the knife all the way into my heart.

I held Sally to me, waiting for her to move and show me she was still alive, but I knew that wasn't going to happen.

Abraham pressed on Shakespeare's wound and he talked to Shakespeare, telling him it was all OK and he was going to be just fine, his sweetheart was sitting right beside him. Then he'd wink at me and he'd go on, saying, "She's right here, she's doing fine too, she's just a little bit worried about you."

I realized I had never been called a sweetheart before, and I liked the sound of it. I'd never had a sweetheart before Shakespeare, and I couldn't help but smile. Abraham saw me and he winked again, and I thought, *And my sweetheart is about to die, right now, right here, in front of me, on the same day my sister died.*

Breath in.

Breath out.

Breath in.

Breath out.

Every time the breath fell in, I thought, *Look, he's still alive, and if he's alive, I still have a sweetheart.*

And every time his breath fell out I thought, *That could be the last one, that could be my sweetheart's death*, and each breath in was a precious moment of life.

Breath in.

Look, he's alive, he's alive, he's alive.

Breath out.

Don't die, don't die, please don't die.

I remembered lying on top of him, both of us naked, and whispering to him, *If you die, I'll kill you.*

So holding Sally to me, I leaned in real close and I whispered to him, saying, "Shakespeare, it's Jane. Listen to me. I know you can hear me, so listen closely, Shakespeare, I have something I want to say to you, and you need to hear it."

I whispered to him what he had said to me.

"Shakespeare, only the dead stay down."

Monty, Shady, and Tommy Deuce arrived with the wagon, all of them having escaped the artillery blasts. I told Monty to toss out all the trade goods except the blankets and the robes, so he and Shady threw out the crates of barbed arrowheads and hatchets and the beads and the tobacco and geegaws, everything, leaving just our kits and a few tools and the food stores.

Tommy Deuce smashed up one of the crates and a splint was made from it, Monty then straightening Shakespeare's leg and strapping the splint to it. Shady came up the hill dragging a lodge pole. He broke it up and threw a blanket over two halves, and with Shakespeare's riata he tied the blanket to the poles and made a stretcher. While Abraham kept pressure on the wound, they lifted Shakespeare onto the stretcher and then lifted him into the wagon as gently as possible, each of them calling out instructions to the other.

I sat in the snow holding Sally to me and I watched while Monty climbed in beside Shakespeare.

Tommy Deuce, who was wearing his mackinaw over his bare chest now, came over to me. "Oh, ma'am, this is good news. Look what I found when I was pressing on his chest." He held up a small book. "This was in his shirt pocket. The bullet went straight through it but I think it slowed the bullet down and kept it from doing more damage."

I don't know why, but I asked, "What book is it?"

As if it mattered.

"I don't know," Tommy Deuce said, "I can't read."

He handed the book to me. It was all covered in blood but I could read the title. It said, *Romeo and Juliet by William Shakespeare*, and there was a bullet hole right through the middle of it.

I held on to the bloody book, rocked Sally in my lap, and hummed to her as best as I could. Her skin was so white. I told myself, *She doesn't get to have a life, but she's at peace now. She's at peace.* I tried to imagine her with Ma and Pa and Jamie and they were all out looking for wild plums or picking fruit from the prickly pear or having a picnic among the bluebonnets, talking and singing, and maybe Pa was tossing her around and she was laughing. Somehow I could believe that better than I could believe in angels and golden streets.

Monty looked at Shakespeare's wound, climbed out of the wagon, and came over to me. He said, "It's good it's cold, that keeps him from bleeding so much. But the bullet's still in him. We need to get it out."

"Have you done that before?"

He shrugged. "Once or twice."

He went back to the wagon and I watched as they all gathered around Shakespeare. I couldn't see what they were doing and I didn't want to know. I kept waiting for one of them to come over and tell me he was dead now, but they worked away. I imagined they were using knives or some kind of tool or utensil to get in and find the bullet, maybe their fingers, and it was more than I could take.

I felt numb, as if my heart was lying on the hillside somewhere, covered in snow, stone-cold dead.

I rocked Sally and at some point I realized there were fewer and fewer gunshots, and I'd lost track of the horses being killed. I looked down the slope of the hill and there were hundreds of dead horses near the rocky ledge, a few still struggling. Several soldiers walked through them and put them out of their misery with a gunshot to the head, just like they'd done with the suffering helpless who had been writhing in pain. I was glad they weren't being left in agony, any of them, and that seemed like a small act of kindness.

And I thought, *If Shakespeare dies I think that's what I'd like, a small act of kindness, someone just putting a bullet through my brain, and maybe I could go back to picking leaf buds off of cattails with Sally and the rest of the family.*

I realized Monty was standing in front of me and I looked up and he said, "Here, maybe you want to keep this."

He held a bloody bullet in his bloody hand. At first I didn't want to touch it, but then I reached out and he put it in the palm of my hand and he said, "He's OK, so far."

His hand and his fingers were large and I thought, *What a beautiful strong hand Monty has, I've never noticed that before.*

Then he said, "Maybe you want to get out of the snow, it's very cold."

"No," I said. "I'm fine here."

"You want a drink of water or maybe something to eat?"

"No, I'm fine."

I held Sally and I rocked her. He backed away and went to the wagon and they all huddled together by Shakespeare.

We were on the crest of a slight rise and on the far side was all of the dead horses and those folks killed in the rout, and on the near side I could see the village, some of it still burning and some of it smoldering now. The soldiers had the families under guard at the edge of the village.

At some point, an officer rode up to us and wanted to know who we were. Abraham explained we were Comancheros here to trade with the Comanches, but we had really been looking to recover my sister who had been stolen some months back, and he pointed to me and told him my sister had been killed in the battle.

He dismounted and looked at Shakespeare in the wagon. Jack Straw's body had been brought over near the wagon by Shady and Tommy Deuce and covered with a blanket. The officer pulled back the blanket and looked at him too, then he come over to me.

He knelt down in front of me. "What's your name?" I didn't answer him, and he said, "I'm sorry about your sister. How old was she?"

"One of your goddamn soldiers shot her."

"I'm sorry about that."

"You can go to hell. You and your whole goddamn army." I didn't say it angry because I didn't have the strength for that. I just told him the truth.

"I understand." He stood up and walked back and talked to Abraham and the hands, and then he mounted up and rode off.

Abraham came over. "They'll be pulling out soon and he says we ought to join them, says it's a long journey back to their fort, says if we stay here the warriors will come back and kill us. They may think we led the soldiers here."

It made sense, but in spite of all the dead bodies and the burning village, it seemed peaceful on the top of the rise and I didn't want to leave. The snow had stopped but it was still gray, and smoke was blowing all around. I felt like I was in the middle of a cloud somewhere and all my insides were gray, like the smoke, but I felt like I belonged on the top of this small hill.

Abraham knelt down in front of me again. "Miss Jane, it's time. What do you want to do?"

I realized I was still the trail boss, so I said, "Bury Jack Straw here but make a sign for his grave and I want it to say, 'Jack Straw, Horse Marine.' Then go get the bodies of Woman-Who Waits and One-Eye, and we'll bury them up here as well."

In my stone-cold-dead heart I hoped One-Eye would roast in hell. I wanted to leave him dead in the snow, unburied, so the coyotes and vultures and wolves could get to him, but I figured that wouldn't be fair to Woman-Who-Waits. Besides, I realized, One-Eye died doing the same thing Pa had hoped to do, save his family, and I couldn't make sense of it all. And although I didn't wish him well, maybe One-Eye and Woman-Who-Waits could all go berry picking with the daughter they'd lost, somewhere in the afterlife. If there was an afterlife.

Abraham said, "What do you want to do with Miss Sally?"

I hadn't heard her called Miss Sally in a long time. Pa would call her Missy and sometimes Miss Sally, and now here Abraham was saying it. I began to weep and he put his hand on me, and I said, "I can't let her go."

"Then you just hold on to her."

❧ ❧ ❧

Jack Straw's grave was dug and the hands gathered around. Tommy Deuce said a few words, then nearby they dug one larger grave and put Woman-Who-Waits and One-Eye in it. Before they covered them up I called Abraham over and I said, "Put Sally in with them too."

He looked at me. "Miss Jane, you sure about that?"

"Yes," I said. "I saw how she and Woman-Who-Waits held on to each other. Bury them together."

I held my hands back and he gently lifted her away from me, then he set her down on the snowy ground. He uncovered her and he carefully straightened out her body and her deerskin dress and he wiped her face clean with snow using his neck scarf again. He folded her hands over her chest and smoothed out her hair and then he rearranged her robe, folding it carefully around her and covering her up so she was a little bundle.

He stood up, holding her in one arm, and he reached down to me. "Why don't you come with us?"

I took his hand, and his hand was so large and black and mine looked like a child's hand in it, so small and white, and I was grateful for his strength and his kindness.

He pulled me up and my legs were so numb I could barely stand. I was stumbling as we walked, so he put his free arm around me and he walked me to the grave.

The hands were all standing around with their hats in their hands. Abraham knelt and carefully placed Sally between Woman-Who-Waits and One-Eye, just like I'd done with Jamie, then he stood up and we all stood there in silence for a long while. He began to sing some spiritual I'd never heard before, about wading in the water, about children dressed in white and red and blue and being led by Moses and the Israelites, about coming through and being redeemed.

And then, I don't know where he come from, but Preacher was there, standing by the grave, and he said his text would be from Ezekiel.

The Lord is my portion, saith my soul, therefore will I hope in him. The Lord is good unto them that wait for him, to the soul that seeketh him.

He talked about the need to hope and wait and seek, then went on to say some kind words about Miss Sally finding peace and being home at last, and how much her sister must have loved her to have looked for her so long and hard, and how they all hoped her sister would find peace as well.

He concluded by saying love of the Lord was found through suffering.

And then he was silent.

In that silence, I felt arms wrap around me and hold me, and for a brief moment I felt a sense of peace and I figured it was Abraham holding me. I was grateful for his touch, and in that touch I sensed the ground underneath me falling away and I was just in space, drifting, feeling nothing but kindness and well-being, and I put my hand out to touch his arms around me, but there were no arms there.

I looked, and Abraham was a few steps away from me, not close enough to hold me, and then I swore I could smell Ma's scent in spite of the smoke and the gunpowder, but there it was. I listened for her voice and wanted to ask where she'd been, but I knew where she was.

And if she should speak again, I wondered, what would she say?

But I figured I already knew the answer to that as well.

Wasn't life a mystery.

While I was marveling at this, Monty began some Spanish song, maybe something he'd sung for his daughters. I couldn't understand the words but it was real sweet and Shady knew the song and joined in with him.

Then there was silence again and I tried to sing but I couldn't get the words out, but lo and behold, Tommy Deuce began singing when I faltered, and who would have thought he knew "Wild Mountain Thyme."

And we'll all go together to pluck wild mountain thyme, all around the blooming heather. Will you go, lassie, go?

My knees went out from under me. Abraham stepped forward and grabbed me and held on to me, and I was sobbing and leaning into him. Then Tommy Deuce was done singing.

Abraham held me for the longest time while I wept. When I was finally quiet, he said, "Miss Jane, we're all going to give you a few minutes alone with Miss Sally."

I nodded that I'd like that. He let go of me real gently and backed away from the grave, and I saw him nod to the hands. They all pulled away and returned to the wagon and stood there, checking in on Shakespeare and acting like they weren't watching me.

I didn't know what to say or do. I stood there awhile and tried to memorize where we were in case I ever had the chance to come back. I looked at the dead horses and the corpses in the snow and the smoldering village, then I looked at the small bundle and hoped Ma wouldn't be mad at me for not bringing her home.

I apologized to everyone for how it had all turned out and how we'd come so close, but it was going to go badly no matter what, because Sally wasn't going to want to leave Woman-Who-Waits and Woman-Who-Waits wasn't going to want to lose her.

Who knew where home truly was for Sally.

With whoever loved her, I guessed.

I wanted to blame God, but I was past being angry at him. I figured even he must be bewildered at how everybody could be so cruel to one another, and didn't it seem that giving everyone free will had all been a disastrous mistake. But then I remembered the dove Maria holding me, and Big Mike coming to my rescue, and Abraham washing my face and holding his hand out to me, and I remembered the first kiss Shakespeare had given me.

The touch and the kiss and the rescue. Maybe that's where the Lord was.

I told Sally I was sorry she wouldn't get to go to fandangos or learn to ride a horse or be tossed by Pa or have her hair done up by Ma, and I asked her to forgive me for taking so long to get to her, and I wished her love and peace and Godspeed. I hummed "Wild Mountain Thyme" and got through it, and then I pulled the blue ribbon that Shakespeare had given me from my hair and I knelt down and placed it on the little bundle of her.

I stood and turned away from the grave. Abraham was by my side in an instant. He held me upright as we walked back to the wagon while the hands came over and covered the bodies with a buffalo robe, then filled in the grave.

Abraham lifted me into the wagon and sat me down next to Shakespeare, who was still struggling for breath, and I said to Abraham, "Thank Preacher for me, tell him it was a real sweet service."

Abraham looked at me. "Miss Jane, he wasn't there."

I told Abraham, "He had to have been there because I don't know those words from Ezekiel by heart. How could I have made them up?"

"If you saw him, Miss Jane, then I'm sure he was there."

He brushed back my hair and he said, "Now, I want you to sit here and hold on to Shakespeare's hand. He'll know you're there, and you need to talk to him. Your job is to keep him with us."

I told him, "Thank you," and when he went to pull his hand away I held it tighter and he looked at me and I said, "Abraham, I'm sorry about your family."

He smiled and he looked at our hands together. "We're all in this together, ain't we, Miss Jane."

Only it wasn't a question, it was the truth.

Then we let go and I took Shakespeare's hand like he said, and I had to smile, because Monty had bandaged Shakespeare's chest using yards of gingham cloth.

Abraham tied Ghost to the back of the wagon and then he pulled Shakespeare's saddle and bridle off of his dead horse and threw that into the wagon as well.

When the hands were finished with the grave, they all mounted up, and with Monty driving the wagon we headed down the hill, me holding Shakespeare's hand and looking back at Jack Straw's and Sally's graves. I felt bad that the last thing I said to Jack Straw was that he was a fool. I wished I had stood at his grave and apologized and told him he was as brave as any Texas Ranger, and thanks, though saying thanks didn't seem enough. And goodbye. And I promised myself I'd go through his kit and see if I couldn't find out where his sister lived.

We joined the caravan of prisoners and horse soldiers, and we headed east.

THIRTY-FIVE

The band of prisoners was in dreadful condition. Many were still barefoot or naked and they huddled together with someone who had a blanket or robe to share. Some of the children were injured and without family, so we did what we could by pulling those most hurt into the wagon, as well as the injured mothers holding babies, and a few of the injured old men and women. We could only get so many in with us and we gave away our robes and blankets to whoever needed them most. Some were grateful and some gave us fierce looks as if we were the ones who had attacked their village, but I guess they felt about us the same way I felt when our farm was raided.

Shady drove the wagon. Monty climbed back and made up a poultice and together we bandaged their wounds as best we could with the bolts of gingham and calico, but there were so many of them. I felt heartsick at their suffering.

A military surgeon attending to the wounded bluecoats came back at one point and looked in on Shakespeare and said we'd done all that could be done, just keep changing his bandages. He said his leg had been splinted fine but it would take time to see if his brain would recover from the blow of the horses smashing into each other.

He took time attending to the helpless in the wagon, looking at the wounds and checking our bandages. But as he got out of the wagon he just shook his head, and then I heard him ordering someone to find more blankets and bring them back to the prisoners. He walked among those following, he and his assistants, doing what they could for the other wounded. Several of the bluecoats dropped back from their formation and dismounted and lifted the weakest ones onto their horses and then walked beside them, leading them, or lifted them up and rode with them, holding them. I thought, *What kind of a world is this where there is such cruelty and such kindness at the same time?*

Then at night, some of the officers came back and grabbed some of the women and began to drag them up to their tents. I screamed at them to stop, getting out of the wagon and grabbing at them, but they knocked me down and threatened me, and when the hands came over to help, the officers told them to back off or our mules might end up dead, then where would we be when the warriors caught up? Besides, they said, why didn't the hands just help themselves?

I was furious, and when I complained to the surgeon, he just shrugged and said they were soldiers, what did I think was going to happen? You couldn't close herd all of them. "Besides," he said, "they'll get better rations with the officers than if they stay back with the prisoners."

It made me sick at my stomach. What these men were doing was no different than what had been done to Ma, and I felt helpless and angry all over again.

We traveled for I don't know how many days with Shakespeare coming in and out of consciousness, sometimes out of his head, saying things like, "Get him some water" or "Keep her still" or "Oh my God no, oh my God no," sometimes weeping and sometimes struggling to yell, his voice croaking as if he was crying out from underwater. I figured he was back in Corpus Christi reliving the loss of his parents or his little brother, and I realized all those Shakespeare stories was his way of maybe figuring it all out, just like the Bible was to some others. I had been short-sighted and should have seen that sooner.

Sometimes he'd drink some water and then seem to sleep, then maybe there'd be a scrap of a clear conversation, then he wouldn't know who I was and he'd panic, and in his struggle to get up I was afraid his wound would start bleeding again. I'd lie on top of him to hold him down, and I thought the wagon would never stop rocking and surely it was going to make him bleed more.

Sometimes he'd cough up blood, so I'd prop him up and I'd wipe it away as best I could. Then he'd sleep or go unconscious again, then he ran a fever for I don't know how long, and then chills, and he'd be struggling to get up again and my weight wouldn't be enough and one of the Comanche women would crawl over and would help me hold him down. I was grateful for her kindness and her help.

There were days of heavy snow and then light snow and then clear blue skies with the sun making the snow look like it had lights sparkling in it. I held Shakespeare's hand, and in spite of their being so many in the wagon, I talked to him the whole time, just like Abraham told me to do. I told him all about Pa making it home from the war even though he was wounded in the leg and that's why he limped, and how Jamie made up stories about knights that were better than *Pilgrim's Progress*, and we both thought Christian was a fool to leave his wife and kids behind to look for the Celestial City, and what kind of a man would do that, and how Sally liked to chase the chickens.

When I wasn't helping the mothers with their children, I'd wash his face and comb his hair and Monty and I would clean him up and change his bandages. It was all very awkward with so many in the wagon and it was hard getting food down him, but we managed to do so when he was conscious for those brief moments.

When Shakespeare was sleeping, I would weep and feel sorry for myself, then I'd look at the women and children next to us and I'd shake that off and think about how hard these families had it, the women still wailing in grief over family they'd lost, the painful cries rolling over us all.

At night, the wagon was like a pack of puppies all huddled up together. I gave Shakespeare's bedroll away and I pulled my bedroll over the two of us and pretended we were husband and wife sleeping next to each other. One time I whispered into his ear, "When this is all over and we're together, you can have me anytime you want me," and I blushed and I told him it was our secret and he wasn't to tell anyone I'd said that.

Sometimes I couldn't breathe for fear he was going to die and I would just sit in the wagon, scared to death, holding my breath, and one of the Comanche women would sit next to me and hold my hand, but another would look at me darkly and I could tell she wished us ill, just like I'd wished so many of them ill.

We rolled into the fort one snowy afternoon and an officer come to tell us there wouldn't be any empty beds in their infirmary because of their own injured and we would need to push on into town, only a few miles distant, thank you very much.

The women and the children and the old men climbed out of the wagon and I wondered what would happen to them. Some of them said something to me in Comanche and I spoke to them as well, and the one who would look at me fiercely got out of the wagon and she looked hard at Shakespeare, and I knew she was wishing him dead.

She reminded me of myself, and I regretted it.

Monty snapped the reins and our own outfit kept on, passing the prisoners as they filed onto the parade grounds, all of them being held as ransom to force the band to come onto the reservation. They were in terrible shape and some of the weaker ones had died along the way, and as much as I hated the Comanches for what they'd done to my family, you wouldn't do to a dog what had been done to these helpless ones. I didn't know what ought to be done about it all, but none of it seemed right. I was glad I wasn't one of them, and I felt ashamed for feeling that way.

⚜   ⚜   ⚜

It was a small town we come into and I never even caught the name. We pulled into a livery stable and I told the boys I didn't know what was to happen next, but they were still on the payroll. I hauled out the strongbox that held my money and Shakespeare's and I paid them what they were owed. I said I would pay for their hotel for the next several days, unless they wanted to leave.

They put Shakespeare on the stretcher and lifted him out of the wagon, Monty and Shady on one side of him, Tommy Deuce and Abraham on the other. Folks on the boardwalk stopped to stare at us as we trailed down the middle of the street, me leading the way and the snow coming down again. I thought, *What a sight we must make, all of us dirty and covered in blood, hauling what looked like a dead man, carrying our kits as well, and all of us, out of habit, still heavily armed.*

When we got Shakespeare into the small lobby of the hotel, the clerk was very dismayed and he said, "I hope the man on the stretcher isn't going to die."

"We hope that as well," I said, "but if he does, you'll be the first to know." Then I told him, "I want a room for the two of us together, and these boys need rooms as well and it's all to be put on my tab. "

He looked at Monty and Shady and Abraham. "We don't take niggers or beaners or savages."

I took him in, staring at him, and I said, "I may not look very dangerous but I've killed six men and one of them was a U.S. soldier, and these men here have been through hell, fire, and high water so you can eat steak at night, much less they've saved my life, and I swear to God if you don't give these men a room I'll add a no-account clerk to the list of people I've killed because I don't give a good goddamn anymore."

I pulled out the Schofield and pointed it at him, and then Tommy Deuce spoke up. "This here is the Comanche Kid, called that because the other five she killed was Comanche warriors, so if I was you, I'd do what she says, because if she don't kill you, I'll kill you myself." And at that he pulled out his Colt and held it on the clerk as well.

We all got rooms and the hands hauled Shakespeare upstairs, then took him off the stretcher and put him on the narrow bed. The room was small and cramped, but there was a chair in a corner and a pitcher and basin on a dresser, and a lamp, and it was all we needed. I told the hands to go get something to eat and I'd stay with Shakespeare until one of them came back, then I'd take my turn.

They all left and I pulled the chair over by Shakespeare's side. I held his hand and I began to talk to him, assuming he could hear me.

"I been thinking about the future. As soon as you snap out of this siesta you're taking we need to discuss where we go from here. I've got Ma and Pa's place, but I don't know if I want to live there after what happened, but I do want to go to their grave and tell them about Sally and have them meet you, and I'll tell them who you are and how I feel about you and how you saved my life by riding straight into One-Eye when he was firing at me.

"Also, while we're traveling, there will be some beautiful sunrise on maybe the Trinity or the Colorado, and we'll be having coffee in the morning, because I want it to be someplace pretty, and you'll ask me to marry you, and I'll tell you yes. Then maybe we could go to your place in Corpus Christi and I could see where your parents and your brother are buried and you can tell them about me, and who knows, maybe we have two spreads between us or maybe we sell it all off and we go to San Antone and we start all over, you being a lawyer maybe and me maybe a schoolmarm. Maybe Abraham and Monty and Shady and Tommy Deuce will all want to go with us, and there's a dove named Maria who did me a big favor and maybe we'll send for her and she'd like to join us as well, but we got a lot to talk about, so I need you to come back, because right now I have a heart that's been battered too much and I can't take it anymore. I'm done with bad luck and people getting hurt and being cruel and everybody losing every-thing that means something to them. I need you to come back and pull the knife out and take this stone out of my chest and put my heart back in so I can live again."

I leaned forward and I put his hand under my shirt and placed it on my heart between my breasts. "Do you feel that? It's beating, but it's not alive."

And then I put his hand on my belly. "Do you feel that? She needs a father, so we're waiting for you and it's time you come home," and I could feel her fluttering like a butterfly against his hand, as if she was trying to wake him up.

"I can't tell you how I know it's a girl," I added. "I just know."

I couldn't think of anything else to say, so I put his hand down. I reached into my pocket where I kept the bullet that had hit him and the arrow that had hit me and the copy of *Romeo and Juliet* that Tommy Deuce had found. The covers of the book was smeared with blood but the pages not as much. I opened it up, and a pressed flower fell out of it. It was a bluebonnet, only it was a white one, not blue at all, a rare white one, and I wondered where and when he had found it and why he'd kept it, so I said to him, "And I want to know what the story is behind this white bluebonnet and why it's in your book."

Then I placed it carefully in the back of the book and I began to read to him, beginning with: *Romeo and Juliet* by William Shakespeare, and everywhere that the words were gone because the bullet had passed through or blood had smeared, I guessed or made up words to fit, trying to make sense out of it. I read into the evening, until Monty came back and sat with him while I went to get something to eat.

After I ate and before I went back to the room, I walked down to the livery stable and I told the stable hand I was taking Ghost out. I went into the corral and I leaned up against her. She stood with her head over my shoulder, real patient like she always was, and I told her how worried I was about Shakespeare, as if she didn't already know that, having followed behind the wagon day after day and listening to me talk and weep and so on. I told her I needed her to do something for me and, oh, by the way, I was going to change her name and I hoped she didn't mind, but it's a good name, a better name, something closer to the truth of who she was, as if you could ever name that truth. She said she was up for anything, so I said, "Then let's go."

I put a hackamore on her and I led her out of the corral and down the street, past whiskey mills where there was music playing and shouts and laughter and arguments, past a tonsorial parlor with a red-and-white pole, past a house with a red light with boys at the door seeking entry, and a dry goods store, and there was a small church and I could hear a preacher speaking to the congregation at an evening service, his words coming out into the street, and the snow was falling and it was cold and gray and the moon looked like a pale coin behind the clouds.

I stopped at the door of the church and I listened, and I could have sworn it was Preacher's voice, and that baffled me. The preacher, whoever he was, said what his text was, and the words stayed with me they were so remarkable. I listened for a while, and the voice was talking vengeance and repentance and forgiveness and redemption, and I could hear cries of "Amen!" and "Hallelujah!" Then there was the sweet singing of a hymn as I left the door and continued on down the street through the snow and the cold, the song following after me.

Through many dangers, toils, and snares we have already come. 'Twas grace that brought us safe thus far, and grace will lead us home.

When we reached the hotel, I led Ghost up onto the boardwalk and then straight into the lobby and the clerk started yelling, "What are you doing? You can't do that! What do you think you're doing?"

I said, "She's spending the night with us."

He yelled I couldn't do that and he was going to call the sheriff and such and such, and as I led Ghost up the stairs I said, "Then I'll shoot the sheriff after I shoot you," and he kept yelling, "You can't do that! You can't do that!"

I called down to him, "Do you remember what I told you?"

"Yes."

"What was it?"

He said, "You don't give a good goddamn."

"That's right."

And then he said, "You're going to have to clean up after her!"

"I surely will."

Ghost took the stairs slowly and didn't stumble because she's an Appaloosa and they're clear-footed. I led her down the hall and I opened the door of our room, and when Monty saw what I was doing he didn't say a word about it, he just said, "He's been real quiet. I see you in the morning," and he left, shutting the door behind him.

There wasn't much space but I turned Ghost so she faced Shakespeare. I took her reins and tied them to his hand, the same hand I'd placed on my heart, and then I sat back down next to him.

I told him, "You need to listen to Spirit, that's her new name. Her name's not Ghost anymore, her name is Spirit. You just hold on to her reins and you can say anything you want to her, or you can just listen and she'll talk to you, although she doesn't always use words. Sometimes it's just a feeling, you know? A feeling, and it doesn't make sense, like when I first met you, and it didn't make sense, but I had a feeling for you. Or when you kiss me, it isn't just a kiss, it's something more than that, like talking, isn't it? So everything is going to be OK. You just listen to Spirit, and everything will be OK."

Then I remembered the words I'd heard, standing outside the church door, but I kept them to myself, like a secret I was afraid to confess.

A new heart also will I give you, and a new spirit will I put within you; and I will take away the stony heart out of your flesh, and I will give you a heart of flesh.

Then I picked up *Romeo and Juliet* and continued reading to him, and I read far into the night.

When I woke up the next morning, I was still in the chair and the book was in my lap. I lifted my head, and out the window I saw the snow had stopped and the day was bright and the sky deep blue. I felt something, and I looked down, and the reins were on the floor and Shakespeare's hand was on my belly.

I looked at Shakespeare and he was looking straight at me, his blue eyes open and clear and bright, like the sky, and he had that soft smile.

She was fluttering under his hand and I said, "Her name is Bluebonnet Hope."

"O brave new world," he said, "that has such people in it."

My heart began to race and I remembered Jamie talking about some king pulling a sword out of a stone and that's what I felt like, like something cold and hard and sharp was being pulled out of my heart of stone, and it could beat now and push blood through it and through my whole body, and I felt hot and I couldn't catch my breath but I pretended to be calm and I said, "Hi, Roy."

He said, "I put the white bluebonnet in there sometime after I met you because it's rare, like you."

"You heard me?"

"I heard everything."

I was holding real still like I was in some china shop and if I moved too quick everything would break. "Strange thing to do after meeting some kid, wasn't it?"

"I knew you were a girl."

"Yeah, you told me that once. You said I was too pretty to be a boy."

He said, "That too."

"What else?"

He smiled at me. "We were both nightriding the herd not too long after you'd joined up and it turned cold as hell and you didn't have your mackinaw on, and when we stopped to talk, I looked at you and that band around your chest didn't work as well as you thought."

I blushed and I started weeping and I hit him on his broken leg with the book and he yelled and I knew the china wasn't going to break. I climbed on top of him and hugged him and kissed him and I was sobbing and he was holding me to him and running his hand through my hair, saying, "There, there, Janey, there, there." And every time he said my name I couldn't breathe because I was so happy it hurt too much.

ABOUT THE AUTHOR

J ames Daniels is the author of four professionally produced one-person plays, *Sam Houston: Standing in His Own Blood*; *Edwin Booth: The Falconer's Voice*; *Custer Rides*; and *Wyatt Earp: Last Man Standing*. Jim's path to writing began in the theatre. He has been a professional actor and director for more than forty years, having acted at such theatres as Shakespeare and Company in Lenox, Massachusetts, the Oregon Shakespeare Festival, the Cleveland Play House, Missouri Repertory Theatre (now Kansas City Repertory Theatre), the Houston Shakespeare Festival, and the Asolo Theatre of Florida (now Asolo Repertory Theatre). His production of *Othello* was performed at the Kennedy Center in

Washington, D.C., and his play about the Mexican-American War, *So Far from God*, was last presented at Chicago Shakespeare Theater. Jim was director of performance for the Western Michigan University Department of Theatre for twenty-five years and retired as professor emeritus, then taught under a five year contract as a Senior Lecturer in Acting at the University of Texas Department of Theatre and Dance. Jim received his MFA in acting from the Florida State University/Asolo Conservatory for Actor Training in Sarasota, Florida. He served in the infantry in Vietnam with the Eighty-Second Airborne and in the artillery with the First Infantry Division. Jim and his wife, Patricia, live in Austin, Texas.

Made in United States
North Haven, CT
21 October 2022

25743417R00214